Love's Bold Journey

Patricia Matthews

PINNACLE BOOKS LOS ANGELES

This is a work of fiction. All the characters and events portrayed in this book are fictional, and any resemblance to real people or incidents is purely coincidental.

LOVE'S BOLD JOURNEY

An original Pinnacle Books edition, published for the first time anywhere.

First printing, October 1980

ISBN: 0-523-40661-4

Cover illustration by John Solie

Printed in the United States of America

PINNACLE BOOKS, INC.
2029 Century Park East
Los Angeles, California 90067

The First Time . . .

Rachel got up, as if in a dream, and without mind or will of her own, allowed Rankin to lead her to the bed. There, he began undressing her. He did it skillfully, as if all the fasteners and appurtenances were familiar to him. Rachel was mesmerized by his actions, by his easy confidence, his subtle skill. Before she fully realized it, she was nude, lying on the bed, staring up at him.

Rankin stared down at her with heavy-lidded eyes. His mouth seemed too full and sensuous to be a man's, and yet, it was capable, as well she knew, of evoking the most exquisite pleasure in a woman. It curled up slightly, forming a smile that seemed to be mocking.

"You are a very beautiful woman, Rachel," he said huskily. "A *very* beautiful woman."

Rankin undressed himself, and Rachel, watching with a mixture of embarrassment and fascination, saw that his classic good looks were only enhanced by his physique. And then he was in bed with her, caressing her tenderly and artfully.

Rachel felt her body responding to his caresses eagerly, and her mounting desire overwhelmed any reservation. Now, now she was to learn what it was like to be a woman, truly a woman! . . .

Other Pinnacle Books by Patricia Matthews:

Love's Avenging Heart
Love's Wildest Promise
Love, Forever More
Love's Pagan Heart
Love's Daring Dream
Love's Magic Moment
Love's Golden Destiny
Love's Raging Tide
Love's Sweet Agony

THE IRON HORSE

Across the prairie,
slowly dreaming,
endless seeming,
stretch the rails.

Wooden ties and steel tracks
ribbon the land,
men's backs
were broken here.

Buffalo stand in shaggy surprise,
reflected in their wild eyes,
the engine cries,
thundering across the land.

Spewing cinders,
trailing steam,
nightmare from an Indian's dream,
the Iron Horse gallops
from sea
to shining sea.

Patricia Matthews

CHAPTER ONE

Rachel Bonner felt tired, dirty, and near to suffocating in the stuffy confines of the small railroad car. After so many hours on the train the wooden seats felt like iron under her bottom; and the seemingly endless monotony of the long journey was enough to make her want to scream aloud.

She and her uncle and aunt, Julius and Mildred Deever, were the only people in the car, and they had little to say to one another. To the Deevers, Rachel was an unwelcome guest, a poor relation they had been unwillingly burdened with, and they made little attempt to hide their feelings.

With a sigh Rachel peered out of the grimy window. She was a gently rounded girl of twenty-four, with soft brown hair and large hazel eyes. She had a fair, fine complexion, and the ghost of last summer's exposure to the sun could still be seen in a few remaining freckles.

With another sigh she took her gaze from the window. There was nothing to see out there, nothing but miles of empty prairie. She couldn't even open the window for a little fresh air, because cinders from the engine would fly in, blackening the passengers' faces and even burning holes in their clothing, if they didn't take care.

Why on earth would people come out here to settle in this great empty space?

But evidently a great many *were* coming. Rachel opened her reticule, took out a yellow poster she'd picked up in Omaha, and read it for the tenth time:

CHEAP FARMS! FREE HOMES!
on the line of the
UNION PACIFIC RAILROAD!

A land grant of 12,000 acres across the best Farming and Mineral Lands in America.

3,000,000 acres in Nebraska! The Garden of the West, now for sale! These lands are in the central portion of the United States, on the 41st Degree of the North Latitude, the central line of the Great Temperate Zone of the American Continent; and for grain growing and stock raising unsurpassed by any in the United States!

Colonists and Actual Settlers can buy on ten years' credit. A deduction of 10% for cash!

O. F. Davis, Land Commissioner, UPRR Company, Omaha, Nebraska

Rachel looked up from the poster, staring off in thought. She had seen hundreds of potential farmers and settlers in Omaha—eager husbands, excited children, and anxious wives, all sitting patiently in waiting rooms near their pile of personal belongings, talking to each other about the farms they were going to have for their very own.

The train began to slow. At the risk of a cinder in her eye, she opened a window and craned her neck out to see what was happening. She had heard horrendous tales of wild Indians ambushing trains out here.

The man called Hawkeye Smith dropped his saddle and gear with the sigh of relief of one who had carried a heavy burden a great distance, and walked up the small grade to stand on the track.

He squinted long, steel-gray eyes, scratched at the stubble of week-old blond beard which hid an otherwise attractive face, and peered eastward, down the track. Stretching before him, as far as he could see, was a twin set of rails, disappearing on a horizon which was a sea of grass, unbroken by hill, tree, or bush. Hawkeye dropped to his knees and placed an ear to one of the iron ribbons, then smiled, for he could hear the faint humming which told him that an approaching train was just over the curve of the horizon.

Standing up, he said aloud, "Well, it looks like I won't have to walk to Plum Creek after all." Then he blushed, because there was no one to hear his words. He had been in the habit of talking to his horse, and logic told him this was no different; but reason alone could not stop him from feeling foolish for speaking aloud.

From his pack he took a yellow and black checkered flag, a private signal that Union Pacific had provided for the buffalo hunters, which would ensure that the engineer would stop for him.

Moments later the train appeared. It was approaching at about thirty miles an hour, a most respectable speed, but the vastness of the terrain lent an illusion of languor to its progress. Against the vaulting sky the silhouette of the train seemed tiny, and even the smoke which poured from its diamond stack made little impression upon the vast panorama.

Hawkeye could hear the train quite clearly now. The chugging of its engine carried to him across the wide, flat plain the way sound travels across water. He began waving the checkered flag, and he could tell by the sound that the engineer had spotted him, for the steam valve was closed and the train began braking. Moments later, as the great engine neared, Hawkeye realized how vast this land really was, for the train which had appeared so puny before was now a behemoth, blocking out the sky. It ground to a reluctant halt, puffing black smoke, wreathed in tendrils of white steam which, in the fading evening light, purpled as it drifted away.

Two faces appeared in the window of the engine cab, both round, red, and decidedly Irish. One face sported a large, walrus-type moustache. The man grinned down at him.

"Hawkeye, my bucko! Sure, and I thought it was you. I told Donovan the same."

"O'Brien," Hawkeye responded. He tossed his gear on the fireman's platform in front of the tender. "Am I glad it's you at the throttle, and not that black-hearted John Patterson!" Hawkeye also got along well with John Patterson, and his fireman, Olag Anderson, but he thought it best to engage in a bit of diplomacy.

"Aye," O'Brien replied. "For, Orangeman that Mr. Patterson is, he would like as not have passed you by, and that's a fact now. Tell me, lad, what are you doing out here afoot?"

"I was tracking a stand of buffalo," Hawkeye said. "Ran into an Indian hunting party doing the same thing, and they got a mite miffed at the competition. They took out after me, and my horse was killed in the ruckus."

"Them heathen redskins ought to be chased clear out, now that we are civilized," O'Brien said, shaking his head. "Nebraska is a state now, come March One of this year."

"So I heard," Hawkeye said.

"Yessirree, we're living in a great time, Hawkeye. The building of this here railroad is a mighty fine thing. 'Tis a shame old Abe himself couldn't be alive to see it coming about."

"Mr. O'Brien, what is the meaning of this delay?" a voice said stridently from behind Hawkeye.

Hawkeye turned to see a well-dressed, portly man of around fifty striding toward them. He stood there, red-faced and blustering, making a great show of looking at the gold watch that hung from his vest. Hawkeye felt an immediate antipathy toward the man.

"This young gentleman here is Hawkeye Smith," O'Brien said. "He's a buffalo hunter for the Union Pacific. Hawkeye, this here is Mr. Julius Deever, the new construction foreman for the UP."

"I'm pleased to meet you, Mr. Deever. I heard a man was coming to take Miller's place. We all felt pretty bad about his murder, and we're hoping that the fellow who did it gets caught."

Hawkeye extended his hand, but Deever pointedly ignored it. Instead, he again made a point of looking at his watch; then he thrust the timepiece into his vest pocket, clearing his throat in annoyance.

"Mr. O'Brien, kindly get us started again, if you please."

"Yes, sir, Mr. Deever," O'Brien said. "Right away. Hawkeye, you just hop on board, and we'll haul you wherever you want to go."

"Thanks, O'Brien," Hawkeye said.

Julius Deever strode back to the first car and resumed his seat next to his wife, Mildred. A plumpish woman with long-suffering eyes, Mrs. Deever had a disconcerting habit of jumping nervously whenever something frightened her, and she was frightened of many things, including her husband.

Rachel asked, "Why did we stop, Uncle Julius?" Her voice had a soft Southern drawl, though she was trying hard to overcome it, not wanting to take it with her into her new life.

Before Deever could reply, the front door of the car opened again and a tall man in a buffalo robe stepped in. Rachel was attracted by his rawboned good looks, and a magnetism that she found exciting; but she was repulsed by the prairie grime which covered him, and even from this distance she could smell the ripe scent of buffalo and the odor of wood smoke.

He walked down the aisle, tipping his hat as he passed the two women. "Mr. Deever," he said. "Ladies."

"Sir!" Deever puffed up with outrage. "This is a private car, for the use of Union Pacific employees."

"Sorry, but you'll just have to suffer my presence," Hawkeye said, undaunted. "I'd be in the way up in the engine cab, and the other cars are loaded with supplies. Besides, I'm an employee of the UP, under contract to supply them with buffalo meat."

Deever glared and opened his mouth to speak again, but Hawkeye walked on to the far end of the car, selected an empty seat in the last row, and settled down into it. He pulled his long legs up so that his knees were resting on the seatback in front of him, reached up and casually tipped his hat forward, then folded his arms across his chest.

"Do you know that man, Julius?" Mildred asked her husband.

"He's a buffalo hunter," Deever said with a contemptuous sniff. "He provides meat for the work crews. Those men are the scum of the earth." He took out his watch and looked at it. "It'll be dark in an hour. We'll be stopping at Willow Station for supper. Hopefully, he'll get off there."

"Sorry to disappoint you, Mr. Deever," Hawkeye drawled from the back of the car. He didn't remove his hat or change position as he spoke. "Hawkeye Smith is going right on through to Plum Creek."

Deever coughed behind his hand and aimed his glare out the window. Rachel hid a smile behind her hand. She reached into her bag and took out a pencil and a sheet of paper. She had been keeping a diary since they started west; though, as she didn't actually have a diary, she was making do with loose sheets of paper, intending to bind them together into a book later.

She began writing.

April 15th—On the train, bound for End of the Track.

We are at sea. How else can I describe it? For there is no more adequate comparison with the plains of Nebraska than to say we are at sea, though in fact it is the middle of the continent. It is a world without features; an empty sky, an empty earth, with the twin black rods of steel stretching front and back from horizon to horizon, and the green plain rolling from side to side, touched by the skirts of heaven.

There have been only a few things to see during this long, weary day. Tiny yellow flowers, I know not what kind, bloom by the trackbed, as if even they hunger for the occasional human company which passes by. They are quite pretty, although I suspect that their beauty lies only in their ability to break up an otherwise monotonous landscape. Also, we occasionally see tiny dots beside the railroad, which grow more and more distinct as we draw near, until they become strange little houses, constructed of sod; then, too quickly, we flash by them, and they recede behind us, until they are indistinguishable from the ground from which they sprang.

Uncle Julius is very pleased about his assignment as construction foreman at End of the Track. Aunt Mildred is resigned, as always, to obeying his every wish and command, and to seeing to his comfort, all without the slightest expression of affection or even gratitude from Uncle Julius. He is a strange, cold man, with a sly, cruel streak to his character.

He continues to taunt me with the fact that the South lost the war, as if he alone were responsible. How I long for the time when I shall have saved enough money to be on my own! How I wish Aunt Mildred had the courage to join me!

Just now a strange man named Hawkeye Smith joined us on the train. Uncle Julius says he is a buffalo hunter. He is a little frightening in his strange buffalo robe, and he smells of buffalo and heaven knows what else!

Rachel stopped writing, her face flushing. Whatever had possessed her to write something like that? She thought of scratching it out, but the light was now too dim to continue writing, so she folded up the sheet of paper and put it in her bag, along with the other sheets of paper on which she had recorded her impressions of the trip.

She glanced across the aisle at her aunt and uncle. Julius Deever was sitting with his arms folded and his eyes closed. Her aunt was staring out the window, although by now it was too dark to see anything.

It wouldn't have mattered if it hadn't been too dark, Rachel mused, because her aunt wouldn't have seen anything anyway. Rachel had a theory about her aunt's long, silent periods of observation. She thought that Mildred Deever looked outward with such intensity only to prevent anyone else from looking in.

Mildred was her father's sister. She had married Julius Deever twenty years earlier; she had been approaching spinsterhood, and Deever was a way to avoid that fate. Deever had come to Mississippi to work on the railroad that ran from Vicksburg to Jackson, and he was impressed by the Bonner plantation. Deever did not understand the Mississippi law of primogeniture, and he thought that by marrying Mildred Bonner he would come in for a share of the Bonner wealth.

There was no share of the plantation, but there had been a very healthy dowry, which Deever had squandered in foolish investments within a year of their marriage. Deever returned to Ohio after the marriage, harboring a sense of injustice over "getting cheated out of the plantation," and when the War Between the States began, he took an intense pleasure in seeing the South brought to its knees.

Rachel's father had been killed at Shiloh, and her mother was killed during the siege of Vicksburg. When the siege was lifted and the river reopened, Rachel left the South to go to her only relative, her father's sister. She had little choice—the plantation house had been burned down, the earth scorched. She had journeyed alone up the Mississippi, then up the Ohio, until she reached her aunt's home at Cincinnati. Julius Deever was still away at war, and Mildred, whose own marriage had produced no children, gladly took her niece in. By the time Deever returned, Rachel's presence in the household was an accomplished fact, though Deever was a man of such ill-humor and insensibility that Rachel often wished she had never moved in with them.

The rear door of the train swung open, and the conductor entered.

"We're coming into Willow Station, folks. An hour stopover for supper."

"Will there be a sleeper coach at Willow Station?" Deever asked.

"Nope. Sorry, Mr. Deever," the conductor replied. "This here train don't normally take anyone but emigrants. It was just fortunate for you that this empty coach was made available for UP employees."

"Surely, sir, you don't call these accommodations fortunate?" Deever said, looking around the car in disgust.

"Yes, sir, if'n you knew how the emigrants have to travel. You should've waited until tomorrow. There's a First Class train making up to leave Omaha then."

"I couldn't wait until tomorrow," Deever said importantly. "Every day is precious to me, and to the UP. I'm needed there. You should know that."

"Yes, sir, I do know," the conductor said. "We can maybe pick up some pillows at Willow Station.

That might make your travel a mite more comfortable."

"Do what you can," Deever said sourly. Then, in a softer voice, "Why is *he* riding in this car?" He jerked his thumb back over his shoulder at the sleeping form of Hawkeye Smith.

"He's got a railroad pass, Mr. Deever, same as all the buffalo hunters."

"I don't approve of sharing my car with a foul-smelling buffalo hunter," Deever said, wrinkling his nose in distaste.

"I'm sorry, sir, but that's Dr. Durant's orders. All buffalo hunters have a pass to Second Class any time they want. You see, wasn't for them, there wouldn't be enough food to feed a crew the size of the UP's. Why, I imagine it's something like trying to feed an army."

"Speaking of food, what will the fare be at Willow Station?"

"Fried beef and potatoes, most likely. That's purty near what it always is."

The train began slowing, and Rachel peered through the grimy window to see what there was to see. There were dozens and dozens of tents and several crude wooden buildings. Lamps and campfires were everywhere, so she could see quite well, and she was astounded at the number of people who were gathered by the railroad depot to watch the arrival of the train.

"Mr. Deever, if you-all go into the First Class dining room in the station, you'll get jimquick service, I reckon, seeing as how you'll be the only First Class passengers there."

"What about our 'guest'?" Deever asked, twisting his mouth at the word and pointing again toward the rear of the car.

"Sorry to disappoint you again, Mr. Deever," Hawkeye said, standing up and stretching. "I do appreciate your kind invitation, really I do. But I'll have to mess with the train crew."

"I assure you, sir, that it was *not* meant as an invitation," Deever said with a sneer.

Hawkeye grinned lazily. "Well then, no harm done by the fact that I can't accept, is there?" He chuckled, then tipped his hat at Rachel and Mildred Deever, and left the car.

"Is that man so dense as to be totally unaware that he was not invited?" Deever said to no one in particular.

"I very much doubt he misunderstood, Uncle," Rachel said, hiding her smile.

The dining room to which the passengers were escorted was a low wooden building, windowless on each side, but with a large window and door in front. A boardwalk stretched across the dirt road to a short flight of wooden steps that led to the door. The building did not seem large enough to hold all the occupants; and once inside, the noise level was nearly unbearable. Many of the emigrants were foreigners, and the strange babble of their tongues mixed with the hearty-voiced banter of the American settlers and the alternate laughter and tears of the children. The room was brightly illuminated by four suspended clusters of oil lanterns. In the First Class dining room the tables had white linen, silver, china, and crystal, to make quite an attractive setting.

"Disgusting," Deever said, looking out over the emigrants crowding the main dining hall. There were two very long, common tables in the hall, both crowded to capacity, and other emigrants lined the walls, hoping they would find an opportunity to grab something to eat before the train pulled out.

Deever said, "There really should be a partition built to separate decent people from this rabble."

"I think they should let the poor people who couldn't get a seat out there come in here," Rachel said spiritedly. "After all, there's plenty of room for them in here, and they may not get anything to eat, otherwise."

"They should have thought of that when they tried to save money by traveling emigrant fare," Deever grumbled. "They certainly can't expect First Class service at those rates."

Rachel, feeling sorry for the people who were traveling in the emigrant section, noticed one particular man and woman and their two children, and her pity, strangely, turned into a kind of envy. The family was obviously poor, yet it didn't seem to trouble them in the least. Their faces reflected excitement over their adventure, and more than that—love for one another. Here, in a sudden and unexpected flash of insight, Rachel saw absolute and total happiness, and she would have given anything to be that women—not because she wanted a husband and family, but because she wanted to know what it was like to experience such joy.

With a sigh she turned back to the table. The

food was relatively bland, though filling, and Rachel ate it without complaint.

That was more than she could say for her Uncle Julius, and indeed, his complaining so unnerved her that after she finished eating, Rachel excused herself from the table and left the room. There was a chill in the air, and she pulled her shawl tightly around her. Free of her aunt and uncle, she decided to take a look around the town.

Willow Station was among those towns known as "Hell on Wheels," so called because they sprang up overnight like mushrooms to cater to the whims and tastes of the gandy dancers, or track workers. The towns had little to offer save liquor tents, bad restaurants, gambling houses, and prostitutes. Rachel encountered one of the latter soon after she left the dining hall.

"You're going to have to work the other side of the street, honey," a woman's voice said to her out of the shadows. "I've got this side staked out for myself."

"I beg your pardon?" Rachel said, startled, whirling around.

The woman stepped out of the shadows into the light. She was strangely pretty. Strangely, because Rachel had never seen eyes as dark, or lips as shiny. And then she realized that it was an exceptionally heavy application of makeup that illuminated the woman's face.

"Oh, excuse me, honey, my mistake," the woman said. "Are you a passenger from the train?"

Rachel nodded. "Yes."

"Well, it ain't none of my business, and I don't

even know why I'm bothering to tell you, but it ain't wise for a—a good woman to walk around here at night all alone."

"I'm not afraid," Rachel said stoutly.

"Then you're a fool, honey."

"*You're* out here alone," Rachel pointed out.

The woman threw back her head and laughed. "Yep, I am at that. Well, I've got to get back to work, so I'll say good night."

"Wait . . . What kind of work do you do?"

"What?" the woman laughed again, then peered at her closely. "Bless you, honey, I think you really don't know."

"How could I know? But I'd like to." A sudden, wild thought had just popped into Rachel's mind. If she could get a job here, she wouldn't have to continue with her aunt and uncle. She could rid herself of Julius Deever. So she was curious to know just what kind of work a woman could do in a place like this.

"You're sure you want to know?"

"Of course I do, or I wouldn't be asking." Rachel was becoming annoyed at the woman's evasiveness.

"I'm a whore, honey," the woman said bluntly, and turned on her heel and walked away, leaving Rachel staring after her.

She was shocked, but she felt more foolish than anything else. How could she have been so stupid? What else could a painted woman be doing on the street alone at night?

Rachel shook her head hard, then continued her exploration of the town. She felt a sense of security despite the prostitute's warning, because the train was sitting at the station with its cylinders blowing off steam in a regular, puffing rhythm, and the sound dominated everything. So long as she could hear that sound, Rachel reasoned, nothing could happen to her. But her sense of security was false, as she all too soon discovered.

"Well now, what have we here?" a man said suddenly, stepping into her path.

His abrupt appearance frightened Rachel, and she let out a gasp of surprise. Then, as she looked at him, her fear deepened, for his looks did little to reassure her. He had a shock of wild, stringy black hair, and his eyes picked up the reflection of the many fires and glowed as if illuminated by some satanic light. He had a huge, beak-like nose, which seemed to bloom from his face, and from his mouth, thin and mean, came the sour odor of whiskey. He had a long, unkempt beard, which he scratched with long, dirty fingernails.

"Pardon me, sir," she said, summoning all her courage. "You are blocking my way, and I wish to return to the train."

"You ain't going nowhere, girlie, not until I'm finished with you," he said.

"What do you mean?" Rachel whispered.

"I'll soon show you what I mean," the man snarled. In the light of the glowing campfires she could see his lewd smile. His hands began to fumble with the front of his breeches. Rachel was still aware of the sound of the train, and the fact that it was so near, yet so far, seemed only to heighten the fear she experienced as the man moved toward her with sliding steps.

CHAPTER TWO

"Leave the girl alone," a quiet voice said from behind Rachel.

"Who the hell are you?" the man demanded, peering into the shadows.

"The name is Hawkeye, friend," the voice said, "and if you don't want to find out how I earned that name, I suggest that you back off from the little lady and be on your way."

The words were followed by the click of a rifle bolt, and Hawkeye's tall figure emerged from the shadows, with his long rifle pointed negligently at the man accosting Rachel.

"Well now, Mr. Hawkeye," the man said harshly. "My advice to you is to find your own woman. I seen this one first, and I intend to stake her out for myself."

"You either leave now," Hawkeye said in a matter-of-fact voice, "or I'll shatter your kneecap with a rifle ball, and you'll never walk like a man again. Not that you're much of a man to start with."

The man seemed to grasp the peril of his situation for the first time, and his eyes took on the flat, opaque look of fear. He took his hands away from his trousers and shoved them out, palms up. "I . . . I ain't armed," he stuttered. "You wouldn't shoot an unarmed man, now would you?"

"I would," Hawkeye said flatly, "if you don't skeedaddle." At no time had he raised his voice, yet every word he spoke had a lethal quality to it, like the quiet, ominous click of his rifle being cocked.

"I . . . I'm going, mister, I'm going!" The man started backing away. As he did so, his breeches, which he had loosened, fell down around his knees, exposing long red underwear. Frantically, he reached down, pulled them up, and hurried away at an awkward hobble. Rachel began to laugh, partly from relief.

"Well, Miss Deever, it's good to see that you are able to retain your sense of humor," Hawkeye said dryly. "Most women in your predicament would be so frightened they would have swooned dead away."

"I can't help laughing," she said. "He looked so ridiculous pulling his breeches up, then running away like that, holding them up."

"He was a comical sight, wasn't he?"

"And I want to thank you," Rachel said. "I guess I should have had better sense than to wander about on my own, but I was curious to see the town."

"Miss Deever, I'd be most happy to show you around," Hawkeye offered.

"No, thank you, I do believe I've seen enough for one night. I just want to get back to the train. And my name isn't Deever, it's Bonner."

"Oh? I'm sorry," Hawkeye said in surprise.

"When I saw you with the Deevers, I thought . . . well, I naturally assumed that you weren't married. I should have known a pretty girl like you would have to be married, wouldn't she?"

Rachel started to correct him; then, for a reason she couldn't fathom, she decided not to. Let him think she was married, it would do no harm for the moment.

"I would feel better though, ma'am, if you'd let me walk you back to the train. This can be a pretty rough place, as you've just found out."

"Thank you, Mr. Smith," she said sweetly. "I would be obliged to you."

When they returned to the train, Hawkeye touched the brim of his hat. "I'll leave you now. You have a nice trip to End of the Track, Mrs. Bonner, and I do hope to have the pleasure of meeting you again some time."

"Oh? But I thought . . . Aren't you going on through?"

"No, ma'am," Hawkeye said politely. "I've had a sudden change of plans. I'm staying here for a spell. Good night to you, ma'am."

"Good night," Rachel said. She was disappointed that he wasn't accompanying them, a feeling that mystified her.

Hawkeye smiled at her, touched the brim of his hat one more time, then turned and strode back toward the cluster of tents and wooden shacks that made up the town. Rachel watched him for a moment, this big man in the stained hat and shabby buffalo robe, with his long rifle held in the crook of his arm. He had the look of a bear—and smelled like one, she thought wryly. Yet, despite his size, he carried himself well, walking with the grace of a cat, and he was extremely capable; he had just demonstrated that.

Finally she turned and entered the railroad car. The car was dimly lit now by lanterns that hung at each end, and by the cherry glow of the wood-burning stove, which took the chill out of the April night.

The conductor came toward her. "Miss, I've got some pillows and blankets for you and your folks."

"Thank you," Rachel said, taking the proffered bedding and making herself comfortable in one of the seats. She had almost dozed off by the time the Deevers returned. The train started up again, pulling away from the station in a series of jerks which quickly smoothed out, and as the wheels clacked over the rails, sleep overtook Rachel.

She had no idea how long she had been asleep when the dream came. There was a man in her dream, nameless and vague to be sure, but a man nonetheless. In the dream the unknown man's hands touched her breasts and caressed her until her nipples, like tiny, budding blooms, rose in response. Then those same hands explored her smooth skin to the dimple of her navel before moving farther down, across the curve of her thighs, and on to her most private part. There, knowing fingers played upon eager flesh until that which her consciousness would have denied burst upon her in sleep, awakening her to exquisite delight and deep embarrassment.

She sat upright, darting a look around the car to see if she had been observed. Her aunt and uncle were both asleep. Involuntarily, her glance jumped to the rear of the car, before she remembered that Hawkeye Smith wasn't on the train.

She had been asleep, but that was little excuse and no consolation. How could she dream such a dream?

Rachel's innocence went as far as her virginity. No man had known her intimately, thought there were many who had desired her and would have paid any price for the privilege. But Rachel knew herself to be a woman with passionate feelings, and she fought a constant battle to control that side of her nature. However, she did take pride in the fact that she could arouse a man's interest, and was not above playing at the game of flirtation.

The engineer blew the train whistle, a lonely sound rolling across the vast prairie. Rachel recalled the first time she had ever heard a train whistle in the night. She had been a very little girl, and the newly built railroad passed just north of the Bonner plantation on its night run from the Mississippi River to Jackson. The whistle was a strange and frightening sound to her then. It had awakened her, and she had cried. .

"Why are you crying, Princess?" her father asked, coming into her room to check on her.

"I'm afraid of the dragon," she said.

"The dragon?" He hid a smile behind his hand. "What dragon, Princess?"

The train whistle's mournful sound came again. "*That* dragon. Daddy, why does it scream so?"

Her father laughed softly. "That's not a dragon,

darling Rachel. That's just a choo-choo train out on that new track, and it'll be passing this way every night from now on." The whistle blew once more. "Hear it?" her father asked. "It's saying 'gooood niiight, sleeep tiiight.' "

And again the whistle sounded. "Gooood niiight, sleep tiiight," her father intoned over the sound of the whistle.

"Gooood niiight, sleeep tiiight," Rachel imitated him, giggling, and from that time, the far-off, lonely wail of a locomotive whistle always spoke to her in her father's voice.

Now, on the train chugging across the prairie, Rachel adjusted her pillows. Outside the window, in the moonlight, she saw the black shadows of a small stand of buffalo as they lumbered away from the track. They had evidently been the cause of the engineer blowing the whistle, and when Rachel saw them she thought of Hawkeye and wondered again why he had changed his plans. He had originally said that he was going on through, yet he had remained behind in Willow Station.

She also wondered what he looked like when he was cleaned up—if that ever happened.

Had Rachel been in the back room of the Chicago House Saloon at that particular moment, she would have seen what Hawkeye Smith looked like cleaned up. Or at least she wouldn't have had long to wait, for at that moment Hawkeye was sitting in a large brass bathtub, happily scrubbing away the residue of four weeks on the prairie. His dirty clothes had been given over to Ling Chou, operator of a laundry next door to the Chicago House, and a clean pair of breeches and a shirt hung over the back of a nearby chair. A cigar was elevated at a jaunty angle from Hawkeye's freshly shaven face, and he was trying to wash his back while at the same time singing, "The dew is on the grass, Lorena . . ."

"If you'll stop that infernal racket, Hawkeye, I'll wash your back for you," said a woman's voice.

Hawkeye glanced up and grinned widely. "Hello, Kate. What's the matter? You telling me you don't care for my singing?"

"Is that what you call it? I've heard coyotes do better," Kate Muldoon said, taking the washcloth from him and starting on his back.

"Ahhh," Hawkeye said in blissful appreciation. "A little more to the left, if you don't mind. There, that's it! Of course I call it singing. My horse liked it."

"Uh-huh, and where is your horse now?"

"Dead," Hawkeye said. "Indians got him."

"That's your story. If the truth were known, your singing probably did him in."

"Ah, Kate, 'tis a cruel woman you are."

"Don't spout blarney at me, Hawkeye Smith."

"Blarney, is it? And you with a name like Kate Muldoon, and hair as red as a sunset on snow."

Kate grinned. "The hair is as phony as the name, and you know it. Clara Wilson came out here with brown hair, and with the help of a little hair dye and a lot of experience, she became Kate Muldoon."

"And why not? After all, the gandy dancers are

mostly Irish. It's a good thing you're following the UP, Kate, and not the CP. I think you'd have a bit of trouble becoming Mại Ly."

"I've heard that the Chinese workers on the CP bring their own whores right along with them, as well as their own cooks."

"That's true, Kate, that's God's truth," Hawkeye said. "Ah, that feels good, damned good. You know, you wouldn't have to be a whore, you could make a good living just scrubbing backs."

Kate laughed heartily and squeezed the washcloth out over Hawkeye's head, letting some of the soapy water run down over his face.

"Watch what you're doing, woman! You'll put out my cigar!"

"And why not?" she said in a teasing voice. "It would clear the air of all this foul smoke."

Hawkeye grinned, and dunked his cigar in the water to extinguish it, then tossed it aside. "Listen, have you had your supper yet?"

"Such as it was."

"Fatback Charlie is frying a chicken for me. Would you like to join me?"

"However did you get Fatback Charlie to agree to kill one of his chickens?" she asked in astonishment. "I swear, the way he fusses over them, a person would think they were all pets or something."

"Fatback Charlie and me go back a long way."

"I figured it was something like that." She smiled seductively. "What do you plan to do *after* supper?"

"I plan to get a little sleep."

"Alone?"

"I said sleep. It has to be that way, I'm afraid," he said sadly. "I'm a little strapped for funds."

"Now when have I ever asked *you* for money?" Kate asked, pouting.

"I know, Kate, you're very good about that. But Katie girl, you have a living to make, just like everyone else."

Kate ran her fingers into his hair, then moved them down to his ear. "I can give away a sample now and then, can't I?"

"Well, sure. But it seems to me it's a little more than a sample when we get together." He grinned lazily. "But after all, it's yours to give away."

"That's right," she said emphatically. "Anyway, you've offered to share one of Fatback Charlie's chickens with me, and you can consider that payment, if you like."

"Kate, you have a deal, even though I'll be getting by far the best of the bargain."

The door opened suddenly, and a short, thin man wearing sleeve garters and a top hat came in. He was carrying a tray upon which sat a bottle and a glass. "Here's your drink, Hawkeye."

"Thanks, Bennie," Hawkeye said.

Behind Bennie, Fatback Charlie, a huge, bald-headed man, belly-hung but obviously strong, with a scar twisting its was across his flat face, came in.

"Your supper's ready," Fatback Charlie said. When he spoke, he sounded like a train engine letting off steam.

Hawkeye, still sitting in the bathtub, looked at the three people standing around him. "Uh . . . Thanks."

"Pardon me, but I was told that I could find a Mr. Smith back here," a new voice said, and a fourth person came into the room. He was dressed like an Easterner, and appeared somewhat embarrassed to have walked in on a naked man in a bathtub.

"Now just a minute!" Hawkeye snarled. "What the hell! Is there a sign outside that door that says Willow Station Depot? Can't you people see I'm taking a bath here?"

"Hell, we can all see that, Hawkeye!" a voice roared mirthfully from the saloon, and his yell was followed by a raucous chorus of laughter. Hawkeye craned his neck around the people grouped around the tub, and realized that he was indeed visible to any of the saloon patrons who cared to look in his direction, since the door was standing wide.

"Bennie!"

"Yes, Hawkeye?"

"Leave my drink, and get back to tending bar. And close that damned door after you!"

"Yes, sir," Bennie said with a straight face, his eyes jumping with amusement.

"And you, Fatback, take Kate along and set the table for two. She'll be joining me for supper."

"Sure, Hawkeye."

"And you, whoever you are," Hawkeye growled, leveling a finger at the stranger.

"I am sorry to burst in on you like this, old man," the Easterner murmured.

"Well, never mind. It's too late now." Hawkeye waited until everyone but the Easterner had left the room. Then the stranger winked at Hawkeye, and they both whooped with laughter.

"Steve King, how the hell are you?" Hawkeye exclaimed.

"Well, I must say I'm doing much better now that I've found you," Steve King said. "I heard you were out on a buffalo hunt and wouldn't be back for a time."

"I wasn't supposed to be back just yet, but I ran into a band of Indians who changed my travel plans somewhat."

"I heard that, too. You must point them out to me if we ever meet. I'd like to thank them for saving me from spending any more time in this godforsaken place."

"It isn't all that bad here," Hawkeye said with a sly twinkle in his eye. "We have all the conveniences of a big city. Baths," he held his hand up and let water drip back into the cup, "liquor," he pointed at the bottle and glass, "and women and food. What more could a man ask for?"

"Ah, yes, what more indeed?" King said sarcastically.

"Let me get dressed, and then we can talk."

Hawkeye stepped out of the tub and began drying himself off. His well-muscled, finely formed body was covered with a network of scars, including one on his right side which was about the size of a silver dollar, puffed out in a growth of white scar tissue. It looked as if someone had daubed him with a handful of clay.

"Comanche war lance," Hawkeye said, noticing

the direction of King's glance. He touched the scar. "It didn't heal back too pretty, but it never bothers me, and didn't leave me in the least lame."

"How did you get it?"

"I was playing a little game with Mean-to-His-Horses."

King stared. "A *game*?"

Hawkeye smiled, a slow, crooked smile. "Yeah. Just that, a game. We were throwing the lances at each other, trying to see how close we could come. Mean-to-His-Horses miscalculated a mite, and hit me in the side."

"What did you say to him?"

"Nothing."

"*Nothing?*"

"Nothing," Hawkeye repeated. He was dressing now. "You have to understand the way an Indian thinks. Not too many white men can, but I can, because I've lived with them off and on for about four years. You see, if I had said anything, whined about it, I would have been a poor sport. Not only that, I would have been a woman, because I complained about pain. And I would have made Mean-to-His-Horses lose face in front of his tribe. So I just pulled the lance out of my side and threw it back at him."

King was fascinated. "Then what happened?"

"Then, Horses pretended that he had just noticed my injury, we both pretended that we didn't know how or when it happened, and he had his medicine man treat it."

"Remind me not to play games with Indians," King said with a little shudder. "I'm sure they'd end up calling *me* a woman."

Hawkeye chuckled. "You know, the funny thing is, there's nobody alive who can withstand pain like an Indian woman, least of all an Indian man." He became brisk. "Now, my friend, what brings you here?"

"There's a new foreman on the way to End of the Track."

"You came all the way out here just to tell me that? Hell, I met him."

"Julius Deever?"

"The very one. In fact, he was on the train that just went through here tonight. I was going on through along with him, until I got word that some Eastern dude was around asking about me."

"What was your impression of him?"

"I think he's a pompous ass, for one thing." Hawkeye grinned suddenly. "But he's got a damned good-looking daughter."

"Deever doesn't have a daughter."

"Sure he does, I met her. Her name is Rachel Bonner. It's just my luck that some lucky fellow has already married her."

King laughed, shaking his head. "I see you haven't changed much when it comes to good-looking women. But Rachel Bonner is Deever's niece, not his daughter. And she's not married."

"But . . ."

"But what?"

"Never mind." Hawkeye gestured. "I suppose she was just having a little sport with me."

"I don't know what the devil you're talking about, but I'm not here to discuss Rachel Bonner. What's your opinion of Julius Deever?"

"Like I've already said, he's a pompous ass, overly taken with himself and, I suspect, a bully to his wife and niece."

"I thought your opinion of him might not be too high, and I'm inclined to agree with you. But Hawkeye, you have to be very careful not to let personal considerations get in the way of our job . . . and Julius Deever is likely to figure quite prominently in what we have to do."

"Is he in on it?"

"No, no," King said. "You're the only one in on this end, and we hope to keep it that way."

"Good!" Hawkeye had finished dressing and was running a comb through his long hair. To anyone who had seen him before, the transformation was amazing. Instead of a foul-smelling, shaggy creature of the plains, there now stood a handsome young man. He said, "Steve, do you think we can pull this thing off?"

"We can do it," King said emphatically. "Don't forget, Hawkeye, there are millions of dollars at stake. And I mean millions!"

Hawkeye laughed wryly. "Here we stand talking about millions, and I scarcely have enough to pay for a meal."

"Do you want a little money?" King asked, pulling his purse from his inside coat pocket. "I can let you have a few dollars."

"No, you'd better not," Hawkeye said, waving the money off. "It's better that I get along without much money. It's expected of me. I want people to think of me as just what I seem to be—a buffalo hunter."

King nodded. "I suppose that's best. After all, if the wrong person ever got wind of what you're up to, you could be in grave trouble."

"I could be dead," Hawkeye said in a flat voice.

CHAPTER THREE

It was called End of the Track, as if that were the name of a town. Many of the towns along the railroad had begun as End of the Track, and then graduated to a real name—Columbus, Grand Island, Fort Kearney, Willow Station, Plum Creek, North Platte. Some End of the Track towns vanished when the tracks moved on, so that nothing was left of what had once been a thriving community.

There was little to distinguish this End of the Track from other "Hell on Wheels" towns Rachel had seen along the railroad right-of-way. It had the same canvas tents, wooden structures, and hybrid combinations of the two. The majority of the structures were saloons, gambling houses, or brothels, set up to relieve the workers of their pay as soon as they had earned it. There were a few buildings that passed as hotels, and one rather substantial-looking building with "The Roundhouse" painted across the front.

Rachel stood on the station platform with Aunt Mildred and a mound of luggage, looking around in the gray morning light at this place which was to be their new home. They were tired and sore from riding on hard seats for so long, and Rachel longed for a bath.

The train had arrived just before seven o'clock and was sitting on the track behind them, popping and snapping as the heated gearboxes and connecting rods cooled. At every town they had passed through, everyone had turned out to meet the train, and the platforms were crowded with all sorts of people: townspeople and newly arrived passengers, miners in broad hats and great boots, buffalo hunters in robes, carrying long rifles, farmers in homespun clothing, nervous emigrants in the quaint dress of their home countries, and children, laughing, shouting, sometimes crying.

"I've located our quarters," Julius Deever said, bustling up to the two women. He had left them shortly after they arrived, to report his presence and find out where they were to stay.

"Which—which tent is it?" his wife asked. She brushed her hair back with the back of her hand, and looked with distaste toward the row of unattractive tents.

"It isn't a tent," Deever said importantly. "We have a private car parked on a siding, just for our own use."

Rachel saw the look of relief on her aunt's face, but she also saw that Deever hadn't even noticed; he had been so insensitive as to put his wife through all that anxiety for no reason. He could have told them that earlier!

"Here's the wagon I hired," Deever said, as a

mule-drawn wagon approached. A withered old man who looked to be in his seventies was driving. Deever motioned imperiously. "Over here!"

The wagon drew to a halt before the platform.

"I showed you which car was mine," Deever said to the driver. "Load this luggage and take it and the ladies over there. Mildred, I have some important business to attend to. I'll see you later. Rachel, as you will be boarding with us, I shall expect you to attend to the cooking and the cleaning. And please do not dally about, now."

"Yes, Uncle," Rachel said obediently. She felt resentment rising in her, but didn't voice it. She had known what to expect.

Deever hurried away, swollen with self-importance, and the wagon driver and the two women began to load the wagon. Most of the articles were easy enough to handle, but there were two great trunks which seemed to be more than the three of them together could manage.

"Ladies, are you wanting those two trunks on that wagon?" A large, powerfully built man approached them. He was easily six feet, three inches tall, and had massive arms and shoulders that gave him the look of a giant. He had dark, curly hair and a dark bush of whiskers, though the area immediately around his mouth was clean shaven. His eyes, Rachel noted, were a snapping brown.

"Yes," said Mildred Deever. "But I'm afraid we have no money to pay you. My husband—"

"Ma'am, you're out west now," the man said. "Out here we do for our lady folks just because it's the proper thing to do." He picked the trunks up from the platform, one at a time, and handled them as easily as Rachel had the lightest valise. "Now, I reckon I'll have to go along with you to unload them, too. Go ahead, Mr. Jenkins, you can take 'em now."

The driver climbed up onto the wagon seat, clucked to his mule, and the wagon began to move.

"I want to thank you, Mr., uh," Rachel started.

"Simmons, ma'am. Will Simmons."

"Yes, Mr. Simmons," Mildred said. "My niece and I both are very grateful."

"I'm only too glad to be of help, Mrs. Deever," Will Simmons said easily.

"You know who we are?" Rachel asked in surprise.

"Yes, ma'am, I sure do, Miss Bonner. Your uncle is the new construction foreman. Fact is, I'm a gang boss myself, and I'll be working for him."

They were walking alongside the slow-moving wagon as they conversed.

"Well, there's your new home," Will said, with a nod of his head.

The "new home" was a dispirited-looking railroad car, badly in need of paint, and coated with dirt and rust.

"Oh!" Mildred said. "Oh, dear." She put her hand to her mouth and stared despairingly at the dilapidated car.

"I reckon it does strike you as kind of strange, I mean living in a railroad car and all," Will said. "But it's real roomy on the inside, and best of all, when it rains the water doesn't run through the floor like it does in most of the tents and buildings here at

End of the Track. And it can be hooked up to the locomotive and pulled on to the next End of the Track, when we're finished here. Convenient, you see."

"Mr. Simmons, what is that big building over there?" Rachel asked, pointing to the structure they were walking past.

"That building, ma'am? That's the Roundhouse."

"I thought a roundhouse was where engines were turned around, and always a round building? I don't see any tracks leading into that one."

Will laughed. "It's just called the Roundhouse, ma'am, it's not really one. What it is, is a restaurant. A pretty fancy one, for around here."

"A restaurant? I must say it certainly has the look of a fine restaurant, much nicer than any I've seen so far."

"Yes, ma'am, I reckon that's true. The Roundhouse sort of caters to the rich folks from back east, the railroad investors, who come out here to see how their money is being spent. Of course, anyone is welcome to eat there, if they like, but the meals are so expensive that not too many of the workers go there."

"Have you ever eaten there?"

Will smiled sheepishly. "Well, yes, ma'am, one time I did, just to see what it was like. But the truth is . . . I'm saving all my money. I'm getting pretty good wages from the UP, and I got a place to spend it."

"Oh? You have a wife and children?" Rachel asked.

"No, ma'am." Will shook his head. "I don't want

to take a wife, not until I have something to give her. That's the idea, you see. I'm saving my money to buy land."

"Land?"

"Yes, ma'am. I intend to buy a right smart chunk of land and start me a farm. 'Course the first few years, it'll all be a struggle, mind, but I figure with three or four sons, why, by the time they're old enough to help me work it, I'll have me a showplace. Yes, sir, a real showplace."

Will's eyes, which were naturally bright anyway, took on a fervent glow as he talked of his dream, and so intense and eloquent was he that Rachel could almost visualize his farm in her own mind.

"Well, I certainly hope you get everything you want, Mr. Simmons," she said.

"Well, I . . . Thank you, ma'am," he said, obviously moved by her comment. He cleared his throat. "I'll just get these big trunks inside for you, and then get out of your way. I know you two ladies have lots of things to do, what with just getting off the train and all."

"Thank you again, Mr. Simmons," Rachel said, marveling anew at the ease with which he was able to handle the heavy trunks.

There was a broom of sorts in the car, a tied sheaf of sagebrush, and Rachel went to work after Will left. Mildred, worn out from the long trip, stretched out on the bed and went right to sleep, despite the cloud of dust that Rachel's sweeping raised.

After she was done, Rachel drew some water

from a nearby pump and began washing the windows and walls, and by noon the car was relatively livable. It was certainly much improved over the condition in which they had found it. After she finished with the rest of the "house," she took care of her own room. It was at the far end of the car, very small, but adequate for her needs. She unpacked her one suitcase, hung her clothes up to air out, and she was settled in.

But she wanted a bath. More than just about anything in the world at that moment, she longed for a bath, for the dust and smoke and dirt and grime of the long journey seemed to have settled on her like some oppressive weight.

The car had a small bathroom, with a wooden tub large enough to bathe in. Of course, the water would have to be hauled in from the pump, a fire would have to be laid in the wood stove, the water would have to be heated, and afterward the water would have to be scooped out, bucket by bucket. It was all extremely inconvenient, but nothing was too much trouble if the final reward was the chance to bathe. So she built a fire, heated the water, filled the tub, and finally, gratefully, she settled in, luxuriating in the warmth and the fresh feeling of water and soap.

Then, wearing a clean though somewhat wrinkled cotton dress, Rachel felt like a new woman. She set out to explore End of the Track. Exploration of the town itself didn't take long, for one liquor tent looked pretty much like another from the outside, and of course, she had no intention of going *inside.*

There were a couple of supply stores, a barber shop, a restaurant similar to the ones she had been eating in for a week now, and the Roundhouse.

The Roundhouse intrigued Rachel. It was two stories high, and dominated End of the Track. No matter where in town a person might be, what caught the eye first was the Roundhouse. Finally, as she had known she would from the very first, Rachel went inside to look around.

Rachel gasped when she saw the dining room. It was the most beautiful public dining room she had ever seen. It reminded her of the dining room at Bonner Plantation when it was set for a party. Large chandeliers hung from the ceiling. They were lighted by kerosene, and they glowed with a soft, gold light with the hundreds of glass facets exploding in spectrums of rainbow colors. The tables were covered with beautifully worked damask cloth and laid with bone china, which seemed to shine with some soft, inner light. The eating utensils were of silver, and the stemware of delicate, fine crystal.

"You idiot!" a woman's angry voice exploded from the kitchen. "Look at what you've done now!"

Rachel was startled by the voice, and she took a step back toward the front door, looking toward the kitchen in alarm. Two people came through the door, a young girl still in her teens, and a woman of around thirty. The older woman was well dressed, wearing a maroon gown which showed an amazing—no, a shocking amount of cleavage. She had yellow hair and was pretty, but it was a beauty without softness. She was heaping abuse on the younger woman. Her breasts, clearly visible in the low-cut dress, rose and fell as she yelled, and Rachel feared they were about to spill over the top of the dress.

"You can't do anything right, can you?" the yellow-haired woman screamed. "Just look at what you've done! You have just ruined this tablecloth!" She held up a white tablecloth and waved it threateningly in front of the girl.

"I'm sorry, Miss Thompson," the girl said miserably. "I have no idea how wine got into that flask. It was empty only this morning. I would certainly have been more careful if I had known. It won't happen again, I promise you."

"Oh, I agree! It sure as the devil won't happen again," the older woman snapped. "Because you're fired!"

"Miss Thompson, please don't fire me," the girl pleaded. "I need this job. You know my pa was killed in a construction accident. Ma is sick, and this is the only way we have to earn a living."

"You should have thought of that before you were so clumsy. This tablecloth is ruined. There is no way to get a red wine stain out of it."

"There is a way you can get it out," Rachel said, and almost as soon as the words were uttered, she regretted them, for they sounded much louder than she had intended, and earned her a long, unfriendly stare from Miss Thompson.

"What did you say?" Miss Thompson said.

"I—I . . . Uh, excuse me for butting in," Rachel said hesitantly. "I couldn't help but overhear, but I do know a way to get a red wine stain out of a cloth."

"Butt out," Miss Thompson said. "This is none of your affair, whoever you are."

"No, no, Marie, allow the lovely young creature to speak," a man's voice said.

Rachel glanced to the back of the room and saw a tall, handsome man in his mid to late thirties. He had wavy brown hair, insolent blue eyes, and a somewhat world-weary look about him. He had none of the ruggedness or strength she had noticed in Hawkeye Smith or Will Simmons. In fact, his classic good looks were almost feminine. Yet, Rachel sensed something about him. A current of menace seemed to flow through him. She instinctively knew that he could be dangerous to men—and to women. And yet that danger intrigued her.

There was something else about him as well. In this raw, primitive world of the West, she had grown accustomed to seeing men dressed in homespun or buckskin or other filthy, prairie-type clothing. This man was dressed as elegantly as any of the wealthiest planters who had visited the Bonner Plantation before the war. And not since then had Rachel seen anyone so strikingly handsome, who could do full justice to such attire.

"My name is Ewell Rankin," he said easily. "I own this place," his glance moved to Marie Thompson, "and everything in it."

Rachel noticed that the woman looked quickly toward the floor, color rising in her cheeks, and she knew that Ewell Rankin included her in his claim of ownership.

"And who might you be?" Rankin asked.

"Rachel Bonner," she replied. "My uncle, Julius Deever, is the—"

"The new construction foreman," Rankin interrupted. "Yes, I've met Julius. But I didn't know he had such a lovely niece. The company wired that he was due in today."

"The company?"

"Credit Mobilier," Rankin said. "Credit Mobilier is handling the construction of the UP, and I am their liaison. This is sort of a sideline of mine," he said, waving his hand around the restaurant. "But having a place like this helps me in my job, for I must impress my guests favorably if I am to operate properly. But enough of that. You were about to tell us how to take the wine stain out of the tablecloth."

"It can't be done," Marie Thompson said emphatically.

"Oh, but it can," Rachel said quickly. "My mammy showed me how."

"Your *what*?" Marie said, with a scornful laugh.

"My . . . my mammy."

"Well, well! I do believe we have a gen-u-ine Southern belle in our midst, Ewell."

"Marie, would you kindly be quiet and allow Miss Bonner to speak?"

"Ewell, can't you see what she's trying to do?" Marie said, a note of desperation creeping into her voice. "She's just trying to worm her way in here!"

"The way things look right now," Rankin said coldly, "perhaps that isn't a bad idea."

Rachel suddenly realized that the other woman was jealous of her. The thought surprised her. Why should Marie be jealous of *her*? And yet it pleased her too, in a way she wasn't that proud of.

"*Would* you like a job here?" Rankin was saying. "Is that why you're here?"

"I . . ." Rachel broke off, gazing around. Curiosity alone had driven her in here, but perhaps she *would* like a job here. "Yes," she said. "Yes, I think I would like to work here."

"Show Marie how to clean that tablecloth, and the job is yours," Rankin said with a smile.

"Oh no, it isn't!" Marie said stormily. "Ewell, I won't stand for it!"

"You will stand for whatever I say, my dear." His voice was even colder. When Marie, intimidated, dropped her glance, he said more easily, "Besides, you just fired Becky, so you're going to need a replacement."

"I don't care," Marie said sullenly. "I won't have this Miss Pushy working for me."

"What are you worried about, Marie? Are you feeling threatened?"

"Threatened? Of course I'm not threatened! But I don't want her here. If she goes to work here, I leave. It's as simple as that."

"Miss Bonner, can you clean the tablecloth?" Rankin asked.

"Yes," she said.

"Tell Becky how to do it."

"Sprinkle it with lots of salt," Rachel said. "Then dunk it in cold water. You'll be able to scrub the stain out."

The girl took the tablecloth and went back into the kitchen.

"Well?" Marie demanded, staring hard at Rankin.

"Well what?"

"You heard what I said. If you hire this girl, I'm leaving."

"Then goodbye, Marie."

"Goodbye?" Marie exclaimed, blinking. "Ewell . . . Do you know what you're saying?"

"I always know what I'm saying," Rankin said with a wolfish grin. "I'm telling you goodbye. You did say you were leaving, didn't you?"

"Ewell Rankin! You can't just throw me out like used dishwater." Marie's hands were clenched at her sides.

"It strikes me that it's the other way around, my dear. I'm not doing it, *you* are."

"It's . . . It's a matter of *principle*," Marie said. "After all, I do have *some* rights around here. I am more than just a hostess, you know."

"You are *nothing* but a hostess," Rankin said harshly. "And the only rights you have are what I give you."

"I . . . I see," Marie said faintly, her eyes glistening with sudden tears. "In that case, I shall leave."

The sound of an approaching train could be heard. Rankin smiled. "If you hurry, Marie, you can catch the next train out."

"I will be on it, Mr. Rankin. You can count on that!" Marie threw back her head, dashed the tears from her eyes, gathered up her skirts, and whirled away. She ran to a flight of stairs at the back.

Rankin raised his voice. "Marie!"

The woman looked back hopefully. "Yes?"

"Just take the clothes you came with. The rest of the gowns are the property of the Roundhouse."

The expression on Marie's face hardened, and Rachel thought that she had never seen such hatred in anyone's eyes. Then the woman hurried on up the stairs.

There was a squeal of delight from the kitchen, and Becky came running in. "It worked!" She held the tablecloth up for them to see. "See? It's as good as new!"

"I knew it would," Rachel said.

Rankin, who had been about to enter a small office off to one side, turned back and came over to her. "So your mammy knew what she was talking about."

"Yes," Rachel said.

"Did she teach you any more tricks?"

"Like what?" she asked warily.

"Did she instruct you on how to act as hostess for a ball, things like that?"

"Well, yes, of course she did. Every Southern girl knows how to be a hostess."

"Good! You're hired. You can act as hostess for the Roundhouse."

"I'm not sure what a hostess does in a place like this."

"It's very simple," Rankin said with a smile. "I give parties here. You see, Miss Bonner, building something on the scale of the Union Pacific Railroad takes money, a great deal of money. The purpose of the Roundhouse, basically, is to provide a nice place to entertain investors when they come out here to see how their money is being spent. And, of course, we also cater to the First Class passengers who ride out as well. All you have to do is supervise the staff and see that things run smoothly. In essence, you will act as hostess for whatever parties I give. Now, can you handle that?"

"Yes," Rachel said. And as she spoke, she knew that all along she had been hoping for an opportunity such as this, so she could save enough money to be able to leave the Deevers. And to have the opportunity come so unexpectedly was a godsend! She said, "Yes, I'm sure I can handle it."

"Then it's settled."

"There is one thing . . ." She was troubled by the rough manner in which he had discharged Marie Thompson.

"What's that, my dear?"

"I feel bad about taking Miss Thompson's place, about the abrupt way she is being sent away."

Rankin gave a negligent shrug. "I would have gotten rid of her soon, in any case. Of late, she's begun thinking that the Roundhouse is hers to run as she pleases. And I can't have that."

Rachel was silent for a moment. It would be foolish of her to turn down the job because of the sudden firing of a woman she'd never seen until today. She said, "There is another thing. I want to rehire Becky." She was rewarded by a wide smile of relief on the young woman's face.

"That's your bailiwick," Rankin said, shrugging

again. "Now, go get your things and move in. Your room will be the one Marie is vacating."

"Oh!" Rachel said, clapping a hand to her mouth. "Oh, no . . . I don't think I can do that."

"Why not?"

"I will have to keep living with my aunt and uncle."

Rankin's face darkened for just a second, then he nodded. "Well, I don't suppose that will pose any problems, if that's the way you want it. Just so long as you get to work on time."

"I will," she said. "I promise, I will."

"Good. You can start this afternoon. As soon as—"

"I'm going now, *Mister* Rankin!" Marie Thompson said icily, marching determinedly past them, carrying a small bag.

"Goodbye again, Marie," Rankin said blandly.

"Goodbye to you, sir! If I never see you again, it will be too soon!" she said, slamming the door behind her.

"Now that she's gone," Rankin said, "you can select the gown you will wear tonight."

"The gown?"

"Come along, I'll show you."

Rachel followed Ewell Rankin up the flight of stairs down which Marie had just come. At the top there was a long carpeted landing, with several doors opening off to either side.

"The other rooms are for our guests," Rankin explained. "This is my room, and right next to it is your room. If you want it."

He opened the door, and Rachel stepped inside, then gasped at its unexpected loveliness. It was nearly as large as the railroad car she was to share with the Deevers. It had a huge canopied bed, a dresser, a chifforobe, a sitting area, and a large brass bathtub.

"Oh, it is grand!" Rachel breathed.

"It's yours to use any time you want it, my dear. It comes with the job."

"Was Marie Thompson sleeping with you?" she asked abruptly, shocking herself with the ease with which she was able to voice the question.

"Of course," Rankin said amusedly.

"Mr. Rankin, if that, like this room, is a part of the job . . ."

Rankin laughed heartily. "It's not a *requirement* of the position, Miss Bonner. So don't worry your pretty head. Now, about the dresses?" He opened the door to the closet, and Rachel gaped in wonder.

"I have never seen so many gowns, nor such beautiful ones."

"Pick one out for tonight." He gestured expansively.

"They are all so lovely. How can I?"

"Here," Rankin said. "I think you'll be gorgeous in this one." He selected a dress of pale gold silk with a very full skirt and held it up for her inspection. "I'll have someone bring it to you at the railroad car, so you won't need to carry it."

"No," Rachel said hastily. "I'll come over here to dress."

Rankin smiled knowingly. "I hoped you would say that."

And as he looked at her, with that secret knowledge in his eyes, Rachel felt a sudden and inexplicable chill, as if she were without her clothes. It was a thrilling, though frightening, feeling.

CHAPTER FOUR

Rachel was sure that Julius Deever would be very angry when told of her new job at the Roundhouse. He did begin to puff up in that way he had, which always reminded Rachel of a toad, and she said hastily, "I told Mr. Rankin that the only way I would take the job was if I could live here, and continue to do my chores."

He gasped at her. "Rankin? Ewell Rankin? What does he have to do with it?"

"Why, he owns the Roundhouse, he hired me."

The anger drained out of him then. He glowered at her for a moment before saying sourly, "All right. So long as the work gets done here."

"It will, Uncle Julius, I promise."

"Although why he'd hire a ninny like you is beyond me. Oh, well." He sneered. "It won't last long anyway. Rankin's a shrewd fellow. He'll soon learn how useless you are, and get rid of you. A hostess indeed! Hah!"

* * *

The gold gown Rachel wore the first evening was as low-cut as the one Marie Thompson had been wearing, and even when she was fully dressed, Rachel felt half-naked. She was extremely aware of the twin mounds of white flesh that rounded up above the dipping neckline of her dress, and she felt an unaccustomed coldness with so much skin exposed to the night air. Then, strangely, she felt warm, for it seemed to her that every man in the Roundhouse had eyes only for her décolletage.

Despite her discomfort in the dress, Rachel was excited; for to step into the Roundhouse out of the dusty squalor of End of the Track was like taking a trip through time and space. Outside, there were the rough and tumble gandy dancers, pioneers, hunters, settlers, and similar types. Inside the Roundhouse, men and women dressed like ladies and gentlemen of class; their language was refined, and elegance was the watchword. It was as if she were back home on Bonner Plantation, before the war.

There were several important personages from the East staying at the Roundhouse. Some of them, Rachel was to learn, were from Credit Mobilier; others were from banks, or influential newspapers. There were even a couple of congressmen present.

The first evening had gone without incident. Rachel had been uncertain at first, but the staff was well trained and efficient, and Rachel really had very little to do. Now, as the staff was cleaning up after the evening meal—pheasant under glass—she stood back in the shadows and watched. The last of the important guests had left the dining room, and Ewell Rankin strolled over to chat with her. He was smoking a long, thin cigar with a mild and pleasant aroma.

"My dear, how did you enjoy your first evening?" he asked.

"Mr. Rankin, I enjoyed it very much!"

"Now, that is something that is going to have to change," he said, taking the cigar from his mouth and pointing at her with it.

"What?" she asked in some alarm.

"Your calling me Mr. Rankin," he said, smiling. "I am Ewell to my friends, and I certainly hope you will become my friend."

"You are my employer," she said diffidently.

"Can't I be your employer *and* your friend?"

Rachel had to laugh. "Yes, I suppose you can."

"Good," he said heartily. "Then that's settled. Now, I should like to take you for a little drive before you return home."

"A drive?" she said warily. "Where to?"

"Oh, a short way out on the prairie, just to show you a few of the local sights."

Rachel laughed again. "Ewell, I have just crossed hundreds of miles of prairie. Believe me, there's nothing all that great to see."

"Oh, but there is," he said smugly. "If you'll allow me to show you."

"I . . . I don't know. I really should be getting home."

"Are you that anxious to return to your uncle? Julius Deever doesn't strike me as being interesting to be around."

Rachel was surprised by his perception, but she thought it best not to show it. "Very well," she said gravely. "But only for a short drive, mind you."

"I promise. Only a short drive. In fact, we can leave now. There is nothing more you have to do here tonight."

"I must change clothes."

"That isn't necessary, either."

"But I'll catch my death," she protested, unconsciously placing a hand across the exposed tops of her breasts.

Rankin nodded, blue eyes aglow. "I can see where you might have some cause for concern. But a warm shawl will take care of that problem. And I have buffalo furs to wrap you in. You will be warm enough. Trust me."

"Very well," Rachel said dubiously.

Rachel informed the staff that she was leaving, then followed Rankin out the side door. A surrey was parked just outside, pulled by a large, beautiful black horse. The horse's coat shone gleaming black and silver in the bright moonlight.

Rankin gave her a hand up, then got in himself. "Here, make yourself warm and cozy."

He gave her a shawl, then held up a buffalo blanket while she got under it. When he tucked the blanket around them, she discovered that the arrangement kept them quite warm, despite the fact that their breath made clouds of steam in the chill night air of spring.

"Where are we going?" Rachel asked, as Rankin clucked to the horse and they started down the road at a brisk pace.

"To see the sights," Rankin answered with no further explanation.

They traveled on in silence for a while longer. Finally Rachel spoke. "I'm still sorry about Marie."

"Sorry?" Rankin elevated an eyebrow at her. "Sorry about what?"

"Well, that you and she broke up, because of me. I know that she meant something to you, and I feel somehow responsible."

"I told you she was about to be discharged anyway. And what makes you think she meant anything to me?"

"Well, you were . . . I mean, you did say . . ." She felt her face burn.

"Oh, I see," Rankin said. "I know what you are trying to say, my dear." He put his hand over hers, as if to add special emphasis to what he was about to say. Rachel knew that it meant no more than that; and yet, that contact under the buffalo robe made her feel a bewildering sense of excitation.

"Rachel, I know you are a lady from a refined background, and with a fine sensibility, so I shall try to explain this to you in a way which won't be offensive to you."

"You—you don't have to explain anything to me," she said hastily. She could scarcely hear what he was saying, because all her senses were concentrated on the contact of their hands, and because of the roaring sound in her ears.

"Men have needs," he went on, ignoring her protest. "You see, men have more animal natures than women, and they are unable to resist certain . . . uh, temptations, shall we say? Women like Marie who can satisfy these physical urges are often available, and yet a woman like Marie could never be all that a man needs. For that, he needs a woman like you."

"I hope you aren't expecting me to take her place," she said.

"No, no, of course not. Such a thought demeans," he said suavely. "Rachel, with you such a relationship would be so much more, for you have so much more to offer."

"I would prefer to talk about something else," she said nervously, and she snatched her hand from his.

"Of course. If I have upset you, Rachel, I beg your forgiveness." He stopped the surrey, and Rachel noticed that they were beside the railroad track. "Now, look out there," he said. "Isn't that a pretty sight in the moonlight?" He pointed to the north.

The plain before them ran unbroken to the horizon, and from side to side, as far as she could see, it glowed silver in the moonlight. The gently undulating waves of grass looked so much like the sea that Rachel felt as if she could leap from the surrey and frolic in the surf.

"It *is* magnificent," she admitted. "I've seen the Gulf of Mexico, and I thought I would never see anything as vast as that, but this matches it. There is so much . . . so much space here."

"Some day this will all be fields of grain," Rankin said.

"Ewell, *you* have visions of farming, too?" she asked, surprised that he should make such a statement.

He laughed. "Good God, no! Such dreams are for the pilgrims and emigrants who are flocking here by the thousands. But they will turn the land into farms, and towns, and cities, and the men who control it now will be rich."

"Oh. And you want to control it now, is that it?"

Rankin laughed again. "My dear Rachel, I *do* control it now."

Rachel heard the far-off, lonesome wail of a train whistle. "Listen, I hear a train."

"Yes, that will be the Midnight Flyer, coming to End of the Track. I brought you out here to see it."

"I thought you brought me out here to see your land?"

"That, too," he replied. "But you came here on a train, and you mentioned that you had watched the prairie from the window of your car. I thought you might like to see how your train looked to anyone watching it go by."

"I've seen trains before. There was a track that ran by my father's . . ." She started to say *plantation* but because she was trying to shed her Southern image, she blurted out, "Farm."

"Even on your father's farm, Rachel, you couldn't have seen anything like this. On this stretch of track, with no people and little game to worry about getting in the way, the engineer opens the throttle full speed, until it's time to slow for End of the Track. They pass by here doing sixty miles an hour."

"Sixty miles an hour!" Rachel exclaimed. "But how do they stay on the track at such a speed?"

She heard the whistle again, and she could tell that the locomotive was moving very fast, for it was no longer far-off and mournful, but quite close now.

She gazed down the track and saw the yellow headlight, growing larger, ever larger, as the train pounded toward them. She could hear the puffing of steam and see the black smoke boiling out of the stack.

Rachel gasped. "Oh! Will the horse bolt?"

"No, he's accustomed to it. Here she comes, right on time."

The engineer of the Midnight Flyer blew his whistle in greeting, and the great train rushed past them at sixty miles an hour, smoke and steam trailing back in long wisps, great driver wheels pounding at the rails, sparks flying from the firebox. The blast of air and noise from its passing shook the surrey until it bobbed like a cork riding on rough water. The lighted windows of the cars streamed by so fast as to be almost one long blur of light. Within a moment the last car flashed by, and Rachel saw the red and green lamps at the train's end already receding in the distance.

"Oh, my!" she said in awe. "I don't believe I've ever seen anything that exciting in my whole life!"

At that moment, with her skin still tingling and her blood churning from the excitement of the speeding train, Rachel felt Rankin's arm go around her, and his lips press against hers. The kiss was not demanding, yet it was dizzying in the sensations it evoked. It was the kiss of a man who was skilled at amatory delights, and thus immensely stimulating. And then Rachel felt his hand around her breast, thrust down into the low-cut dress, so that the flesh of her breast was burning against the skin of his palm. It left her senses reeling and her mind spinning.

"Please. Please don't!" she murmured, pulling out of his grasp and turning her head aside. She was trembling violently.

"Very well," he said easily, sitting back. "I've no wish to force myself on an unwilling woman."

"It's not that I'm unwilling—I mean, ungrateful," she said, correcting herself quickly, "for the job. But, as I told you, there are certain duties of Marie's that I don't intend to inherit."

"Then I shall not press the issue," Rankin said without rancor. He took the reins and clucked at the horse, and they started back toward End of the Track.

Rachel sat very still under the buffalo lap robe, but at the moment she had no need of it. Her body was a tumult of raging emotions. She realized that she had been sexually aroused by the handsome man beside her. She closed her eyes in despair as she attempted to block out the wild and uncontrollable urges that threatened to overwhelm her. She thought of the train, of the smoke and fire and flash of its passing, and like the terrible energy that drove such a machine, her own passions propelled her toward the inevitable and ultimate consummation of her own desires.

Three days later the track workers were paid, and End of the Track literally exploded. All work stopped at two-thirty in the afternoon. The gandy dancers took their pay to the saloons and brothels of

End of the Track, as if determined to spend it as fast as was humanly possible.

Rachel finished her chores in the railroad car, and then started across End of the Track to the Roundhouse.

Pistol shots suddenly rang out, and she screamed, and jumped in quick fear. Then she heard a roar of loud and raucous laughter, and looked toward the sound. A man was trying to win a wager by shooting a whiskey bottle tossed into the air, but his efforts were unsuccessful.

"Do it again," the drunken shooter said. "Toss it up again, and I'll show you bastards that I can do her."

"I tell you what, Charlie! Throw rocks at it!" one man yelled, and everyone hooted laughter. Charlie responded by shooting at his heckler; fortunately, his aim was no better than before.

"Hey!" another man shouted, spotting Rachel walking past. "Hey, fellers, look at this! That there's the Roundhouse lady!"

Several pairs of eyes turned in her direction, and she was suddenly very self-conscious.

"Hey, Roundhouse lady, we got paid today. We got cash money, so how about we spend a little of it with you? Our money's good as the rich folks' money!"

"That's right," said another. "Hey, I know what! It takes a heap of money for the likes of her. What say, boys, we hold us a raffle? Everybody put up a dollar, and the winner gets the money to buy her services."

"Services?" Rachel frowned. "I don't understand."

"Aw, come on. Sure you do. They ain't no big mystery about it. We'll pay you to go to bed with the winner of the raffle, just like you do with the rich dudes in the Roundhouse."

"No!" Rachel was scandalized. "Dear God, is *that* what you all think? Is that what everyone thinks I do at the Roundhouse?"

"Think! Lady, we *know*. Now, how about it? Are you going to be a good girl and go along with the lucky gent what wins the raffle?"

"No!" Rachel said angrily. "Absolutely not! I'm not that kind of woman! You're all wrong, and I'll thank you to remember it!"

"Aw, hell, let her be!" one man said disgustedly. "The girls at Jane's Gilded Palace will do me just fine."

"They ain't none of them this purty."

"Maybe not, but they're a heap more friendly."

There was a general chorus of agreement and, much to her relief, their attention swung away from Rachel.

But ahead of her, directly in her path, a full-scale brawl was in progress, and she had no wish to make her way through another rowdy crowd of men. So, hoping to avoid another unpleasant incident, she turned off the boardwalk and started down between a row of tents, stepping over the ropes and pegs that held them secure, moving through the alleyways, following a roundabout way to the restaurant.

She had circled almost all the way around End of the Track, passing through an area she had never seen before, when she happened upon a most shocking scene. The back flap of one of the tents was raised and tied back, exposing the interior. Inside, on a mat of furs, lay a naked man and woman, locked in a lovers' embrace, oblivious to everything around them. Although she had never been witness to such a scene before, Rachel knew exactly what she was seeing.

She halted, shocked to be sure, yet curious also. And then her curiosity was replaced by another, far stronger sensation. She felt her heartbeat quicken. Sudden warmth radiated out from her loins, and she experienced a sudden and inexplicable weakness in her knees.

The thrashing inside the tent grew more frenzied, and though the day was mild, Rachel felt such a heat suffusing her body that she began to perspire. The pair in the tent began moaning in unison, and then, with a few convulsive quivers, the thrashing was stilled entirely.

Rachel stood rooted to the spot, vaguely ashamed of herself, yet seemingly incapable of moving. Suddenly, she felt a prickle of apprehension, for she realized that the man was none other than her Uncle Julius!

At her involuntary exclamation, Julius Deever looked up and saw her. "What the hell!" he shouted in dismay and anger.

"Uncle, I . . . I was just taking a shortcut," Rachel said miserably. "I'm sorry, I didn't mean to . . ." She broke off, whirled about, and ran blindly away.

Unfortunately, she ran the wrong way. Within a

short time she found herself at the far side of End of the Track, away from the living quarters, the saloons and the restaurant, and in the equipment area, where the construction materials were kept.

Confused and momentarily lost, she found herself in an open storage depot, where a vast number of cross-ties were piled high in mountainous stacks. She walked down a lane formed by the ties and leaned against one of the stacks to catch her breath. Her mind worked hard at trying to sort out what she had just witnessed.

What would her uncle do to her? What would he do to Aunt Mildred? Should she tell her aunt what she had seen? No, this was something best left between her and Uncle Julius.

Finally, with that decision made, she began to calm down. What did she have to fear? After all, Julius Deever hadn't caught her in a compromising situation—she had caught *him*. If someone should be concerned, it should be Julius Deever.

Rachel regained her breath and her composure, and even managed a small, triumphant smile. Yes, this might very well work to her advantage in the end. Not that she would try to blackmail him, for she had no intention of doing that. But if he was worried about what she might do, he might decide to bully her less.

"Well now, Roy, what do we have here?" a male voice said behind her.

Rachel felt a quick chill. She looked around but didn't see anyone. She called out shakily, "Who's there?"

"Just us chickens," the same voice said. He appeared abruptly from behind the stack of railroad ties, dirty and unkempt, holding a half-empty bottle of liquor. He leered at her. "My name is Poke. And this here is Roy." Another disreputable individual appeared. Both men had evil, close-set eyes and demonic grins framed by filthy beards.

"What are you doing in here?" she demanded.

"Naw, girlie, that ain't the right question. The question is, what are *you* doing in here?" Poke said. "We'uns are 'sposed to be here to guard against anyone trying to steal the materials."

The man called Roy said, "Hey, Poke, maybe she's one of them whoors come to us since we can't come to her this payday."

"Is that the way it is, girlie?" Poke said. "You one of them whoors from Jane's Gilded Palace?"

"No," Rachel said angrily, "I certainly am not!"

"Roy, you ever seen one as purty as this one is? Tell the truth now."

"I ain't never."

"Me neither. Strikes me we got us a chance here to have some sport."

"I told you, I am *not* what you think," Rachel said, trying in vain to keep the tremble out of her voice. Fear had squeezed her throat so tight she could barely speak. Her glance darted about frantically in search of a way to escape, but the men had her way blocked.

"Poke, if'n she ain't one of them whoors, we can't do nothing with her."

Poke laughed cruelly. "Hell, Roy, if she was one of them whoors, we couldn't do nothing anyway. Without being paid, they don't play. But being as she ain't a whoor, why then, we don't have to pay her."

"What are we gonna do?" Roy asked, licking his lips.

"Grab ahold of her," Poke said, reaching for his belt, "and I'll show you."

Rachel opened her mouth to scream, but no sooner had she done so than it was stuffed with a foul-smelling rag.

"That'll keep you from screeching when you start to enjoy it," Poke said, chuckling.

Rachel felt her flesh bruise as her clothing was torn and pulled from her, and she realized when she felt a sudden shock of cold air, that she was half-naked. She was shoved down hurtfully onto the ground, gravel and wood chips grinding into her skin, but concern over the pain faded quickly as she saw the grinning face of Poke looming over her. She closed her eyes tightly and waited, flesh and mind contracting, for his brutal penetration of her body.

CHAPTER FIVE

The dreaded contact never came. Instead, Rachel heard a dull thump and a groan of pain, and opened her eyes to see Poke's body collapse on the ground beside her own. Behind Poke, standing wide-legged as an avenging angel, the giant form of Will Simmons loomed menacingly.

Looking down at her, Will reached down and jerked the gag from her mouth. Rachel coughed and gasped.

"Miss Bonner, are you all right?" Will asked anxiously, averting his gaze from her exposed body.

"I . . . I think so, Will. But if you hadn't come when you did . . ." She shuddered.

All of a sudden she remembered that there were two of them, and raised her head. "Will, be careful! There's another one!"

Will grinned and jerked his thumb toward a second prone figure. "Do you mean that one?"

"Yes, that's him—" Abruptly, she realized her near-naked state, and tried to cover herself with her hands.

Will turned his face away in quick embarrassment. He stooped to pick up her torn dress, and held it away from him between two fingers. With his gaze still averted, he handed it to her.

"They tore it a mite," he said grimly. "But you can cover yourself with it."

"Thank you, Will," Rachel said primly.

"What were you doing around here anyway?" Will asked, as she hurriedly pulled her dress on. "You ought never to come to this place. It's not safe for a lady."

"I was on my way to the Roundhouse to work," she said. "But there were so many rowdies that I was afraid to go through them, so I tried to circle around. Then, somehow, I wound up back here, and those two stopped me."

"That's why you have no business coming this way," he said in a scolding voice. "No matter how rowdy the boys get on payday, nothing like this would happen to you on the main street. It's only when a sorry pair like these come across a lady out all alone that they get up nerve enough to try anything. Now, come on. I'll walk to work with you."

"All right," she said meekly. "It was foolish of me, I realize, and I appreciate your help, Will. Very much."

As they walked toward the Roundhouse, they could hear the shouts, the laughter, the loud, off-key singing, and the occasional gunshot which Rachel was to learn always marked the celebration of payday. She flinched nervously at every outburst of sound.

"You musn't think too badly of them men, Miss Bonner," Will said with a tolerant smile.

"Those men tried to *attack* me," she said angrily. "How else should I think?"

"Like I said, I don't mean those two sneaks. They'll never bother you again, I can promise you that. No, ma'am, I wasn't speaking of them. I was talking about the gandy dancers. They're doing a job here that's bigger than anything in the history of this country," he said. "They're laying five or six miles of track a day, every day, and by the time this railroad is through there'll be more land opened up than there is in all the states of the Union now."

"But why are they so . . . well, so unruly today?"

"Miss Bonner, you have to understand what their life is like out here. It's hard. They're rousted out of bed at five-thirty in the morning and hustled through the dining car for a ten-minute breakfast. Then they start laying iron. They get twenty minutes off for lunch, work until six in the evening, then get their suppers. They have calluses on their calluses, aching backs, pains in every muscle of their body. They sleep on a board which is not as long as they are tall, or as wide as they are broad, and they're given one blanket that they share with the bedbugs. For all this they get paid thirty dollars a month, most of which they already owe to the company store for tobacco or other such necessities of life, and the camp followers are around for the rest. By tomorrow morning the entire payroll will have changed hands, and the men will go back to work without a penny left."

Rachel stared. "But why? Why do they do it?"

Will chuckled. "We have over five thousand men in this camp. I guess that means there are five thousand reasons. But the rest of the people in the country can just be thankful that they are willing to do it. When the railroad is finished, a person will be able to travel from New York to San Francisco in a week's time. One week, Miss Bonner. Think what the people who crossed this great country in covered wagons and on horseback would think of that. It's amazing, truly amazing. Well, here's the Roundhouse. And there's Mr. Rankin." His voice was shaded with disapproval, and Rachel was about to inquire as to the reason. But before she could speak, Ewell Rankin saw them and came hurrying toward them. He took in her dishevelled appearance in a sweeping glance.

"Rachel, what the devil happened to you?"

"I'm all right, Ewell," she said shakily. "Thanks to Mr. Simmons here."

"A couple of hardcases tried to get funny with her," Will said, still in that distant voice. "I rousted them."

"Who were they?" Rankin demanded, his voice hard as steel.

"I don't know," Will said. "I didn't recognize them."

Rachel recalled the two men calling each other by name, but now that her initial outrage had cooled, she decided not to mention it. What purpose would it serve?

"Have you ever seen them before?" Rankin asked her.

"No. And I hope I never see them again."

"Don't worry, my dear, I'll see that you're never bothered by such scum again." In a gesture that struck Rachel as unconscious Rankin loosened the pistol in his holster.

"Will, thank you again for escorting me to work," Rachel said warmly.

"Yes, thank you, fellow. Allow me to recompense you for your trouble." Rankin took some gold coins from his pocket and held them out. Will recoiled as though struck.

"No need for that," he said harshly. "I didn't help Miss Bonner for money."

"Suit yourself, fellow." Rankin shrugged and returned the money to his pocket.

Will turned to Rachel and touched the brim of his hat. "Ma'am," he said, and strode off.

"I'll have Becky draw a bath for you," Rankin said. "You'll feel better for a bath and change of clothes."

"Yes. Yes, I'm sure I will. Thank you, Ewell."

"I'll see you upstairs."

Becky took special pains in preparing the bath, so that as Rachel sat in the tub she was surrounded by frothing bubbles and embraced with the aroma of pleasing perfumes. The silken sensuousness of the bath washed away not only the filth from the ground, but also the lingering repulsion of her encounter with the two men.

When Rachel finally stepped out of the tub, she walked nude toward the clothes closet. Catching her reflection in the mirror, she blushed as she realized that Will Simmons had enjoyed the same view. But beneath the blush there was a feeling of womanly pride as well, for she knew that men enjoyed looking at her. In fact, she was no longer embarrassed by the low-cut gowns she wore; instead, she even derived a degree of delight from them. She laughed softly to herself, took a silken robe from a hook, and wrapped it around her, restoring some decorum.

Becky had laid out three dresses on the bed, and now Rachel studied them. One was white and demure; the second, blue and elegant; and the third, red and daring. She looked at them closely, one finger pressed to her cheek and her hazel eyes taking in every detail.

There was a knock on the door.

"Come in, Becky."

The door opened, and Ewell Rankin stepped in. "It isn't Becky," he said. "I just came to see if you were all right."

"Yes, I'm fine, thank you, except for one thing. I can't seem to make up my mind which one of these I should wear tonight."

"My dear Rachel, it really doesn't matter," he said amusedly. "When you come downstairs, all eyes will be on you, not on your dress."

"Still, a woman likes to wear a dress that is right for the occasion."

She leaned over to pick up one of the gowns, and as she did so, the neck of her robe dipped forward slightly, affording Rankin a glance at her breasts, two delightfully curved mounds of pink flesh tipped by tightly drawn nipples.

Rachel glanced up and saw the direction of his glance. A quick heat flared inside her, flashing through her body like summer lightning. She felt a rising excitement at the prospect of being in a situation which appeared to be fraught with peril, yet was actually quite safe. For surely she was safe with Ewell Rankin. She had never met a more polished or cultured gentleman.

And yet, he was a man, after all, quite a virile man, she was sure.

She smiled shyly, and then, boldly, coquettishly, began untying the belt that held the robe together. She timed the action perfectly, so that she stepped behind the dressing screen just at the instant when her modesty would have been compromised. She passed the robe across the screen, handing it to Rankin, at the same time displaying her bare shoulders.

"Ewell, perhaps you would hand me the dress *you* prefer," she said, gazing innocently over the top of the screen. "After all, I can't come out from behind the screen now, until I'm dressed." Rachel was amazed at her boldness and a touch ashamed at her wanton behavior, yet she couldn't seem to stop herself.

Rankin looked over at the screen, then saw something that Rachel wasn't aware of. He discovered that her naked form was clearly visible in the mirror behind her. Smiling, he stared pointedly at her reflection.

Rachel saw his look, then gasped as she recognized her error. At that moment her control of the situation slipped away with dizzying suddenness.

She made a desperate lunge for the robe he had cast aside, but as she did so, she inadvertently upset the screen, so that she stood before his burning gaze.

"Please, Ewell," she said in a small voice. "Look the other way. Please!"

Rankin was upon her in three quick steps. He stood before her, staring at her with undisguised desire in his eyes. He was so close now that she could feel his warm breath on her face and smell the tangy aroma of the brandy he had drunk earlier.

"I'm sorry, my dear, but it isn't that simple," he said huskily.

She made an effort to cover herself with her arms and hands, but he brushed them aside, then put his hands on her and pulled her hard against him. She jumped involuntarily, shocked at the unexpected turn of events.

"No, Ewell, please! I didn't intend for it to go this far. I only wanted to—" But her entreaty was interrupted by his kiss.

She pushed against him, trying to struggle free of his grasp. He was too strong for her, and her struggles were in vain. She was aware of his hands kneading and squeezing her buttocks. A wanton excitement raced through her body, overcoming any fear and shame she felt. Rankin's lips pressed even more firmly against hers, with a slight, pleasant pain, and she opened her mouth to his.

With a brazen hunger that surprised her, she allowed her hands to stop resisting, and instead began to explore the male body pressed against her. With a giddy sense of arousal, she felt the hard bulge in front of his breeches.

Then, quite inexplicably, Rankin stepped back, and stood gazing down at her with a small, almost victorious smile on his full mouth. Rachel was puzzled, and she stared back at him questioningly.

Rankin strode to the bed and picked up the red dress. "This one will do quite nicely, I think," he said, tossing it to her. "You'll sleep here tonight," he added firmly. "I'll not take the responsibility for your returning home, not with that payday bunch roaming about."

Rachel suddenly remembered the incident with her uncle, and she knew that she didn't want to return to the railroad car tonight.

"Yes, you're right. I think that would be best, Ewell."

"I'll see you downstairs," he said, and, with a slight nod, he left her to battle the urges still shaking her body.

There were more people than normal in the Roundhouse that evening. Some of the gandy dancers, those who apparently had no love for the rowdiness of the liquor tents nor the gambling tents, nor the services of the soiled doves in the brothels, spent their hard-earned money on an elegant supper, eaten off fine china and served by refined young ladies. Those who came to the Roundhouse were freshly scrubbed, and the few who had suits wore them, evidently in the hope that the short time spent at supper would help them to forget the two weeks of backbreaking labor between paydays.

There were a few wealthy people from the East present, too, but most of them avoided the Roundhouse on paydays because of the presence of the rougher element. Thus, although the supper hour was more crowded than usual, the after-dinner crowd of wealthy tycoons lingering over cigars and brandies was conspicuously absent. Because of that, Rachel's work period was shortened; and when the final table was cleared away, she went into the kitchen, as was her usal custom, to prepare her own supper.

"Miss Bonner, Mr. Rankin told me to set a table for you in your own room," Becky informed her. "So that's what I did."

"Well, thank you, Becky," Rachel said, pleased. Yes, a nice leisurely supper in her room would be just what she needed to end this hectic and rather strange day. "Where *is* Mr. Rankin? I would like to thank him."

"I don't know." Becky shrugged. "I haven't seen him for a spell."

"Well, if you do happen to see him, tell him I said thanks very much," Rachel said.

She walked over to look out through the kitchen window, and saw the red sun dying in the west in an explosion of color. There might be only a few surface features to enjoy out here, she thought, but the sunsets were undeniably magnificent. And the stars at night were beautiful as well. It was as if the sky tried to compensate for the starkness of the windswept prairie by providing extra beauty for anyone who bothered to look.

She climbed the stairs at the rear of the Roundhouse and crossed the landing to her room. Before she could reach for the knob, the door was opened from the inside. Ewell Rankin stood there, a charming smile on his handsome face.

"Come in, my dear," he said, stepping back and sweeping his arm around in a gesture of invitation. "May I say that I find you exceptionally lovely tonight?"

There was something insinuating in his smile, and then Rachel noticed that the table had been set for two.

"I thought we would eat up here tonight," Rankin went on. "It will be more private. I hope you don't mind?"

"If I did mind, would it matter?" she asked tartly.

"Of course it would," he said smoothly. "As I have told you, I don't wish to press myself on an unwilling woman."

Careful, Rachel, she told herself; this could be leading to more than you bargained for!

"I am not unwilling," she said.

"Good!"

"For you to join me for supper," she added quickly.

"Of course, I understand. What else would you mean?"

"I just wanted to make sure that you didn't misunderstand."

"Well then, shall we dine?"

They ate slowly, leisurely, and although Rachel ate the meal and held up her end of the conversation, the food had little taste, and the words no meaning. There was only one thing on her mind, and it burned into her consciousness like the scorch of a branding iron. She knew she was on a one-way ride, and all she could do was hold on to see where it took her.

After the meal, Rankin poured a brandy for both of them. Rachel accepted hers gingerly, and drank it quickly to allow its warmth to spread through her and relax the nervousness she was experiencing.

Rankin leaned across the table. "Are you sure you want to do this?"

"Do what?"

His smile was knowing. "My dear Rachel, please don't play the innocent with me. It doesn't become you."

He touched a finger to her cheek, then tipped her face up to his. He leaned farther across the table and kissed her. The kiss was warm and tender and knowing, and within an instant Rachel uttered a small cry and returned it with fervor.

"The bed is over there." He motioned with his head.

Rachel got up, as if in a dream, and without mind or will of her own, allowed him to lead her to the bed. There, he began undressing her. He did it skillfully, as if all the fasteners and appurtenances were familiar to him. Rachel was mesmerized by his actions, by his easy confidence, his subtle skill. Before she fully realized it, she was nude, lying on the bed, staring up at him.

Rankin stared down at her with heavy-lidded eyes. His mouth seemed too full and sensuous to be a man's, and yet, it was capable, as she well knew, of evoking the most exquisite pleasure in a woman. It curled up slightly, forming a smile that seemed to be mocking.

"You are a beautiful woman, Rachel," he said huskily. "A *very* beautiful woman."

Rankin undressed himself, and Rachel, watching with a mixture of embarrassment and fascination, saw that his classic good looks were only enhanced by his physique. And then he was in bed with her, caressing her tenderly and artfully.

Rachel felt her body responding to his caresses eagerly, and her mounting desire overwhelmed any reservation. She *was* twenty-four, after all. Often, her nights had been troubled by longings so intense as to be painful. Now, now she was to learn what it was like to be a woman, truly a woman!

As though they did not belong to her, her hands began to explore his body, touching him with the delicacy of a butterfly's wings, then grasping him with a boldness she wouldn't have believed possible had she not been so swept up in the ecstasy of the moment.

"Ewell, please! Please make love to me now," she whispered throatily. "I want you now."

Rankin moved over her, then into her. There was a sharp, brief pain when he entered her, but it was quickly lost in a sensation of pleasure so strong that she cried out from the joy of it. His movements established an easy rhythm, and she felt her own body moving in response, in a quickening counterrhythm, until finally, with a powerful shudder, she felt an explosion of ecstasy inside her that completely overwhelmed her senses, wrenching a sob of pleasure from her throat. So lost was she in her own release that she took little note of Rankin's own frenzied climax.

She lay beneath him for a time, feeling his weight on her, enjoying the feel of a man in her arms. It had been a most pleasant experience, yet some element seemed to be lacking—tenderness, perhaps. And yet it could be that her expectations had been too high. Ewell Rankin was male, all male, and all the men she had known, except her father, scorned tenderness as an unmanly emotion.

She stroked his shoulder with her hand, and he kissed her again, brusquely this time, rolled over and lay beside her. They were both silent, save for their labored breathing, which was just beginning to return to normal.

"Ewell, do you think I am a wicked woman?" she asked suddenly.

Rankin raised up on one elbow, eyebrow arched in amusement. "No, of course not. Whatever made you ask such a question?"

"I enjoyed what we did. I can't begin to tell you how much I enjoyed it."

"I enjoyed it, too," he said with a slight shrug. "It is supposed to be enjoyed."

"But *women* aren't supposed to enjoy it."

Rankin smiled somewhat cynically, and touched his lips to her forehead. "That's nonsense," he said forcibly. "I would never marry a woman who didn't enjoy what we just did together."

Marry? Was he asking her to marry him? Rachel wondered. But she didn't voice the question, because she didn't know what his answer would be.

In fact, she didn't even know what she wanted him to say.

CHAPTER SIX

It was late summer, and it was raining. It wasn't a gentle rain, it was a cloudburst, a once-a-year rain which usually came to the Great Plains in early September, dumping more water on the prairie within twenty-four hours than had fallen during the previous four months.

It had started just after dark, and Hawkeye Smith was caught out in the open without shelter and with no place to go. The raindrops blew into his face like pellets, and although he drew his slicker tightly around him, and spread the brim of his hat, all his efforts were practically useless.

He had been tracking a stand of buffalo. He was more than twenty miles from the new End of the Track, and more than forty from the town that was now being called Connersville, named after the track foreman, Miller Conners, who had been murdered there.

Hawkeye had been to Connersville a couple of times during the past two months and, always from a distance, he had seen Rachel Bonner. She was working at the Roundhouse, and that was a place Hawkeye thought it best not to patronize in his present circumstances. So he had not talked to her. With the railroad's insatiable appetite for fresh meat, perhaps a good stand of buffalo would provide him with enough money so that he could legitimately go to supper there.

The trouble was that the buffalo herds were getting increasingly difficult to find, and it was necessary for him to roam far afield in search of them. And that was how he had ended up here, a long way from the railroad, in the midst of a driving rainstorm.

The sky split with a brilliant bolt of lightning, and in the harsh white light, Hawkeye saw a cluster of Indian tipis ahead. Who were they? Were they a hunting party who would find his presence unwelcome? Or were they friendlies?

Hawkeye hoped to hell they were friendlies. If they were, they would offer him food and a warm, dry place to sleep. But if they weren't friendly . . . what then? Well, he certainly represented no threat to them at the moment. He wasn't shooting buffalo, and he had no armed men with him. The worst thing they could do, he decided, was turn him away. They would find no honor in counting coup upon a solitary, soaked-to-the-skin white man on a stormy night.

"Come on, horse," he said. "Let's go get something to eat and somewhere dry to sleep—I hope."

The horse wouldn't have a dry place, Hawkeye knew, even if he was welcomed. The horse would be tied in a remuda, and if the animal was fortunate he would be tied where he could graze. Well, no matter, the horse didn't know what he was saying anyway, Hawkeye thought with a chuckle.

Another lightning flash illuminated the Indian village just as he reached it, and in the glare Hawkeye spotted the unmistakable blue horse-and-lance symbol on one of the tipis. He grinned broadly in relief; that was the personal insignia of Mean-to-His-Horses.

Hawkeye called out in the language of the Sioux, "Ho, the camp! I am a friend in need!"

Some of the tipi flaps opened, and he glimpsed the warm wink of fires inside. He could also smell the rich aroma of buffalo stew, simmering in a half-dozen pots.

A deep voice answered, "Who calls in our tongue?"

"I am Lance-in-the-Side," Hawkeye replied. "I have come to see my old friend, Mean-to-His-Horses."

"Ho, Lance-in-the-Side! Come, I am here, my friend. I am here!" One of the tipi flaps opened even wider, and Hawkeye saw the silhouette of a tall, straight man, standing in the opening. The silhouette waved an arm, indicating that he should enter.

"Where is the remuda?" Hawkeye asked.

"Do not concern yourself, Lance-in-the-Side. My daughter will tether your horse."

"Your daughter? Bright Fawn? But she is too young for such work."

"Ho, wait until you see her!" Horses said.

A shadow slipped out of the tipi, and hurried

through the rain to take Hawkeye's mount. Bright Fawn was lithe in form and stood as tall as Hawkeye's shoulders. She took his horse without a word and hustled him away to the remuda. Hawkeye ducked into the tipi, grateful to be in out of the rain at last.

"It is good to see you, my friend," Horses said. Mean-to-His-Horses was a very tall Indian, perhaps even an inch taller than Hawkeye, and broad of shoulder and chest as well. He put one hand on Hawkeye's shoulder.

"I am pleased to see you as well, my friend," Hawkeye responded. He had never learned Horses's true age, but he figured that the Indian was older than he by several years.

There was a fire in the center of the tipi, and most of the smoke was drifting up through the hole at the top. But a great deal of it was trapped inside the tipi, and it had already started to burn Hawkeye's eyes and nose and lungs. He knew that he would grow accustomed to it after a while. Neither Horses nor anyone else in the tipi seemed to notice.

Hawkeye gazed around. There was a pale, orange glow from the fire, and it was shadowed by the amount of smoke that stayed inside, so the interior of the tipi was very dim. But he could see Quiet Stream, the wife of Horses, and he saw a papoose sleeping in a small crib.

"What is this?" Hawkeye asked gravely, pointing to the baby.

Horses smiled, and sat down, inviting his guest to do the same. The smoke was less bothersome at that level, and Hawkeye was grateful. He accepted a plate of stew put in his hands by Quiet Stream.

"That is my son, Stone Eagle," Horses said proudly. "He is a fine, strong boy, with a voice as loud as thunder. He will become a mighty hunter."

"And the girl who took my horse," Hawkeye said. "Could she really be Bright Fawn?"

"Yes," Horses said. He smiled again. "She has grown strong and beautiful, and is a great joy to her mother and to me. Next spring, the young men will be bringing presents for her."

"Two more springs," Quiet Stream said.

"Woman, this is her sixteenth spring. You think to keep your daughter with you always? I tell you, even now the young braves have an eye for her. If we do not give our consent now, I fear she will go of her own accord. Then what will we get for her? Nothing, that is what. We will lose a daughter and receive no payment for her."

The subject of the conversation stepped back into the tipi at that moment and looked shyly at Hawkeye.

"Daughter, do you remember Lance-in-the-Side?" Horses asked. "He lived with our people for four years."

"I remember him," Bright Fawn said.

"Bright Fawn, can this be you?" Hawkeye said. "When last I saw you, you were very small, no bigger than this." He held up his hand at about the height of a man's waist.

"Then I was a little girl," Bright Fawn said. "Now I am a woman."

Bright Fawn was wet from having secured Hawkeye's horse, and she untied a small bag and took out a dry dress. Without the slightest embarrassment, she stripped her wet dress over her head and spread it out near the fire to dry, then put on the dry one. But in those few moments her naked form was completely exposed. Hawkeye felt his throat go dry and he tore his gaze away, but not before he had seen that she was, indeed, a lovely woman.

"You are farther south than usual, Mean-to-His-Horses. Why is this?" Hawkeye asked, as he ate the stew. In the Indian way, he ate with his fingers and then licked them appreciatively, and smacked his lips to make a point of showing how much he was enjoying the meal.

"I have heard of an Iron Horse which pulls many wagons," Horses was saying. "I am told that it belches fire and smoke, and goes faster than the wind, and travels upon a trail of iron. It is a thing of the white man, I am told."

"Yes, Horses. The trail of iron is called a railroad track, and the Iron Horse which pulls the wagons is called a train."

"I wish to see this thing," Mean-to-His-Horses said.

"Why?"

"Because I am a man who uses his eyes to see many things. Such a thing must truly be wonderful to behold."

Hawkeye finished the stew and put his dish down. He smiled at Quiet Stream. "You can still make magic with food," he said, and she smiled in appreciation of his compliment. He wiped his hands and looked at his Indian friend. "You are right. It is a magnificent thing to see. But there are many Indians who have no wish to see the Iron Horse come. They are frightened by it, and they have attacked it."

"I know," the Indian said. "I am told that the Iron Horse kills the buffalo and the deer and the antelope. This is not good for the tribes, for we must have these things to live."

"The train can kill the buffalo and the deer only if the buffalo and the deer are on the railroad tracks. The train cannot leave the tracks."

"Have you seen this thing, this Iron Horse?" Horses wanted to know.

"Yes, I have seen it many times."

"Is it frightening?"

"Only to foolish people. Clever people know that it cannot leave the track, and can do them no harm."

"I know of some Crows who tried to capture one," Horses said. "I was told that they were killed by the Iron Horse."

"Yes," Hawkeye said. He had heard the story too. In fact, although three Indians were killed in the attempt, it was the kind of story that the UP men could gloat over, since they had little regard for Indian lives anyway. "They did not understand the Iron Horse, and what they did was foolish."

"What did they do? I have not heard how they were killed."

"They stretched a rope across the track," Hawkeye said. "Three men stood on each side of the track and held the rope taut as the train approached.

They thought they would be able to stop it. They did not realize that the Iron Horse has the power of many hundred horses, and cannot be stopped by six men holding a rope."

"Yes," Horses said, nodding gravely. "They were foolish. They should have been on horseback. Then they would have had the strength of the horses to add to their own."

"No," Hawkeye said quickly. "Mean-to-His-Horses, in the village where I lived four happy years with you, all of the people who lived there then, and all their horses combined, could not stop the Iron Horse with a rope."

Horses reared back. "Aiyee, this must be a creature of great strength!"

"It is, my friend. Believe me."

"It is good that you know so much of this Iron Horse. Tell me, my friend. Why do you know so much?"

Hawkeye sighed. He had hoped it wouldn't come to this. "I work for the railroad, Horses."

"Do you make this thing go?"

"No."

"Do you build the trail of iron?"

"No."

"Then what work do you do?"

"I kill buffalo," Hawkeye said.

Horses stared at the ground for a moment. Finally he spoke. "You are my friend, but my heart is truly saddened that you would kill the buffalo and leave them on the plains, as I have heard the white men are doing."

"No," Hawkeye said. "I am not one of those.

Those are rich men from the East. The UP has brought them out here and arranged hunting expeditions for them. They are killing the buffalo because they think it is a sport. I kill the buffalo for the same reason as the Indian. I kill the buffalo for food and hides."

"I cannot find fault with you, Lance-in-the-Side, for killing the buffalo for food. But I am angry at those who kill for sport."

"There are many white men who share your anger," Hawkeye said.

Horses pondered for a moment, then he smiled. "I have the solution."

"What?"

"Let those who hunt for sport continue to do so. Then you can use the buffalo they kill as food and fur, the way it was intended."

"I wish we could do this, my friend. But the buffalo we use for food must be killed near End of the Track, where the workers are. The buffalo which are killed for sport are killed at places convenient to the hunters. When we can, we do bring the carcasses in. Often, though, with the hunters for sport, the buffalo are not killed, they are merely wounded. Then they go off to die and are lost."

"But surely the white men who hunt for sport follow a wounded animal?"

Hawkeye spread his hands. "Not always, I am afraid."

"It is difficult for the Indian to understand such people," Horses said, frowning.

"It is difficult for *me* to understand such people."

"You are a red man."

"My skin is white."

"Your heart is red," Horses said.

They talked a while longer, even after Quiet Stream and Bright Fawn lay down to sleep.

"You may sleep there, by the door," Horses finally said. "When the rain stops, it will be hot and you can catch the breezes of the night."

"Thank you," Hawkeye said, and he spread out a fur and blanket pallet near the tipi flap, and within a short time was sound asleep.

When Hawkeye awoke later that night, he realized that it had stopped raining and, as Horses had predicted, it was hot. The flap was drawn back, and moonlight flooded in. He was grateful for the slight breath of air. Then he saw Bright Fawn standing in the spill of moonlight.

At first he couldn't be certain that she was naked, because he had only the soft light of the moon in which to see her. Then she turned slightly, and her body was highlighted and made all the more mysterious and intriguing by the subtle shadows and lighting of the night.

Hawkeye made a guttural sound in his throat, and she walked softly up to him. Hawkeye knew then that she had been waiting for him to wake up. Quietly and without fanfare she gave herself to him, without reservation. Her body was lithe and supple, soft and warm, and even at the age of sixteen she knew how to arouse and please a man. Of course, Hawkeye thought, Indians didn't place such value on a maiden's virginity as did white men.

He gasped, his body arching, and all thought left

him. Bright Fawn rose and straddled him, settling into an ever-quickening rhythm.

It was strongly physical and immensely satisfying, but it was much more than that. It was as if their passions were perfectly orchestrated to move in harmony, so that there was a tremendous sense of mutual need and fulfillment.

After their desires were satisfied, they went back to sleep. Hawkeye awoke once more in the middle of the night. The moon still shone brightly, sailing high in the velvet sky. It spilled a pool of iridescence through the tipi opening and onto the robe-covered ground. Bright Fawn had returned to her own pallet, and was breathing softly.

Hawkeye was alone once more. He lay there, thinking about the strange events of the night. Unbidden, the thought of Rachel Bonner intruded into his mind. He gave a rueful shake of his head, turned over on his side, and drifted into a deep sleep.

CHAPTER SEVEN

Rachel moved out of her uncle's railroad car long before the Deevers relocated to the new End of the Track. When she told them she would be moving into a room at the Roundhouse, she expected some sort of row, but surprisingly none came. Then she remembered Julius Deever and the woman in the tent, and she smiled. That secret knowledge undoubtedly had a great deal to do with keeping her uncle mute.

Connorsville was now losing population rapidly, as the camp followers and the workers moved on to the new End of the Track. Finally the Roundhouse itself was moved, lock, stock and barrel, to the new location.

Ewell Rankin had already gone ahead to End of the Track, and was overseeing the construction of a new building there, while Rachel was supervising the loading at this end. At the moment she was standing in the middle of a large number of crates, bossing the operation of loading them onto a flatcar.

"Now, be especially careful with those two boxes," she said, pointing to the two in question. "They contain the chandeliers."

"Yes, ma'am," one of the workers said with a patient sigh.

The freight agent, a man named Philpott, had been watching the loading, marking each crate off on a sheet of paper as it was loaded. Now he walked over to Rachel to show her the papers.

"Miss Bonner, there're two more crates here than the bill of lading calls for."

Rachel frowned. "What does that mean?"

"Well, it means that you can't load 'em. You're going to have to decide which ones you want to leave behind."

"I don't intend to leave any behind!" she snapped. "Mr. Rankin is expecting every crate to be delivered to End of the Track, and that's just what I'm going to see to."

"But there's no way we can do that," the agent said doggedly.

"Let me see that." She snatched the bill of lading from his hand. She studied it for a moment, then looked at the crates and counted them quickly. "Oh," she said with an exasperated sigh. "How could this have happened?"

"I have no idea, lady," Philpott said. He took off his hat and wiped the sweat from his forehead, then squinted up at the sun. "You know, there ain't nothing hotter than Nebraska on the day after a rain like the one we had last night."

"Yes, I quite agree with you," Rachel said impatiently. "But the weather is not my concern right now, Mr. Philpott. My concern is getting all of these crates on that car so we can ship them to End of the Track. Now, can't you just make an exception this one time?"

"Nope. Don't see as how I can, Miss Bonner," the agent said obstinately.

"But I *must* get them there!"

"Well, ma'am, you could get another bill of lading drawn up and maybe ship 'em out tomorrow."

"Tomorrow? No, absolutely not! There is no way I'm going to leave any of these crates out overnight. They are all much too valuable."

"Sorry, Miss Bonner, but orders is orders."

"What seems to be the trouble?" someone asked, and Rachel glanced around to see Will Simmons approaching.

"Will, am I glad to see you!" she exclaimed. "Maybe you can make this stubborn man see reason."

"He's got no say over me in this," Philpott insisted.

"First, what is 'this'?" Will asked. Rachel quickly explained the problem to him.

"The answer is simple," Will said, smiling broadly. "Philpott, you just load those two extra crates onto one of my cars as unspecified dunnage."

"Can't do that," the agent complained. "That ain't the way it's supposed to be."

"Unspecified dunnage, Mr. Philpott," Will said firmly. "That'll take care of the problem."

Philpott grumbled a bit more, then capitulated. "Which two crates do you want to go that way, Miss Bonner?"

"Those two," she said, pointing to a pair near the track. "They don't have anything but bedding and towels, so nothing will be broken. Will, I don't know how to thank you."

"Well, it's nearly lunchtime, Miss Bonner," he said. "So maybe you could have lunch with me. I know it's not the same as eating at the Roundhouse, but the food at Mabel's is a little better than that in the railroad house."

Will's invitation surprised Rachel. She was sure that he knew that she was considered Ewell Rankin's woman. But it was this very knowledge which made her decide to accept. After all, as long as he fully understood the situation, there could be no misunderstanding.

She smiled brightly. "Why, thank you, Will. I should be delighted to have lunch with you, but only if you start calling me Rachel."

"Well . . . All right." He shifted uncomfortably from one foot to the other, then said shyly, "Rachel."

"There, see, it wasn't that hard!" She slipped her arm into his as they started off.

The Roundhouse had been torn down, and most of the lumber had been shipped to End of the Track to be used in the construction of a new Roundhouse. With the demolition of the Roundhouse, Mabel's Restaurant was now the most substantial building left in Connersville. A new hotel was under construction, and it would be larger than Mabel's when it was finished, but for the time being, Mabel's reigned supreme.

The cost of a meal in Mabel's kept out the

rougher element—they would rather spend their wages on cheap women and cheaper liquor—so it was quiet and orderly when Rachel and Will Simmons entered.

Mabel was the widow of Miller Conners, the construction foreman after whom Connersville was named. She was a large, red-faced woman, with a ready smile for everyone.

"Will! How nice to see you," she said, beaming. "And Miss Bonner, what a pleasant surprise! I never thought I'd see you in here."

It struck Rachel as an honest remark, with no offense intended. Rachel smiled in return. "I'm a working girl. I haven't had time to do all the things I would like to do, so that's one reason I haven't been into your place yet."

"Don't I know that, honey?" Mabel said, laughing. "Don't I know that?" She poured mugs of coffee for them without being asked. "I've got some awfully good apple pie today, Will. You know, the kind I used to make for you and Miller?" A shadow crossed her plump face.

"I can tell you right now that whatever I eat for lunch, I'll be saving room for the pie," Will said. "Miller always did say that he married you for your apple pie, and after tasting it, I can see why."

Mabel laughed heartily. "Bless your heart, Will Simmons! If I thought it'd win me another husband, blessed if I wouldn't serve it with every meal."

"Ah, Mabel, what would a husband do for you now, except steal this fine restaurant you've started," Will said.

"The restaurant doesn't keep me warm at night,

Will," Mabel said, and left, still laughing at her own jest, while Rachel and Will pondered over what to order.

"Were you and Miller Conners close?" Rachel asked.

"We were," Will said solemnly. "We were friends before we ever came out here, and when we met here, we just picked up where we left off before."

"What happened to him? I mean, I know he was killed, but what happened? And why?"

"Well, they said it was probably some drunken gandy dancer," Will said, frowning. "But I've never believed that. I've got my own idea about what happened, why he was killed."

"What is your idea?"

Will looked at her, then gazed around the restaurant, as if to make sure that he wasn't being overheard. "I've got to be careful who I tell. A fellow might wind up the same way as Miller, if he didn't watch out."

"Surely, Will, you aren't afraid to tell me?"

"No, no," he said hastily. "I'm not afraid to tell you. But I'm afraid of *who* you might tell."

"Why, I won't tell anyone! Why should I?"

"It has to be that way, Rachel. You can't tell your uncle, or Ewell Rankin, or anyone. I mean it."

She leaned across the table. "Now you simply *must* tell me, Will. I'm dying of curiosity. And you have my solemn promise that I won't tell a soul."

"Well," he began in a voice a little above a whisper, "I don't know *who* did it. But I think I know why. You see, I was with Miller Conners when he figured the cost per mile of construction. In fact, I helped him put the figures together. We cut it right down to the bone, and the figures we arrived at were thirty thousand dollars per mile."

"Whew!" Rachel said explosively. "That's a lot of money."

"Yes, it is. But the bosses said that the standards we figured on weren't high enough. They sent Miller back to the desk, and he figured it all over again, using a wider road bed, heavier gauge steel, more ties, and better ballast."

"That must have come to a lot more."

"Quite a bit more. In fact, the second set of figures came to fifty thousand per mile. That's one million dollars for every twenty miles."

"Good heavens! I had no idea the costs of building a railroad were so enormous!"

"Building a railroad is costly, and they *are* spending fifty thousand per mile. The trouble is, the railroad is being constructed according to the standards of Miller's *first* proposal."

"What?" She stared. "Are you sure, Will?"

"Sure as I can be," he said grimly. "You see, I saw the specifications for the first proposal, and the specifications for the second as well. I know what the budget is, and I know what standards are being used for the actual construction." He took a deep breath. "Miller knew too, of course, and I think he went to someone he shouldn't have and mentioned it. That's when I think he was killed, *and* the reason why."

"But . . . but who would do such a thing?" Rachel asked in bewilderment.

"Someone who has a lot to gain. Someone who is

involved with the construction company, and has the opportunity to pocket the difference in money."

"The construction company. That's Credit Mobilier, isn't it?"

"Yes," Will said quietly.

"But what you're saying can't be true, Will! Ewell is the liaison for Credit Mobilier. Surely you aren't suggesting . . ."

"I'm not suggesting anything, Rachel. I'm just pointing out a few facts. I'm sure Ewell Rankin has nothing to do with it. After all, his job with Credit Mobilier is really just to entertain the visiting bigwigs, and see to it that they are happy with their investments."

"I'm sure that if Ewell had anything to do with something as crooked as all that, why, I would know about it. And murder? Oh, no!"

"I'm sure you're right, Rachel," he said soothingly. "I don't know all the facts, and someone who knows only half the facts is more dangerous than someone who knows nothing. That's what my old daddy used to say." He grinned. "Now, let's have a good meal and forget all about such unpleasant matters."

He motioned to Mabel and ordered for both of them. The topic of conversation changed then, and Will began talking about his dream of having a farm of his own someday.

"This land out here, Rachel, is ideal for wheat," he said enthusiastically. "A young man, say my age, could get a good start now, and by the time he was sixty, he could be well off, and have something for his children."

"Where do you plan to have this farm of yours, Will?"

"I've got a piece of land in mind already. It has a creek running through it, so there'd always be water, even during a dry spell. And the soil is good and rich, and there's hardly any timber at all to be cleared away. You could just about go in there and poke holes in the dirt with your fingers and drop in the seeds. It's about twenty miles from here."

"Why don't you just homestead it?"

"I can't," Will said glumly. "It was part of a grant given to the railroad. The UP did own it. Now someone else does."

"Is he farming it?"

He looked away. "It belongs to Ewell Rankin. It's his land. I'd have to buy it from him."

"Oh," Rachel said slowly. "Yes, I knew that Ewell had bought a good deal of land. But I'm sure he'd be willing to sell. He bought it as an investment."

"Oh, he's willing to sell, right enough. I've already looked into it. But I've got to raise a lot more money before I'm ready. And then I'm going to make my move."

"I wish you all the good fortune possible, Will," she said sincerely, putting her hand across the table to touch his.

Will almost blushed as he gazed down at her hand. Rachel choked back a desire to laugh, not because she wished to make sport of him, but because his shyness seemed strange in such a powerful man.

"I'll be ready then to take that wife I was talking

about," Will said in a choked voice, without looking at her.

"I'm sure any woman would be more than happy to share such a life with you," she said quickly. "Oh, here comes our lunch."

Rachel was looking toward the steaming plates being brought to the table, and so didn't notice the sudden look of happiness on Will's face. But she had made the remark in such total innocence that she might not have understood the meaning of his expression if she had observed it.

CHAPTER EIGHT

The new Roundhouse was, if anything, even more imposing than the old one had been. It was larger and it had a stage, something the old one did not have. The stage had been Rachel's idea. She asked Ewell Rankin to let her bring in a professional show troupe to celebrate the opening.

"Go ahead, if you want to. I see nothing wrong with that," he said with a shrug.

"And Ewell, can we please open it to everyone? Just for opening night?"

"Why the hell should we do that?" he asked in astonishment.

"Oh, I don't know. Call it a goodwill gesture," she replied. "I know there are many people who would like to see inside the Roundhouse, at least one time. This would be their opportunity to do so."

"There is no rule saying anyone can't come in."

"I know, no stated rule. But there is an unwritten rule, and you do all you can to discourage people you don't want."

"It's true, there are a lot of people I don't want in

here," he said harshly. "The whole idea of a place like this is to keep out the rabble."

"Please, Ewell, just this once. I'm sure everyone will be well behaved, and it *will* create goodwill."

Rankin stared at her for a moment, then grinned. "All right. But I swear, the way I let you boss me around, Rachel Bonner, people will begin to think we're already married. You can have this open house, but you must make all the arrangements. I can't be bothered."

"You won't be, I promise." She was enthused over the project of putting together a show. "It will be the most wonderful thing that has ever happened out here. You'll see. People will talk about it for years to come."

"That remains to be seen," he said in a grumbling voice. Then he smiled grudgingly. "But what the hell! If it makes you happy . . . Now, you take care of things, my dear. I have a number of important meetings to attend. In fact, I probably won't be back until quite late tonight."

"I know, you have business to take care of." Rachel sighed. "Don't worry about me, I'll be all right."

Rankin kissed her goodbye and left at once. Rachel hadn't said anything in response to his comment, "people will begin to think we're already married," but the phrase hadn't been lost on her. Did that mean that he planned to marry her? She was almost certain that it did. But the exasperating fact remained that he had never *asked* her!

In truth, Rachel wasn't at all certain that she wanted to be married. Yet if she didn't marry him, then the life she was leading now was no different from that of Marie Thompson's. Marie had been both Ewell's hostess and his mistress when Rachel arrived. Recently, she had heard that Marie Thompson was working in a brothel somewhere. Was *she* going to end up the same way?

No, no, of course not! She gave a sharp shake of her head, scolding herself for being silly.

After all, Marie's situation with Ewell had been totally different. Ewell was going to marry her, and he had never had any such intentions toward Marie Thompson.

Then an unwelcome memory intruded into Rachel's thoughts. "I am more than just a hostess, you know," Marie had said that day.

"You are *nothing* but a hostess," Ewell Rankin had replied contemptuously.

Had Marie been gulled into thinking he would marry her? Did *she* think she was more to Ewell than she was? Had he allowed her to think that?

Rachel didn't want to think about it, and as soon as the thought was born she put it away, yet she couldn't help but wonder if her position was really any more secure than Marie's had been.

Of course it was, she finally decided. After all, Ewell was very open about his relationship with her, and he had told her often that things were different between them. She had to believe that, she told herself. There was absolutely no need for her to feel apprehensive and guilty.

Thus reassured, Rachel turned her attention to the program she had designed for the show.

PROGRAMME

Opening remarks by Mr. Ewell Rankin

1. Song	Chicago Singing Society
2. Whistling Solo	Mrs. Harriette Brown
3. Athletic Exhibition	Anaheim Turner True
4. Recitation	Nell Regan
5. Whistling Solo	Mrs. Harriette Brown

The acts were listed in the order recommended by the troupe, and it was they who had recommended that the word *program* be spelled "programme," as "it adds a degree of charm and class to the proceedings," Mrs. Harriette Brown's letter had stated. Mrs. Brown's whistling solos were the feature attraction of the troupe, which wasn't surprising, since Mrs. Brown was also the troupe's manager.

During the next few days, Rachel had posters printed and distributed, not only around the new End of the Track, but back in Connersville, Plum Creek, Willow Station, and most of the other towns along the UP right-of-way. She scheduled the show for the next payday, at which time the maximum number of workers would be able to attend. Within a few days the news of the upcoming performance had reached as far east as Omaha.

"How would you like to go out to Rail-End with me today?" Rankin asked Rachel a week before the show.

"Rail-End? You mean where the track is being laid?"

"Yes. I have some business to discuss with your uncle. I thought you might like to visit with him."

"I have no wish to see my uncle," she said stiffly.

"But I *would* like to visit Rail-End. I've never seen the tracks being laid."

"Well, then by all means come along. We'll be leaving in about an hour, so hurry and get ready."

"I'll be ready," she promised.

End of the Track, the town, was not actually located at the extreme end of the rails. That would have been impossible, due to the speed of the daily progress of the railroad. The towns which were called End of the Track were the farthest spot forward that actual railroad passenger service extended. And it was there that the supplies and material were stockpiled to supply the work trains and the crews which were at the actual railend.

When Rachel and Ewell Rankin boarded the special car which was attached to the end of the supply train, Rachel saw that there were several soldiers on board. Also on board was a very handsome man, tall and blond, whom she didn't know—although she had the strangest sensation that she did. He nodded politely, but he didn't speak, and when Rachel and Rankin took their seats near the rear of the car, the silent young man sat in the front, looking quietly through the window.

One of the soldiers, a colonel, was sitting across the aisle from them, and he smiled and spoke to them.

"How do you do, Colonel?" Rachel said.

The colonel looked startled. "I'm surprised, ma'am, that you recognized my rank. Not many ladies can tell just by looking at the uniform."

"I've seen a great many uniforms," she replied.

"Oh? Was your father a military man?"

"Yes," Rachel said shortly. "Though not by choice. He was killed at Shiloh."

"Oh, I'm sorry to hear that. What unit was he with? I was at Shiloh with General Grant."

"My father was on General Johnston's staff," Rachel said coolly.

"Johnston?"

"Albert Sidney."

"Oh! Please forgive me. You mean your father was a Confederate. It was most indelicate of me to tell you that I was with Grant. I do apologize."

Rachel realized, belatedly, that she had begun evincing hostility toward this man. She forced herself to smile. "Colonel, I'm certain that the danger was just as great for the men on your side of the lines as it was for the men on my father's side."

"It was indeed," the colonel said. "You can thank your lucky stars that you weren't there."

"But I was there, in a manner of speaking." Once again, her voice had become curt. "Our fate at Vicksburg was little better."

"I . . . I daresay it was," the colonel said in confusion. He cleared his throat, nodded awkwardly, and turned away to stare out the window.

Rachel also fell silent, and although she did not want to, she could not help but think of Vicksburg during the war. She could vividly remember the scream of the shells as they fell on the city, and the sounds of the explosions as the bombs burst in the streets and homes and other buildings in the beleaguered town. And she could remember the hunger. Most of all, she could remember the hunger, as the citizens of Vicksburg and the defenders alike were slowly, slowly starved into surrender by the relentless Union army. The Federals had held the city under bitter siege and wouldn't let anything in or out, until the inhabitants were reduced to eating horses, mules, dogs, and in all too many cases, rats, to survive.

"Tell me, Colonel," Rankin asked the man across the aisle. "How is the Army coping with the Indian situation?"

Rachel became alert. "Indian situation? What Indian situation?"

"Nothing for you to worry your pretty little head about, ma'am," the colonel said patronizingly. "The Army has everything under control."

"Ewell, what is he talking about?" Rachel demanded.

"Oh, it's a plan the government has worked out," Rankin said negligently. "The Army has been ordered to move all the Indians out of a certain area."

"My goodness, whatever for?" she said. "They haven't been causing that much trouble, have they?"

Rankin shrugged. "I think the government is afraid that they might in the future."

"Oh, Miss Bonner, I think your friend is being much too modest," a new voice said, and Rachel glanced up to see that the blond man she had seen earlier had come back to speak to them. There was still something hauntingly familiar about him, but she couldn't put her finger on it.

"You see," the young man went on. "Your . . . uh, friend . . ." He gave a scornful twist to the word. "Your friend, Mr. Ewell Rankin, helped develop the plan which would push all the Indians back from the tracks for a distance of one hundred miles on either side. The UP is afraid that Indians in that area might discourage settlers from moving in. And that would mean that the UP wouldn't be as likely to sell its land so easily. Am I not right, Rankin?"

As the young man had begun talking, Rankin had stiffened, his face darkening. In a low, intense voice he said, "Smith, this is a private conversation, and your comments are not welcome."

Of course, Rachel thought, Hawkeye Smith! How different he looked now from the way she had last seen him. He was handsome, well-dressed, clean, and—she was certain—he smelled much better. She flushed at the thought, grateful that he was not looking at her.

Hawkeye said dryly, "Oh, I'm sure my comments are not particularly welcome."

Rankin batted a hand at him. "You are paid by the UP to hunt buffalo, Smith, and nothing more. You are certainly *not* paid to establish policy, or to be critical of that policy. May I suggest that you leave that job to those who are trained for it, and who have the intelligence to do it?"

"Intelligence, is it?" Hawkeye said scornfully. "There was certainly nothing intelligent about this move. The Indians were giving the railroad very little trouble. Amazingly little, when you consider what the railroad is doing to them."

"Oh? And just what is it that the railroad is doing to the poor Indians?" Rankin said sarcastically.

"For one thing, the damned track cuts right through their best hunting ground," Hawkeye said.

"And what game we haven't slaughtered, we've driven away. The number of buffalo that have been killed to bring the railroad this far is greater than all the buffalo killed by all Indians in this century. We can't go on killing these animals like we have and expect them to survive. The Indians knows this. Their very existence depends on the buffalo."

"That all sounds very fine and noble, but I've come across idealists like you everywhere I've ever been." Rankin's face wore a sneer. "You would do anything under the sun to halt progress. You're worried about a few buffalo and a few hundred Indians? I consider myself one of the builders of a new and prosperous nation. I don't have time to worry about your Indians, not when they stand in the way of progress."

"I'm all for progress too," Hawkeye said, "but must this new nation you're talking about be built on the death of an old one?"

"I have no wish to exterminate the Indians, if that's what you're saying. I just want them to move out of the way."

"Then they will fight," Hawkeye said strongly.

"If the Indians do that, sir, we'll be ready for them," the Army colonel interposed.

Hawkeye sighed wearily, realizing that he had not made the least impression on them. "Excuse me, gentlemen, Miss Bonner," he said, tipping his hat, and returned to his seat in the front.

The conversation changed now, ranging over several subjects during the next hour, but Hawkeye didn't leave his seat to join them again. Rachel saw that he just sat quietly, ignoring everyone.

She had listened to the heated exchange between Hawkeye and Ewell Rankin in some confusion. It seemed to her that they were both right, and that only added to her confusion. She would have liked to talk to the buffalo hunter about it, but she knew that would not only scandalize the colonel but anger Ewell as well.

So she remained in her seat until they reached Rail-End. There, Rachel was overwhelmed by what she saw. There were more than a thousand people at work. Never had she seen such activity.

The first thing to catch her attention was the work train. Not the one she had come in on—that was merely the resupply train, and she had seen it many times in the past few months. But the work train always remained at Rail-End. This was the first time she had ever seen it.

The work train consisted of a dozen cars, each one designed to serve a special purpose. There was a car filled with tools; one outfitted as a blacksmith shop; another with rough dining tables, kitchen and commissary; others with built-in bunks; and at the end, several flatcars loaded with rails, spikes, fish-plates, bolts, and all the other necessary road-building materials.

Rachel walked up ahead along the train, fascinated by what she saw. Soon she came upon the work in progress.

"Make way, make way, new rails!" a man shouted.

A light car, pulled by a horse, rushed down the rails until it reached the very end. The horse was unhitched, then hitched up to an empty car which had been shoved over to one side, and the car started back for a fresh load of rails.

In the meantime, two men grasped the forward end of one of the rails and started ahead with it; the rest of the unloading crew took hold two by two, until the rail was clear of the flatcar. Then, at a word of command, it was dropped into place, right side up, while a similar operation had been going on with the rail for the other side. Behind the track layers came the gaugers, men with a measured length which they used to space the rails at the exact distance. Behind the gaugers came the spikers.

The spike drivers gave out a grunting exhalation of breath to accompany the rhythmic ring of their sledgehammers, and as they worked they sang. The song they were singing now Rachel had heard before, but this was the first time she had ever heard it sung at the site of its birth—the actual laying of the rails.

Drill, ye tarriers, drill
Drill, ye tarriers, drill.
Oh, it's work all day,
No sugar in your tay,
Workin' on the U Pay Ra-ailway!

"Down!" the track boss shouted, and another set of rails dropped into place. It seemed to Rachel an impossible pace for the men to maintain, yet the new rails were being laid down every thirty seconds.

"Why, Rachel!" It was Will Simmons's voice. She turned back. Wearing stained work clothes, Will was standing near one of the flatcars, holding a rolled piece of paper in his hand. He had been talking to one of the rail bosses.

Now he came toward her. "What are you doing at Rail-End?"

"Hello, Will," she said, walking to meet him. "I just came out to see Rail-End. You know, I've never been to where the actual work is being done."

"Interesting, isn't it?" Will was smiling with pleasure at seeing her. "Are you looking for your uncle?"

"No," she replied. "Ewell came out here on some business, and he asked if I wanted to come along. This is fascinating, Will. Absolutely fascinating."

Will gazed around proudly. "There hasn't been a feat like this since the building of the pyramids of Egypt. And this is much more practical. Rachel, would you like a cup of tea, or coffee? Or maybe something to eat? There's a tent pitched over there for the visiting bigwigs. Just go on in over there, you'll find somebody. They'll be happy to serve you."

"Thanks, Will. At least over there I won't be getting in anyone's way. My heavens, I had no idea they worked so fast."

She walked away from the track and the workers, toward the tent Will had indicated. It was located about fifty yards from the right-of-way. Just before she reached the tent, she heard a gunshot.

"Goddamned thievin' redskin!" a voice yelled. "I'll shoot his eyes out!"

A young Indian came running out of the tent. Rachel didn't think he could be more than fifteen. He leaped down into a gully, then ducked behind a large rock. Rachel saw that he was clutching a slab of bacon. His eyes were wide with fright.

"Lady—Miss?" A short, fat man wearing a cook's apron had charged out of the tent. He held a revolver in one hand. "Did you happen to see a red-skin skunk come running out of this here cook tent?"

"Yes, I did."

"Where did the bas—Where did he go?"

"He ran down the gully. That way," Rachel said, and for some reason she didn't quite understand, she pointed in the opposite direction.

"Thanks," the cook said. He grinned savagely. "Stick around for the entertainment. When I catch 'em, we'll have us a necktie party. It's been nigh onto a week since we hung one of them thievin' redskins." The cook pounded off down the gully, running in the direction Rachel had pointed.

She was suddenly startled by the sound of a strange language spoken behind her, and she whirled about to see Hawkeye Smith, speaking in an Indian tongue.

Rachel was mortified. Hawkeye knew she had lied!

The Indian youth, in response to Hawkeye's coaxing, left his hiding place and raced up the gully in the opposite direction from the way the cook was headed.

"What . . . what did you tell him?" Rachel asked, somewhat timidly.

"I told him that the white woman had just saved his hide, and for him to skeedaddle while he still had the chance."

"Would they really have hanged him?"

Hawkeye's mouth took on a bitter twist. "They average about one a month."

Rachel was scandalized. "But that's terrible!" She shook her head. "I'm glad that I lied to that awful cook!"

"So am I, Miss Bonner, so am I," he said softly, looking directly into her eyes.

Under the impact of his intense gaze, Rachel felt herself grow uneasy, as a surprising warmth spread through her body. She was both annoyed and mystified. No one had ever made her feel like this just by looking at her. What was it about this man, this Hawkeye Smith, that affected her so?

CHAPTER NINE

By telegraph to the New York *Tribune,* from our special correspondent with U.P. Construction, from End of the Track, Nebraska:

The population of End of the Track has swollen to better than five thousand people in the last month as the railroad prepares to push across eastern Colorado and into Wyoming. In the storage depot here, more than 100,000 ties are cut and curing, waiting for use. Other materials are stored here, too, much like the material which accompanies a mighty army prepared for battle. In fact, the U.P. might be compared to an army, and the battleground the untamed wilderness which lies just ahead.

End of the Track is an amazing town, consisting of, among other things, a large and comfortable hotel, filled with well-dressed guests. Everyone seems to have gold watches attached to expensive chains, and many wear patent-leather boots. One might think they are wealthy bankers, but would be astonished to learn that they are but clerks, ticket agents, freight agents, conductors and engineers.

One of the many houses of ill repute is known as King of the Hills. It is gorgeously decorated and brilliantly lighted. The ground floor is always crowded, the people talk loud and fast, and everyone seems bent on debauchery and dissipation. The women, especially, seem wanton, and the men eager to enter this whirlpool of sin.

The managers of the saloons rake in greenbacks by the hundreds every night. There appears to be plenty of money here, and plenty of fools willing to spend it. The women are expensive articles, and come in for a large share of the money thus squandered. In broad daylight one may see them gliding through the dusty or muddy streets in the finest dresses, carrying fancy derringers slung to their waists, with which they are dangerously expert.

And yet, in this den of debauchery, there appears to be the promise of some culture, for Miss Rachel Bonner, hostess of the Roundhouse, a restaurant of impeccable standing, has engaged the traveling troupe of Mrs. Harriette Brown to provide entertainment for one and all. The entertainment is of the highest moral and intellectual quality, and should go a long way toward establishing a civilizing influence for the inhabitants of End of the Track.

Rachel read the story in the New York paper only seventy-two hours after it was published. It gave her a thrill to see her name in such a large and fine newspaper, and an equal thrill to realize that only a short time after it hit the streets in New York, she had a copy at End of the Track, which was nearly on the Colorado state line. Truly, she thought; this was an amazing time in which to live.

And tonight was the night!

Mrs. Brown's troupe of players had arrived on the afternoon train, and had been greeted by most of the population of End of the Track, or so it had seemed. The reception had been warm indeed, and Mrs. Brown was most enthused.

Rachel was happy with the way things were going, because, although it was payday, the number of drunks and disorderly citizens seemed much less than normal. In fact, most people appeared to be on their best behavior, and Rachel attributed this to the fact that they were anxiously awaiting the show she had arranged for them.

There was only one thing to dampen her happiness, and that was that Ewell Rankin had done nothing to help her. Not only had he not helped her, he hadn't even been supportive. Though she said nothing about it, Rachel was hurt by his lack of interest.

Rankin seemed more and more disposed to occupy himself with mysterious business meetings, often with Julius Deever, and even more frequently with Credit Mobilier people from the East. He was also less attentive to her. Most of the time now he seemed preoccupied and, it seemed to Rachel, deeply troubled.

His attitude distressed her, but when she tried to

discuss it with him, he refused. The result was a growing feeling of guilt in Rachel, guilt that she was allowing him continued liberties with her, while not definitely establishing just what their relationship was. She simply could not accept the thought that it might be nothing more than the relationship that had existed between Ewell and Marie Thompson. She would *not* accept that!

And yet, what could she do about it? Should she demand that he make his intentions known? It was a question she had spent many hours pondering during the last few days, without reaching any firm conclusions.

Now, though, that question and others nagging at her would have to be put aside. The only thing on her mind was the success of the show tonight. She had gone over the stage and the lighting with Mrs. Brown that afternoon, making sure that everything was in satisfactory order for the evening's performance.

The show was nearly two hours away but already a crowd was collecting outside the Roundhouse. With all the tables removed, and the chairs placed in neat, orderly rows, the ground floor of the Roundhouse could accommodate fifteen hundred people. It appeared that many were already waiting to purchase tickets.

Rachel went up to her room to bathe. She stood looking down at the big brass bathtub, as two of the girls employed by the Roundhouse poured hot water for her. Steam rose from the water, and it looked so inviting that Rachel could scarcely wait until the girls left. Finally the tub was full, and she dismissed them with a word of thanks.

Rachel added scented oil to the hot water, and the fragrance of violets rose richly to her nostrils. She inhaled the evocative scent as she slipped out of her robe and into the tub. The steaming water stung her skin, and her body turned pink from the heat as she lay back against the side of the tub.

Rachel stayed in the tub until the water began to cool, washing luxuriously with a soft linen cloth and scented soap. As the last of the heat faded, she reluctantly stood up, reaching with one hand for the pitcher of cool water that sat on a low chair beside the tub. She stood, pouring the pleasantly tepid water over her body, washing away the soap, feeling the pleasant, wet slide of the water over her breasts and belly; then she reached out for the towel, which was draped over the back of the chair.

"I believe you're looking for this, my dear," said Ewell Rankin's amused voice, as he handed the towel to her.

"Ewell!" she exclaimed, taking the cloth from him and instinctively covering herself with it. "What are you doing here?"

He laughed at her modest gesture, and reached out and pulled the towel away. "Who has a better right? The girls told me you were bathing, so I thought it would be a good time to pay you a short visit."

"Well, it's not a good time!" she snapped. "A lady has a right to privacy during her bath!"

"A lady, it it?" he said mockingly. "What about *my* rights?"

Rachel drew herself up, and attempted not to feel at a disadvantage in her nude state. "Your rights? What are you talking about? What right do you have to come barging in on me like this?" Something about his manner made her uneasy, and that, in turn, sparked her temper.

"I have the right of prior consent," he said easily.

"Prior consent?" She stared at him. "What in heaven's name does *that* mean?"

Rankin laughed. "It means you've already given yourself to me. That's prior consent."

He reached forward and put his hands on her bare shoulders, then let one hand trail down onto her damp breast. As he did so, the nipple hardened to a point.

Rachel sucked in her breath and suppressed a shiver. Even when he angered her, this man was capable of arousing her.

"Ah, you see," he said lazily. "We are alike, Rachel. You enjoy dalliance as much as I do."

If the truth were known, she thought, she probably enjoyed it more; for Ewell Rankin, for all his skills in the erotic arts, entered into lovemaking with a sense of detachment that she often found infuriating.

"There is more to lovemaking than enjoyment, Ewell."

"Oh? And what would that be?"

"You know what that would be," she said angrily. "Ewell, we can't—I can't just go on being your mistress. I must know that I am something else, something more!"

"And what would that something more be?"

"Am I to be your wife?"

"Of course," he said casually.

Her heart began to beat faster. "When?"

"When I am ready, not before." He added curtly, "Now is not the time to talk of such things."

Rachel stepped out of the tub and retrieved the towel from where Ewell had dropped it. Wrapping the cloth around her, she said, "Now is not the time for anything else, either. I have to get dressed for the show tonight."

But even as she made this statement, Rankin put his arms around her, sliding his hands down her wet back. His hands cupping her buttocks, he pulled her against him and covered her mouth with his. She wanted to stop him, but his knowing hands and skilled kisses quickly disarmed her and she leaned into him with a sigh.

"Do you see what I mean, my dear?" he said. "You are a creature of the flesh. You don't need the promise of a wedding to become aroused. You like the bed as much as I do. You won't stop me from having you. Not now, not at any time. You don't have the will or the strength to stop me."

The mocking words, the gloating note in his voice angered Rachel, and she shoved him away forcibly, then hastily retreated a few steps.

"You're wrong," she said emphatically. "I'll show you. I'm not like that. I'm not at all like that."

Rankin's smug smile never left his face as he advanced toward her. She backed away from him, but the backs of her legs came into contact with the bed, and she fell upon it.

Rankin was over her then, on top of her, already

opening his breeches. He forced her thighs apart and drove into her, despite her efforts to fight him off. And though she mouthed protests, she was unable to deny the lubricity of her desire, and his entry was made easier by that fact.

This Rankin was not the same man who had visited her bed before. Always before he had shown considerable skill, though remaining somewhat detached and aloof. This time, he took her with an edge of cruelty he had never shown before. He was rough with her, and his brutal thrustings pounded her hard against the mattress.

Rachel, growing really angry now, tried to fend him off, pushing as hard as she could against his chest, but it was all to no avail. He continued his cruel lovemaking, almost with the savagery of an attack. The subtle variations and ways he had used in the past to orchestrate her sensuality and build her passions were abandoned this time in his selfish quest for sexual release.

During the attack—in truth, it was nothing more than that—Rachel suddenly saw Ewell Rankin in a new and unflattering light. He was no longer the desirable lover she had thought him to be. The quick spurt of passion which had flared as he entered her was extinguished by his uncaring assault, and she endured the rest of the act with quiet, controlled rage.

When finally Rankin had satisfied his lust, he rolled off her and lay beside her, laboring for breath. Rachel felt unclean, and hot with shame. Without a word, she got out of bed and returned to the bathtub, where she slipped back into the water which, like her own passion, had grown cold.

Rankin sat up in the bed and gazed at her, that insolent, superior smile still on his face. "I believe you said you were going to show me you weren't *like that*?"

"Never do that again," she said quietly. She was surprised at her lack of hysteria over the cheapening encounter, but she was also happy to discover that she no longer felt a slave to her own sensuality.

Rankin was scowling. "If our arrangement is to continue, my dear, then I will not be denied. Not now, not ever."

"And I shall no longer be your concubine, without assurance of a wedding."

He laughed cruelly. "Why? Why lock the barn door after the horse is gone? Your virginity is no longer intact, my dear. It is too late to make an honest woman of Rachel Bonner."

"Get out of here!" Furious, she threw the washcloth at him. "I wouldn't marry you anyway, not after what just happened!"

He ducked, avoiding the washcloth easily. "I will leave, for the time being. I must say that I admire your show of spirit. It does add a touch of spice. But remember, so long as you remain under my roof, you belong to me. Just as Marie did."

"Then, sir, I shall not remain under your roof any longer," she said coldly. "I'll take up lodging in the hotel this very night, as soon as the show is over."

"Suit yourself, my dear." He shrugged. "You may stay the night, and move in the morning."

"I have no intentions of staying the night, Mr. Rankin. Now kindly leave this room."

He gave her a mocking salute, then stepped out into the hall and closed the door behind him. Rachel could hear his cruel laughter as he walked down the hall.

She fought hard to hold back the tears so close to the surface. How dare he do this to her today, of all days! This was to have been a very, very special day. She had worked so hard to make it so. And now he had spoiled it for her.

Yet in the back of her mind there was a tiny voice of joy. She didn't love Ewell Rankin, and she hadn't from the beginning. It had taken something like this to make her realize the fact. She had been a willing participant in the erotic acitivity, she couldn't deny that; and except for the episode tonight, she had liked it. In fact, she admitted candidly to herself, she had loved it. So, in order to ease her pangs of guilt, she had convinced herself that she wanted to marry him. But she hadn't really wanted to, and now that it was clear that he had no intention of wedding her, she realized what a load had been lifted from her.

Then why leave? After all, if she could be this honest and admit that she didn't love Rankin in the first place, could she not go all the way, and admit that even if she didn't love him, she did enjoy the sexual part? And, once admitting *that* to herself, why couldn't she just let things go on as they were going?

No! No, a hundred times no! She had *thought* she had been in love with him, and that had been some justification for her behavior. But she would not allow herself to be so controlled by the sensual side of her nature that she would abandon all moral principle. It was true that she could never recover her virginity. But she *could* recover her chastity.

No one who saw Rachel come down the stairs just before the show was to begin could have sensed the personal turmoil she had gone through earlier. Everyone knew that she was beautiful, but most of the gandy dancers had seen her only from a distance. Most of them had never seen her in a gorgeous gown, with sparkling jewelry and perfectly coiffed hair. She was, one news reporter recorded, ". . . as radiant as an angel, descending from heaven to tread where mere mortals dwell!"

The crowd that had come to see the show was scrubbed and dressed in their finest, and amazingly well behaved. They cheered and applauded and whistled when Rachel came down, and for a moment she didn't realize that she was the recipient of the ovation. When she did realize it, she colored with embarrassment, but secretly she was pleased.

She didn't see Ewell Rankin anywhere, and she was grateful for that. This was *her* moment. She had conceived the idea for the show, she had booked it and promoted it, and she didn't want anything to detract from her enjoyment of it. She smiled brightly at the crowd, curtsied, then went backstage to seek out Mrs. Harriette Brown.

Mrs. Harriette Brown was forty-five at the very least, Rachel was sure, although the woman steadfastly maintained that she was twenty-five. She wore her hair piled high on her head and very heavy make-up with lips as red as blood and eyes grotesquely outlined in black.

Rachel was surprised to see that the males of the troupe were almost as heavily made up, including the "athlete," Anaheim Turner True. True was dressed from head to toe in flesh-colored tights. He wore a pair of short breeches over the tights, so that from a distance it seemed that he wore nothing but the breeches. His act consisted of lifting tremendous weights, and he was broad-shouldered with strong muscles, although Rachel suspected that Will Simmons might be stronger.

"The makeup is very important," Mrs. Brown explained. "For without it, the bright limelight of the stage would wash out all the features of the face."

"The crowd is growing restless," Rachel said. "Are you ready to begin your performance?"

"Isn't Mr. Rankin going to announce us?" Mrs. Brown asked.

Rachel remembered then that Ewell was scheduled to make the opening address, but as she hadn't seen him since he'd left her room, she made an instant decision to eliminate him from the playbill. "No," she said. "He won't be able to. We'll go right into the show."

"Then *you* must introduce us," Mrs. Brown said firmly.

"Me? You want me to get out on the stage before all those people?" Rachel was appalled. "I can't do that!"

"Of course you can," Mrs. Brown said blithely. "After all, you're responsible for bringing us here. Now it is up to you to see that we are properly introduced." She added haughtily, "In fact, I insist upon it."

Rachel looked at the curtain that hung across the front of the stage. A small crack of very bright light shone beneath it. She sighed, straightened her shoulders, took a deep breath, then boldly pushed the curtain aside, and stepped out onto the stage apron. The crowd immediately began to applaud, and the noise was deafening. The lights were so bright that Rachel could see nothing but a white glare. From somewhere she summoned the courage to introduce Mrs. Harriette Brown's traveling show troupe.

After the introduction, Rachel hurried from the stage and made her way to the back of the big room to enjoy the performance.

She loved the singing by the Chicago Singing Society—a chorus made up of the entire troupe—and she enjoyed the whistling solo. The audience seemed to appreciate those two performances also. They were less appreciative of the athletic exhibition. Possibly, Rachel thought, it had to do with the fact that most of the audience was men who worked ten hours a day with their muscles, and there were probably few who didn't feel that they were as strong as Mr. Anaheim Turner True.

The best-liked feature was Nell Regan's recitation, called "The Baggage Coach Ahead."

One stormy night as the train ran along,
 all the passengers had gone to bed,
Except a young man with a babe on his knee
 who sat with bowed-down head;

The innocent babe began crying just then,
as though its poor heart would break,
"Make that child hush its noise," an angry
man said. "It's keeping us all awake."
"Put it out," said another. "We don't want
it in here. We've paid for our berths and want rest."

But never a word said the man with the
child, as he folded it close to his breast.
"Oh where is its mother? Go take it to
her," one young lady softly said.
"I wish that I could," was the man's sad
reply. "But I can't though, for she is dead."

As the train rolled onward, a husband sat
in tears,
Thinking of the happiness of just a few
short years.
A baby's face brings pictures of a
cherished hope now dead.
And the baby's cries won't wake her, in
the baggage car ahead.

Every eye filled with tears as the story
he told of a wife who was faithful and true;
He told how he'd saved up his earnings for
years, just to build a home for two;
How when heaven sent them their sweet
little babe, their happy young lives were blest,
His heart seemed to break when he mentioned
her name, and in tears tried to tell the rest.

Every woman arose to assist with the
child; there were wives and mothers on that train.
And soon was the little one sleeping in
peace, with no thought of sorrow and pain.
Next morning at the station he bade all
goodbye. "God bless you," he softly said,
And each had a story to tell in their home
Of the baggage car ahead.

More than a few of the burly gandy dancers, perhaps thinking of their own wives and children in far-off places, dabbed self-consciously at their eyes during the recitation. Mrs. Brown's final whistling solo, a bright and cheerful melody, was just what was needed to lighten the mood once again.

During Mrs. Brown's last number, Rachel, feeling the need to escape the closeness of the large crowd, stepped outside for a breath of fresh air. It was dark, and a crisp, cool breeze was in the air, a herald of autumn, as welcome to her lungs as water to a thirsty person.

The Roundhouse stood on the edge of town, and fifty yards away was a small hill. Rachel had often walked to that hill at night, for from it she could look out over all of End of the Track, or watch the moon on the timeless prairie.

The sounds from the town carried well through the night air. From the Roundhouse she could hear the faint cheery notes of Mrs. Brown's whistling, and counterpoint to that were the sounds from the other establishments of End of the Track—a woman's high-pitched laughter from one of the saloons, or perhaps a brothel; an argument of some kind between two men down at the depot; the ringing of iron on steel as a blacksmith worked late. All were signs of a vital community.

Rachel reached the hill and started up. If she walked down the other side of the slight slope, it would be as if she were all alone. Sometimes she did that, for the illusion of total solitude cleared her mind and made it easier to think about whatever was troubling her. And tonight she was troubled indeed. She had committed herself to leaving Rankin, and likely the Roundhouse. How was she going to earn a living now? She shuddered at the thought of living again with Julius and Mildred Deever. She would do almost anything to keep from returning to them!

She reached the crest, took one step down the opposite side, then froze in quick and numbing terror. For there, in the faint moonlight, painted in fierce warpaint, were more than a score of Indians astride their ponies!

They gazed up at her, apparently as startled as she was. Then one muttered what was apparently a command in a guttural voice, and as one, the Indian ponies charged up the hill directly at her!

CHAPTER TEN

A scream rose in Rachel's throat, but got caught somewhere inside, and her throat constricted painfully. She whirled toward the hill, knowing that it was useless, and began to run. Behind her she heard the beat of hooves, and then she was roughly seized and thrown to the ground.

She was so frightened that she barely felt the fall. Everything horrible that she had ever heard about Indians raced through her mind: scalping, attacks on white women, kidnapping, tortures!

The Indian who had thrown her down dismounted from his horse and stood over her. His painted face and fierce eyes filled her with new terror. Slowly he bent over her, his mouth widening in an expression that might have been a smile or a grimace, she could not tell. The rest of the band gathered around her, and she wildly looked from face to face, hoping to find one less terrifying than the rest; but each face was stony, fiercely stoic, and unfriendly.

Rachel heard herself moan softly. What would they do with her? Was she going to die here on the prairie? Better that than to be carried away to their village. She shuddered.

The Indian reached for her hair, and she flinched, but did not pull away. She had heard that the Indians admired stoicism, and with all the strength within her she tried not to show her fear.

With an expression of wonder, the brave roughly pulled down her hair, spreading it like floss, examining the texture and the soft color with curiosity. Most of the other braves had turned away and had begun a discussion among themselves in a guttural, tentions were. They were going to put the torch to torches, and Rachel abruptly realized what their intentions were. They were going to put the torch to End of the Track! *My God!* she thought. If they set the Roundhouse afire right now, hundreds of people would be killed!

Her captor was still examining her, pulling at her clothing and showing signs of a more intimate investigation, when one of the other braves called to him. For a moment, he looked away, calling something back in his strange language.

Rachel acted instinctively. Twisting her body, she threw him back and in an instant was up and running; but she had taken only a few steps before she was seized by the ankles and thrown to the ground again.

She lay there for a moment, stunned and shaken. What could she do? How could she warn End of the Track? She could scream, but the hill would cut off the sound, and besides, End of the Track was so noisy they would have difficulty hearing her.

She felt herself being turned over, and made no

attempt to struggle. It was a different brave, and he held a long-bladed knife in his hand. Was he going to scalp her? Rachel closed her eyes and breathed a fervent prayer, waiting for the slice of the knife. Then she heard a sharp, guttural shout, and the Indian with the knife moved back. Cautiously, Rachel opened her eyes, and saw that the one with the scalping knife had stopped, looking back down the slope.

Another Indian was coming toward them. Rachel sat up, staring. His face was fire-lit by the torches, and the red ochre on his cheeks had the look of blood.

Had he intervened to save her? But why? It didn't make any sense! Or did he want the pleasure of scalping her himself?

"I am Quannah-teh," the Indian said. "I have told them you are a good woman."

The dancing shadows and the paint on his face made it impossible for her to see his features clearly, but Rachel suddenly recognized his eyes. She had looked into those same eyes when they were wide with fear. He was the Indian youth whose life she had helped to save.

"You were the one at the cook tent, aren't you?" she asked. "At Rail-End?"

"I am that one," he replied. "I have told them how you saved my life, and they will now give you your life in exchange. You will not be harmed."

"Thank you," Rachel said. "Does that mean that I can go?"

"No," Quannah-teh said. "Not until we have finished what we came to do."

"What . . . what are you going to do?"

"We are going to burn the white man's village," Quannah-teh said quietly.

"Quannah-teh, you can't do that!" she said. She stood up, rubbing her wrist. "Please, you mustn't do that!"

"Be quiet, woman," Quannah-teh said sternly. "I have bought your life, but I cannot promise your safety if you try to stop us."

"Quannah-teh, there's a show going on in the Roundhouse right this minute. If you set fire to it, many, many people will die."

"That is good. The whites are our enemies. It is good to kill many enemies."

"But you don't understand," she said desperately. "If they are killed this way, the Army will be so angry that every Indian in the territory will be hunted down and killed. Even the innocent Indians who know nothing about this."

One of the others spoke to Quannah-teh, and Quannah-teh answered him. Then he said to Rachel, "This is Blood Knife. He is our chief. Blood Knife says he is weary of woman's talk. If you talk more, your life no longer belongs to me."

"Quannah-teh, tell Blood Knife what I said," she pleaded. "Don't let him burn down the Roundhouse. Don't kill all those innocent people!"

Blood Knife spoke again, his voice harsh and angry, and Quannah-teh responded. This time he evidently told his chief what Rachel had been saying, because the tall Indian leader stepped up to the crest of the hill and looked toward End of the Track and the Roundhouse.

"Please, Quannah-teh," Rachel said. "Don't let them do it."

Blood Knife spun about and spat several words out, pointing a finger at Rachel.

"Please, woman, you must say no more," Quannah-teh said, and even as he spoke, Blood Knife took his knife out and strode over to her. Scowling, he spoke to her.

Quannah-teh translated. "He says if you speak once more, he will kill you."

Rachel put her fingers into her hair and pulled it to one side, offering her scalp to Blood Knife. "Then kill me," she said defiantly. "But don't set a torch to the Roundhouse."

Blood Knife drew his knife back, and Rachel willed herself not to flinch away. Then, suddenly and inexplicably, the Indian chieftain began to laugh. He said something to Quannah-teh, and Quannah-teh also laughed.

"Blood Knife is glad you are not his squaw. You do not know when to be quiet," Quannah-teh said with a tight smile. "He has named you Brave-Woman-with-Running-Tongue. He will not kill you."

"But will he burn down the Roundhouse?"

Quannah-teh shook his head in wonder, then relayed the question, and Blood Knife made a gruff reply.

"What did he say?" Rachel demanded.

"He says we will burn only the big house that the Iron Horse comes from, and the piles of wood that make the path of the Iron Horse grow," Quannah-teh said.

Rachel knew that he meant the depot and the storage area where the building supplies for the track and the trestles were kept. Both would mean serious losses and delay the construction, but it would not mean the terrible loss of life that would ensue if they carried out their threat to burn down the Roundhouse.

"At least that's something," she said in relief. "Tell your leader that I am grateful."

"Will you give us your word that you will remain here?" the young Indian asked.

She reluctantly shook her head. "I must tell the truth. I will warn my people if I have the chance."

Quannah-teh again translated, and a moment later two Indians approached her with rawhide thongs. They bound her hands and feet and left her on the ground. Then all the Indians mounted their horses. As she stared up at them a strange thought came into her mind. How magnificent they looked! They were lean and muscular, and despite all the things she had heard about them, they were honorable people. She had seen evidence of that tonight. Her life had been spared in honor, and, in honor, the lives of hundreds of others were also being spared.

All of a sudden Blood Knife yelled at the top of his voice, a sound that sent a shiver down her spine. The Indians drummed their heels against the flanks of their ponies, then galloped off toward End of the Track. Rachel could watch them, but there was nothing she could do about it. They hadn't gagged her, and she tried to scream a warning, but she knew that the sound was lost in the night. And she was sure that the inhabitants of End of the Track would not hear the hoofbeats until it was too late.

The mounted Indians were now nearing the Roundhouse. Rachel held her breath. Would they go back on their word at the last minute?

No! She breathed a sigh of relief as she saw them ride past the Roundhouse, splitting into two groups. One group rode toward the open storage yard, while the others thundered toward the train depot.

Then she saw torches tumbling over and over in the air, little points of yellow light. The torches landed, and for a long moment she thought perhaps they hadn't caught. Then a pile of ties blazed up, followed almost immediately by the roof of the depot.

The Indians were discovered then, and she saw a man outlined in the flames from the depot. She could see streaks of fire erupting from his gun, and in a second she could hear the dull reports of the gunfire. The shooting alerted others, and men began piling out of tents and the Roundhouse. Other guns began firing, and to her ears it had the sound of a steady fusillade. The Indians were galloping away. As far as she could ascertain, none had been killed.

She heard a shout carried on the wind. "Fire! Turn out, turn out! The depot is on fire!"

She heard the incessant clanging of the firebell, and then the alarmed shouts of the townspeople as they ran to fight the fires. The Roundhouse rapidly emptied, and from her vantage point on the hill, Rachel saw figures gathered around both fires. There was small likelihood that the depot or the railroad ties could be saved, but at least the townspeople had been alerted in time to save the rest of the town. Fortunately there was little wind.

Rachel struggled to free herself from the bonds, but was unable to do so, although finally she managed to get to her feet. Hobbled as she was, she couldn't walk, so she tried hopping forward, but lost her balance and fell headlong. Unable to break her fall, she hit the ground quite painfully; then, because she was headed downhill, she bounded and rolled for several more feet. The rocks and scrub brush cut and bruised her, but she was grimly determined to get back to End of the Track, so she struggled to her feet and tried again, only to fall and tumble downhill once more.

About halfway down the hill, she had to rest for a bit. She sat there and watched the fires burn bigger and brighter, sending huge pillars of orange, glowing smoke billowing hundreds of feet into the black night sky.

"Watch it!" a voice shouted. "Sparks are beginning to spread to the tents!"

Even as the warning came, one of the saloon tents ignited from a burning brand and blazed up. The bucket brigade, using water from the depot water tank, formed a line to work on that fire as well. The saloon tent burned down almost by the time the line was formed.

Rachel got up and started hopping forward again. She managed about ten yards this time before she fell. She got right back up and started over; each painful fall, each bruising tumble, meant that she was getting closer to End of the Track, and someone who could free her.

She had made it to the bottom of the hill when she saw a man coming around the back of the Roundhouse. He was running, carrying several empty buckets, and Rachel realized that he had taken them from the Roundhouse kitchen to supply the bucket brigade.

"Help!" she screamed at the top of her voice. "I'm over here. Help me!"

The man skidded to a halt, and looked toward the sound of her voice. He dropped the buckets and took a few hesitant steps in her direction, then stopped again. "Where are you?" he called between cupped hands.

Rachel had fallen again, which explained why he couldn't see her. At first she started to stand up and shout again, then something stopped her. What if he didn't help her? What if he was like one of those two dreadful men who had attempted to rape her? She couldn't do anything to fend him off. She was tied hand and foot, while all the people of End of the Track were occupied with more pressing matters.

"Where are you?" the man shouted again, and this time Rachel recognized the voice. Will Simmons!

"Will! Thank God it's you," she said. She struggled upright.

"Rachel, is that you?" Will said in astonishment, starting toward her on the run.

"Yes, yes! Will!"

"What the devil?" Will exclaimed, as he reached her and saw how she was bound. "Who did this?"

"Indians," she said succinctly.

"Indians?"

"The same ones who fired the depot and the storage area. Oh, Will, it's awful! It looks like the whole End of the Track will be burned to the ground.

Will pulled a knife from his pocket and sawed through the thongs on Rachel's hands, then kneeled down to slice through the bindings around her ankles.

"It *is* pretty bad," he said gravely. "It looks like the UP is going to lose a lot of money. But it could have been worse. I think we'll save most of the town, and I haven't heard of anyone being killed. If they had torched the Roundhouse, there would have been a heap of folks burned to death. Thank the good Lord they didn't know about all those people in there!"

Rachel started to tell him that the Indians had known about the Roundhouse and had left it untouched, but then she decided to say nothing. It would serve no useful purpose, and she doubted that he would believe her, anyway.

"How did the Indians come to tie you up, Rachel?" he said, standing up.

"It got stuffy inside the Roundhouse, and I thought it would be nice to step outside for a bit. I walked up the hill, as I often do, and stumbled onto them just as they were about to ride down."

"You're fortunate, is all I can say. I've no idea why Divine Providence saw fit to spare you, but for some reason He did. You being a white woman, it's God's wonder they didn't kill you, or worse!"

There was a loud, crashing sound from End of

the Track and they turned to look toward the depot, just in time to see the roof cave in.

"Rachel, I have to get back and help save what I can," Will said. "It's too late for the depot, but we can save the tents and maybe even salvage some of the ties. Will you be all right?"

"Yes, now that I'm untied, I'll be just fine. I'll go clean up and tend to the cuts. None of them are serious."

"I'll come see you when the fires are all under control."

"I'll be fine, Will. Don't worry about me. You go on and do what you have to do."

Will touched the brim of his hat, and ran back to pick up the buckets he had dropped, and hurried back toward the center of the town. Rachel followed more slowly, limping slightly.

The bucket brigades were now concentrating on the buildings and tents that had not caught fire, trying to contain the fire to those places where it had already taken hold. Many were working in the storage yard, moving the cross-ties that had not caught fire, and splashing them with water.

Rachel watched for a few minutes, then went in through the kitchen door to the Roundhouse. There, in the kitchen, she found the huddled company of players from Mrs. Harriette Brown's Troupe. They were all standing together in the middle of the room, as if seeking safety in numbers, peering nervously through the windows as the orange flames leaped against the night sky outside. Rachel was amused to notice that Anaheim Turner True looked as terrified as the others. They all jumped in fright when the door opened to admit Rachel.

"Oh, dear, oh, dear! You scared me half to death!" Mrs. Brown said, wringing her hands together.

"I'm sorry," Rachel said, suppressing a smile. "Is everyone all right?"

"All right? I should hope not!" Mrs. Brown said indignantly. "Those were wild Indians out there, do you realize that? Savages! We could all have been scalped! Why, I had no idea! I mean, I wouldn't have come out here. Oh, I shan't sleep a wink this night for fear that we shall all be murdered in our beds!"

"You need have no fear," Rachel said dryly. "They won't be back. They accomplished what they came to do."

"How do *you* know that?" Mrs. Brown asked. "You'll excuse me for not putting much faith in your assurances, Miss Bonner, but I do recall your letter of invitation stressing the fact that civilization had come out here. If those red-painted creatures are civilized, I should like to see your idea of savages."

Although Rachel did not say so, she considered "those creatures" more civilized than many of the so-called civilized people she had encountered out here. But Mrs. Brown wouldn't understand that, so there was no point in talking about it. Besides, Rachel suddenly felt very, very tired, and she pulled a chair out and sank into it with a sigh.

"Oh, my goodness!" Mrs. Brown exclaimed, for

the first time taking note of Rachel's bedraggled condition.

"My dear, whatever happened to you?" Mrs. Brown asked in distress.

"I, uh, fell down the hill trying to get back to town," Rachel said lamely.

"You mean you were out *there*, when those savages rode in? But you are hurt. Nell, get a can of hot water and a washcloth," Mrs. Brown said, suddenly all brisk efficiency. "Frank, go quickly and fetch a bottle of whiskey. We'll use it on the cuts."

"I'll be all right, honestly," Rachel said weakly.

"Hush now. Fortunately, none of the cuts appear to be too severe," Mrs. Brown said. "But you are fortunate, young lady, running downhill at night. You could have been badly hurt, maybe broken something."

"I know," Rachel said.

"And with those savages rampaging out there!" Mrs. Brown shuddered. "What if they had happened upon you?"

"I know," Rachel said.

With something concrete to do, Mrs. Brown seemed to have forgotten her own fears, and Rachel sat quietly, allowing the woman to tend her. None of the cuts were very serious, but it was worth suffering Mrs. Brown's ministrations to calm her and her troupe down.

"Mrs. Brown, I haven't had a chance to tell you yet. Your whistling solos were marvelous tonight," Rachel said. "I'm sure that you will be long remembered hereabouts."

Mrs. Brown laughed merrily. "And I am equally sure that *we* shall remember this place for a long time to come. Am I not right, children?" she asked the others, and received murmurs of agreement.

"And Nell," Rachel said, "your recitation was wonderful."

"Thank you, Miss Bonner," Nell said, blushing.

"And your song, Mr. Ruggs. And you, Mr. True. Your athletic exhibition was fascinating. In fact, the whole performance was magnificent."

"Thank you for your kind praise," Mrs. Brown said. She beamed with pride. "You know, in all modesty, I must confess feeling a little proud of myself tonight. We went on in the finest tradition of the theater. Not even a savage Indian attack prevented us from finishing our performance."

Rachel smiled to herself. The performance, she knew, was already over before the Indians rode in; and if it had still been on, she was sure it would have come to a sudden stop. Yet the memory of their abject fear diminished with every passing moment, so that by the time Mrs. Brown had finished with Rachel, the troupe was chattering away among themselves, convinced of thir undaunted courage.

"Wait until we give our next performance in New York," Ruggs said. "They won't believe us when we tell them what we went through here."

"Do you think Miss Sylvia Rehan's troupe would perform out here?" Mrs. Brown asked.

"I do not," Ruggs assured her stoutly.

"I'm sure not," Mrs. Brown said. She smiled in self-satisfaction. "She hasn't the spirit for such an adventure. We may be the only legitimate theater that would be so bold."

Rachel stood up. She was very tired, and she wanted to get some things together and move into the hotel. She had made up her mind not to spend the night here, and she was afraid that if she didn't get moving, she would become so overcome with fatigue that she would postpone it.

Just as she had made up her mind to go upstairs, Will Simmons pushed open the kitchen door. He smelled of smoke and his face was blackened. He smiled wearily. "Well, we lost the depot," he said. "But we saved almost all the ties, and only one tent went up."

"Really? But the ties were burning so, I thought they would all go," Rachel said.

"That was just one pile," Will said. "We got the rest of them pulled out of the way and doused down with water. We lost maybe ten thousand, but more than ninety thousand were saved."

"That is good news, isn't it, Will?"

"I'll say. It saves the company at least ten thousand dollars. But enough about that. Are you all right, Rachel?"

"I'm fine, thanks to Mrs. Brown here."

"I told her how fortunate she was that she didn't have a more serious fall," Mrs. Brown said primly.

"Fall? That was the least of her worries," Will said. "She was just fortunate that—"

"Will," Rachel said quickly, to forestall his telling about her encounter with the Indians.

"—she wasn't scalped," Will rushed on. "I don't

know why the Indians just tied her up like that. It's a mystery, all right."

"Tied her up? *Indians?* What are you talking about?" Mrs. Brown demanded.

"You mean she didn't tell you?" Will laughed admiringly. "Miss Bonner was captured by those redskins. The same ones who set fire to the depot."

"My word, girl, you said nothing!" Mrs. Brown said, swaying as if about to swoon.

"I didn't want to cause you any concern," Rachel said. "Anyway, as you can see, I wasn't hurt. Now, Mr. Simmons, if you would, please, I could use some help."

"Of course," Will said easily. "What can I do to help?"

"I would like you to help me move out of the Roundhouse," Rachel said. "I'm moving into the hotel."

Will studied her intently. "Of course I'll be glad to help you move. But don't you think you should wait until Rankin returns, so he'll know you're all right?"

"I have severed all personal and professional ties with Mr. Rankin, so I fail to see why he should be concerned with my welfare. Now, please, Will. Just help me leave this place."

"You mean you won't be working here anymore?" Mrs. Brown asked with raised eyebrows.

"That's exactly what I do mean."

"Well, my dear, I am glad we were only scheduled to do the one performance. You can rest assured that we shall be on the morning train out. Especially if you will no longer be working here," Mrs.

Brown said. She frowned. "I must confess that I was never too taken with Mr. Rankin. He didn't seem to be concerned about our performance at all!"

"Rachel, I know it isn't my place to say so," Will said gravely. "But I want you to know that I think you are doing the right thing. I didn't think that a nice woman like you should work in a place like this from the beginning."

There was a note of self-righteousness in his voice that annoyed her, but she was too tired and too dispirited to dispute him. Let Will Simmons think what he would. It would stop him from asking questions, questions that she didn't wish to answer.

CHAPTER ELEVEN

"There!" Rachel said, throwing the last garment into her trunk. "That does it."

"But what about all the dresses in the closet?" Will wanted to know. "Surely you don't mean to leave them?"

She scowled at the gowns in the closet. They had been the club wielded over Marie Thompson. Rachel was determined not to give Rankin such leverage over her.

"They aren't mine. They belong to Ewell Rankin."

"They do?" Will looked at the dresses with an incredulous expression. "What would a man want with dresses?"

Rachel began to laugh, almost hysterically. "What indeed?" She managed to choke off the laughter. "Come on, Will. I want to be quit of this place before he returns."

Will swung the trunk easily upon his shoulder and started for the door. Just as Rachel began to open the door for him, she heard Ewell Rankin's voice on the stairs.

"Get back!" she hissed, pushing Will back into the room. "It's Ewell!"

"You aren't afraid of him, are you?" Will asked. "I'll see to it that he doesn't harm you, Rachel."

"It's not that I'm afraid of him," she said crossly. "I just don't want to get into a discussion with him, that's all. He might try to argue me into staying, and my mind's made up."

"All right," Will said. He set the trunk on the floor and waited patiently as Ewell Rankin and whoever was with him came up the stairs. Rachel said a man's voice just outside the door.

"Shouldn't we go down to your room, Ewell?" said a man't voice just outside the door.

"No," Rankin answered. "If we do, someonc might happen down the hall and overhear us. If we stay here in the hall, we'll spot anyone coming up the stairs."

"But what about these rooms?" the man said. "This one here, for instance?" The doorknob turned as someone tried to open it.

"Rachel's door is locked," Rankin said. "That means she's gone. She told me she would be. And if someone is in the other rooms, they're too far away to hear us."

"If you say so," the other man said. "Now, what's on your mind, Ewell?"

"Bert, how would you like to make eighteen thousand dollars?"

"I know that other voice," Rachel whispered to

Will. "He's staying here. That's Bert Parker. He's an engineer for Credit Mobilier."

"That's a lot of money," Bert Parker was saying. He laughed uncertainly. "Who do I have to kill to get it?"

"Nobody," Rankin said.

"Then where does the money come from?"

"The Indians tonight opened the way. When I turn in my damage report, I'll indicate a total loss of a hundred thousand cross-ties. We actually lost about ten thousand, but UP will be billed another twenty thousand dollars anyway. Two thousand dollars is all we need to replace the burned ties. That leaves eighteen thousand."

"That's all there is to it?"

"That's all," Rankin said.

"How much of the eighteen thousand is mine?"

"All of it."

"I'm not sure I understand, Ewell. How about the others in Credit Mobilier? How about you?"

"The others won't know about it. I can fix the books so that their smartest bookkeepers won't be able to find it."

Bert Parker laughed. "You're planning to steal from Credit Mobilier?"

"I am. Why not? Why are you laughing?"

"I just happen to think it's humorous, stealing from the biggest bunch of thieves ever assembled. I should know, I work there. They've double- and triple-billed the UP on just about everything. They've milked the federal government out of land and money, and now *you* are going to steal from *them.* What makes you think you can get away with it?"

"The reason I can get away with it is because they're so busy doing their own stealing, they don't have time to mind their own fences. Believe me, I can do it. The question is, are you interested?"

"Hell, yes. For eighteen thousand, you bet I'm interested. But what about you? What do you get out of it?"

"From that I'll get nothing, it's all yours. But in return I want you to draw up some plans for me. Very special plans."

"What kind of plans?"

"Plans for trestles. Beginning with Eddison Gulch."

"Plans for that trestle are already drawn."

"I know that, but I want you to draw it again. I want you to draw up new plans, and shave ten percent off the cost."

"The only way I can see to do that is to eliminate ten percent of the support structure."

"Will it stand up with ten percent of the support structure eliminated?"

"Sure. It's designed to a safety factor of two." Bert Parker laughed. "Though UP is paying for a safety factor of four."

"Good!" Rankin said. "And after you finish with that one, do the same thing for Midnight Canyon, Kimberly Pass, and Tyson Gorge."

"Let's see if I have this straight, now. The UP is paying three hundred thousand per trestle, Credit Mobilier is stealing a hundred and fifty thousand of that, and you want to take off the top another fifteen thousand per trestle. Is that it?"

"That's about it."

"That's sixty thousand dollars."

"Yes."

"Well, it doesn't seem fair, now does it? I mean, I only get eighteen thousand to do all the dirty work. You get sixty, and you do nothing."

"You'll get the eighteen thousand right away. I won't collect my money until the trestles are built. And even then I'll have to manipulate the funding very carefully to cover my tracks. I don't think it's that unfair."

"I'll get mine right away?"

"That's right," Rankin said. "We'll have to reorder the ties right away, won't we? Every mile we gain on Central Pacific means money. We aren't going to wait around for new ties."

"Yes, you're right about that. You're a real tricky fellow, Ewell. You've got yourself a deal. You get eighteen thousand to me next week, and I'll give you some revised trestle plans in exchange. But what about Julius Deever? What will he say when he sees that the plans have been revised?"

"Don't worry about Julius," Rankin said. "I'll take care of him."

"Mr. Rankin!" a third voice called, floating up from downstairs. "You're wanted down at the depot!"

"All right, I'll be right there." Then, in a softer voice to Parker, "Come along with me, Bert. Who knows what fresh opportunity we might come across?"

Bert Parker laughed uproariously. "Yes, sir! And to think that my old daddy went out to California during the gold rush days to try to make his strike. I tell you, *this* is the real gold rush!"

"And this is just scratching the surface, Bert . . ." Rankin's voice receded as the two men outside the door walked away.

Rachel and Will had been listening with growing disbelief, and were quiet for several minutes after the pair were gone. Finally Rachel spoke. "Did you hear all that, Will?" she asked in an awed whisper.

"Yes," Will replied, equally as quiet. "My Lord, Rachel, do you realize how much money Credit Mobilier must have stolen by now?"

"Millions," Rachel said, letting her breath go explosively. Limbs weak, she sank down onto the trunk. "Millions and millions of dollars!"

"Yes, and I know now that I was right about Miller Conners," Will said thoughtfully. "Remember I told you we were building to his minimum standards, but billing for higher standards? He must have gone to someone with his story."

"You could be right. I'm willing to believe almost anything after what we just overheard."

"Well, that settles it! I have to find someone not involved and report this!"

Rachel stared at him as if he'd suddenly lost his wits. "Are you serious? After what happened to your friend Conners, you're going to report this? To someone not involved? Who would that be? It seems to me just about everyone is involved in this corruption!"

"Well . . . I don't know. Maybe your uncle?"

"Julius Deever? Ha!" Rachel said scornfully. "What good would that do? For all we know, he's in cahoots with them as well. Didn't Ewell just tell that man not to worry about Uncle Julius? In fact, the more I think about it, the more I'm convinced that my uncle is mixed up in this." She recalled how surprised she was when Deever learned of her involvement with Ewell Rankin, but said nothing about it. What else could that mean but that they were involved together?

Will was saying, "Well, I must talk to somebody. I can't just let it go as if I hadn't heard anything."

"You can't do anything else, Will." Rachel saw the determined set of his face, and she smiled at him, reaching over to put her hand on his. "Don't you see, Will? It could be very dangerous for you."

"I don't care," he said stubbornly. "It's my duty, as I see it."

"Well, I care! I wouldn't want to see the same thing happen to you that happened to Miller Conners."

Will's face brightened perceptibly, and he looked at her with a strange expression on his face. "Are you serious, Rachel? Would you really care what happened to me?"

"Of course I would! What a silly question!"

"Well then, in that case, I won't tell anyone what we overheard. At least not until I've thought about it some."

"Good!" she said. She got up. "That makes me feel much, much better, Will." She opened the door and peered outside. "I think it's safe to leave now. They're gone."

Will swung the trunk up onto his shoulder and followed her out of the Roundhouse and over to the hotel.

"Thank you, Will, she said, as he put the trunk down on the floor of her room. She smiled brightly at him. "I don't know what I would have done without you tonight. You always seem to be there when I need you, and I want you to know how much I appreciate that." Without thinking she leaned over and kissed him lightly on the cheek.

Will blushed, and touched his fingers to his cheek where she had kissed him. Rachel laughed, and to Will her voice sounded like the chimes of a delicate wind bell. "Why did you do that?" he asked in a hushed voice.

"Why? Because you are very special to me, Will Simmons," she said in some surprise. "And because I can't think of anyone else I'd rather kiss at this moment."

"Rachel, what will you be doing now that you've left the Roundhouse?"

Rachel sighed, and sat on the bed. The springs creaked as she sat down, and Will looked away in an agony of embarrassment. He hoped that no one had heard. It wasn't seemly for him to be in this room alone with her. People would talk. And if anyone heard the bedsprings creak, they *really* would talk!

"I don't know what I'm going to do," Rachel said thoughtfully. "To tell you the truth, I really haven't given too much thought to it yet. It's all happened so suddenly." She gave him a sober look. "If you hear of a job I could do, tell me about it, will you?"

"Yes, Rachel, I surely will."

Rachel yawned, and then began unbuttoning the bodice of her dress. "I'm very sleepy now, Will. Would you excuse me, so I can retire?"

"Of course," he said hastily. "Of course I will." He moved quickly to the door and opened it. "Be sure to lock the door behind me now, Rachel."

"I will, don't worry." She smiled sleepily. "Thanks again for being around when I needed you, Will. Good night."

"Good night, Rachel."

There was carpet on the floor of the upper landing of the hotel, and carpet on the stairway going down. But Will Simmons didn't need carpet—he was walking on air.

Rachel had all but confessed to him that she reciprocated his love. She had told him that she would be very sorry if anything happened to him. She told him that he was very special to her, and that she needed him; and if all those hints weren't enough, she had even kissed him.

Will had been enamored of Rachel Bonner from the moment he set eyes on her. She was a pretty woman, to be sure, but looks were not all that important to him. What was important was the fact that she was a strong woman, so that she could bear him sons and help him with his plans. She had not only physical strength, but strength of mind and spirit as well. How many women could have stood up to the sight of marauding Indians, let alone survive with undaunted spirit an encounter such as she had experienced? Very few, he was sure. She had proved that she had the strength to make a fine settler's wife.

And that was what Will had in mind for her. It was his intention to ask her to marry him. Oh, how wonderful it would be! They would settle on the land and build a sod shanty. He would put in all the crops that he and Rachel could handle together the first year. Later, when the children started coming and grew old enough to help, he could easily increase his acreage.

Will hoped that she would give him many sons. One of the first things that he had noted about her was that she was built well for bearing babies. He knew how to look for that in a woman, and had checked for that in every woman he had ever considered for a wife. Of course, he had no way of telling whether Rachel would give him sons or daughters. Sons! She would simply have to bear him sons! It had to be that way!

As he left the hotel, some of his good spirits left him. He really wasn't ready to take a wife yet. If he married now, he wouldn't even have enough money for the first crop, much less the price of the land he needed. There had to be a way for him to get the money he needed. Now that he had found the woman he wanted for his wife, he could not wait any longer.

No, he couldn't wait any longer. Rachel no longer had a job, and she might even decide to leave End of the Track. If she did that, he would never find her again. Also, someone else might ask her to marry him before he did.

But surely she wouldn't marry just anyone who came along. She would wait for him.

Or would she? She might be too frightened to remain here, especially now that she had learned what kind of a man Ewell Rankin was. She might be so frightened of Rankin that she would do anything to get out of here.

Will had always known that Rankin was a no-good, and a slick gent with the ladies. Will had wanted to warn Rachel about him, but he hadn't been able to find the words. It had hurt him when she started living at the Roundhouse. Oddly enough, Will had never been angry with her. He blamed himself. If he had warned her about Rankin, she would never have moved in with him.

It was Ewell Rankin that he was angry at. He had sullied Rachel, and now it was clear that he was a crook.

Ewell Rankin . . .

Will skidded to a stop, his thoughts churning. The conversation they had overheard. Yes, that was it! That was the way to get the land he needed!

But that would be crooked, he thought. Yet there was no other way that Rankin could be made to pay for his misdeeds. There was no one Will could trust with what he had learned; no way he had of knowing who was and who was not hooked up with Rankin.

What was wrong with Will—*and* Rachel—benefiting by making Rankin pay, at least in a small way, for his crimes? It would be an ironic justice!

Will had been brought up to believe in law and order and a rigid moral code. To get ahead in the world a man had to work hard so that he might prosper by the fruits of his labor. Well, he had worked hard all his adult life, and where had it gotten him? To buy the land he wanted, to have the woman he wanted, he would have to work and skimp for the Lord knew how many more years! And the more he thought of it, the more he feared that Rachel wouldn't wait that long. Will knew, dimly, that he would have continued to plow along if she hadn't entered his life. But now, to have his farm and Rachel, he had to seize the opportunity that presented itself. He would be a fool not to!

Will waited in the shadows and watched Ewell Rankin from a distance. Rankin was still at the burned depot, picking over the smoking, smoldering remains, laughing with the few men who still lingered about, as if the destruction of the depot had never happened. In fact, Will thought, Rankin would probably devise some way to make money from it.

It was quite late now, and the crowd which had turned out for the fires had long since left the streets. Even the saloons were closed. The only sounds were the soft strumming of a guitar somewhere, and the conversation of the men at the depot.

Finally, Will heard Rankin bid the others good night, and a few moments later all the men had gone off in different directions. Rankin came directly toward where Will lurked. Just as Rankin came abreast of him, Will reached out a long arm, grabbed him by the neck, and yanked him off the street.

"What the holy hell!" Rankin bellowed, and as he spoke, his hand was going for the pistol at his belt. Will had anticipated that, but even with the element of surprise on his side, he very nearly didn't knock the gun from Rankin's hand in time, so fast was the man's draw. The gun went skittering away in the dust, and Will slammed Rankin roughly against the clapboard side of the barbershop.

"Will? Will Simmons? You? What the devil is the meaning of this? I can have your ass fired for this!"

"That's as may be, but you and me, Mr. Rankin, have a little business to discuss."

"Business? What business could you have with me, fellow?" Rankin struggled to get free, but Will increased the pressure of his grip on Rankin's neck, and Rankin gasped for breath. "Dammit, man, you're strong as a bull. You're strangling me!"

Will eased his grip slightly, but he doubled his free hand into a fist and held it cocked so that Rankin could see it. He said, "We'll talk business here and now."

"What business are you talking about?" Rankin said angrily. "And why like this? Couldn't you come to see me at my office tomorrow?"

"No, Rankin, this isn't office business. You see, I have the goods on you, and to keep me quiet it's going to cost you."

Rankin loosed a scornful laugh, which was a mistake, because Will jerked him away from the wall of the barbershop, then slammed him back hard enough to knock the breath from him. "This is no laughing matter, Rankin," Will said through gritted teeth.

"No," Rankin said hastily. "No, I can see that. So what do you want to talk to me about?"

"About the ninety thousand cross-ties that you are going to claim were burned, when if fact it was only ten thousand. And about the four trestles. You're paying to have the plans changed, and you're pocketing the difference."

Rankin sucked in his breath, going still in Will's grasp. "How—how did you know about that?"

"I was in Miss Bonner's room, and overheard you and this Bert Parker."

"Rachel's room?"

"Yes," Will said. He started to add that Rachel was also present and had overheard the incriminating conversation, then realized that that would place her in jeopardy. "She asked me to go to her room and take her trunk over to the hotel."

"Hell! I see," Rankin said.

"Now, Mr. Rankin. As you can understand, I am serious. It should be worth a great deal to you to see that I remain quiet about what I know."

"Who are you going to tell?" Rankin said with a sneer. "The Union Pacific? The police? The Army?"

"No," Will said. "I thought that the higher-ups at Credit Mobilier might be interested in knowing that you're stealing from them as well as from the UP. I know many people at Credit Mobilier. If I go to enough of them, I figure I'll find the right one to tell."

"I see." Rankin sighed. "All right, Simmons. What do you want?"

"Not much," Will said. "Just enough money so that Miss Bonner and me can start a farm."

"You and Rachel are going to start a farm?" Rankin asked in disbelief.

"Yes."

Rankin laughed harshly, but when the expression on Will's face turned hard, he sobered. "I'm sorry, Simmons. It's just that I have a hard time imagining Rachel Bonner on a farm with you, or anyone else, for that matter. Are congratulations in order? Are you wedding her?"

"I am."

"Well, I'll be damned," Rankin said softly. "Well, then you must congratulate the bride for me. I can see where you might be in need of some money, but the problem is, I don't have much available cash. It's all tied up, you see."

"Then untie it," Will said tersely.

"I can't, there's no way to get it as quickly as you seem to think . . ." As Will's grip tightened, Rankin added hastily, "Wait now, wait! I just had an idea. You *do* want to farm?"

"Yes," Will said simply. "It's all I ever wanted."

"Do you remember that piece of land you once looked at back near Connersville, the land you wanted to buy from me?"

"I remember," Will said, his breath quickening.

"Come to my office with me now, and I'll sign

the deed over to you now for that piece of land. We'll call it my wedding present to you and your . . ." Rankin paused for a moment, smiled, and then said, ". . . bride."

"Yes!" Will said, his voice thickening with excitement. "You sign that land over to me, and the blackmail is finished. You'll not hear a word from me again."

"Blackmail? Don't demean yourself. It isn't blackmail at all, my dear fellow," Rankin said smoothly. "As I told you, consider it a wedding gift. After all, it's the least I can do for someone who is getting me out of a sticky situation."

Ewell Rankin laughed, and there was an unpleasant undertone to his laughter that Will, in his pleasure at getting what he wanted so easily, did not take note of. In fact, he was so happy that he laughed right along with Rankin.

CHAPTER TWELVE

Rachel went down to breakfast at six-thirty the next morning. She ate early for a specific reason. She had high hopes of going to work for the hotel today. Of course, she knew that she wouldn't be earning nearly as much money as she had been making in the Roundhouse, but if the hotel would throw in room and board, it would be decidedly better than going back to live with the Deevers. *Anything* would be better than that!

As she ate her breakfast, she looked around. The hotel restaurant was doing a brisk business. The customers, while not of the class that frequented the Roundhouse, were a respectable lot. They were mostly business and professional people; she saw only a few gandy dancers.

With a practiced eye Rachel watched the waitresses at work. She had hopes of getting employment similar to what she had been doing at the Roundhouse. She already knew that the hotel did not employ a hostess. Of course, the hotel was not in the same class as the Roundhouse, yet Rachel felt that she could increase the efficiency of the restaurant operation to the point where the additional wages paid her would make her hiring worthwhile. At least that was the point she intended to try to make with Mr. Finley.

One of the waitresses approached her table. "Miss Bonner, you wanted me to tell you when Mr. Finley arrived in his office?"

"Yes, I did," Rachel said, dabbing her lips with a napkin. "Has he come in?"

He just came in," the waitress said. She smiled. "And good luck."

Rachel sat back. "Now what makes you say that?"

"You're going to ask him for a job. Am I right?"

"That's right. But how did you know that?"

"The news is all over town that you left Ewell Rankin and the Roundhouse last night. That means you're going to have to find another job, and for someone like you, this is the only other place in End of the Track. So, good luck."

"Thank you."

Taking a final sip of coffee, Rachel left the dining room and went down the hall to Marcus Finley's office. She knocked on the door.

"Come in," a wheezing voice called from inside.

Rachel pushed the door open and stepped inside. She saw a large, fat man standing beside a desk. He smiled at her, flashing a gold tooth.

"Well, well, well! Miss Rachel Bonner," Finley said. He laughed a wheezing laugh, and his large paunch shook like jelly. "You've come to see old Marcus Finley, have you?"

"Yes, I have."

"Sit down, sit down." He waved a hand expansively. "Ain't often I get to see a lovely young lady such as you in my office. How about a cup of coffee?"

"No, thank you, Mr. Finley. I've just finished eating breakfast."

"Hope you don't mind if I have a cup myself."

He went to a small wood-burning stove and, with a potholder, took a blue pot off the stove and poured black coffee into a chipped mug. While he was thus engaged, Rachel took the opportunity to look around his office. It was dominated by a large roll-top desk, and a long, leather-covered divan. Both the desk and the divan were piled high with papers. On the wall was a calendar which was a month behind, and a wall clock which was fifteen minutes ahead. There was a gun case holding three rifles; the gun case hung on the wall above a moth-eaten, stuffed buffalo head, which had one eye missing.

"Now then," Finley said, returning to his desk. He sucked at the coffee through pursed lips, making a slurping noise as he drank. Finally he placed the cup down and expelled his breath with a sighing sound. "Now then, what can I do for you?"

"Hopefully, Mr. Finley, it's the other way around . . . what I can do for *you*."

He squinted at her. "And what might that be, now?"

"Well, as you probably know, I moved into your hotel last night, and I had my breakfast here this morning."

"Yup," Finley wheezed. "I know all that."

"At breakfast, I took the liberty of looking around. You don't have a hostess here, do you?"

"A hostess, you say? What might that be?"

"A hostess is someone who could supervise your kitchen and waitresses. In fact, supervise your maids as well. A hostess would take work off your hands, and I'm sure would mean better service for your customers, and increase your income considerably."

"A hostess, you say. Pretty fancy name, that." He slurped more coffee. "And I reckon you have someone in mind for this, uh, hostess job?"

"Indeed I do. Myself. I held a similar position at the Roundhouse."

"Now, I know that. But then Rankin provides special entertainment for his people over there. We don't offer such special entertainments here."

"That doesn't matter. That was the least of my duties there. My job was to supervise the kitchen and dining room. And that is what I propose to do for you here."

He nodded ponderously, and pursed thick lips. "What kind of arrangements did you have with Rankin?"

"I had a salary, of course, and he provided room and board."

"I'll bet he did. And you'd expect the same arrangements here."

"Yes, something like that."

Finley's smile was more a leer than anything else. "You would be willing to work here, with the *exact* arrangement you had with Rankin?"

All at once Rachel sensed what he was getting at.

She had been so eager for the job that she had not been thinking clearly. She said warily, "I'm not certain that I know what you're implying, Mr. Finley. I would work for a reasonable salary and room and board, yes."

"That wasn't my meaning." His gaze swept her up and down. "What I'm getting at, would we have the same kind of relationship that you and Rankin had? Agree to that, and we might work something out."

"I'm sure I don't know what you're talking about, sir," Rachel said coldly. She stood up. "At any rate, I seem to be wasting my time here."

"Well now, Miss Bonner, you'd hardly expect any other kind of offer, it seems to me." He wheezed lewd laughter. You're a pretty piece. Me and Rankin agree on that."

"I am scarcely interested in what you and Ewell Rankin agree on. It seems you're two of a kind, that's clear. I made a mistake coming to you. I'll find a job somewhere else, thank you."

"Will you now? Check around and you'll probably come back to me. Of course, you might try the Hoghead Saloon. And don't forget the King of the Hill."

Rachel's face flamed with outrage and shame and she stormed out of his office, his cruel laughter spurring her on. She was so furious that she stalked past Julius Deever without seeing him.

"Rachel!" Deever called out.

She stopped and faced around. "Uncle Julius! What are doing here?"

"It seems to me, Rachel, that the question should

be, what are *you* doing here? I have just learned that you left Mr. Rankin's employment."

"I did."

"Then I would consider taking you back with us, much as it might go against the grain. You are related to Mildred, after all, and she's feeling poorly of late. She could do with a little help around the house."

"It isn't a house, it's a boxcar," she said scornfully. "And if you had any compassion at all, you'd send Aunt Mildred back home."

"Don't prattle to me of compassion, young lady," Deever said sourly. "You're the one who deserted her in her time of need. And now I demand that you return, as a dutiful niece should."

"I have no intention of returning." Rachel responded.

"Oh? And pray tell me how you intend to support yourself. You didn't get a job here, did you? Did you?"

"No." Her glance slid away.

"Nor will you find work anywhere else at End of the Track. You have no choice, Rachel. Surely you must realize that."

Rachel sighed. Perhaps he was right. She was at the end of her rope. She could not find employment here, and she did not have enough money to leave End of the Track and seek work elsewhere. He was right; she had little choice. She would have to move back in with the Deevers . . . at least until something else came along.

Resignedly, she said, "All right, Uncle Julius, I will come back."

"Now, that's more like it," Deever said, smiling triumphantly. "I'll expect to see you for the noon meal. In fact, it would be nice if you could get there in time to prepare it."

Rachel turned away from Julius Deever and trudged up the stairs to her room. She was deep in despair. What a comedown from being the hostess at the Roundhouse and bringing in a show, which was written up in a New York newspaper, to being out of work, dispirited, and returning to the one place she wanted more than anything to avoid. She wondered if she had made a mistake in leaving Ewell Rankin and the Roundhouse. But she didn't wonder about it for very long. She had been right to quit that arrangement. Maybe she was going back to a miserable existence with the Deevers, but at least she was recovering her self-respect.

She had just unpacked her trunk that morning before going down to breakfast, and now she had to repack it. She had bought two nice dresses of her own while working for Rankin, because she did not like to feel that he not only owned her but everything that she wore. She looked at the two dresses now, and clucked softly to herself. They were very expensive. If not for the dresses, she wouldn't be in such dire need of money. There would certainly be no opportunity to wear them for a while. She could store them away in the bottom of the trunk.

She finished packing, then gazed at the trunk in speculation, wondering if her uncle would pay to have it moved to the boxcar. Probably not, she concluded. And, as it was too heavy for her to move herself, that meant that she would have to pay someone to do it, taking more of her few remaining dollars.

The few dollars she did have left, she intended to keep a secret from Julius Deever. Then, if she could earn a little money working part time, even as a serving girl in one of the eating places, by spring she might have enough to leave. She thought of Mabel's Place, back in Connersville. Maybe she could get work there. But even as she thought of it, she realized how many people had left Connersville when the track moved on. Connersville was very nearly a ghost town now, and there was probably hardly enough business for Mabel to support herself, much less hire a waitress.

No, Rachel decided, she would have to save enough money to go all the way back to Omaha, or St. Louis, or even Cincinnati. At the moment that seemed an impossible task.

There was a knock on the door. It was a heavy knock, and she wondered if Julius Deever had come to hurry her up. With slumped shoulders she walked over to open the door, and saw a smiling Will Simmons.

"Will! I thought you'd be at work!"

"No more work for the railroad, Rachel," he babbled. "I have the most wonderful news! Oh! First, let me give you this." He had been holding a bouquet of flowers behind his back. Now he handed it to her.

"Will, what on earth?" She stared at the flowers in astonishment.

"They're awful pretty, aren't they?" Will said with a foolish grin. "They came in by train from

Council Bluff a short while ago. They raise them there in a glass house, even in the wintertime."

"Yes, I know. It's called a greenhouse," she said amused by his patient excitement. "But what is the occasion?"

"That's part of the wonderful news," Will looked around conspiratorially, then stepped closer and lowered his voice. "Do you remember what we over-heard last night?"

Rachel had not thought about it again until this moment, but as soon as Will mentioned it, she did remember. "Of course. How could I forget?"

"Well, I got to thinking about it after I left you. And you're right. There doesn't seem to be anyone I can go to with this story, not anyone who would be-lieve me and do anything about it. But, on the other hand, it didn't seem right just to let Rankin get away with it, either. No, sir. So, I hit on a plan."

"A plan?" Rachel went tense. She didn't like the sound of this. "What kind of a plan?"

"A most wonderful plan, as I'm sure you will agree." He smiled broadly, proudly. "I blackmailed him, Rachel."

A cold feeling started in her stomach. "You did what?"

"Ewell Rankin." Will put a finger across her lips to shush her. "I blackmailed him."

"You . . . You blackmailed Ewell Rankin? How did you manage to do that?"

"It was easy, easier'n I thought it would be. I just went up to him, and I told him that I overheard him making all those plans with that other fellow, Bert Parker—"

"Oh, Will, you didn't mention that I overheard?" she asked apprehensively.

"Well, no. I thought of it, but then it came to me that that might put you in danger, and I wouldn't do that to you, Rachel."

"Thank goodness!" she said in relief.

"Anyway," Will was going on, "it worked! He gave me just what I wanted, and Rachel, we're all set up now."

"Set up?" Rachel stared at him, feeling utterly stupid. What on earth was he going on about?

"Yes," Will said exuberantly. "That's the why of the flowers, Rachel, I want you to know that I've never bought flowers for any woman before."

"They are beautiful, Will, and I thank you very much. But I still don't see . . ."

"Rachel, the flowers are for marrying."

"For marrying?" she said in a small voice. "What did you say?"

"I said the flowers are for marrying," Will swept on. "I've bought a wagon, and a team of good mules. I also got a cow, 'cause we'll be needing fresh milk and butter. And I've got a hundred little chicks. That'll provide our eggs before too long. I got seed, and a good plow, and enough flour, coffee, beans and bacon to last us the winter—"

"Wait, wait!" Rachel tried in vain to stop the flow of words.

"—and if we get started now, I'll have time to throw up a sod house before the real cold weather sets in. Come spring, I'll get the first crop in. The good Lord willing, Rachel, by summer you'll be birthing our first young'un."

"Mr. Simmons!"

"*Mister* Simmons?" Will said in a hurt voice. "You've been calling me Will all this time."

"Will . . ." She took a deep breath, not knowing whether to laugh or cry. "Let's get this all sorted out. Are you asking me to *marry* you?"

"Well, yes, Rachel," Will said with a puzzled look. "I thought you had that understood all along. I'm sorry, I reckon women like for their menfolk to propose all proper-like. It's just that, well, we have a lot of work to get done before the first snow flies, and I reckon I was getting ahead of myself." He dropped to one knee. "Rachel, I went to Ewell Rankin and all, for us, you and me. So now, I'm asking you nice and proper—will you become my wife?"

My God, Rachel thought, *I can't believe this!* It couldn't be happening! And yet there he was, on one knee, a silly grin on his face, asking her to be his wife.

Thoughts racing, she tried to think of a way to refuse him without hurting his feelings. Will was a good man, a kind man, and she cared for him as a friend; but she had never thought of him in a romantic way.

Oh, why couldn't life be simple? Why couldn't she love him? It would be so easy to say yes, and it would solve so many of her problems. Why not accept his proposal?

"Rachel?" Will said plaintively.

"Oh, Will, do get up from there," she said crossly. "I can't stand to see a man on his knees!"

He got awkwardly to his feet, and she could see by his expression that she had hurt him.

"I'm sorry, Will," she said, putting her hand on his arm. "It's just that you've taken me by surprise."

A frown crossed his face. "But you know how I feel." He looked at her searchingly. "You haven't given me an answer yet."

Rachel turned away, unwilling for him to see her eyes. "Let me think for a moment, Will. A woman doesn't like to rush into something like this."

She went to the window and stared blindly down at the street below. Hadn't she been ready and willing to marry Ewell Rankin? On the balance, Will was certainly a better man than Ewell. There was a goodness about him that Rankin certainly did not possess. Will was honest, kind, and caring, all qualities that Rankin did not possess. Strangely enough, she could not blame Will for what he had done; it might strike some people as dishonest, but in her opinion it was no more than Rankin deserved.

And since Will said he was set up now, he certainly should be able to provide for her. But farming? It struck her as a hard life, especially out here and starting from scratch. If he wasn't so set on farming, it would not be so bad. Maybe she could just agree to go with him for a while; maybe in time she could talk him out of farming.

No, she couldn't go off with him! It wouldn't be fair to either of them. If she loved him, it might be different.

She looked back over her shoulder. Hat twisting and twisting in his big hands, he was still waiting for her answer.

Will was not at all bad looking, she told herself. In his rugged way, he was handsome. Maybe she could learn to love him, in time. She knew that a great many marriages started off without love, and then love developed. Could it happen that way with her and Will?

All at once, she remembered the couple she had seen at the train depot in Willow Station. She recalled being envious of the woman, because she and her man were going west as pioneers to establish a new life for themselves. Never had she seen such happiness as on that woman's countenance.

Could she ever be like that? Could Will be her man, the way that settler was that woman's man?"

Rachel considered the alternative. If she did not wed Will, she would have to return to the Deevers, or go humbly to Ewell Rankin and beg him to take her back. The first she had no desire to do, and the second she would never, never do! She recalled Marcus Finley's words about the King of the Hill saloon. That, of course, was unthinkable. Against such choices, the prospect of marriage to Will Simmons suddenly became attractive.

She made her decision and turned around. "Yes, Will. I'll marry you."

"You'll never be sorry, Rachel," he said fervently. "I'll make you happy. I promise you that."

Rachel kept her voice steady. "I'm sure you will."

"Whaoo!" Will let out a yell and jumped up, clapping his boot heels together.

Rachel had to smile. There was something boyishly appealing about him in that moment. Then he became businesslike. "We'd better get going. I told the preacher that we'd be over to see him this afternoon."

Rachel felt her temper stir. He had been assuming an awful lot! Then she smiled wryly at herself. She should be pleased that he was so eager.

"We can put the wagon, mules, and everything else on the evening train, be in Connersville by noon tomorrow, and be on our own land by sundown! Is your trunk all packed?"

At her speechless nod, Will hoisted the trunk easily upon his shoulder, and held the door open for her. She smiled tremulously at him as she passed, but again, she did not know whether to laugh or cry.

Well, no matter. She was committed now, for better or worse. Wasn't that what the marriage vows said?

CHAPTER THIRTEEN

Rachel, who at five o'clock on the previous afternoon had become Mrs. Will Simmons, shifted her position on the hard board seat of the wagon, trying to restore some circulation to her sore, cramped legs and her numb buttocks. She turned to look behind them, but no matter in which direction she looked, she could see nothing but the gently rolling prairie.

It had been four hours since they left Connersville. Four hours of travel had taken them, by Will's estimate, barely ten miles. Only ten miles in four hours! Had they been traveling by train they would have covered nearly two hundred miles in that length of time. Their slow progress galled Rachel.

"Will, how much farther is it?" she finally asked.

Will smiled at her, and covered her small hand with his big, rough palm. He was still in excellent spirits, and this infuriated her.

"Anxious to get to our own place, aren't you, girl? Can't say as I blame you. I'm just as anxious. In truth, it'll be dark when we arrive, and there'll be little enough for you to see. But this I promise you: come morning, you'll see the sun rise on Edenland."

"Edenland?"

"That's what I've decided to name our farm. After the Garden of Eden, you know?"

"Yes," she said dryly. "I know about the Garden of Eden, and this hardly seems to be it."

"But that's what it's going to be for us," Will said proudly. "A Garden of Eden. I'll spend the winter making improvements on our house, and maybe add a barn. Come spring, I'll be ready to put in our first crop."

"Our house?" Rachel said, her spirits brightening at the prospect of at least finding a house at the end of this journey.

"Yes. Of course, it's not up yet, but I'll have it up before the first snow, that I promise you. Wait until you see it, Rachel. There's nothing cozier than a sod house, when it's freezing outside. We'll be as warm as a bug."

"A . . . a sod house?" Her spirits sank as she recalled the sod shanties she had seen from the train on the way out here. "We're going to live in a sod house, one you haven't even built yet?"

At her tone he squeezed her hand reassuringly. "There's no other kind of house that can be built out here. There's no lumber, unless you have it shipped in, and that costs a fortune."

"I see," she said dispiritedly.

Will laughed. "Don't worry about it. You'll be proud enough of it, and ready enough to move in when it's finished, considering we'll be sleeping out in the open for the two or three weeks it'll take me to build it. Nothing over our heads at night but the stars."

"I'm sure I'll be proud of it, Will," she said dutifully. Since he was obviously filled to bursting with pride over what he had accomplished, and intended to accomplish, what else could she say? But . . . Edenland? There was more of the dreamer in Will Simmons than she had thought. She wrapped both arms around his and leaned against him. "You're my husband, Will, and whatever you do is fine with me."

Will beamed. "I don't think there's a happier man in all of Nebraska than me right now. What more could any man want than what I have?"

"'I'm glad you're happy, Will."

"I should say I'm happy! All I have to do is count my blessings. I've got two sections of land in my name, all free and clear. That's twelve hundred and eighty acres, Rachel. I have a team of fine mules, a cow, seed corn and wheat, a plow. It's a steel plow, too, not cast-iron. And on top of all that, I have the finest wife in the territory!"

"At least I should be grateful that you rated me up there with the plow," she said teasingly.

"What?" He was thrown into confusion.

"Never mine, Will. I was joshing."

"Oh . . . But it's not only me who has everything needed to get a good start. Guess what I bought for you this morning in Connersville?"

"What, Will?" Perhaps she had really misjudged him. Perhaps he did have some understanding of her need for an occasional object of beauty, something that wasn't just functional.

"It's back there under the canvas."

"What is it?" She turned and leaned back to raise the canvas covering their goods.

"No, don't mess with that covering. I've got it fixed to keep off the rain in case that happens. I'll tell you what I bought."

"Then tell me, Will! You know about the curiosity of a female."

"Well, sir." He pursed his lips. "Let's see now. I bought you a stove, a tin wash boiler, two iron pots, a teakettle, two pie pans, a steamer, a coffeepot, a coal-oil can, a gridiron, four tin cups, four plates and four forks. That's in case we have company, you see. Aside from all that, I bought you a washbasin, a pepper box, a lamp and a bucket." As he finished the inventory, he smiled at her, waiting for a word of praise.

Rachel's initial reaction was one of disappointment. She had expected a new dress or something equally frivolous. Then she scolded herself. She did not need a new dress, and the items he had described were infinitely more important for their well-being. She suspected that within a month of being a settler's wife, she would not trade even one of the things Will had mentioned for all of Ewell Rankin's dresses back in the Roundhouse. For some odd reason, that thought struck her as humorous, and she laughed aloud.

Will misunderstood her laughter, saying, "I figured you'd be happy." He looped one arm around her shoulders and pulled her close to him.

Rachel felt the strength in his arm, and she recalled again the scene in the railroad depot between the settler and his wife. She tried now to experience that feeling herself, and did succeed in feeling some sense of contentment. Will clearly loved her, and despite the long wagon trip, some of his excitement over building Edenland infected her, sparking her enthusiasm.

Soon, weariness overcame Rachel and she leaned against Will and dozed off and on. The weather had been rather pleasant, since it was now into autumn, and they had not suffered from the pitiless heat of the full summer sun. As she dozed, Rachel's thoughts moved ahead to the coming night. Will had yet to make love to her; they had ridden the train all night after getting married at End of the Track, so there had been no opportunity. She was certain that Will would not come close to being the skillful lover that Rankin was. Yet the thought of her husband's splendid physique stirred a sexual response in her, and she began looking forward to their first night together under the stars.

When the sun dropped out of sight in the west, the prairie lost heat rapidly, and it became cold. Rachel murmured, shivering, and Will found a blanket and wrapped it tightly around her.

She slept more soundly now, dreaming of a time and place vastly different from her present circumstances. It was a pleasant dream but it fled from her mind and memory at the sound of Will's voice. "Rachel!" He shook her gently.

She muttered a protest, and he shook her again. "Rachel, we're here!"

"What?" She came reluctantly awake and sat up to gaze around.

There was little to see. It was night, and the moon was but a slender crescent, shedding little light on the rolling prairie. There were no hills or trees or even rocks to fix into her mind, only a vast darkness stretching away from her.

And the wind. The wind had blown ceaselessly since they left Connersville, a low, stupefying moan, but now it seemed louder than during the day. It made Rachel feel apprehensive.

"Is this your Edenland?" she asked.

"Yes, Rachel. We're home. We're home at last."

Will stepped down from the wagon seat; the wagon creaked and bent under his weight. Rachel thought he was coming around to give her a hand down; instead he began unhitching the mules.

"Walk around and unhitch the cow," he called to her. "There's a creek about twenty yards off to our right. Lead her down and let her have a good drink, then bring her back here and tie her to the wagon for the night. Don't want her wandering off until she gets used to the place."

"Will . . . where are we going to sleep?"

"Sleep? Like I told you, under the stars. I'll throw a buffalo robe on the ground under the wagon, and we'll pull a couple of blankets over us. We'll sleep fine, you'll see. But it'll be a spell before we're ready to bed down. We have too many chores to tend to first. You go ahead and water the cow, like I said."

Rachel climbed down from the wagon seat. She was sore in every muscle, and she felt the cold wind blow against her legs as her dress hiked up. She untied the cow and led the animal away into the darkness. The cow found the creek before she did, lowing at the scent of water.

Before the cow was done drinking, Will loomed up in the darkness, leading the pair of mules.

He had an empty bucket in one hand. "Here," he said, "fill this and take it back with you. We'll need water in the morning. There's a small pan in the wagon for the baby chicks. Some of them may have died, but that's to be expected. Water them. I'll scout around for some buffalo chips before I return to the wagon. We'll need them for a fire in the morning."

Rachel brushed the hair out of her eyes. "Buffalo chips?"

"Sure. Buffalo chips make the best fuel to be found out here. I once suggested that the UP use chips instead of wood. It would be much cheaper."

"Yes, I suppose it would," she said disinterestedly. She was so tired, and it seemed that they were to spend the night performing chores. She filled the bucket as instructed and started back to the wagon, leading the cow.

"Rachel," he called after her. "The flour and baking soda are in the larder box on the side of the wagon. If we're to have bread for breakfast, you'll have to knead the dough tonight."

"All right, Will," she said dully.

She tied the cow to the wagon, found the flour and baking soda, and began mixing the dough for bread. It was so dark she could barely see what she was doing, but she kept doggedly at it. It was some time before Will returned, and she was beginning to worry, but finally he appeared, carrying an armload of buffalo chips.

"I found a real gold mine," he said happily. "We have our own private supply of these things."

"That's good," she said, looking at the pile of black buffalo droppings with distaste.

"I'd better go wash up," Will said. "You'll not be wanting me to come to you smelling of buffalo chips, that's for sure."

Will spoke casually, but his remark reminded Rachel that this was, in effect, her wedding night, and her cheeks felt warm in the dark, as she thought of what was soon to take place.

Did Will know of her arrangement with Ewell Rankin? He must know; everyone else at End of the Track seemed to know. Will might be an innocent in many ways, but he was not *that* innocent.

She wondered again what it was going to be like going to bed with Will. Since Rankin had been her first man, she had little experience for comparison. Rachel knew that Will would not have Rankin's erotic finesse. But perhaps he would make up for that in other ways. Surely he would not be as remote, as detached from her, as Rankin had been. She wondered about Will's own experience. Would she be his first woman?

No, of course not, not at his age. Men weren't like women. They were expected to have many experiences with different women. Rachel had heard that all her life, and she had no reason to disbelieve it. But long ago she had thought of a question which she had never been able to answer satisfactorily. If men were expected to have many sexual experiences, and women were expected to remain virgins, then with whom were the men supposed to have their experiences? With whores? Out here, that certainly seemed to be the case.

Will returned from having "washed up." He walked over to the wagon and raised the lid of one of the other sideboxes. He took out a large buffalo rug and a couple of blankets, dropping them on the ground under the wagon.

"You can fix us a bed, then get into it and keep yourself warm," he said. "I'll be along after a while. I've got a bit more to do yet."

"Will!" Rachel gave a little laugh of vexation. "What else *is* there to do tonight? The stock have been watered and cared for, the stuff for the morning's cookfire has been collected, the water has been brought up, the bread dough mixed, and the bedding got out. What other chores can there *possibly* be?"

"I've got to lay out our house."

"Lay out the house? In the middle of the night? Will, don't be ridiculous!"

"I'm not being ridiculous," he said stoutly. "Night is the best time to do it. This way, I can get it all laid out with straight walls, lining them up with the North Star, don't you see?"

She sighed in resignation. "All right, Will. You get the house marked out. I'll make our bed and get into my nightgown."

Will had not waited for her approval; he was already stepping out across the ground, sighting on the North Star to give him the desired alignment of the walls—straight north and south, then straight east and west.

Rachel watched his striding shadow for a few minutes, then opened her trunk and found her nightgown on top, precisely where she had put it when she packed yesterday. As soon as she took it out, she realized that there was nothing to protect her modesty as she took off her dress to put the nightgown on. Then she laughed wryly at herself. The night was dark and Will's attention was, at the moment, concentrated on something else aside from her nakedness.

Even so, she stepped around to the other side of the wagon from Will before she slipped out of her dress, petticoats, and underthings. For a brief moment, she was totally naked. It was the first time in her life that Rachel had been naked out of doors. The unaccustomed caress of the wind on her bare skin was chilly and yet, strangely, sensual.

She slipped the cotton nightgown over her head, settled it down into place, then got down under the wagon and made their bed.

Lying on the buffalo robe, the blankets up to her chin, she looked through the spokes of the wagon wheel at Will. He was nothing more than a moving shadow as he paced back and forth across the prairie, counting off the steps and using sticks to drive into the ground to mark the outline of their sod shanty.

He made Rachel think of a soldier pacing on guard duty. She narrowed her eyes to slits and tried to imagine a house there. First a sod house, then a wooden frame, and later, perhaps, even a fine brick home, with a white picket fence, several tall shade trees, and a flower garden, with neighbors and parties.

Could Edenland ever be as fine as Bonner Plantation?

She had almost dozed off by the time Will finished pacing off the house, but she woke up with a start when he returned to the side of the wagon and began removing his clothes. From her position beneath the wagon bed, she could only see him from the knees down, and she saw his breeches come off to reveal legs clad in long flannel underwear; then, a moment later, she saw the long underwear come off, too. When he slipped between the blankets, he was completely nude.

"Pull this up," he said matter-of-factly, plucking gently at her nightgown.

Rachel readily complied, pulling it not only up but over her head. The thought of them both naked, and outside under the stars, was a sensual one to her, and as he came to her and she felt the total skin-to-skin contact of thier bodies, she was flooded by a pleasant feeling of warmth. She felt a rush of affection for her husband. She tingled in anticipation of the remembered pleasure of lovemaking, and felt herself warming toward him, and knew that she would quickly be aroused.

But Will was either without experience, or totally inept. He did not caress her, he did not kiss her—he did nothing whatsoever to help orchestrate her arousal. Indeed, he seemed wholly unconcerned for her needs.

From the prod of his organ against her thigh,

Rachel knew that he was ready. She reached her hand down to stroke him. With a grunt he knocked her hand away and moved over her. With rough hands he pushed her thighs apart and thrust sharply, almost brutally, into her. His penetration, happening so quickly, was painful, and Rachel let out a short exclamation.

Will stopped moving. "You're a virgin? But I thought . . ." He made a pleased sound. "But that's good, that's fine! And don't worry about it hurting, it always does, I'm told, with a woman's first time. That tells me that you're a good, decent woman, and that makes me proud."

Was he that stupid about women? He was not insensitive, she knew that. And yet he was moving again, thrusting into her with rough lunges, hurting her each time. She tried to accommodate herself to his rhythm and recapture the earlier feeling of sensuality, but it was no use.

"Will," she whispered urgently. "Will, wait! Go slower. If you'll only go slower, I can—"

"I can't wait!" he said huskily, his breath coming in short gasps. "I can't wait. You're my wife, and the first woman I've had in . . ."

His breath left him in a whistling grunt, and his movements quickened to a frantic pace. Rachel sighed and lay still, knowing it was useless. In a moment his body convulsed mightily.

He lay still on her for a moment. It was all Rachel could do to keep from pushing him away. She turned her face away from his heaving breath, and stared into a future that suddenly seemed bleak indeed.

He rolled off her finally and lay stretched out beside her. Painting, he said, "Do you suppose a baby will come from this?"

"I don't know," she said dully.

Will raised up onto one elbow and gazed down into her face. "I don't know much about women and these things. I don't know how to tell if what we're doing will get you with child or not. I'll have to depend on you for that."

He put his hand on her cheek, and turned her face toward him. All she could see of his façe was a dark shadow, and she had no inkling of what his expression might be.

He went on, "I do know that what we just did is not something you enjoy, since only men get any pleasure from doing that."

Rachel sighed. "Will, whatever gave you the idea that women don't enjoy making love?"

"They're just not supposed to, everybody knows that," he said stiffly. Then he chuckled. "Oh, I guess some women do, but that kind are whores. It's plain to tell that *you* don't like it. But that's woman's lot in the world, to put up with such things from a man in order to give him sons. That's where a woman's pleasure comes in. There's nothing gives a woman more pleasure than having a baby. It's strange how it all works out, isn't it?"

"Yes, it's strange." Dear God, was this the reason he had married her? To have his children? Was she to be nothing but a child-bearer? She turned her head aside, even though she knew it was too dark for him to see her tears.

"The man, he likes coming to a woman in bed, but the woman must suffer him. It's the way the world is. Then the children come along, and she likes them when they're babies. The man, he likes them all right, but they're more trouble than they are useful at that age. Then, when his sons get old enough to be of help, that's when a man gets his joy from his children."

"Is that the way you see it, Will?"

"Of course. Even the Holy Bible says so." He sighed and lay back down. "It's best we get some sleep. We have a big day, come first light, and that's not too long from now. We're going to have to work from first light till dark from now on."

"All right, Will," she said in a low voice. Not only was she expected to be a breeding mare, she was to be work stock, as well. Was that all she had to look forward to for the rest of her life? Marrying Will Simmons had been a dreadful mistake; she had never regretted anything more in her life.

"Rachel?"

"Yes, Will?"

"I figure this has all been sudden for you, and strange. You're probably having doubts about the whole thing. I'll make it right for you, Rachel, I promise you that. I'll make it right for you. We'll have a good life."

There was feeling and a surprising amount of tenderness in his simple statement, and Rachel took his hand and squeezed it convulsively. In his own way, he was a good man.

She had made a bargain, and she had to do the best she could to make him a good, obedient wife. She had made her bed and she would lie in it, even if it was to be a cold bed.

CHAPTER FOURTEEN

"Roll out, Rachel," Will said. "We have to get busy."

Rachel felt Will leave the pallet, taking with him the warmth she had snuggled up to through the night. She opened her eyes and saw that it was still just as dark as it had been when they went to sleep.

"Will, what is it?" she said groggily. "What's wrong?"

"Wrong?" he said cheerfully. "Nothing is wrong, Rachel. It's just time to get up. This is our first day on Edenland."

As he talked, Will was getting dressed. She watched him sleepily, reluctant to leave the warmth of the blankets. It was chilly out there!

Will said, "The buffalo chips are right here, by the front of the wagon. Get a fire going and start the bread. Bread and coffee is about all we can have for breakfast. We're going to have to ration our food so that what we have will last the winter. Maybe I can find time to hunt now and then, get us fresh meat."

Rachel dragged herself out of the blankets and hastily got into her clothes as his voice ran on. He was so disgustingly cheerful, and she was freezing! And now that she was moving, she realized that her muscles were sore and cramped. She wasn't accustomed to sleeping on the ground, and it was going to take some getting used to.

"The lucifers are in a tin box, wrapped up good in waxed paper and oilcloth. Be sparing with them, they're almost as precious as our food supplies. Call me when breakfast is ready. I'm going to start cutting sod."

He was already in motion. Taking the plow from the wagon, he lugged it over to the mules and began hitching them up. Yawning, Rachel looked to the east and saw a faint streak, not of light actually, but of a lighter hue than the rest of the sky. The stars were beginning to fade. She could not remember when she had been awake at such an early hour.

Will was already at work by the time she got around to starting the fire. She used three matches before she got the fire going. With the first two, she merely held the flame to the edge of one of the buffalo chips, but that did not work. Finally it occurred to her to scrape together a small pile of dry grass. With that she was able to ignite the buffalo chips with the third match. She knew Will would be upset if he learned she had wasted two matches, so she decided not to tell him.

Becoming a pioneer's wife was going to take some doing!

When the chips began to burn, she was concerned that they would give off a foul odor. She had never seen a fire made of buffalo chips, and it seemed logical to her that they would smell. To her surprise, the slightly pungent odor was not at all unpleasant. A short time later the smells of baking bread and boiling coffee permeated the camp area.

The sun was just up and the morning was already warming. Despite being awakened before dawn, Will's disappointing love-making, and her sore and aching muscles, Rachel experienced a degree of contentment. And why shouldn't she? It was going to be a nice day, the odors from the campfire were tantalizing, and some of Will's excitement was infectious. And, probably the most important thing, the life before her might be a difficult one, but at least there was nothing about it she should ever be ashamed of.

By the time Will returned and they had finished their meager breakfast, the sun was well up. Will leaned forward, poured the last of the coffee into his tin cup, and stood up. He swept one hand around, beaming.

"Well, Rachel, now you can see it—Edenland! What do you think of it?"

Rachel took her first good look around. The prairie stretched to the horizon on every side. The only break in the flat expanse was the creek meandering across the property. Now that it was full daylight, she saw that the spot Will had picked for them to spend the night, as well as the area he had staked out for their house, was slightly elevated, so that she was able to gaze down on the twists and turns of the creek. There were several scrubby trees growing along the banks of the creek, and some of them appeared to be bearing some sort of fruit.

Noting her glance, Will said, "Wild plum trees. We can have our own jam this winter. It would have gone good with that bread you baked, wouldn't it?"

"It would have indeed." Rachel had not realized how bland coffee and unbuttered bread could be. She resolved to make some jam as soon as she had time.

"As soon as you have finished with cleaning up the camp, bring the wheelbarrow and spade over to the spot where I'll be working. You can help me."

Rachel went about her chores, stopping from time to time to watch him, astonished at the amount of work one man could do, and the delight Will seemed to take in it. He was cutting strips of sod. Rachel saw that the buffalo grass on the prairie grew from roots as densely tangled as the roots of a tightly potted plant. Will was using the plow to rip out a long ribbon of sod, about a foot wide and three inches thick. After the strip of sod was dug out, he retraced the furrow he had made, this time turning it over so that it lay as one long strip of upside-down earth.

Finished with her own chores, Rachel brought the wheelbarrow and spade over to Will. There were at least a dozen strips of sod exposed. Taking the spade, Will used the sharp edge to cut cleanly through the sod, then moved down about three feet, and made another clean cut. He handed the spade to Rachel.

"Follow my example," he said. "Cut it about every three feet or so. Then load the pieces you've cut into the wheelbarrow. Just be sure you don't break 'em apart when you pick them up and put them into the barrow."

Rachel went to work with the spade. She loaded the barrow and then wheeled it over to the spot where Will had laid out the site of their house by starlight last night. She unloaded the wheelbarrow and went back for another load. All the while Will was busy turning more sod with the mules and plow.

It was hard, backbreaking work of a kind that Rachel was totally unaccustomed to. The sun, well up now, grew hot and perspiration ran down her in rivulets, but she kept grimly at it, determined not to complain.

She was glad to take a break, however, when Will suggested she prepare the noon meal. She noted ruefully that blisters had already formed on her hands.

After they had eaten they resumed work, and continued until sunset.

This set the pattern for the next two weeks. Every day Rachel rose before dawn, prepared breakfast—she found time to make wild-plum jam which made their simple breakfast better—worked on the house, prepared all their meals, watered and fed the cow and the chickens, and did what seemed to be endless other small chores. By nightfall, she was exhausted and ready to go to sleep after supper.

That first night under the stars also set the pattern for their nights. Will was never too weary to take her every night with the same brisk determination that he had for building their house. Rachel soon recognized, with sour amusement, that Will was more interested in impregnating her than he was in any pleasure he might derive from the act of coupling with her. After a few attempts to get him to change his love-making techniques, she gave up, realizing that it was hopeless. Will was shocked at some of the suggestions she voiced to him. "It is not seemly for a woman to speak of such things, Rachel! Do you want to shame me?"

So she learned to open herself to him and then lie as still as a stone until he was finished and rolled away from her, when she could go to sleep.

But at least the house slowly began to take shape, and she was toughened now, and able to keep pace with Will. The blocks were laid with the grass side down, and the layers were staggered like brickwork. Two rows were placed side by side, making the walls double thick. At the corners, intersection layers were lapped together, then pinned with iron rods which Will had bought just for that purpose. Spaces were left for windows and a door. Finally, the roof was put on. The roof was the same canvas sheet that had covered the wagon. It was reinforced with tightly woven grass and clay from the creek bank.

Standing back and looking at it, Will said with understandable pride, "That'll do us for the winter. Come spring, I'll take the wagon into town for lumber, and we'll build a better roof. But this is fine for now. It's beautiful, isn't it, Rachel?"

"Yes, it is, Will," Rachel agreed.

And to someone who had been sleeping out in the open in weather which had been growing steadily colder, the sod house was, indeed, a beautiful sight. At least it should protect them from the coming winter.

Winter struck the Great Plains with a vengeance four weeks later. It came whipping down from the Rockies, carrying howling winds and freezing temperatures. Ice and snow turned the prairie into an arctic wasteland.

On the night the blizzard hit, the Midnight Flyer was twenty miles out of Connersville, headed west with its speed reduced to a crawl. Mike Donovan was the engineer at the throttle, and he had to poke his face out of the cab into the freezing wind every minute or so to see where they were going. The blowing snow let him see very little. Behind the engine, in the eight cars, more than a hundred passengers were huddled around the wood-burning stoves in an effort to keep warm.

The fireman, a huge man known only as Sparks, grumbled as he shoveled fuel into the maw of the engine. "If you ask me," he said sourly, "we should've stayed back in Connersville."

Donovan snorted. "And what would we be doing with the one hundred souls bound for End of the Track? There was no place for that many people in Connersville. You know that."

"But what if we get stuck out here, in the middle of nowhere? We'll all freeze to death."

" 'Twouldn't be the first train I was stuck on," Donovan said amiably. "Why, I mind the time I was . . ."

Donovan broke off as he saw an orange glow alongside the track ahead, reflected against the falling snow. He pulled the whistle cord and closed the throttle. The train slowed to a stop next to the fire and the tall man standing beside it.

"Hawkeye! Man, you ain't got the sense of a goose! What are you doing out here on a night like this?"

"I might ask the same question of you, Mike Donovan. I've got a load of fresh buffalo meat," Hawkeye Smith said. "Happened onto a good stand. I was just praying that this storm wouldn't stop you, but late as you are, I was beginning to sweat it."

"A little snow like this never stops Mike Donovan," the engineer said proudly.

"Would you mind carrying the meat on to End of the Track?"

"Be happy to be of service, lad." Donovan blew the whistle, three shorts and a long, to summon the train crew to the front of the tracks.

Hawkeye climbed up into the cab, shaking himself like a wet dog to get the snow off his tall frame. "Have them load my horse on too, will you, Mike? I'll ride up here with you so I can stay close to that firebox and thaw out."

"Be glad to, lad." Donovan leaned out the cab window to shout down to a brakeman to load Hawkeye's horse into the horse car.

"Have you ridden along the tracks, Hawkeye? Are they clear?"

"They were when I came along. There hasn't been time for any drifts to build up. But it's snowing like Billy-be-damned out there. You'd better get a hustle on."

"Aye, that we'd better." He yelled down to the crew to hurry with the loading. As soon as he got the signal, the engineer opened the throttle again and the train moved forward with a jerk and a clatter of couplings.

Sparks said in his grumbling voice, "At least with you riding the cab, Hawkeye, maybe I won't have to listen to this man's blarney."

"Blarney, is it?" Donovan said good-naturedly.

"Aye, blarney it is," Sparks said in an exaggerated mimicry of Donovan's brogue. "You was minding the time you got caught in the great blizzard, and—"

"Now don't you be trying to tell my story for me," Donovan interrupted.

"And why not? I've heard it enough times so that I can probably tell it better'n you, Mike Donovan."

"That may be true enough," Donovan retorted. "But I lived it, boyo. And only those what have lived a thing like that can tell it proper. The time I was talking about, Hawkeye me lad, was the Great Blizzard of—"

"Eddison Trestle coming up soon," Sparks said.

Donovan said, "So it is. I suppose I'll have time to finish my tale on the other side." His expression turned grave. "I hope they listened to my report of the last time I crossed Eddison Trestle."

"Your report?" Hawkeye asked interestedly. "What report are you talking about, Mike?"

"I don't like Eddison Trestle. I don't trust it for a goldanged minute. Nor any of the four they just finished building, if the truth were known."

"What's wrong with them?" Hawkeye demanded.

"They don't feel right," Donovan replied.

Sparks laughed. "I told him he was crazy. I can't

tell any difference, and nobody else I've talked to had noticed anything wrong, either. Now, how Mike can take a twenty-ton engine across a trestle, and then say it doesn't *feel* right, is beyond me."

Hawkeye had to admit that he couldn't feel anything different as they rolled onto the trestle, but Mike Donovan grew tense as the train crawled across the span. The bridge was about three hundred feet long, and its lattice-work of trestle spanned a gulch that was fifty feet deep. It had just been completed two weeks ago, eliminating the detour around Eddison Gulch.

"Ah!" Donovan sighed gustily. "Here comes the end of it, the saints be praised!"

Suddenly there was a loud cracking noise, and the bridge began to tremble so badly that even Hawkeye could feel it.

"My God, she's going!" the engineer shouted.

He opened the throttle to full, and the engine rammed ahead and off the bridge. But instead of pulling the cars clear, the sudden jolt of speed snapped the coupling, so that the engine separated from the rest of the train. The trestle began to topple, and all the cars behind the engine and tender tumbled into the deep ravine. The engine, suddenly deprived of its load, rocked down the track at a dangerous speed.

"We've lost the cars, Mike!" Hawkeye shouted. "Stop the engine, man!"

Donovan slammed the throttle into reverse to start the great driver wheels spinning backward. The sudden reversal sent up a shower of sparks, and the inside of the cab was bathed in an orange glow.

Hawkeye watched in stomach-wrenching horror as the cars behind them tumbled into the gulch, one right behind the other. They crashed together into the ravine with a thunderous noise.

Donovan stopped the engine right at the edge of the gulch, where the twisted rails came to an end. Hawkeye leaped out before the engine came to a complete halt, and ran back to what was left of the trestle. The rails were twisted and bent out of shape, and the trestle had completely collapsed. Huge timbers had snapped like matchsticks.

But the collapsed bridge, Hawkeye saw, was nothing to the carnage below. There, red-hot stoves had ignited the splintered cars into a colossal bonfire. Even those people who were relatively uninjured in the crash found that their situation was little better than the seriously injured, because they were trapped in the wreckage and unable to escape the flames. Their wails of terror joined the moans of the injured, so that the horrible sound of the victims' screams rose even over the roaring and crackling of the flames. It was a scene out of hell, and the wind-driven snow added a macabre touch.

Hawkeye clambered down the rocky sides of the gulch, soon feeling the fierce heat of the flames. Lying on its side, not yet on fire, was one of the passenger cars. Hawkeye could see people inside at the windows; they were injured and dazed, but still alive. Whether or not they lived depended on their getting out before the car went up in flames.

He yelled back up the slope, "Sparks, throw down your axe! I have to chop into the side of this car! There's no damned time to lose!"

"Right away!" Sparks shouted back. "I have a couple of shovels, too."

"Bring them down. Anything will help."

Hawkeye reached the back door and tried to open it, but it was jammed from the fall, and he could not budge it. And the fire was eating its way closer.

"Hurry up!" he bellowed.

"Get us out! Mister, please get us out!" someone called from within the car.

"Don't worry, we'll get you out," Hawkeye promised, but he had to wonder if it was possible to save them.

At that moment he heard Sparks yell for him to watch out for the axe. Sparks sent it skittering down the slope, along with two shovels. As Hawkeye turned, he saw Sparks coming down after them, followed by Mike Donovan. Hawkeye scooped up the heavy axe and began chopping at the side of the wooden car. Within a very short time, there was a large enough hole for those inside to squirm through. Hawkeye, Sparks, and Donovan began helping them out.

The passengers were in shock, and even those who were not seriously hurt were of little help. Finally, Hawkeye managed to convince them that they should all stay in one place, off to one side and out of the way, until as many could be rescued as possible.

"My baby!" One woman was crying hysterically as Hawkeye pulled her through the hole. "My baby is in there, trapped under one of the seats! I couldn't move it. Dear God, please get him out of there!"

"I'll get him out, ma'am," Hawkeye promised.

"Hawkeye, look!" Donovan exclaimed. "The other end of the car has caught. It'll go up like a torch any second now."

"No!" the woman screamed. "I have to get my baby out!" She broke free of Hawkeye's grip and tried to crawl back into the car.

Hawkeye seized her arm and pulled her back. "Lady, you can't go in there!"

"I won't leave my baby!"

"Mike, hold her," Hawkeye said. He stuck one leg into the hole.

"Lad, you can't go in there!" Donovan shouted in alarm. "In a few minutes this car's going up like the others!"

"I have to try," Hawkeye said doggedly. "Where were you sitting, ma'am?"

"I was sitting in the back," the woman said. "On the right-hand side, the side that's on the bottom now."

"That's the part that's already on fire," Donovan warned.

Without any further delay, Hawkeye wormed his way through the jagged hole. The car was lit inside by the eerie, wavering glow of the other burning cars. Smoke was starting to fill the car, making it difficult to see or breathe.

Hawkeye tripped over someone's leg.

"Pardon me," he said automatically, then he looked down to see who he had stumbled over. It was a man, and his open, staring eyes told Hawkeye that he was beyond help.

The stove was in the center of the car, but when

the car had crashed into the ravine, a large drift of snow had poured in through a rupture, and the fire in the stove had been immediately extinguished. That was what had prevented it from catching fire as the other cars had done.

"Hallo!" he called. He wished now that he had asked the woman for the child's name, or even how old he was. He had no idea whether the child was old enough to respond to his voice even if he was conscious enough to hear.

"Hallo!" he called again.

"I can't get loose, mister," a small voice said.

"Where are you?" Hawkeye called.

"I'm here," the voice said. "Can't you see me?"

"Not yet. But you just keep talking like that, and I'll find you. What's your name, boy?"

"My name is Billy Harper, and I want my mama."

"Your mama's just fine, Billy, but she's worried about you, and she sent me to fetch you."

"I'm scared," Billy said in a quavering voice.

"So am I, Billy, so you're not alone in that."

Hawkeye saw the boy now, and saw what was holding him. Miraculously, the very thing that held him trapped had also saved his life. A heavy steel axle from one of the other cars had crashed through the roof of this one, but an overturned wooden seat had deflected the axle, so that Billy, who was underneath the seat, was unharmed. The weight of the axle was such that it was easy to understand why the boy's mother had been unable to free him.

"Will you get me out, mister?" Billy asked.

"I'll get you out, you can believe that."

The fire was so close now that he could feel the scorch of the blazing heat. Billy was temporarily shielded from the heat by the overturned seat, but Hawkeye knew that would not last for long.

He took hold of the axle and heaved with all his strength, but it would not budge. He tried to pry the seat out, and failed again. Frantically, he cast around and found a length of plank that had been torn loose by the car's tumble into the ravine. He jammed it under the seat and pried until the veins stood out on his neck. He felt it give a trifle.

"Billy, are you hurt anywhere?"

"No, sir," the boy said in a whimpering voice.

Hawkeye realized that the shock, which had been keeping Billy reasonably calm, was wearing off, and the realization of his predicament was driving him toward panic.

"Son, you're going to have to help me now," Hawkeye said urgently. "When I lever the seat up, you're going to have to crawl out. I can't help you. Do you understand?"

"I can't move."

"You'll be able to when I lift the seat. Now, get ready."

"All right, sir," Billy said stoutly. "I'll try."

"That's all I ask." Hawkeye put all his strength into the plank lever, and the seat rose a few inches. "Now, Billy!" he said with a grunting breath. "Slide out now!"

The boy scrambled out from under the seat on his belly. The instant he was clear, Hawkeye let the seat fall back. He reached down and picked Billy up in his arms. The boy was light; he appeared to be about six years old.

Hawkeye fumbled his way through the thickening smoke to the hole in the side of the car. At his shout hands reached in and he gave Billy up to them, then squirmed through himself. Just as he stepped clear and away from the car, the lower end, where Billy had been trapped, collapsed in on itself, the flames shooting high.

"You made it just in the nick, lad," Mike Donovan said. As Hawkeye's glance went to the miserable huddle of people, the engineer added glumly, "I just made a count. Forty-seven all told. A few managed to get out of the other cars."

"How many badly hurt?"

"Nothing bad with this group. A few scratches, burns, a broken limb or two." His gaze dropped to the ground. "The ones badly hurt, lad, didn't make it out, may the Good Lord receive them in heaven."

Hawkeye glanced back at the pile of burning wreckage. It was still now, the only sounds the crackling of the flames. Donovan was right. Anyone left inside those cars was dead by now.

Hawkeye turned away resolutely. "There's nothing more we can do here, and it's getting damned cold. Most of these people are in shock, and this weather will do them no good. We have to get them to End of the Track and a doctor's care. I'd suggest you throw off the wood from the tender, except for what we need to make the rest of the run, and we'll load them on the tender."

"Aye," Mike Donovan said softly. In the leaping firelight Hawkeye saw the shine of unshed tears in the engineer's eyes. " 'Tis a sad night, a sad night indeed."

Then the engineer's glance went to the wreckage, and his expression hardened. "My feeling was right, Hawkeye. This trestle and the others are not safe. Below standard, I'd say. Aye, lad, there's been dirty work afoot here."

"You could be right, Mike," Hawkeye said thoughtfully. "The trouble is, now how do we prove it? But maybe this disaster will open a few eyes, although I very much doubt it."

CHAPTER FIFTEEN

The pile of buffalo chips by the corner of the sod house was growing low. There were plenty more out on the prairie, but they were under at least two feet of snow.

Rachel selected three from the dwindling pile, and was standing up to go back inside when she saw something moving in the near distance. Shading her eyes, she peered into the snow-glow and saw that it was quite clearly a horse and sleigh. She gasped aloud. It had appeared out of nowhere, like an apparition. Yet the sleigh was real enough, and she could make out several people in it. She had seen no one since they had come to Edenland more than three months ago, and she did not know whether to be elated or frightened.

"Will?" she called tentatively. Then, louder and with more urgency, "Will!"

Will had been digging a root cellar, and he hurried around to the front of the house at her call.

"What is it, Rachel? What's wrong?" he asked apprehensively.

"Nothing's wrong. At least I don't think so." She pointed to the approaching sleigh. "But it looks as if we're about to have company."

"They'll be wanting some coffee, I expect," Will said glumly.

"Coffee! They'll be wanting and getting more than that in *my* house, Will Simmons! They'll stay to supper, if I can persuade them!"

"Rachel, I don't know," he said worriedly. "We've got to get through the winter, and—"

"Will, whoever they are, they'll be the first human beings beside ourselves that either of us has seen since we came out here. Now if you and I have to miss a meal in order to make up for it, I'll settle for that. But I intend to serve them supper!"

"All right, all right!" Will began to smile. "I know what store women set by such things. We'll feed them. We'll manage. It will be nice to have some company, at that."

"Thanks, Will," Rachel said, and impulsively she kissed him on the cheek, then hurried into the house.

There were few enough comforts in the sod house. The table was made from a packing crate, but they did have four cane-bottom chairs. The bed, like the house, was made of sod, although it was covered with dried grasses and blankets and buffalo fur, and was actually quite comfortable.

The stove was Rachel's prize possession. It was a very fine stove, and served both to cook the meals and heat the house. There was also a lantern, but their supply of coal oil was limited, so they did not use it more than was absolutely necessary. What light came into the house during the day filtered in through the window, which was covered with oil-cloth to let in some light, yet keep out the weather.

But despite all their efforts to keep out the weather, the melting snow on the roof seeped through, and Rachel could hear the constant sizzling sound of water dripping on the hot stove from above. Yet the house was remarkably cozy, for the sod proved to be good insulation against the cold.

Rachel wondered briefly what type of meal she could prepare. Then she remembered that there was some buffalo meat which would do nicely. Will had killed two buffalo shortly before the first blizzard struck. The meat was wrapped up and stored on the roof of the house, where it would keep frozen throughout the winter.

She had just started the water boiling when Will ushered their visitors inside. There was a man, a woman, and two children, a boy of ten and a girl of eight.

"Rachel, this is Mr. and Mrs. Watson. It seems they're our next-door neighbors, five miles to the east of us."

"I'm glad to meet you," Rachel said, smiling happily at the prospect of another woman to talk to. "And who might you be?" she asked, looking at the children.

The girl ducked behind her mother's skirts and peeked out at Rachel, but the boy wasn't in the least shy. "My name's Jimmy," he said. "She's Ginny."

"Well, Jimmy and Ginny! I'm awfully glad to meet the both of you."

"Do you have any sweets?" Jimmy asked boldly.

"Jimmy!" his mother scolded. "Mind your manners, young man!"

"It's all right. I'm sorry, Jimmy, I don't," Rachel said. Then she brightened. "But I'll be making a dried-apple pie for supper. You'll like that."

"We don't want to put you folks out any for supper and the like," the man said. "It's just that I saw the house once, uh, a month or so back, and I told the missus, perhaps we ought to drop by some day and visit with you folks."

"Well, we're glad you *did* come by," Rachel said. "It's been so long since I've visited with anyone. And of course you're staying for supper! I'll be awfully put out if you don't stay."

"Well, Zeb?" Mrs. Watson said, looking at her husband.

"If you're sure, Mr. Simmons, that we won't be putting you out none," Zeb said to Will.

"I don't rightly have any say in the matter." Will grinned. "I don't think Rachel'd give me any peace if you didn't stay, so I'd count it as a favor if you would."

"All right," Watson said. "We'd be right pleased to stay for supper."

"Hoorah!" Jimmy cried. "I can taste that apple pie right now!"

"Is there anything I can do to help you?" the woman asked. "I'm Mary, by the way."

"And I'm Rachel. I'm making a buffalo stew. You could peel a few potatoes and cut up some onions, if you'd like."

"Say, would you folks like a sack of potatoes?" Zeb Watson said. "We had a fine crop of them last year. You can pay me back come summer, when your own potatoes are in."

"Well, I don't know," Will said dubiously. "I'd hate to be a bother to a neighbor."

In truth, the potatoes they had bought in Connersville were running low, and they had begun to ration them.

"No bother, it's what good neighbors are for. Everybody borrows when they're first getting started out here. Why, you haven't even had a chance to get your first crop in yet. I know you could use a few things." Watson smiled. "I just happen to have a sack in the sleigh."

"And I've got some vegetables that I canned from the garden in early summer," Mary Watson said. "I can bring some of them over the next time we come visiting."

"Mary, that would be wonderful!" Rachel said warmly. "We thank you very much." If Will would not accept their generosity, she thought, I certainly will.

As the two men sat at the table and chatted, Rachel studied Mary Watson covertly as the woman peeled the potatoes. Mary was of an indeterminate age, anywhere from Rachel's own age, twenty-five, to perhaps thirty-five years old. Her brown hair was tied back in a bun, and her dress had been chosen for warmth, certainly not for fashion. Her face was lined, and there was a look of weariness in her features that Rachel suspected was permanent. Her hands were red and worn.

Rachel had to wonder if, in time, she would look like this pioneer woman. She well knew that the life of a settler was hard. In fact, as they did not have a mirror, Rachel had little idea of what she might look like now.

Before too long, the aromas of stew and dried-apple pie filled the little sod house. Rachel sank down onto the edge of the bed and beckoned Mary over to sit with her. She asked, "Are there many other settlers out here?"

"Oh, yes," the other woman replied. "Why, last week at Christmas, there was a party over at the Hogans', and I'll bet there were some thirty people there."

Rachel said in astonishment, "You mean Christmas was last week?"

"It was."

Rachel sighed. She raised her voice. "Will, did you know that Christmas had come and passed, and we didn't even realize it?"

"I'm sorry, Rachel, I guess I plumb forgot," he said sheepishly. "When we have young'uns of our own, we'll have to keep better track of things like Christmas."

Rachel was silent. She was pregnant; she had known that for some time. In fact, she was sure that it had happened that first night under the wagon. She did not quite know why she hadn't told Will—probably as some sort of punishment, since she well knew how delighted he would be. She was far from sure about her own feelings in that regard.

Will was speaking to Zeb Watson. "You see, when we came out here, I thought of just about everything we'd need, except a calendar. I don't even know what day today is."

"It's January 3, 1868," Watson said.

Will smiled broadly. "Rachel girl, it's the new year! I'm obliged to you, Zeb. I'd better mark out some form of calendar, so I'll know when to start the spring planting."

"If you folks need any seed corn, anything like that, I have some to spare."

"We'll make out fine, thank you, Zeb."

"Since you folks have been out here all by yourselves, I'll just wager you haven't heard any of the news, have you?"

"Nothing since we've come to this place," Rachel said.

"Well now, let's see. President Johnson was found not guilty, you know," Mary said. "They were all talking about it at this Christmas party at the Hogans'."

"President Johnson? Found not guilty of what? I didn't even know he'd been on trial."

"Not exactly a trial, I reckon. It's called an impeachment, and they wanted to put him out of office. You know, it never set too well with many folks, him being our president. I mean, what with him being a Southerner, and the war not long over."

"He was never that sympathetic to the South," Rachel said tartly. "He was Abe Lincoln's vice-president during the last of the war."

"I know, I know that," Mary said. "But to some people, I guess that didn't make any difference. Anyway, they tried to impeach him. I was never sure quite why. But they didn't succeed, and he's still president."

"Don't bother her with news from Washington,

woman," Zeb said. "Who cares out here about what happens back there? If you want to hear some recent news, the army has just about got all the Indians cleared out of the territory."

"Blood Knife was kilt," Jimmy said importantly.

"That's right," Zeb said. "You know, Blood Knife led a group of redskins into End of the Track last fall and burned it down. I don't know how many people were killed that night."

"No one was killed," Rachel said firmly.

"Oh, but that's not the way we heard it," Mary said, frowning. "This Blood Knife and his savages burned down the opery house there, I think it was called the Roundhouse, and there was a show going on inside. Why, there was hundreds killed! And not only that, but the depot was burned down, and all the ties the railroad had stored there."

"More'n twenty thousand dollars' worth," Watson added.

Rachel realized that they had the story wrong and she longed to correct them, but Will gave her a warning glance, and she remained silent.

"What's this about Blood Knife?" Will asked.

"Oh, yes, him," Watson said. "Well, after he led that raid on End of the Track, the army colonel swore to get him, and they tracked him all the way up into the Dakota Territory. Then, oh, not more'n two weeks before Christmas I think it was, they happened upon an Indian village early one morning and surprised them. Way I get it, they killed nigh on to a hundred of them redskins. Course, it didn't quite even things up for all that they did at End of the Track, but at least Blood Knife himself was killed."

Rachel vividly remembered the night she had stumbled upon Blood Knife and his band of warriors, and she recalled how magnificent they all had looked just before they rode down into End of the Track. She wondered if the young Indian who had intervened in her behalf had been killed. She felt a small tug of grief. Blood Knife had been a man of honor. He and his followers had committed a crime, but nothing deserving of being slaughtered in their sleep.

Will was saying, "I guess that'll just about take care of the Indian problem around here once and for all, won't it?"

Zeb Watson shook his head slowly. "I wish I could say that's true, but there's one out and about now that they say is meaner than Blood Knife ever hoped to be. See, it was actually this other Indian's camp where Blood Knife had run to, when the soldier boys caught up with him. And when the soldiers attacked, they just rode through killing one and all. They killed Blood Knife and a lot of his warriors all right, but they also killed some of this other Indian chief's people, including his squaw and son. The way I hear, this other chief swore that he'll war against the white man until he's run them all off, or until he's killed himself. Now, you know which that'll be. But in the meantime, he's one dangerous redskin!"

Rachel asked, "What's this other Indian's name?"

"His name is Mean-to-His-Horses," Watson replied.

Mary Watson shuddered. "Isn't that a terrible name? It gives me the shivers just hearing it!"

"Oh, and that's not all the news, by any means," Watson, clearly relishing his role of news bringer. "Not by a long shot. There was a terrible train wreck some weeks ago, and it killed nigh on to a hundred folks!"

"A train wreck?" Will sat up. "Where, around here?"

"Not too far away. At a place called Eddison Gulch. The trestle gave way and the cars all tumbled into the gulch. Then they caught fire."

"My God!" Rachel went rigid exchanging glances with Will. "Did anyone survive?"

"Some did, I hear tell. The engine was already across the trestle when she gave way, so the engineer and the fireman survived. Also, there was this buffalo hunter on the train, riding up in the cab, and he made it all right. Then him and the engineer and the fireman got down into the gulch somehow and saved some forty or so. I don't recollect the exact number, but I know they put them on the tender and hauled them on to End of the Track. It was during that first big blizzard we had. They could've all froze."

"What did you say the name of the trestle was?" Will asked in a low voice.

"Eddison Gulch," Watson replied. "It's about twenty miles the other side of—"

"Yes," Will interrupted. "I know where it is."

Will got up without another word and walked toward the door. He stood there for a long moment, then went outside without speaking.

"Will?" Rachel called, concerned. "Will?"

"What is it, Rachel?" Mary Watson asked. "What's wrong with your man?"

"He used to work for the railroad," Rachel explained, getting up. "I'm sure the news hit him hard. Mary, would you see that the supper doesn't burn? I'd better go to him."

"Of course I will, honey," the woman said. "You go on."

Rachel quickly put on her coat, then took Will's with her, since he had gone out in just his shirtsleeves. It was cold and crisp outside, and the brightness of the late afternoon sun reflecting off the snow made her squint. She looked around, and finally located Will walking toward the lean-to barn, his head down.

She hurried after him. "Will?"

He slowed to a stop, turning about. She came up to him and gave him his coat. "Here, put this on. It's freezing out here, you'll catch your death."

Will took the coat and slipped into it, without ever looking directly at her. Fog came from his mouth and nose as he breathed.

"Eddison Gulch, Rachel," he finally said in an agonized voice. "Zeb said that the trestle fell in and killed all those people. At Eddison Gulch!"

"We don't know that it's true, Will. After all, look at the story he told about End of the Track. We know that no one was killed there, and yet he insists that hundreds were."

"But he's right about Eddison Gulch. I know he's right. And it's all my fault."

"No, it's not. How can you believe that it's your

fault, Will? You didn't have anything to do with that."

"I overheard Ewell Rankin and that fellow planning on weakening the structure. I could have told someone and stopped the whole thing."

"No, you couldn't have," Rachel said emphatically. "We went through all that, Will. You know there was nothing you could do. There was nobody you could trust to tell."

"But there should have been *someone*," Will said doggedly.

"I'm as much responsible as you are, then. I overheard them plotting, too."

"That's different, you're a woman."

Rachel almost bit her tongue choking back a sharp retort. She touched his arm. "Will, it's over and done, behind us. We have a new life here. What's past is past. You can't keep torturing yourself about that."

"You're right, of course." Will sighed, then looked back at the house. "It's best we get back, I expect. I wouldn't want our company to think ill of us. They'll be wondering why we both charged off like that."

"They won't think ill of us," she said. "I explained to them that you used to work for the railroad."

"Good for you! Then I won't be asked to explain anything."

Mary Watson was taking the pie out of the oven when they entered the house. It was a deep golden brown, and it filled the air of the little sod house with a rich cinnamon and baked-apple odor.

"The stew appears to be done as well," Mary said.

"Then let's hurry and eat, Mama," Jimmy said. "I want to taste that pie. Ummm, it sure smells yummy!" Jimmy rubbed his stomach and rolled his eyes, and the adults laughed.

"We only have four plates, I'm afraid," Rachel said. "Will and I can wait."

"Nonsense," Mary said briskly. "I'll make the children wait."

"Mama, I can't wait," Jimmy whined. "I'm hungry, really I am."

"Then you can have my plate," his mother said.

"And Ginny can have mine," Rachel said. "Mary, you and I will sit on the bed and have a nice chat until it's our turn to eat."

"That will be nice!"

The two women sat side by side on the bed, arranging their skirts demurely. After a moment Mary Watson said, "I got my seed catalogue the other day. I just love them, don't you, honey?"

"I don't know," Rachel answered. "I don't think I've ever seen one."

"Oh, dear," Mary said in distress. "Oh, dear, you simply can't survive out here without them. It's the best cure for cabin fever there is."

"Cabin fever?"

Mary laughed. "I guess it hasn't hit you yet, your first winter on the prairie. But when you've been out here for seven years as Mr. Watson and myself have, then you'll learn well enough what it is. It's when you think you won't be able to stand it one more day. That's cabin fever."

"I . . . I think I know what you're talking about," Rachel said cautiously. She glanced over at the men and saw that they were engaged in deep conversation. "I'm already feeling that way . . . sometimes. Only I was ashamed to mention it."

"Don't be ashamed, honey. It happens to all of us, especially us women. That's why you should send away for your seed catalogues. They have such bright, pretty pictures of all the spring flowers. Blue and red and yellow. Even in the dead of winter, it makes you think that spring is just around the corner."

"Yes," Rachel said. "I can see how that would be nice. I like to look at pattern books myself."

"Pattern books?"

"You know. To make dresses."

"Oh, yes. Do you have a pattern book?"

"I'm afraid not," Rachel said ruefully. "Not right now."

"I would like to study some new patterns. Mr. Watson will be going into Omaha in the spring for a meeting to organize the Grange."

"What's the Grange?"

"It's a farmers' organization. Zeb heard about it a couple of months ago, and he wrote a letter. He was invited to Omaha for a convention, and he promised to take me and the little ones. The children haven't been anywhere since they were babies, and I can hardly remember when I've been anywhere myself. I'm excited about going, but I'm worried because I don't have anything to wear."

"I have a dress you could borrow. It should do

with a few alterations. I'll let you have it before you go."

"You have a *fancy* dress, honey?" Mary said in astonishment.

"Yes." Rachel laughed. "I don't know if I'll ever get a chance to wear it again. Certainly not out here. Come, I'll show it to you.

Rachel walked over to the corner and opened the lid to her trunk. She rummaged through the things she had there until she reached the bottom, where she found the two dresses she had brought from End of the Track. She pondered for a moment. One had an exceptionally low neckline, while the other was less daring. She chose the more modest one and showed it to Mary.

"Oh, my!" Mary said in a tone of awe. "Oh, Rachel, I've never seen anything so beautiful in my whole life!"

"You may borrow it."

"Oh, thank you! Oh, my!" She snatched the dress from Rachel and hurried over to the table. "Zeb, look at what Rachel said I could wear to Omaha, when we go. Isn't it the most beautiful thing you've ever seen?"

"If you say so, Mary," Watson said indifferently. "Mrs. Simmons, it's most kind of you. You sure you want to do it?"

"I'm sure," Rachel said. She looked at the dress sadly. "I doubt I'll ever have the occasion to wear it again. Anyway, I have another, if the need arises."

"Will, I'll tell you what I'll do." Zeb Watson had already turned back to Will. "I'll throw in six hogs.

Four of 'em are sows, and the other pair boars, plus, mind you, fifty grown chickens, among them a half-dozen roosters. I'm being generous because your missus is being so nice to my Mary."

"If you don't mind, Zeb," Will said, "I'd like a word with Rachel before I decide."

"Go right ahead," Watson said expansively. "I'll just have me another piece of this pie."

Will motioned for Rachel to join him in the far corner of the room, and there he spoke to her in a low voice. "Rachel, I know you have about fifty dollars."

"Why, yes I do. I had that much saved at End of the Track. Why?"

"I need that money."

"You need it? What for?" she asked suspiciously. "What are you up to, Will?"

"From Zeb there, I can buy us another cow and a bull, and six hogs and some more chickens. And all for fifty dollars. That will give us a good start on our livestock, with what we already have."

"Well, I suppose so, Will. You're my husband. What's mine is yours, you know that. But do you mean that my fifty dollars is all the money we have?"

"I only have twenty dollars, and I want to hold onto that, in case of emergency."

"Will . . ." She darted a glance at the table and lowered her voice even more. "I thought you said we were all set after your, uh, arrangement with Ewell?"

"We are, but there was no cash involved in that deal. He just gave us the deed to this piece of land.

The supplies I bought in Connersville was with money I'd saved up, and it took almost all I had."

"I see," she said slowly. So it was down to this. She was just as poor and just as trapped as she had been before she married Will. At least before she had had her personal freedom.

"All right, Will, I'll get you the money."

She went to the east wall and slid one of the pieces of sod out, keeping her back to the others to hide what she was doing. Then she laughed to herself. What did it matter if they knew? In the niche made by the missing sod brick was a small sack holding a handful of gold and silver pieces, totaling fifty dollars. The money had been a hedge against . . . against what? It certainly wasn't enough to get her very far, even if she were free to go. She turned to give the sack to Will.

Grinning broadly, he went over to the table. "Zeb, you've got yourself a deal." He plunked down the sack of coins.

Watson's hand crept toward the sack, then drew back. "Maybe you'd better wait and pay me on delivery."

"No, you take it now. I trust you."

"Well, all right."

The two men got up from the table, and went to hunker down by the stove. Watson fired up a smelly corncob pipe and continued their conversation, ignoring the women.

Rachel and Mary were now free to sit down and eat what was left. Mary prattled on as she ate. Rachel, busy with her own thoughts, did not bother to listen, since no response was really required.

Loaning the dress to Mary Watson and giving all her savings to Will seemed to Rachel to be a symbol of her dreary future. There was no way she could turn back now. She was fated to live out her life here. In that moment she came close to hating Will. And to make matters worse, she was carrying a child.

CHAPTER SIXTEEN

Rachel adjusted the lantern so that a golden bubble of light bathed the inside of the house. Outside it was still dark and cold; in fact, it was almost as cold inside. She clutched her robe tightly about her, fighting the chill, and she stoked the fire until it was roaring in the stove. Then she huddled over it, holding her arms stretched out, luxuriating in the welcome warmth.

Behind her, in bed, Will snored away. Last night, as he had nearly every night since they were married, he had turned to her to "do his duty." Not once, in the whole time they were married, had Rachel been able to recapture the feeling of intense pleasure at being with a man, the feeling she had experienced with Ewell Rankin. Perhaps there was a reason for that. Perhaps it was wicked for a woman to enjoy physical love, and thus it could only be enjoyed by a wicked woman when she was with an evil man. If so, that would explain why Will had never been able to give her pleasure.

Oh, dear God, she prayed silently, *is it to be my*

punishment then, that I am doomed to spend my life knowing the pleasure that a woman can feel, and yet be forever denied that pleasure? She wondered about Mary Watson. Did she enjoy it when her husband took her? Zeb was a man like Will, a good man, and a man of the soil. Did he pleasure his wife, or did he just "do his duty"? Perhaps she should ask Mary sometime.

Despite the misery of her own situation, Rachel smiled at the thought. "Tell me, Mary," she could picture herself saying casually, "does your husband pleasure you in bed? Or do you merely lie there while he does his duty?"

"Oh, my, Mrs. Simmons," Mary would reply in shock, "such things are not for women to enjoy! Oh, my, no! We get our pleasure from the joy of childbearing."

"Is that so, Mary? Then I take it you have never been bedded by an evil man. For believe me, Mary, an evil man can show you pleasure you have never dreamed of!"

Rachel closed her eyes tightly to force such thoughts from her mind. Only then, after her mind was calm again, was she able to resume her morning chores.

The fire was going well now, and gradually an envelope of warmth began spreading through the house. She went to the box behind the stove and removed the pan of bread dough she had prepared the night before. Then, just as she picked it up, her stomach revolted and she had to stop and walk away from the smell of the dough and the heat of the stove, and stand against the cool surface of the far wall.

The Watsons had said that yesterday was January 3rd. That meant that it had been at least three months since last she had the monthlies. And for several weeks now, she had been ill in the morning. There was no longer any doubt in her mind. She was pregnant.

"Rachel, what are you standing over there for?" Will's question hit her like a slap, stirring her to anger.

"I'm going to have . . ." No, no, she could not tell him. Not yet! She could just see him capering about in his male pride, and she'd be damned if she would give him that satisfaction just yet. "I'm going to have your breakfast ready in a minute. But I got heated up being too close to the stove, and I moved over here to cool off."

"Don't make yourself sick now," Will said solicitously. "Fact is, why don't you just sit down and rest a bit? I'll finish making the breakfast."

"No, it's my *duty*," she said bitingly. "I'm all right now."

He gave her a puzzled look, then shrugged and got out of bed to put on his clothes.

"Why *didn't* she tell him? She knew how desperately Will wanted children. The knowledge that she was pregnant would make him the happiest man on the prairie. Besides, if she was four months along, he would know before long, anyway. She could not hide it indefinitely.

But even as this thought crossed her mind, she

knew why she would not tell him now. She could not stand to be around his happiness while she was sunk deep in gloom. This made her feel vaguely guilty, yet there was nothing she could do to keep such thoughts from popping into her mind, so she didn't even try. She would just have to live with her feelings.

"That was a real nice thing, Rachel, agreeing to allow Mrs. Watson to wear one of your fine dresses to the Grange meeting in Omaha," Will said later, as they sat down to breakfast.

"There's no sense in having a dress if it's never worn," she said dully.

"Rachel . . . would you like to be going to that meeting in Omaha?"

"Well, I wouldn't mind. It would be nice to get away for a short time. I'd like to hear some music, see people wearing fine clothes, eat a meal that I didn't have to prepare myself, maybe even hear some laughter."

Will put his big hand over hers and forced her to look into his eyes. "I know you would like to do those things, and I know the reason why. You got used to all that when you worked at the Roundhouse. There, all that was going on all the time. You get used to a life like that, and you miss it. Take me now, I ain't never been around nothing like that, and I don't feel the loss. It doesn't bother me none at all."

His concern for her was so obvious that her resentment melted away. She smiled a small, resigned smile. "Don't fret about me, Will. I'll make out all right."

"Ain't you going to eat your jam and bread?" he

asked, pointing a thumb at the uneaten slice of bread still on her plate.

"No, I think not." She smiled slightly. "I think I may have eaten too large a supper last night, and I'm still full."

"Well, we can't let anything go to waste," Will said, reaching for it. "Soon as you finish up in here, Rachel, you come on out to the root cellar and help me finish up."

"I'll be there, Will," she said with a sigh. She got up and went about doing her morning chores.

The bitter cold of the gray January morning was intensified by the fact that Mean-to-His-Horses had spent most of the night in the sweat lodge. There, sitting in the steaming heat of the burning stones, and with the sweat pouring out of his body to cleanse his soul in order to receive instructions from the Great Spirit, he had thought about what he must do, and now he was ready.

"Today," he said to his warriors gathered around him, "we shall have a great victory. We will count many coups this day."

His warriors shouted in agreement and appreciation. In a few moments they were all mounted; the ponies, like the warriors, were painted for battle. Then, with Mean-to-His-Horses in the lead, they rode out to engage the advancing column of soldiers under the command of Colonel Bowers.

This time the pony soldiers would not catch Mean-to-His-Horses' people unawares. Scouts had warned of the army's approach three days earlier, and Mean-to-His-Horses was prepared. He had chosen ten of his braves to act as decoys, and now they were mounted and ready to depart on their mission.

Mean-to-His-Horses smiled as he heard Quannah-teh, one of the ten decoys, yell to a warrior beside him, "I will get a white scalp for your lodgepole!"

The other warrior answered in a jeering voice, "Ho! Let us hope it is not your own scalp, for that would make me very sad."

Most of the recent snow had melted, but the day was still cold, and patches of snow and ice were still very much in evidence as they rode hard to the spot where they planned to ambush the soldiers. After receiving word about the movement of the pony soldiers, Mean-to-His-Horses had led a foray into Connersville early the day before, and set the torch to a number of abandoned buildings on the edge of town. He knew that burning the buildings would do little damage to the white men, but he also knew that the buildings were unguarded, offering no danger to his band. His purpose had been to make a big show and create a diversion.

Connersville was not his target. His target was the expeditionary force under the command of Colonel Bowers, the same officer who had led the sneak attack against Mean-to-His-Horses' encampment up on the Rosebud, killing his wife, Quiet Stream, and his son, Stone Eagle. Mean-to-His-Horses had been wild with grief over their deaths, but as soon as his grief subsided he began making his plans. He knew that when Colonel Bowers heard of the raid, he would send his troops toward Connersville, under the belief that Mean-to-His-Horses and his warriors would flee in the other direction, and the army could therefore run them to earth.

Before the raid, Mean-to-His-Horses had scouted the area and found an ideal place for an ambush between the army's route of march and Connersville. There, the road ran alongside a narrow stream. On one side of the road was a grassy flat, and on the other side of the stream were some rocky ridges.

Mean-to-His-Horses' plan was to have the decoys make a feint at the pony soldiers, then lead them down that road. Some of his warriors would be hidden in that grassy flat, and they would open fire when the soldiers came within range. The soldiers, naturally thinking they had ridden into an ambush, would leave the road and cross the stream to find cover in the rocks. And that would be where Mean-to-His-Horses and the main body of his braves would be waiting for them.

Mean-to-His-Horses had explained his plan in detail to his braves, and all had agreed that it was a brilliant plan. But he wanted to meditate in the sweat lodge before he definitely committed his tribe to the attack. And last night, in the sweat lodge, the Great Spirit had come to him and told him that he would enjoy a great victory over the white men.

Now his warriors were in position on both sides of the narrow stream. Mean-to-His-Horses was among the warriors on the grassy flat. That was where their first shot would be fired, and there lay the most danger. Mean-to-His-Horses would not dream of placing himself in less peril than the least of his braves.

All of a sudden, the sounds of gunfire rolled across the plains toward them. The brave beside him said excitedly, "Mean-to-His Horses, the battle has begun!"

"To your places," Mean-to-His-Horses commanded. He held his war club high over his head. "Today is a good day to die!"

"Today is a good day to die!" the braves chanted.

Mean-to-His-Horses had a rifle in his other hand, but his blood was too hot, his thirst for vengeance too strong for a rifle. He saw that one of his braves had only a bow and arrow. He called the warrior to him. "Do you know how to use a rifle?"

"Yes, Mean-to-His-Horses," the warrior said.

"Then use it well," Mean-to-His-Horses said, handing him the rifle. "Kill many of the whites with it."

Now Quannah-teh and the other decoys came riding along the road at a full gallop. Then they reined in, turned, and fired a volley at the pursuing soldiers.

Colonel Bowers's soldiers were in plain sight now. Riding at a gallop, they returned the decoys' fire. The decoys scrambled off their mounts and fled into the grassy area. A whoop of victory erupted from the soldiers, and they rode full force toward the flat.

Mean-to-His-Horses stood tall, raising his war club as a signal. His warriors rose out of the weeds, charging toward the soldiers, firing and screaming as they went.

Many of the soldiers had already dismounted to pursue the decoys on foot, and now they found themselves engaged in hand-to-hand combat. Instead of outnumbering the decoys, they were confronted by a number of warriors equal to their force.

Within a short time, most of the dismounted cavalrymen were dead. Colonel Bowers, still ahorse, bellowed a command for his troops to retreat across the stream and into the rocks. They wheeled their mounts and road across the stream, sending up a silver spray of water as they splashed across. Once on the other side, they dismounted to seek cover among the boulders.

There the Indians who had been waiting for them attacked in force and the soldiers, now greatly outnumbered and surrounded on all sides, began to mill about in panic.

Mean-to-His-Horses leaped over the rocks and in and out of gullies, dodging aside as one trooper fired at him, and ran recklessly on. He vaulted up onto a boulder and found himself just above Colonel Bowers, who was firing his pistol and bellowing orders, which went unheeded by his soldiers.

"Colonel Bowers!" Mean-to-His-Horses shouted, speaking the strange-sounding name with difficulty, but clearly enough so that Bowers understood. Horses had practiced saying it many times, because he wanted the colonel to realize that he, Mean-to-His-Horses, knew who he was killing.

Colonel Bowers whirled at the sound of his name. Seeing Mean-to-His-Horses he raised his pistol and fired, but his bullet went wide. Mean-to-His-Horses saw the wild look of fear in Bowers's face—the narrowed pupils, the beads of sweat across his lips, the distended nostrils. It did not move him. He had seen that same look on the faces of his wife and son when Colonel Bowers ordered them killed.

Mean-to-His-Horses emitted a blood-curdling yell and sprang form the boulder to bring the war club down on Colonel Bowers's head, smashing his skull like an eggshell.

The fighting continued until only one trooper was left alive. He was the young soldier who blew the bugle, and he held his instrument in front of him, a pitiful shield, as one of the Indian warriors ran at him.

"No!" Mean-to-His-Horses shouted. "Let the music soldier live!"

"Why?" one brave demanded. "It is his music which makes the soldiers attack."

"Would you attack the fire which sends messages in smoke?" Horses asked. "The music soldier is but smoke to the long knives. He carries messages to them. And I want him to carry a message for me. Who speaks his language?"

"I speak it," Quannah-teh said.

"Tell him that I, Mean-to-His-Horses, have this day avenged the death of my wife and my son. I counted coup upon this man, Colonel Bowers, who stained his hands with their blood. Now I am ready for peace. If the white man will fight me no more, I will fight him no more."

Quannah-teh translated the words, and the young bugler, realizing that he was going to live after all, quickly agreed to pass it on. Then, at a word from Quannah-teh, he leaped onto one of the horses and rode away at a gallop.

As the bugler rode off, the Indians shouted taunts

and obscenities after him, laughing at the spectacle of the young soldier riding away as if demons pursued him.

"Tell your chiefs they mate with horses!" one brave shouted after him.

"No, they mate with dogs! Horses will not have them!" another yelled.

Finally, when the bugler had disappeared on the prairie, the warriors gave another victory cry, then went about the business of taking scalps.

Mean-to-His-Horses watched the mutilation of the bodies in passive silence. He knew that this act would probably enrage the soldier chiefs to the point where they would not accept his offer of peace. Perhaps he should stop it. But he had only to close his eyes to remember the desecration of his own people when the pony soldiers attacked his village.

Finally it was done, and he ordered them onto their ponies. It was time to go.

"No!" he said, as they pointed their ponies in a northeasterly direction. "We will not go that way."

"But that is where we left our village," one brave said. "Our squaws and children are there."

"Do you want to lead the pony soldiers to your squaws and children?" Horses asked.

"No," the brave said. He smiled. "But there are no pony soldiers left."

"There are as many pony soldiers as there are blades of grass. Does a prairie fire kill all the grass? No, there is much, much more. It is so with the pony soldiers as well."

The warriors nodded solemnly at the wisdom of

this pronouncement, and when Mean-to-His-Horses started off in a southeasterly direction, the others followed his lead without question.

Rachel's back was hurting and her hands were black with dirt as she stepped out of the hole she and Will were digging for the root cellar. She brushed her hands together as she stepped up into the light, but that was more a reflex action than anything else. It certainly did not get any of the dirt off.

And that was when she saw them. It appeared to her that there were more than a hundred, all astride their ponies, frightening in their war paint. They sat almost motionless, staring toward the house. They were spread out like an open fan.

"Will!" she called urgently. "Will, come here, quick!"

Will responded to the fear in her voice immediately. He came boiling up out of the hole. His face went pale when he saw the Indians; then he started toward the house.

"Where are you going?" Rachel demanded.

"To get my rifle."

"Will, don't be foolish! You won't frighten away that many Indians with a gun! All you'll do is get us both killed."

He hesitated in indecision. "What do you suppose they want here?"

"I think I know." She was looking toward the barn where an Indian had just emerged, leading their cow.

"Hey!" Will shouted. "Where the hell you going with my cow!"

He started toward the Indian leading the cow, but a half-dozen of the others kneed their ponies over to position themselves between Will and the one with the cow.

"Will, for God's sake, let them have it!" Rachel exclaimed. "A cow's not worth our lives!"

"Have you more cows?" one of the six Indians asked, in stilted English.

"No," Will said. "That's the only one we have."

"I do not believe you," the Indian said. "All white men who farm have many cows.

"We've just started farming," Will said. "Believe me, this is the only cow we have."

"You have pigs?"

Will said, "No, no pigs."

"I do not believe you."

"My husband is telling the truth, Quannah-teh," Rachel said, walking over to stand beside Will.

Quannah-teh peered down at her, then broke into a broad smile. "Brave-Woman-with-Running-Tongue, it is you!"

"Yes. Take the cow, Quannah-teh. But we have nothing else for you. Please believe me."

"I believe you. You do not lie," Quannah-teh said gravely. "I am sorry we must take cow, but we must go a long way, and we have no food. We will eat cow."

"Why can't you kill a buffalo?" Will asked.

Quannah-teh said, "There are no buffalo where we go." He turned to speak to the leader of the band, a very tall and, Rachel could not help but notice, very handsome Indian. The Indian nodded, then spoke in his own tongue.

"Mean-to-His-Horses say we will take nothing else," Quannah-teh said. "He thanks you."

The Indian leading the cow got up onto his pony, and the Indians turned their mounts and rode away with a rumble of thundering hooves.

Rachel heard Will grumble angrily, and sensed that he was about to run into the house for his rifle.

"Don't do it, Will. Let them go."

"Rachel, I can't just stand by and let those heathens steal our only cow!"

"Didn't you just buy another from the Watsons last night?"

"Yes, but that—"

"Will, let it go, please. A cow isn't worth our lives. Besides, what can you do against that many Indians?"

"I could round up some of our neighbors, and—"

"And how long would that take? And even if you could get a few together, what chance would you have? For certain, some if not all of you would be killed! And over a cow?"

Will sighed. "I suppose you're right. Still and all, it galls me." He put his arm around her shoulders and drew her against him. "I'm just sorry I wasn't more of a husband to you."

"More of a husband? What do you mean by that?"

"I should have protected you. Instead, I just let them ride in here, take our only cow, and I didn't do a damned thing about it."

It was her turn to sigh. "Will, there wasn't anything you *could* do," she said in exasperation. "Didn't you hear what Quannah-teh said? That chief was Mean-to-His-Horses. Isn't that the Indian that Zeb Watson said was on the warpath?"

"That's the name he said . . ." He broke off to stare at her. "Rachel, I just realized! You *knew* that young Indian buck!"

"He was with the group who burned the depot at End of the Track. I first met him when he was stealing a slab of bacon." She quickly told him what she knew of Quannah-teh.

"That explains it then. If you hadn't helped him once, we'd both probably be dead now."

"I don't think that follows."

"Of course it does. They're savages! They'd rather kill than do anything!"

"I don't believe that." Rachel drew away from him. "I believe they're pretty much like we are. I know that they do have a sense of honor."

"A sense of honor," Will said scornfully. "They don't know what the word means. You're too trusting, Rachel. Believe me, they'll never catch me outside the house without a rifle, not ever again. I see a red hide skulking around here, he gets a bullet, that's for sure!"

CHAPTER SEVENTEEN

Fatback Charlie set a large steak and a side order of fried potatoes down in front of Hawkeye Smith. Hawkeye took a long swig of his beer and looked at the steak dubiously. With a straight face he said, "You're positive now, Fatback, that this isn't from the same animal I rode in here on?"

Fatback Charlie reached for the steak platter. "You don't want it, I'll find someone who appreciates it," he said in his deep, steam-engine voice.

"You reach for that steak, and you'll draw back a stub for an arm."

"Is that all you can say? After all the work I've gone to cooking it nice for you?"

"It's a grand steak, Fatback. I'll eat it and enjoy every bite, I swear."

"That's better," Charlie said. "I don't have to cook for you, you know. You could get your victuals somewhere else."

"Now, how could I do that? How could you even *think* that? I wouldn't dream of eating anywhere else."

Steve King, the other man at Hawkeye's table, laughed. Fatback Charlie went back to the kitchen, and King took another drink of his beer, then set it down on the table, adding another wet ring to the marks already there.

"You were saying?" Hawkeye said, between bites.

"I was saying that now it's spring, the railroad will come out of the winter slowdown, and start pushing ahead again."

"They scarcely waited for spring," Hawkeye commented. "They started in mid-March. What's the news out of Washington? Are they ready to move on Credit Mobilier?"

"No." King sighed. "Ever since they brought up the impeachment proceedings again, they don't have time for anything except trying to run a good man out of office."

"I thought President Johnson beat that last December?"

"He did," King said. He laughed. "But Johnson's a fighter, you know. He no sooner beat that first try at him than he ups and fires Stanton. Well, that was just like spitting in the Senate's face. So the House tried again, and this time they just may get the job done."

"You're living back in that world," Hawkeye said. "What do you think? Will Johnson be kicked out this time?"

"I don't know. But I have to say that things don't look too good for him."

"Well," Hawkeye said, forking a generous bite of steak into his mouth, "what does that mean to us?"

"It doesn't mean a great deal as far as we're concerned. Lincoln was president when the railroad started. Now there's Johnson, and after Johnson, who knows? But the railroad construction will continue, regardless of who is president. And as long as there's construction, there is going to be a little extra money to be made. And that's where we come in. Nothing has changed."

"Something has changed."

"What?"

"They found that fellow, Parker, a couple of days ago, hanging from the trestle at Midnight Canyon."

"Dead?"

"He wasn't sleeping," Hawkeye said in a dry voice. "There was a note pinned to his breeches, saying that he accepted full responsibility for the change in the plans for Eddison Trestle where the wreck happened. He took the blame for the deaths of all those people, and asked that everyone pray for his forgiveness. He also confessed to altering the plans for Midnight Canyon, Kimberly Pass, and Tyson Gorge."

"I guess the guilt was just too much for him and he killed himself."

"Well, let's put it this way. I guess that's what we're *supposed* to think."

"What do you mean?"

"Maybe someone helped him kill himself. How many people do you think would pin a suicide note to their breeches before hanging themselves?"

"I'll admit it does sound a bit strange," King said thoughtfully. "But Eddison Gulch was a terrible,

terrible accident, and you never can tell what a person will do when he is carrying that heavy a load on his conscience."

"What about us?" Hawkeye said quietly. "Are we going to stick to our original plan?"

"Of course! We can't back away now, Hawkeye. We're too close, and have too much invested."

"I don't know." Hawkeye sighed. "I will never forget the scene of that wreck. You don't know what it was like."

"I can imagine."

"No," Hawkeye said slowly. "I'm not sure you can. I've thought about it a hell of a lot since then. I'm not at all sure we're going about this the right way. I'm not sure at all. There are some things more important than money."

"I agree," King said. "But Hawkeye, we can't lose confidence now. We are almost there, my friend. I can taste it. I can literally taste it!"

"I can too. And it's turning to ashes in my mouth."

"Don't give up on me now! All the work and time and effort that has been put in by so many people will all mean nothing if you give up now. We're all counting on you."

"Oh, don't worry, I'll hold up my end of the bargain."

"Good!" King said. He finished his beer, then pulled out his pocket watch and squinted at it. "I'll be leaving to catch the train for Omaha shortly. Any messages you want me to take back?"

"No," Hawkeye said. "Oh, you can tell them back east, the army higher-ups, that they're being damn fools about Mean-to-His-Horses. He gave the army an opportunity for peace, without any strings attached. Just leave him alone, he said, and he'll leave them alone. And he didn't even demand that the building of the railroad be abandoned."

"You didn't think for a minute that the army would just let it go at that, did you?" King said incredulously. "After all, he massacred fifty troopers, Hawkeye!"

"He defeated them in battle," Hawkeye said grimly. "Bowers massacred the Indians when he rode into Mean-to-His-Horses' village, and he murdered women and children besides."

"Well, don't think that there aren't many who wouldn't like to see that done to every Indian in the country."

Hawkeye scowled at him.

"Now don't get huffy. I'm not one of them. But I can understand why the army couldn't just accept his peace offer, right after such a thing happened."

"Well, they lost their chance. Now there'll be a lot more killing. It's inevitable."

"Hawkeye, how about the railroad? Do you think these Indians on the warpath will interfere with the construction?"

"It could," Hawkeye said with a slight smile.

King rested his chin on his hand, thinking for a moment. "That could cause us problems with what *we* are trying to do."

"You're right about that, friend."

"You know this Mean-to-His-Horses pretty well, don't you? What do you think he'll do?"

"I think that he'll try in every damned way he can to destroy the railroad."

"If he does, they'll run him to earth."

"He'll figure it's a good day to die."

King reared back. "A good day to die? What the hell does that mean?"

"That means that Horses has no fear of the pony soldiers, or of dying. That means that he will war against the railroad, disregarding any consequences to himself."

"What if *you* went to see him? What if you talked to him?"

"What about?"

"About stopping this foolishness. About giving himself up. Do you think he'd listen to you?"

Hawkeye stared. "Are you asking *me* to go see Mean-to-His-Horses, to ask him to surrender?" He shook his head. "Do you think I'm addled?"

"If anyone could do it, you could," King argued. "And consider what is at stake here. That Indian could mess up all our plans if he isn't stopped."

"There's one thing wrong—I couldn't do that."

"Why the hell not?"

"It would be an insult to him."

"Are you worried about hurting his feelings? An Indian's feelings?"

"Nope," Hawkeye said lazily. "I'm worried about my precious hide. I'm worried about getting killed."

"I thought you said he was your friend. I thought you said you could think like an Indian."

"I *can* think like an Indian. That's why I know that if I insulted him like that I would no longer *be* his friend. And if I'm no longer his friend, then I am his enemy."

King laughed. "You know something? Sometimes, Hawkeye, you don't make any more sense than an Indian when you talk."

"I do to an Indian." Hawkeye pushed his plate away and leaned back, firing a cigar. He looked thoughtful. I'm not sure what I'm doing in all this, anyway. I'm killing buffalo, what few are left, and I am involved in something I'm not sure I approve of. It seems to me that I've abandoned just about every principle I ever had. What I should do is go to see Mean-to-His-Horses, not to insult him, but join him."

King looked suddenly anxious. "You're not serious, surely?"

"No." Hawkeye said with a wry laugh. "But tell our friends back east to keep that in mind. It might just give them pause for thought, worry them a little."

King sighed with relief, sitting back. "What are you going to do next?"

"Well, let's see." Hawkeye blew smoke across the table at his friend. "Shortly, I intend to take a bottle of good wine to a room at the top of those stairs. And I intend to spend the night in that room with the bottle of wine and a woman almost named Kate Muldoon."

"*Almost* named Kate Muldoon?" King said quizzically.

"That's what I said," Hawkeye said without elaborating. "And tomorrow . . ."

"Yes? Tomorrow?"

" 'And tomorrow, creeps in this petty pace from day to day.' " Hawkeye laughed at King's expression. "That's William Shakespeare, in case you don't recognize it."

"Oh, I recognize it. I saw Edwin Booth do *Macbeth* back in New York. But I'm a little surprised at you knowing it. And I wouldn't go about quoting Shakespeare to people out here. They might think it a little strange, coming from a buffalo hunter."

"I didn't see Edwin Booth. But I did get my hands on a book of Shakespeare from one of the government's supply shipments to the Indians."

King reared back in astonishment. "Why on earth was the government shipping Shakespeare to the Indians, for God's sake?"

"You tell me," Hawkeye said with a shrug. "Perhaps the politicians back east thought that if an Indian had Shakespeare on his mind, he wouldn't feel the hunger in his belly. Of course, I imagine that it never dawned in their pea-brains that not one Indian in a thousand can read, and the few who can probably have little interest in Shakespeare."

"Something should be done about things like that."

"Horses would probably agree with you on that point." Hawkeye stood up, stretching. "I'll get back to work tomorrow, don't worry."

"I'll try not to. And I'll tell the others when I get back to Washington, so they won't worry, either."

"You be sure and do that. We certainly don't want them to lose any sleep worrying, now do we?"

"No," King said, missing Hawkeye's sarcasm. "We don't want them worrying."

King left the saloon, and Hawkeye went to the bar for his bottle of wine in a bucket. He took it upstairs to his room. The room was empty; Kate had promised to come to him the minute she could get away.

Hawkeye lit the coal-oil lamp, turned the wick down low, undressed and got into bed. With the covers up to his chin, he lay with his arms behind his head, letting his thoughts drift aimlessly.

And after a little his thoughts arrived at Rachel Bonner . . . No, not Bonner. He had heard that she had married some dirt farmer, and he did not even know her last name now. The news had affected him strangely at the time. It seemed such a waste, a fine-looking woman like that resigning herself to a life of hard work and child-bearing. He knew that her relationship with Ewell Rankin had ended badly, and he supposed that was responsible for what she had done. But hell, she couldn't be all that innocent! Rankin was notorious for using women and discarding them as casually as he would toss away a half-smoked cigar.

Hawkeye went to sleep with images of Rachel still in his mind's eye and he was disoriented when he was awakened some time later by a woman's warm, naked body slipping under the bedcovers, snuggling against him. For a dangerous moment he almost spoke Rachel's name aloud.

Then Kate Muldoon said throatily, "Sorry to keep you waiting, honey. But we had a rowdy crowd tonight, and I thought I'd never get away." Her warm breath on his cheek smelled of wine.

"You've been at the wine, I see."

Her mouth moved against his. "Wasn't it for me? You weren't expecting anyone else, were you?"

"No one else."

"I wondered. I thought I heard you speak a woman's name in your sleep."

"A woman's name?" Hawkeye was a little startled. Had he spoken Rachel's name in his sleep? "You must be mistaken, Katie. Right now you're the only woman in my life."

"That's good," she murmured. "I like that."

He put his arms around her and gathered her close. She came against him hard, her lips smothering his. Kate was expert at the art of love, but each time with her seemed new to Hawkeye, and he had never ceased to wonder at such smoldering passion in a woman of her profession. In the beginning he had thought it was feigned, but in time he had decided that it was not false at all.

His hands moved lovingly down her back to the sweet curve just above her buttocks. She squirmed in his grip, the hardness of her nipples prodding at his chest.

"It's been a long time, Hawkeye," she murmured. "A long, cold winter."

"What do you think it's been for me? I've been out there ass-deep in snow, with nothing but buffalo and my horse for company."

"We'll have to remedy that, sweets."

Her strong hands plucked at him urgently, and Hawkeye moved over her. She accepted him eagerly, moaning with pleasure as he entered her. She was wild with need, and soon his own need matched hers. His hands cupped her full breasts as he thrust into her again and again.

"Ahh, Hawkeye! Ah, love! Now, now!"

Her body shuddered in mighty convulsions, as he drove toward his own completion. When they finally lay side by side, sated, she whispered in his ear, "Wasn't that nicer than deep snow, buffalo, and your horse?"

He chuckled, "Much nicer, Kate."

Her fingers brushed his chest in gentle strokes. "Are you going to be around awhile?"

"Not too long, Kate. Now that winter is behind us, I have things to do."

She sighed. "But at least we'll have tonight. And maybe tomorrow night?"

"Tonight, yes. About tomorrow night, I don't know. I can't promise."

"Then we can't afford to waste time, like with sleeping, now can we?"

Her hands and lips were on him again, and he suspected she would bring him to full arousal again within short order.

"I'm not worried about it," Julius Deever said. He was pacing nervously back and forth in Ewell Rankin's office. "As far as I'm concerned, Bert Parker took us all off the hook. I can't imagine why he panicked so, but it sure took the pressure off us."

"You think so, do you?" Rankin said dryly.

"Of course I think so," Deever said. "Especially

with that note he left. Now the government investigators will ease up."

"You're a fool, Julius," Rankin said caustically. He took out a long, thin cigar, snipped the end off with a gold cigar trimmer, then put it in his mouth and lit it. Within a few seconds, the room was filled with aromatic smoke.

"You can't talk to me that way!" Deever blustered.

"I can talk to you any way I like."

"What are you getting at, anyway?"

"It's never been any government investigators we have to worry about. "It's Credit Mobilier."

"Well, won't his confession satisfy any questions they may have?"

"No, Deever, it won't. You see, they feel that too deep an investigation by the government will expose things that would be better left unexposed. They don't take too kindly toward anyone going out on their own."

"I see."

"I'm not at all sure that you do see," Rankin said, blowing smoke. "If you did see, you wouldn't be making asinine statements about how you aren't worried."

"Perhaps there's some cause for worry," Deever conceded. "But surely Parker's killing himself took some of the pressure off."

"It did take some pressure off, yes. That's why it was so convenient." Rankin grinned wolfishly.

"What do you mean, convenient?" Deever peered at him suspiciously. "What are you saying? Are you hinting that he didn't kill himself?"

"He came to see me last week. He was scared, not of any federal investigation, but of Credit Mobilier finding out what he was doing. He talked of going to see them, telling them that I forced him into altering those plans." Rankin's lip curled. "The damned fool."

"Good Lord, he wasn't trying to talk you into going with him to back up his story, was he?"

"Nothing like that. He was trying to scare some more money out of me."

"More money?"

"Right. He said that I had made sixty thousand from his altered plans, while his pay for the altered plans was a mere pittance. He tried to scare me out of twenty thousand more. In exchange, he promised to quit the UP. In fact, he said something about taking off for South America."

"You didn't pay the blackmail then?"

"No. Not this time." Rankin looked off, his face settling into angry lines. "This time I did something about it."

Julius Deever took a handkerchief from his pocket and mopped at his brow. The room was warm, but not warm enough to cause him to sweat so profusely. He coughed. "I, uh, suppose you did the right thing, under the circumstances."

Rankin snapped, "I did the *only* thing! One thing I've learned, Deever. You can never trust a frightened man. And I could no longer trust Parker."

"I just wish such extremes weren't necessary," Deever muttered. He brightened. "At least you took care of the problem."

"Not the whole problem, I'm afraid."

Deever looked startled. "You mean there's more?"

"I'm afraid so."

"What more could there be? I mean, who else knows about what we've done?"

"Well, you for one, Deever." Rankin's cold eyes surveyed Deever over the smoldering cigar.

Julius Deever paled visibly, and the hand holding the handkerchief began to shake. "Ewell, for God's sake! You can't be worried about me! I wouldn't tell anyone, I swear! Why would I? I'm in this thing just as deep as you, not only with the federal government, but with Credit Mobilier as well. You can trust me!"

"I've found it best not to trust anyone." Then he relaxed with a harsh laugh. "But I just wanted to make sure that you understood the situation, and to what lengths I will go to protect myself."

"Oh, I understand, Ewell, indeed I do!" Deever said fervently.

"However," Rankin continued, "there is another person still around who knows about the change in the trestle plans."

"Who? I thought that aside from Parker we were the only ones involved!"

"We are. But a fellow found out what we were up to and came to me threatening to make trouble if I didn't buy him off."

"Why didn't you take care of him?"

"I should have," Rankin said with a cold smile. He put out his cigar, walked over to the window and stared out at the new depot, which had been constructed during the winter. "No, I didn't take care of him. I should have, but I didn't want to stir up a fuss at the time. Since then, I've been thinking that I made a mistake."

"Who is it? Is this fellow liable to cause trouble?"

"I don't know." Rankin turned about and aimed his cruel smile at Deever. "Perhaps I should ask you. After all, the fellow is a relative of yours."

"A relative?" Deever said incredulously.

"In a manner of speaking. He's your nephew-in-law, Will Simmons." Rankin watched Deever's face closely. "He overheard me talking to Parker. Later, he came to me and demanded that I bribe him to keep quiet."

"That clodhopper! I didn't think he had enough brass to do something like that!" Deever said angrily. "He's no relative of mine. When Rachel wed that dirt farmer, I disowned her."

"Then I guess you don't care what happens to him."

"I don't care a damn. Why, do you think he's a threat to us?"

"It's possible." Rankin shrugged. "If he's heard about all those people killed at Eddison Gulch, and he's sure to hear sooner or later, he might get an attack of conscience."

"We can't have that," Deever said nervously. "What are we going to do?"

"Well, I suppose we could just sit back and hope he keeps his mouth shut." He resumed his seat and got another cigar, lighting up. Over the cigar he looked at Deever, his eyes hard and cold. "Or we could do something about it. There's an old saying, I guess you know it, that a dead man never talks."

CHAPTER EIGHTEEN

Rachel set the pail of water down, straightened up, and put both hands on her back. Why should pregnancy make her back hurt so? The baby was not in her back, and yet for the past two months it had hurt constantly.

She was halfway between the creek and the house, and she reached down to pick up the bucket as she saw Will hurrying toward her.

"Rachel, you shouldn't be toting heavy things like that around!" he said in a scolding voice. "You know what Mary Watson told you. The baby is due in about two weeks."

"Will, I'm only fetching water to the house, something I've always done. I can't be calling you for something like that."

"Yes, you can," he said, taking the bucket from her. "I'll be doing my work and most of yours from now on. I don't want anything to happen to our baby."

Together they walked back toward the house. The sun was sinking in the west, and in the muted afternoon light Rachel felt a sense of satisfaction as she viewed the results of their hard work this winter and early spring.

Fields of young wheat and corn were coming along nicely. In the barnyard, pigs rooted and more chickens than Rachel could count clucked contentedly.

Will had even put in a bed of flowers, right in front of the house. Rachel was surprised when he did it, because she had not asked him to and, as flowers were a non-productive crop, she had been sure that he would have said no had she asked him. She had derived a tremendous comfort from those flowers, and at the end of the day, when the chores were completed, she would sometimes sit outside in the soft, mild evenings and just contemplate their beauty, breathing in their soft, pleasant perfume.

Will had done other things for her as well. In addition to the flower garden, he had made a real window, using glass. He got the money for the glass pane by digging a root cellar for one of their neighbors. A mirror had come with the glass, but it was a mixed blessing for Rachel. She was happy to have it, yet she didn't like what she saw when she looked into it nowadays.

Of course there was a reason for the change that had come over Will—he had finally learned that Rachel was with child. From the day that Rachel had told him, the change in Will had been remarkable. Much of the time he worked with a happy grin on his face, singing tunelessly to himself, and he was as solicitous of her as he would be of an adored child. And he no longer performed his "duty" night after night, proclaiming that he was afraid he would harm the baby. Naturally, that would change once the baby was born.

And yet, sometimes Rachel wondered if she was being fair to him. In fact, she was beginning to develop a real sense of Will's worth. She was hardening to the rigors of being a settler's wife, true, yet she did believe that Will was softening somewhat, too, and maybe the changes in both of them would eventually lead them to meet on common ground.

And maybe—just maybe—she could convince Will that patience, understanding, tenderness, and concern were all qualities that a man should bring to bed with him, as well. And if she could do that, who knew what might happen? There might even be room for love to develop.

"You sit out here in the cool of the evening air," Will said, as they arrived at the house. "It's too hot inside for you to cook. I'll make us some soup."

"For heaven's sake, Will!" she protested. "You don't have to cook. I can at least do that much."

"I know you can, Rachel. But birthing a baby is about as hard work as anything I can think of, so you just sit and rest for a spell. I'll take care of everything."

The fact was, Rachel had already worked a full day today and she *was* tired. She welcomed the thought of just sitting for a bit, just to enjoy the flowers and give her back a respite. She sat down into the chair Will brought outside for her, and as she did so, she caught the reflection of the sun on the window glass; it made the glass look golden.

"Will!" she exclaimed. "Look at our window. Isn't it pretty?"

Will glanced at it and smiled. Unexpectedly, he leaned down to kiss her cheek.

"My heavens, what was that for?" Her hand flew to her cheek. "That's not like you, Will."

"I know," Will said. "Rachel . . . I know it was a terrible winter for you, and I know that you, being used to pretty things, an easier life, found it hard. I ain't much for pretty sayings, pretty doing, Rachel, but I want you to know that I love you."

Touched, she reached up and took his hand in hers. "I know you do, Will. And I want you to know that I intend to make you a good wife, and be a good mother to your children."

He shouted laughter. "If I died right now, Rachel, I'd die a happy man! I tell you true."

Rachel squeezed his hand, and Will went inside to prepare their supper, humming to himself. Rachel felt a sense of contentment and peace. Perhaps this is what love is all about, she thought. Perhaps that which she had experienced with Ewell Rankin had been no more than lust, after all. Lust was a pleasure of the flesh, she decided, while love was a pleasure of the spirit. But, almost unbidden, came the unspoken question—why couldn't a person feel the pleasure of the spirit *and* the pleasure of the flesh?

She laughed aloud suddenly. Such philosophical thoughts! Guiltily, she looked around to see if Will had heard her laughter.

Later, just as the sun had turned into a blood-red disc that did not hurt the eyes, and a band of pink and purple painted the scattering clouds, Will came outside with two steaming bowls of soup. He handed one to Rachel, then sat down on the ground beside her, his back against the wall of the house, and began spooning up his soup.

"I understand that the Watsons had a good time in Omaha?" he said.

"That's what Mary told me."

"I've talked with Zeb about it, about this Grange thing. Sounds to me like it might be a pretty good thing for all farmers to join. Especially if Edenland becomes the farm I want it to be."

"If you have anything to do with it, I'm sure it will."

"You know, it's not just for me that I want Edenland to really be something, and it's not just for you, either. It's for him." He leaned over to pat her protruding stomach.

"How do you know it's going to be a boy, Will Simmons? It could be a girl, you know."

"It'll be a boy," he said complacently. "And I don't want him growing up poor and ignorant, like me. I want him to be well-spoke and educated and to appreciate pretty things, like you, Rachel. You were fortunate, growing up like you did on a fine plantation with a rich daddy, and all the things you needed. I know, the war took all that away, and that was a bad thing. But not war nor nothin' can take away what it was like for you as a child growing up."

"I never thought of it that way, Will, but you're right," she said, moved by the simple yet profound wisdom of his statement.

"I ran away from home when I was fourteen. In a

way, that was probably the best thing I could have done for my family, because that left them with one less mouth to feed. Now, I don't want our young'uns ever feeling like that. I want them to have all the . . . what's the word I want?"

"Advantages?"

"That's it!" he said, smiling sheepishly. "I want them to have all the advantages."

As if reluctant to quit the earth, the sun finally set with a brillant burst of color. It glowed intensely for a few minutes, then grew paler, if no less beautiful. Finally, the colors passed from light to dark red through the various shades of purple, and into a pearl gray. The evening star appeared, a bright, polished diamond hanging in the sky; then more stars appeared, and more yet, until the heavens were ablaze with the night's glory.

"Rachel?" Will said softly.

"Yes, Will?"

"At this moment, I wish you weren't with child."

"Why, I thought you were thrilled and happy about it."

"I am, Rachel, I am. Don't get me wrong. It's just that if you weren't with child . . . I could come to you tonight. And I'd try to be gentle and loving, like you're always wanting. Oh, I know, don't think I don't. And I promise you I'll try to change. It ain't easy for a man like me to change in matters like that, but I promise I'm going to try."

Before the stunned Rachel could respond, Will quickly ducked inside the house, as if embarrassed by his confession.

Of all the things he might have said, that was the

last thing she would have expected from him! All of a sudden, Edenland seemed a much brighter place, and she sat on for a little, dreaming of a happier future, before she went in to bed.

When Rachel woke up suddenly, Will was sitting upright in bed. She did not know what had awakened her, but something about Will's stillness sent a shiver of alarm down her back.

"Will?" she whispered. "What is it? Why are you sitting up like that?"

"Shh," Will cautioned.

"And then she heard it, too. There was the muffled sound of horses and the creak of saddle leather. Then the chickens started to cackle.

"Somebody is stealing our chickens!" Will said angrily. He swung out of bed, snatched his rifle from a rack beside the bed, and went storming out of the house.

"Will, wait! You don't know who's out there!"

But he was already out the door. She stood up and started after him. Before she was halfway to the door, the whole world seemed to explode with the noise of gunshots. There were three shots in quick succession—heavy, booming sounds, like shotgun blasts. Will had a rifle, not a shotgun!

"Oh, my God! Will?" She ran outside.

There, clearly visible in the spill of moonlight, she saw his grotesquely sprawled form. He had been sleeping in his long underwear, but the white color was splotched with spreading blots of scarlet.

"Will, Will! Oh, dear God!"

She fell to her knees beside him, but he was still,

his eyes wide and staring, and she knew that he was dead. She looked up through tear-dimmed eyes, and saw two men on horseback. Wide hats shadowed their faces, and they wore long rain slickers, though it was not raining. Both men had shotguns cradled in their arms.

"Who are you?" she demanded. "Why did you do this?"

The horses were still skittish from the shotgun blasts, and were prancing about. As one man got his mount under control, Rachel ran at the horse. She was mindless with rage. She seized the rider's booted leg and tried to pull him from the horse.

He raised the shotgun, and Rachel saw moonlight glint off the metal as it came arcing down at her. She tried to duck away, but she was too late. The gun crashed into her head. A loud noise roared in her skull, and she saw a brilliant flash of blinding light. She fell headlong, and knew no more.

As Bright Fawn squirmed her way through the shallow ravine, the sounds of gunfire rolled toward her, reverberating off the walls of the ravine and filling it with noise, like the mighty rush of a spring flood.

Bright Fawn felt a heavy weight settle around her heart, because she knew what the gunfire meant. They had discovered the hiding place of her father!

Mean-to-His-Horses had returned from his last skirmish with the pony soldiers with three bullet wounds. One of them was in his chest, and when he breathed, Bright Fawn could hear air bubbles coming through the bullet hole. She knew that the air that comes from inside a man is his life spirit leaving his body; and she tried to stop up the hole with grass, but no matter what she did, she could not stop the spirit of Mean-to-His-Horses from escaping.

For a time they had found refuge in an abandoned sod house, but Mean-to-His Horses had insisted that it was wrong for a Sioux to die in a white man's house, so they had moved out of the house and made camp in some rocks and high grass beside a stream. Her father wanted to remain there and rest until he died, and then he could build a wickiup for Quiet Stream and Stone Eagle in the land ruled over by the Great Spirit.

Bright Fawn did not want him to die. She had left him there alone and trudged many miles in an attempt to find some sign of other Indians. She would get them to build a travois, and she would take her father to the Rosebud.

But she had been unable to find anyone, and now she was returning to keep a vigil while Mean-to-His Horses died. But she knew from the sound of gunfire that the white men had discovered his hiding place.

She crept as far down the ravine as she could without being seen. She found a spot where she could hide herself and yet observe what was going on. The first thing she saw was that the white men were not pony soldiers, but a sheriff's posse. At least she saw one man with a star pinned to his shirt; she knew about the white man's sheriff. There were an even dozen of them, most of them huddled behind a ledge. Three of the men were crouched in a position where they could watch her father, who was behind a boulder with just the barrel of his rifle showing. The others were squatted in a semi-circle, smoking, talking, and passing a bottle of whiskey back and forth.

Bright Fawn longed to run to her father and die with him. Yet she was wise enough to realize that the white men would see her and kill her long before she reached Mean-to-His-Horses, and the life force was strong in her.

One of the sheriff's men threw a whiskey bottle against a rock, and Bright Fawn could hear the tinkle of breaking glass. The man wiped his mouth with the back of one hand and scratched his crotch with the other. He moved over behind the men watching her father.

"Hey, you down there, Mean-to-His-Horses!" he shouted. "Come on out where we can see you, or we're coming to get you!"

"He can't understand English," one of the others said. "He don't know what you're saying."

"That daughter of his speaks English well enough. She went to the Indian School, the way I get it. That dirt farmer who spotted Mean-to-His-Horses and told us, he saw the little squaw with him." He raised his voice to a shout. "Hey you, Indian girl! You understand me, all right. Tell your pa to come on out here, and we'll be real friendly." He gave a drunken giggle, and said more quietly, "Yes, sir, we'll be real friendly, all right, all the time we're stringing that savage up by the neck."

The others laughed raucously and fired off shots.

Mean-to-His-Horses returned the fire, and the men ducked down.

The drunken one sneered. "Well, come on, we going to kill us an Injun or ain't we?"

The man wearing a star had walked over. "I'm just a deputy sheriff," he said. "What do you want from me? The whole damned U.S. Army hasn't been able to bring him in yet."

"Well, you won't be a deputy long, if you don't bring him back dead."

"Aw, hell, Jake, you're drunk," the deputy said. He unpinned the badge and held it out. "If you want Mean-to-His-Horses so bad, pin this on and go get him."

Jake hesitated for a moment, then took the badge with a broad grin. He pinned it to his vest. "By God, I will!"

He leaped out into the open and started at a weaving lope toward the boulder that hid Mean-to-His-Horses. He had taken about half a dozen steps when Mean-to-His-Horses fired. The man called Jake spun around, a hole in his chest pumping blood.

"The sonofabitch killed me!" he said, with a surprised look on his face. He pitched forward and rolled down into the gully not too far from where Bright Fawn was hidden.

"Damn him, he got Jake!" one of the men yelled. "Let's get him!"

They all stood and began advancing toward the boulder that sheltered Mean-to-His-Horses, firing as they went. A moan escaped Bright Fawn as she saw her father suddenly stand up, taking a staggering step toward the advancing posse. He raised his rifle and got off one shot before several bullets struck him, knocking him back and to the ground.

Bright Fawn squeezed her eyes shut, tears leaking past the lids. At least Mean-to-His-Horses had died gallantly, standing tall and proud before his enemies. His gentle voice seemed to echo in her mind, "It was a good day to die, daughter."

When she opened her eyes again, she saw that the posse was gathered around the prone body. One man squatted down for a moment, then stood up. "He's dead all right," he said in an awed voice. "Dad you see how he stood right up to us like that? Must have been crazy!"

"All Indians are crazy, didn't you know that?"

Another said, "What are we going to do with him?"

"Is there a bounty on him?"

"Damned right there is," said the deputy sheriff. "Seems to me like there's more'n a thousand dollars on his head. Half is paid by the government, and the other half is posted by the UP."

"How we gonna divvy it up?"

"I'm the one killed him," the deputy said. "Seems to me like I ought to get the biggest share."

The others looked at him with dark scowls, and then the deputy laughed weakly. "Just joshing, fellows. I figure it ought to be cut up into equal shares."

"Yeah," one said. "That's the way I figure it."

"What about the farmer who told us where to find him, where he was holed up?"

"What about him?" the deputy asked.

"Don't he get anything?"

"Was he here, taking his chances on getting shot?" the deputy wanted to know.

"Nope."

"Then he don't get a red cent, not if I have anything to say about it. Now, what about the Indian girl?"

"What about her?"

"The report was, Mean-to-His-Horses had his daughter with him. Seems to me she ought to be around somewhere," the deputy said.

"So?"

"So, if she's around here, I think we ought to try and find her."

"Why?"

"You don't have much sense, do you, Ted? In the first place, like as not there's a bounty on her, too. In the second place, if she gets away, we don't know but what there might be a war party somewhere nearby, coming to rescue Mean-to-His-Horses. There's not that many of us. Colonel Bowers had some sixty men with him, and you know what happened to him. And they was soldiers, by God! Now, do you want to take that chance?"

"No," the other said. "Hell, no."

"Then let's spread out through here and let's find her."

"What do we do with her when we find her?"

One man smiled with a wicked leer. "Well, they do say she's a mighty comely squaw. Could be we might have a little fun first, and then . . ."

"I don't know," the deputy said doubtfully.

"You don't know what?"

"I don't know if I could just up and kill her like that. She's just a young girl, ain't she?"

"She's a damned Indian, by God! Are you too squeamish to take your turn at having a little fun when we catch up with her?"

"Having a little fun with an Indian squaw is one thing, killing her in cold blood is another. Now, I'm in charge of this posse. There'll be no more killing. Now spread out and find her. Call her. She speaks English. Tell her we just want her to give herself up so we can take her back to her people on the Rosebud."

"She's sure stupid, if she believes that."

"Whoever said Indians were smart?"

The men began moving through the area, calling out. They did not know her name, and they shouted, "Indian girl!" Bright Fawn took one last look at her father in order to preserve his memory forever in her mind, and then she turned to go, squirming nimbly through the high grass. So skillful was she that the tops of the grasses hardly quivered at all. Soon she was out of hearing of their voices and she stood, running across the prairie as gracefully as a doe.

Her heart was heavy. She would not go back to the Rosebud; she had no kin left there. She had no idea where she would go. And she did not care.

By dawn, Bright Fawn had traveled quite a distance from the place where her father was killed. She was going east. She had not consciously chosen that direction; she just went the way she was pointed, with no plan or reason.

But now she was hungry. She had not eaten since the morning of the day before. She saw a white man's sod house loom up in the morning light. Perhaps she should stop and plead for something to eat.

No, she decided, it might not be wise to make her presence known. They might be angry or frightened at the sight of her, and they would not give her anything to eat. They might even hold her for the men who killed her father. Or they might even kill her themselves. Since going to war against the pony soldiers, Mean-to-His-Horses had warned her repeatedly that no white man could be trusted—not even his old friend, Lance-in-the-Side.

If she was going to get something to eat at this place, it would be better to get it without them knowing. She would steal her food. The white man did not understand stealing, yet to an Indian, stealing from an enemy was an honorable thing to do.

Bright Fawn slipped stealthily toward the lean-to barn. She heard a rooster crow and knew that there were chickens, so that meant there would be eggs. Then, just as she rounded the corner, she saw a man lying on the ground halfway between the house and the barn, and she froze in sudden fear.

Then she realized that there was no need to be frightened of this man. He was dead. Curiosity overcame her fear for a moment, and she walked over to stare down at him. He was covered with blood. His chest had been riddled with shotgun pellets. She heard a moaning sound, and she glanced toward the house.

There was a woman lying on the ground in front of the house. The woman was moving, a strange sound coming from her. All reservations gone, Bright Fawn ran over to her, and gasped in wonder. The woman was on the verge of giving birth!

CHAPTER NINETEEN

Like a cork surfacing from far beneath the water, Rachel floated back to consciousness. From somewhere close at hand she heard the sound of a baby—a cough and a wailing cry. Then she heard a quiet shushing and the soothing sound of humming. It was not a tune she recognized, but more of a singsong or chant. Evidently it had the desired effect, for the baby stopped crying, hiccuping down to silence.

Rachel realized that she was in bed, but she had no idea why. Her thoughts were fragmented, and she had difficulty remembering clearly. Where was Will, and why hadn't he awakened her when company came? Who did they know with a baby?

She turned her head on the pillow and felt a rush of dizziness and a residue of remembered pain. She lay very still for a moment, hoping that everything would stop spinning.

Finally the dizziness passed, and she opened her eyes cautiously. Across the room a young woman sat at the table, a baby in her lap. On the table was a bowl of milk, and the woman was dipping a piece of cloth into the milk, then putting the cloth into the baby's mouth. The baby mouthed the cloth but seemed to obtain little satisfaction from it, for the tiny face contracted and the child began to cry again.

Where was everyone? Why was she alone with this strange woman and the baby? Rachel felt a sense of unease.

"Who are you?" she demanded.

The woman looked around and smiled. She was an Indian!

"My name is Bright Fawn," she said, speaking English with difficulty. "Who are you?"

"Rachel Simmons," Rachel said crossly. "Bright Fawn, what are you doing here? Where is my husband?"

The smile left Bright Fawn's lovely features, and she looked disconcerted. "You do not know about your husband?"

"Of course not! Why would I be asking if I knew?" She tried to sit up, and was annoyed as another wave of dizziness seized her. What *was* wrong with her?

"I am sorry," Bright Fawn was saying. "I thought you knew. When I find you, I also find a man with long hair here . . ." She gestured to her chin.

"Yes, that would be Will. But what do you mean, you *found* me?"

"Someone hit you here," Bright Fawn said, gesturing to the back of her head. "It made you very sick."

Suddenly, memory flooded back and Rachel

went rigid. Again she could hear the shotgun blasts and see the blood staining Will's long underwear. And she remembered the moonlight glinting on the shotgun barrel as it descended . . .

She moaned in grief. "Oh, dear God! Will is dead!" Tears burned her eyes.

"Yes, your man is dead," the Indian girl said quietly. "I put him in hole in the ground, as is the custom of your people."

Rachel was crying openly now, sobs shaking her body. Everything had happened with such shocking suddenness that she was barely able to comprehend it. In a few short moments her whole life had been shattered. She fell back on the bed and sobbed into the pillow. Why? Why would anyone so wantonly kill Will? Poor Will, and his grand plans! She recalled his last words to her, and the sudden blooming of hope for a better life between them. Now all that was gone, and there was nothing left.

Her loud sobbing upset the baby, and it began squalling. And another realization hit her forcibly. This was *her* baby!

It must be. She cautiously touched herself and found her once-swollen stomach flat and flaccid. How could she have given birth to a baby and not remember?

She sat up, ignoring the dizziness, and held out her arms. "My baby, that's my baby!"

"Yes, it is your baby." Smiling, Bright Fawn got up and came over to lay the child in Rachel's outstretched arms.

It was a boy, Rachel saw at once. The son Will had been longing for.

She dipped her head and kissed the child gently on the forehead. "Hello, little Will." She was filled with a sense of awe, and holding the baby in her arms eased some of her grief. Oh, her heart still ached for Will, yet she also felt an awareness of her responsibility for this tiny new life. This enabled her to get her emotions under some semblance of control.

"The child was being born when I found you," Bright Fawn said. "He is a fine, strong child, but he needs mother's milk."

"Bright Fawn, how long ago was he born? How long have I been unconscious?"

"This is the third day," Bright Fawn said gravely.

"Three days?" Rachel said incredulously. She touched her fingers gingerly to the back of her head and felt a swelling and a small encrustation of blood. "I suppose I should thank God that I wasn't killed along with Will. In fact, I'm sure those two men left me for dead."

"You cannot make milk," Bright Fawn said, reaching out to touch Rachel on the breast. "I have placed the child there many times, but milk will not come."

"Perhaps that's because I was unconscious." Rachel opened the bodice of her nightgown and took out her right breast, which looked pale and swollen, then held little Will to the nipple. He began sucking greedily, and at the strange, sharp, drawing feeling she felt an overpowering surge of love for this infant, *her* baby.

Bright Fawn leaned down. She exclaimed in delight, "Now, milk comes!"

A short time later little Will, fed and contented, was sleeping soundly on the bed, and Rachel, with Bright Fawn's help, sat up. She was weak, but she was also ravenous, and she ate the thick soup the Indian girl brought her with a greedy hunger to match the baby's a few minutes earlier.

After her hunger was somewhat appeased, she looked up at Bright Fawn. The Indian maiden had saved her life, there was not the least doubt of that. If she had been left out there alone, not only would she have died, but the baby as well.

But who was Bright Fawn, and how did she happen by at the most fortunate time?

"Who are you?" she asked.

"I am Bright Fawn," the girl said.

"I know that, you told me. But where did you come from? How did you happen to stumble upon me?"

Bright Fawn's face closed up, and sorrow clouded her eyes. "I am Bright Fawn, daughter of Mean-to-His-Horses. I come from the Rosebud River, many suns north of this place."

"You're Mean-to-His-Horses' daughter? The Indian chieftain who had been warring against the whites?"

"Yes."

"But he is a fugitive. Everyone in the territory is looking for him."

"They look no more," Bright Fawn said simply. "My father is dead."

"Dead? When did this happen? I hadn't heard anything about it."

"It was three days ago," Bright Fawn said. "I hid

in a ravine and watched the white men shoot him, than I ran. I came here to ask for food, and I found you and your man."

Rachel stretched a hand across the table, and placed it gently on the Indian girl's arm. "Bright Fawn, I am so sorry! Believe me, I am. I have been so self-centered and worried about my own troubles, while you've had your own tragedy, just as great. And despite all that, and despite the fact that you were fleeing for your life, you stopped to help my baby and me. What a dear and brave woman you are. I know it wasn't easy for you to do this for a white woman and a white baby."

"Baby is not white, baby is not red," Bright Fawn said with dignity. "Baby is baby."

"Bright Fawn, I wish the men who run our government affairs had your compassion . . . *and* your wisdom." Rachel finished her soup, then stood up, noticing with relief that the annoying dizziness had passed. "Where is Will buried?"

"You will see," Bright Fawn said. "I marked the place with the cross of your Great Spirit, your Jesus."

"Thank you," Rachel said. "When I am stronger, I will go to see it."

"His spirit will welcome you," Bright Fawn said.

By the afternoon of the next day, Rachel felt strong enough to get up from the bed and dress herself. She tired quickly, but after resting a bit, she again felt able to get up. She was determined to see Will's grave. She knew that until she did she would not really accept the fact of his death.

She did not have to walk far. Bright Fawn had buried Will close to where he had fallen, near the flower garden he had planted for Rachel.

Rachel stood, squinting in the bright sunlight, looking down upon the long pile of earth that marked her husband's final resting place. It looked so small, not nearly large enough to hold such a large man as Will.

Tears burned in her eyes, and she turned to the garden and picked a large bouquet of flowers, which she lay at the foot of the wooden cross Bright Fawn had made. The tears spilled unashamedly down her cheeks as she slowly knelt beside the grave, placing one hand upon the sun-warmed earth.

"Will, it's me, Rachel." She felt her voice about to break, and stopped for a moment before she could continue. "You were a good man, Will Simmons, and I know you loved me. I wanted to be a good wife to you, and I really think that I would have been, in time. I even think that in time I would have come to love you. Maybe I already did. I do know that I respected you. I respected you about as much as anyone I've ever known."

She felt the tears flowing down her cheeks and wiped them away with the back of her hand. "Will, I bore your son. I wish you could see him. He's a beautiful baby. I'm going to name him Will Bonner Simmons. The Bonner is to carry on my own papa's name."

She stood in silence foı a few more minutes, then turned back toward the house. She could see a house, a barn, a root cellar, as well as fields of growing corn and wheat, all products of the single-minded purpose of the man who lay in the ground behind her, Will Angus Simmons, one of Nebraska's pioneers—and a murder victim.

Two days later Rachel hitched up the wagon and drove over to the Watsons with the baby, to tell them of Will's death. She had not asked Bright Fawn to go with her, but had left her at home, uncertain of how the Watsons would react.

Mary Watson was most solicitous and offered to come over at once, to offer any assistance Rachel might need, and her husband offered his help in getting in the crops.

"Edenland just may be the best piece of farmland in these parts," Watson said. "The truth is, I would have settled over there instead of here, if I had seen it in time. But by the time I had this farm going good and was looking to expand, why, that land had been given to the UP. But it's mighty fine land, Mrs. Simmons, and I reckon you'll have about the finest crop this year of any farmer around."

"My land, Zeb," Mary Watson scolded. "The poor girl has no interest in listening to farm talk right now. She's just lost her man, for goodness sake! How would you feel if it was you instead of poor Will laying in his grave, and somebody was talking business to me?"

"I'd feel durned good about it," Watson said stoutly. "The trouble with you women is that you don't stop and think about the important things until it's too late. Rachel here has to know that someone will help her with that crop. There could be two, three hundred dollars there."

"I'm sure it means nothing to her right now," his wife said tartly. "Besides, you've not said one word about this pretty little baby boy she brought over here! Couldn't you at least say *something* about him?"

Watson looked at little Will, who was at that moment lying in his wife's lap, looking up at her with big, curious blue eyes. Watson reached a finger down and tickled the baby's chin. "He is a pretty little tad at that."

Both of the Watson children were crowding around their mother, striving for a look at the baby. Ginny was pestering her mother to let her hold the child.

"Do you mind, Rachel?" Mary asked. "She's very good with little ones."

"No, I don't mind," Rachel said, smiling.

"All right, Ginny, you can hold little Will, but you sit down first, then let me put him in your lap."

"It ain't no fair she gets to hold him," Jimmy said, "without I do, too."

"Boys ain't supposed to hold babies," Ginny announced importantly.

"Well, I'm gonna hold 'em, so there!"

"All right, you two, behave!" their mother said.

Ginny sat down and Mary deposited the baby in her lap. "Now you be extra careful." Mary turned to Rachel. "I put some lemonade in a crock in the cellar to cool off. Would you like some, honey?"

"You have lemons?" Rachel said in surprise. "Oh, yes! I've no idea how long it's been since I've had any lemonade."

"Jimmy, run fetch the lemonade," Mary said, and

the boy darted off to do her bidding. "Rachel, have you heard about that murdering Indian, Mean-to-His-Horses?"

"I heard that he was killed," Rachel said. She had not mentioned anything about Bright Fawn to the Watsons.

"That he was," Mary said. "There was a terrible gun battle. His daughter escaped, and now they're looking everywhere for her. When they find her, they may hang her."

"Hang his daughter? Whatever for?"

"Well, she was with Mean-to-His-Horses, you know. They say she killed three or four of the posse herself. Anyway, the posse is out and about, searching every farm and every building. But don't you fret, honey, they'll find her."

"If the posse was really interested in protecting the people, they wouldn't waste time hunting down a harmless Indian girl! They should be out looking for the two men who killed my husband!"

"My land, I'm sure they will, once they learn what happened. After all, honey, we're your nearest neighbors, and even *we* didn't know anything about it until you came here today to tell us."

"I guess you're right," Rachel said in a subdued voice.

Jimmy came sprinting back with a jar. "Here's the lemonade, Ma. Can I have some?"

"You can have some soon as the grownups have been served," Mary said reprovingly. She poured a glass and gave it to Rachel.

Rachel had drunk lemonade many times when shre worked at the Roundhouse, and tasting it now recalled those times. She remembered the good food, the fine clothes, the cluttered people, and the conversation that went beyond weather and crops and the condition of the livestock. How she wished she could go back! Not to Ewell Rankin; she could never go back to him. But she wished there was some way she could resume the kind of life she had known then.

She also remembered the show she had brought to End of the Track, and the excitement of that evening. Oh, if only she could capture that feeling again! A sudden thought struck her.

"Mr. Watson, how much do you think Edenland is worth?"

"Oh, now, Rachel, I couldn't rightly say," Watson said judiciously. "If the crops come in good like it looks like they might, you got two, three hundred dollars right there. And the house and barn, the livestock, the farming equipment, plus the land . . . Edenland should be worth two thousand, somewhere in there."

"Do you think I could get that much if I sold it now?"

"We-ell, if you found a buyer for it, I'd say so, yes." Hand on his chin, Watson squinted at her. "You thinking on selling it, Mrs. Simmons?"

"Yes." Her head went back, her mind made up. "Yes, I am."

Mary Watson said incredulously, "Honey, you mean you're going to just walk away and leave everything you and Will worked so hard for?"

"Without Will . . . it means nothing to me." Rachel spoke to soften the shock Mary felt, but even as she said it she knew it was true. Edenland had been Will Simmons's dream. As his wife, she had helped him build it, and had even, toward the last, began to share it, but she knew she could not sustain that dream on her own.

Yet there was one dream that Will had had that she *could* sustain. He wanted to make certain that his son grew up with the advantages he, Will, had never experienced. She could see that that dream was carried out. But she also knew that it would have to be done some other way than farming.

She said, "There are too many bitter memories at Edenland for me to continue to live there."

"You know, Mrs. Simmons, like I said, I've always had a hankering for that place myself." Watson sighed. "But to tell the truth, I don't have the kind of money it's worth."

"Well, what could you pay?"

Watson studied her closely. "You're sure now, sure that you want to sell?"

"I'm sure."

"I could maybe go to the bank in Connersville and maybe borrow money to take it off your hands. But I'd have to borrow the whole amount, and they wouldn't loan me two thousand, I'm sure of that. Maybe . . ." He hesitated. "A thousand dollars?"

"Zeb!" Mary exclaimed. "I won't stand for it! I'll not let you steal that place from Rachel. She's been our neighbor and good friend. My land, she loaned me her own dress to go to Omaha in. I won't sit here and let you cheat her!"

Watson protested, "I'm not cheating her, woman! I'm trying to be truthful with her."

A thousand dollars, Rachel was thinking. It was more than she had anticipated, and the thought of what she could do with that much money excited her.

Watson said grudgingly, "I'll tell you what . . . I might, *might*, mind, be able to raise fifteen hundred. But that's the best I can do."

"Mr. Watson, the day you come to me with fifteen hundred dollars," she said gravely, "Edenland belongs to you. I'll leave that very night, if you'll allow me to use a wagon and mules to get us to the train depot in Connersville."

"Where will you be going, honey?" Mary asked.

"I don't know. Maybe back east," Rachel said. She had an idea where she was going and what she was going to do, but she had no intention of telling the Watsons. "Or maybe back to End of the Track."

"I'll be over to your place with the money in a couple of days," Watson promised, as Rachel finished her lemonade and took her leave.

It took Rachel over an hour to get back home. She had to stop once and nurse the baby. She sat on the wagon seat, the sun warm on her bared breast as the baby nursed, and looked at the prairie. Here, she had thought, she would spend the rest of her life. It was not to be, and she realized that she had no regrets about leaving. The money she would receive from the sale would buy her freedom.

She laughed aloud with joy. "I'm sorry, little Will. Maybe I'm not being true to your daddy's memory. I would have stayed with him until the end of my days, if he had lived. But I would have done that for him, not for his memory, not for love of the land. Now I have my own life to live, and yours to shape for the future, son. I can't do that here. I hope you can understand that when you get old enough. I simply cannot remain here."

Will's lips made a smacking sound, as he slipped away from her nipple and went to sleep. Rachel rearranged her clothing, clucked to the mules, and completed her journey home with the baby asleep in her lap.

There were several horses in the front yard before the house, and she was both surprised and frightened. She snapped the reins at the mules, and hurried into the yard. There were six men in a knot before the front door. They turned about as the wagon jolted to a halt, and Rachel gasped as she saw Bright Fawn on the ground. Her buckskin dress had been torn until it hung down around her waist like an apron. She was naked from the waist up, and her small, well-formed breasts gleamed like gold in the afternoon sunlight.

Rachel left the baby on the wagon seat, and climbed down to the ground to confront them. "What is going on here?" she demanded angrily.

One of the men tipped his greasy hat politely. "My name is Tom Burns, ma'am. May I ask what you are doing here?"

"What am *I* doing here? I live here. This is my home. But you haven't answered my question. What are you men doing here?"

"Ma'am, we're members of the Platte River Vigilante Patrol," Tom Burns said.

"I don't care who you are, you have no business coming onto my property and abusing my help."

"Your help?" Burns looked startled. "This here Indian girl is your hired help?"

"Yes, she is," Rachel said. "In fact, she is more than help. She is part of my family."

"Look here," one of the others said. "Are you sure this squaw girl ain't the daughter of that murdering redskin, Mean-to-His-Horses?"

"I'm sure I don't know what you're talking about," Rachel lied.

Tom Burns said, "Have you ever heard of Mean-to-His-Horses?"

"He's an Indian chief, that much I know," Rachel said. "But what does that have to do with me?"

"The thing is, ma'am, he had a daughter. She's young and pretty, they say, and that fits the description of this one here. We had it figured we'd hit upon her when we found her here."

"We figured maybe we was doing you a favor, lady," another man said. "She was in your house, and she was baking bread, just like she lived there."

"She *does* live here, you blithering idiot!" Rachel said harshly. "She is my son's nurse. Now will you kindly get off my property?"

Heart hammering in her breast, she walked over to help Bright Fawn to her feet. She pulled the girl's dress up to restore some modesty, then went over to the wagon for the baby. With Will cradled under one arm, she pushed the dazed Bright Fawn toward the house with her other hand. The vigilantes stood around uncertainly, clearly unsure what to do next.

Once inside the door, Rachel ran to the bed, deposited the baby, and reached up to the rack for Will's rifle. She worked the lever to put a cartridge in the chamber, and went back outside, alone. Aiming the rifle toward the ground in the general direction of the men, she pulled the trigger. The rifle exploded with a loud crack, and a puff of dust appeared on the ground, right between the feet of Tom Burns. The bullet whistled through his legs, then whined off into the leaves of the stand of corn behind him.

"I said, get off my property!" Rachel worked the lever again.

"Hold it, ma'am," Burns said placatingly, holding his hands, palm out, toward her. "You don't realize what you're doing here. Somebody could get hurt!"

"I know exactly what I'm doing, sir," she blazed. "And it is my intention that someone *will* be hurt, if you don't get out of here right now!"

"We're going, ma'am, we're going! Just don't shoot that thing anymore," Burns said. "Come on," he shouted to the others. "Let's get the hell out of here while we're all in one piece! This little lady ain't no one to mess with!"

The men mounted up, Burns tipping his hat to Rachel, and they rode away. Rachel stood at the ready with the rifle until they were out of sight. Only then did she relax her vigil, and by that time, Bright Fawn had ventured out of the house behind her.

"Well," Rachel said, thumping the rifle butt down into the dirt. "I'm glad to see *them* gone!"

"They will tell others that I am here," Bright Fawn said. "I think more will come."

"Let them come," Rachel said. "We are leaving this place day after tomorrow."

"Day after tomorrow?" Bright Fawn asked, puzzling over the unfamiliar term.

"Two more days," Rachel said, holding up two fingers. "And you are coming with me, Bright Fawn."

"I hope we live two more days," Bright Fawn said soberly.

CHAPTER TWENTY

In the months since Rachel had left what was then End of the Track, the Union Pacific had pushed on through Nebraska, giving birth to the town of Julesburg in the extreme northeast corner of Colorado, then on through Wyoming and the new towns of Cheyenne, Laramie, Medicine Bow, and Carbon Station. By July 1868, a new End of the Track was laid out, named, ironically, after Senator Thomas Hart Benton. The late senator had spent years advocating a transcontinental railroad that would follow the 38th Parallel, and had fought vehemently against running the railroad farther north; yet, there was a town named for him right on the 42nd Parallel.

Benton, like most of the other towns along the right-of-way, underwent an immediate land boom, as it stood ready to assume its role, albeit a temporary one, as the new End of the Track. Newspaper correspondent John Hanson Beadle, writing for the Cincinnati *Ledger*, penned a vivid description of the town for the newspaper's readers back east:

> For ten hours daily, the streets are thronged with motley crowds of railroadmen, Mexicans and Indians, gamblers, saloon keepers, merchants, miners and mule-whackers. The streets were eight inches deep in white dust as I entered the city of canvas tents and polehouses. The suburbs appear as banks of dirty white lime, and a new arrival in black clothes looks like nothing so much as a cockroach struggling though a flour barrel. The great institution of Benton is the "Big Tent." This structure has a nice frame, a hundred feet long and forty feet wide, covered with canvas, and conveniently floored for dancing, to which and gambling, it is entirely devoted.

There was no water in Benton. It had to be hauled in by the wagonload from the North Platte River, three miles away, and the entrepreneur who had that business was commanding, and getting, a dollar per barrel.

It was to Benton that Rachel and Bright Fawn came after selling Edenland, with its crops and all its equipment, to Zeb Watson. The train ride to Benton took two days, and three times someone had tried to move Bright Fawn back to the emigrant car.

Each time Rachel intervened. "I have paid full fare for her, and as she is the nurse of my child, I intend for her to stay with my child."

Now, on the outskirts of Benton, the conductor came into the car. "Benton!" he announced. "Next stop, Benton. This is the end of the line, folks. Everyone will detrain here."

"Conductor, would you tell me where the Roundhouse is located?" Rachel asked.

"No roundhouse in Benton, ma'am. There's just a loop and a spur to get the engine headed back the other way."

"No, you don't understand. I'm not talking about a real roundhouse, I'm talking about the hotel and restaurant."

"Oh! The Roundhouse. Yes, ma'am, I know what you're talking about. Let's see, there was one back down the line, I recollect. Julesburg, I think. Or was it North Platte?"

"You mean there isn't one here?"

"In Benton? Oh, no, ma'am. Fact is, I don't believe there's one anywheres now."

"I see," Rachel said slowly. "Well then, is there an establishment similar to the Roundhouse in Benton?"

"Ma'am, I don't know what it is you're expecting." His curious glance took in Bright Fawn and the baby. "I mean, seeing as you have the little tot, and all. But there are twenty-three saloons, two restaurants, one hotel, and one . . . uh, well . . ." The conductor's face was bright red. He finished lamely, "There's another place I can't be mentioning to a lady. I'm sure you wouldn't be interested."

Rachel hid a smile behind her hand. "Thank you for your information, conductor."

As the train chugged to a stop, she turned to Bright Fawn. "I'll take little Will and see if I can find us some transportation. You see to our luggage."

Bright Fawn handed her the baby, and Rachel made her way to the end of the car, where the conductor was dropping a boarding step down for the passengers' use. Rachel stepped out onto the station platform and looked around. If anything, Benton had a rawer look than the other End of the Tracks she had seen, and was certainly noisier and wilder. Even now, in the middle of the afternoon, she heard gunshots and cries up the dusty street. It seemed to her that the farther west the railroad moved, the less civilized the towns became.

Just then she saw a buckboard draw up alongside the platform, and a woman stepped out, turning back to direct the driver to load her baggage onto the train. The woman was dressed rather gaudily for the surroundings, and carried a parasol against the sun.

Rachel hurried over to engage the buckboard and driver. After she had made arrangements, she turned to find the woman staring at her curiously.

Then her painted face bloomed with a smile. "I know you! You're Rachel Bonner. You used to work at the Roundhouse, didn't you?"

"Yes." She stared at the woman, but she did not look familiar.

The woman laughed. "You probably don't remember me, hon. You'd have no call to. I used to come into the Roundhouse all the time. I'm Rose Foster. One day you just up and disappeared. I always wondered what happened to you."

"I left the Roundhouse to get married."

"That explains it, then. What a cute baby!" She chucked Will under the chin. "Are you and your husband moving to Benton now?"

"My husband is dead."

"Oh, hon, I'm sorry. Really I am. Listen, is there anything I can do?" She laughed in some confusion. "I guess most people ask you that, don't they?"

"Only those with kind hearts," Rachel said, smiling. "And I thank you for your concern."

Just then two young women strolled toward them across the station platform. Rachel recognized one of them—Becky, from the Roundhouse.

"Becky!" she exclaimed. "How grand to see you!"

"Miss Bonner!" Becky smiled with pleasure. "What are you doing here?"

"I'm here looking for work. Will, my husband, was killed, and now I have a baby to support."

"Oh, what a beautiful baby! May I hold it?"

"Certainly. I'm calling him Will, after my husband."

Becky started to reach for the baby, then she jerked her arms away. "Before I touch your baby, maybe I ought to tell you that I work for Rose." She looked away.

Rose Foster laughed. "You mean you *did* work for me, hon. Nobody works for me now. I'm getting out of the business for good, the moment I get on that train for St. Louis."

"Becky, I don't understand. So you work, or worked, for Rose—what does that have to do with anything?"

"Don't you know? Rose is . . . well, you know!"

Rachel said, "I'm not sure that I do."

Rose laughed again, a shrill laugh this time. "What Becky's trying to tell you, hon, is that she's become a soiled dove since last you saw her."

"Oh!" Rachel, understanding now, smiled at Becky, and held the baby out. "You can hold him, Becky. I want you to."

Becky's face beamed with a wide smile. "Gee, thanks, Miss Bonner. You're swell!"

"It isn't Miss Bonner anymore."

"Oh, that's right. You did get married," Becky said. "What's your name now?"

"It's Rachel, just plain Rachel."

"Oh, Judy!" Becky turned to the girl with her. "Isn't this the most beautiful baby? Don't you wish you had one?"

"Hardly," Judy said, with a rueful laugh. "Babies and our profession don't go together."

Becky sighed. "Well, we don't have a profession now, anyway."

Rachel said, "How did you get into this . . . uh, profession, Becky?"

"I know what you must think of me," Becky said with downcast eyes. "But I didn't have any choice. My ma finally went back east, and I've been sending her money so she won't be a burden on my sister and her husband. Ma thinks I'm still working at the Roundhouse. Trouble is, there ain't no Roundhouse. I had to do something, and Rose, she was nice enough to take me on at her place."

"I did well by her, too, did well by all my girls," Rose said. "They all had rooms, plenty to eat, and I ran an orderly house. No drunks or rowdies allowed."

"But Rose is leaving now," Becky said dolefully. "So it looks like we'll all have to be on our own, nobody to look after us."

Rachel studied Becky closely. She was prettier than she had been when working at the Roundhousc, but she had lost what innocence she had had.

Rachel's mind was racing. She glanced at Rose Foster. "How many girls do you have working for you?"

"Six. Six of the best."

"Then why are you leaving?"

"The only reason I *would* be leaving." She winked bawdily. "I found me a rich swell. He fell in love with me. I'm going back to marry him, can you feature that? The dream of every working girl."

"Well," Rachel said doubtfully, "I certainly wish you all the best."

"You say that like you're maybe thinking I won't take to it too well."

"You say he's rich?"

"I'd say he is. He owns a bank."

"Are you in love with him?"

"In love with him?" Rose laughed heartily. "Honey, I'm in love with every man who's ever bedded me. Mr. Wilson is better than some and not as good as others, but if I need to be in love with the fellow, why, I'm sure I can work that out, too."

Rachel realized that she shouldn't be critical. Hadn't she married Will Simmons to escape, without being in love with him? Yet she had survived, and probably would have remained with him if he had not been murdered. No, she had no reason to judge Rose Foster!

She said, "Becky, why isn't there a Roundhouse here? What happened to Ewell Rankin?"

"I don't know, Miss . . . Rachel. He just came into the Roundhouse back at the last End of the Track and announced that he was closing the Roundhouse for good. He paid everybody off, and the next thing I heard, he was on the train headed back east. Far as I know, nobody's seen him since."

Rachel said curtly, "As far as I'm concerned, it's good riddance!"

The baby started crying, and Becky tried to quiet him. Bright Fawn had come up unnoticed, and now she reached over to take Will from Becky. Startled, Becky said, "Hey! What do you think—?"

"It's all right," Rachel said quickly. "This is Bright Fawn. She's little Will's nurse." The baby stopped squalling the moment Bright Fawn took him.

Becky shied away from the Indian girl, moving closer to Rachel. "What are you going to do here in Benton, Rachel, with the baby and all? It's a pretty wild town. No jobs around for a lady like you."

"I don't know how much of a lady I am anymore. How about you, Becky? What are you going to do?"

Becky grinned sheepishly. "I guess I'll just go on doing what I've been doing. The thing is, I suppose I'll have to open a crib. I'm sure not looking forward to that, but I don't have much choice. I couldn't go anywhere else, I don't even have train fare."

"A crib? I'm sorry, what does that mean?"

"It's not very nice, for a working girl," Rose Foster said. "A girl going into business for herself needs a room of some sort, and she shuffles the customers in and out as fast as possible. But she's on her own, if you catch my meaning. If some gent decides he doesn't want to pay up, or if he gets nasty . . . why, there's not much a girl alone can do. She won't have a bouncer like I had. There won't be a nice, genteel bar, where gentlemen drink like gentlemen. You can't have all those things unless you have a house, like I did."

"What about your house?" Rachel asked.

Rose Foster frowned. "What about it?"

"Who's taking it over?"

Rose shrugged. "Nobody. I'm closing it up. It costs money to run it, which none of my girls have. And there's nobody around who can run it. You have to know what you're doing to run a good house."

"What would it cost to take it over and run it?"

Rose got a thoughtful look. "Honey, what are you thinking?"

"I'm thinking of taking over your house."

"Girl, do you have any idea what you'd be getting into?" Are you willing to sleep with any man who comes along?"

"No. No, I don't think I could do that," Rachel said slowly. "But I don't see that that would be necessary, not if I had enough girls working for me. I was the hostess at the Roundhouse, and I handled that fine. I can't see that there would be all that much difference."

"Oh, there's a difference, right enough. There's a *big* difference. Working at the Roundhouse, you could at least walk the street without women spitting at you, or turning away when they see you coming."

"I faced some of that when I worked for Ewell Rankin," Rachel said, remembering. "Many people had the wrong idea about my duties there. And now that I think about it, maybe they weren't too far wrong. I think I was just more naive back then."

"You think you've changed that much?"

"My eyes are wide open, at least."

"Honey, there's still a difference. There, at least you could put up a front of being a proper lady. Running a house, you can't do that. You would be the madam of a whorehouse and everyone would know it. You prepared to face that?"

"Yes," Rachel said resolutely. "I'm prepared to face that."

"Why? You mind telling me?"

Rachel looked over at her son in Bright Fawn's arms. "Because of him, because of my son. I made a promise to his father, over his grave, that Will would grow up with more advantages than his father ever had. That will take money, and this seems to be the only way I can earn it. There's nothing else open for me. I'm determined to do what I have to do."

"No matter what others may think of you?" Rose

said. "You may not lay on your back along with your girls, but folks will think you do."

"I don't care what others think," Rachel retorted. "I've seen a few examples of the ways of the 'good' people. Let them think what they will."

"What about men?"

"What about men? I told you, I won't be selling myself, so what will I have to do with men?"

"You may not sell yourself, hon, but operating a whorehouse is going to reduce your chances of finding a good man to marry almost to zero. Why do you think I'm jumping at my chance? I'm thirty-two years old, and this is the only proposal I've received since I became a whore."

"I have no desire to get married," Rachel said firmly. "Nor do I wish to enter into a relationship with another man. I've known two, one good man and one bad man. I was hurt both times. It was not the good man's fault that I was hurt, but I was hurt all the same."

Rose's laughter was harsh. "Hon, broken hearts can be mended. Take my word for it. I've had my heart broken any number of times. It's always mended."

"That's as may be, but I'm not going to pass up this opportunity to make money. Now, how much will it cost me?"

The buckboard driver came back just then. He had taken Rose's luggage to the baggage car, and was now carrying Rachel's trunk. He put it in the back of the buckboard and looked inquiringly at her.

Rachel said to Rose, "How much?"

"You can probably get started for about a thousand dollars. Do you have that much?"

"Yes," Rachel said simply.

Rose gave a startled look, then she shrugged. She had a watch hanging from a chain on her bodice. She opened it. "I have about an hour before my train leaves. I left my tent in the hands of someone to sell for me, but I'll let you have it for five hundred, if that's all right with you?" At Rachel's quick nod, she continued, "Good! Then I'll ride back with you, and advise you how to set up." She climbed into the buckboard and patted the seat beside her for Rachel. Then she beckoned to Becky and Judy. "Girls, you and the Indian climb in. It looks like you ladies aren't going to be out on your tails after all."

"Oh, Rachel!" Becky clapped her hands enthusiastically. "Oh, you have no idea how happy this makes me!"

"Well, let's just hope it works out," Rachel said. "After all, this is new to me."

"There's nothing new about it, hon," Rose said matter-of-factly. "It's the oldest profession in the world."

At about the time Rachel was riding through the alkali streets of Benton, two men whose lives had crossed with hers in the past were preparing to meet each other in the back room of the Fort Sherman Officers' Club, in Cheyenne, Wyoming.

One of the men was relatively short, somewhat stocky, with reddish brown hair and a full beard. In June and July of 1863, he and Rachel had both been at Vicksburg, Mississippi. Rachel had been inside the beleaguered city, dodging cannonballs and bursting shells, and trying to find something to eat. The man had been outside the city, directing the firing of those same cannonballs and shells which were making Rachel's life so difficult.

Then, he had been a general in the U. S. Army. Now, he was a candidate for the presidency of the United States, and most people agreed that he would probably win. His name was Ulysses S. Grant.

The other man whose past had crossed Rachel's —more recently—was a tall, handsome, slender man with blond hair and searching blue eyes. He, like the general, had an interesting and varied past. He had lived with the Indians, had been a fur trapper, a wagon-train guide, a scout for the army, and a buffalo hunter for the Union Pacific Railroad. He was also a United States marshal, now working on a special assignment. His assignment required absolute secrecy—to all who met him, he was nothing more than a buffalo hunter for the UP.

Just before General Grant left Washington on a campaign tour through the West, he had been summoned to the White House for a conference with President Andrew Johnson. President Johnson had beaten down the impeachment proceeding in May, surviving by a count of thirty-five to nineteen, one less than the vote needed for conviction. President Johnson had not been nominated to run for reelection, and was interested now in an orderly transfer of power to his successor. His own party had nominated Horatio Seymour, but Johnson knew that Grant would probably be the next president, and it was to Grant that he entrusted the secret of Hawkeye Smith's mission.

Hawkeye Smith, Johnson had told Grant, was the advance man for a network of marshals and secret agents in the investigation of crooked manipulations and corruption in the building of the railroad. President Johnson had asked Grant to meet with Smith when he got to Wyoming, and General Grant had agreed.

When Hawkeye stepped through the door of the Officers' Club, he saw General Grant standing near the window at the rear of the room, looking out over the Wyoming landscape. Hawkeye was surprised at how short the general was. He was a hero of the first magnitude, a man whose name was immediately recognizable, yet he was surprisingly small of stature.

"General?" Hawkeye said tentatively.

Grant turned around and smiled; and when he did, there was a complete change in the man. Instead of seeming small and rather insignificant, he took on an aura which was larger than life. One did not notice his short stature then, for he seemed easily six feet tall.

"Mr. Smith!" Grant said, with obvious pleasure. He waved his hand. "Sit down, Mr. Smith. It's Hawkeye, I believe?"

"That's what I'm called." He laughed easily, taking the chair offered.

Grant sat across from him. "Andy Johnson tells me that you're onto something out here?"

"Yes, sir."

"What exactly have you found out?"

"To begin with, General, there is a lot more money being spent than there is railroad being built."

"That's often the case," Grant said with a wry grimace. He took a cigar case from his pocket and held it out to Hawkeye, who took one. Both men fired their cigars. Grant leaned back. "All right, Hawkeye, give me some details."

"The train wreck at Eddison Gulch was a prime example. The UP paid for a trestle strong enough to be more than adequate. They got one that was weak, below standard."

"I recall that," Grant said gravely. "A tragic thing. But it seems I also recall some fellow killing himself and taking the blame for that."

"Maybe."

"What do you mean, maybe?"

"General, quite simply, I am not authorized to investigate such an incident, although I would dearly love to do so. In my judgment, I would say that Parker did *not* kill himself. He was involved, sure. After all, he drew up the plans for the trestle. But I think others were in on it, and they killed him, then set it up to make it look like he killed himself, taking the blame on his shoulders."

"I see," Grant said slowly. "But just who are these others?"

Hawkeye sighed. "I don't know. I get close to them and they slip away, like quicksilver."

"Andy seems to think that some congressmen may be up to their hocks in this mess. Do you think that's possible?"

"I don't know, General. Steve King could probably tell you more about that. I'm working from this end. I can tell you about one rather strange thing I have discovered."

"What would that be?"

"It would appear that there's a double graft going on here."

"A double graft?" Grant leaned forward, blowing smoke. "Can you explain that?"

"Sir, I think that the construction company is cheating the railroad, and that someone *within* the construction company is cheating the construction company in turn. No honor among thieves, as it were."

"I see." General Grant ground out his cigar. "Hawkeye, I have to tell you that some of my top advisors—Schuyler Colfax, who is running for vice-president on my ticket, for one, and Congressman Ames, for another—are telling me that I should not encumber the grand destiny of the railroad in any way."

"What exactly does that mean, sir?"

"The way it's told to me, the important thing is that the railroad be completed. It doesn't matter if it costs two times or even three times the original estimates. The end result will be of such benefit to the country that we can afford to turn a blind eye to a little graft."

"I see." Hawkeye studied Grant closely. "So what do you intend to do, General?"

"If I am elected president, you mean?"

"Yes, sir."

Grant smiled broadly, and tugged at his whiskers.

"I will command you to keep up the good work, sir."

The general got to his feet, and held out his hand. Hawkeye took it, and they shook.

"Of course, Horatio Seymour may be the next president," Grant said with a sly grin. "In which case, it won't matter a damn what I say or think, anyway."

"General Grant, Seymour will be president of these United States when the buffalo fly!"

General Grant laughed uproariously, slapping his knee. "Mr. Hawkeye Smith, I like your style, sir. Are you sure you wouldn't like to quit what you're doing now and come campaign with me? I could use you, and if I'm elected I could find a place for you in my administration."

"Thank you very much, sir, but I'm happy where I am. Maybe not too happy with what I'm doing, but I could never live and work in Washington City."

"I dare say, Hawkeye, I dare say." Grant got a faraway look in his eyes. "There's something to be said for a man who can see a clear objective and commits himself to that goal. It's like a military operation." He stepped to the table and drew on it with his fingers, as if illustrating a point. "You see a critical railroad junction here, and it is held by the enemy. Your task is to take that critical railroad junction. Ah, well! If only national politics could be so simply illustrated."

"You will do well, sir. Of that I have no doubt."

"And you, Mr. Smith. You will serve your country well, too. Of that, *I* have no doubt, sir."

CHAPTER TWENTY-ONE

As Rachel listened to the receding whistle of the eastbound train, she began to wonder if she might not have made a mistake. Rose Foster was on that train headed for St. Louis, with five hundred dollars of Rachel's money in her reticule. Rachel now had less than a thousand dollars left to pay for the additional expenses that would be necessary in setting up her establishment.

"Well, Rachel," Becky said, "what do you think?"

Becky swept her arm around in a grand gesture, taking in the structure which had been Rose's bordello. It was gloomy inside. Although it had a wooden floor, the walls and ceiling were of canvas. Even the rooms in back where the girls worked were little more than areas partitioned off with canvas, holding narrow beds and wash basins.

"I don't know," Rachel said heavily. "It isn't the most imposing place I've ever seen."

"You should see how the girls without houses work," Judy said. "Usually they don't have anything more than a large cardboard box to serve their customers." She shuddered. "No ma'am, Miss Rachel, I'll take this place any time."

Jason, the bartender Rachel had hired, brought her a glass of wine. She accepted it, nodding her thanks. She had not tasted wine since her days at the Roundhouse. She thought of the Roundhouse as she took a sip of the wine.

"Um-mm, you know what I'd really like," she said musingly. "I'd like a place like the Roundhouse."

Becky laughed. "Who wouldn't? But you'd have to be filthy rich to have something like that."

"What is this Roundhouse people keep talking about?" Judy wanted to know.

"It was a grand, elegant restaurant and hotel," Becky said expansively. "We had a kitchen serving the best meals this side of Chicago. I don't know how many folks told me that. We had grand rooms upstairs for the guests." Becky signed pensively. "And once Rachel even got a first-class show out from back east."

Judy asked, "How many girls did it have?"

"No girls." Becky laughed. "It wasn't that kind of a place!"

"It should have been, seems to me," Judy said. "With a place like that, why, you could have made a million!"

"Yes, Judy," Rachel said. "A place like the Roundhouse could have made a million dollars with girls. But this place can be made to pay. I intend to see that it does."

"But this place ain't nothing like that," Judy said

scornfully. "It's just a tent, nothing elegant about it."

"But it could be made elegant," Rachel said thoughtfully, raising one hand to rest her chin on it. "And I'm going to make it into an elegant place."

"But Rachel, have you got that much money?" Becky asked in an awed voice.

"I don't know, since I don't know how much it might cost me."

"I'd figure it would cost you around fifteen hundred," said a man's voice behind them. "And likely another fifteen hundred for the kind of furnishings you'd need."

Rachel spun around at the sound of the strange voice. A man stood just inside the doorway. He was tall and swarthy, with a thin moustache above a mouth set in a bemused smile; his dark brown eyes shone gold in the reflection of the scattered lanterns. He wore a black jacket that hung open and a black string tie. His hat was flat and wide-brimmed, unlike the high-crowned hats most of the men wore. He had a pistol holstered on his hip, and Rachel noticed that the long jacket was arranged in such a way as to allow him quick access to his gun.

"Who are you, sir?" Rachel demanded. "And why should our discussion be any of your affair?"

"My name is David Spencer," the man drawled. He came toward her. "And I suppose you're right, ma'am. Your discussion is none of my affair, Mrs. Simmons. I just thought I'd provide an answer to your question. I'm sorry if you took offense."

Pausing before her, David Spencer touched the brim of his hat. It appeared to be nothing more than a courtly gesture, yet it seemed to Rachel that there was a touch of mockery about it. In fact, his whole manner seemed mocking, as if he were privy to some joke on the whole world, but was keeping it to himself.

"How do you happen to know my name?" she demanded.

"I've admired you in the past, always from a distance, of course. But when Rose told me you'd taken over her old place, why, I just naturally had to come and pay my respects."

"Did Rose also tell you that I would be managing it only?" she asked tartly.

"Oh, I wouldn't be getting any wrong ideas," David said easily.

"Is what you said true? Would it take another three thousand to make this a really nice place?"

"Only an estimate, of course. But it's not far off the mark, you can be sure. Do you have that kind of money?"

"No," Rachel said honestly, swallowing her dismay. She turned away from his probing gaze, taking another sip of wine. "No, I don't have anything near that kind of money."

"Well," Becky said with a sigh. "It was a nice idea."

"Yes, it was," Judy said. "I would have really enjoyed working in such an elegant place."

"Why don't you go to a bank?" David suggested. Without asking permission, he walked over to the plank bar and poured himself a whiskey.

"Yes, why don't I?" Rachel said sarcastically. "I

can just see myself going into a bank and asking to borrow money for a brothel!"

David took a swallow of his whiskey, then wiped his mouth with the back of his hand. His hands, Rachel noted idly, were long and thin and graceful looking. She had never seen hands quite like those on a man.

"Your brothel will make money, won't it?" David asked.

"I certainly intend for it to do so. Money is the only reason I'm going into the business."

"Money is the only reason bankers are into the banking business," David said. "They don't care *how* you earn the money. They only care *if* you earn the money to repay the loan. They want a return on their investment, that's all."

Rachel stared at him. "You're serious, aren't you? But even if you're right, I don't even know a banker."

"I know a banker!" Becky suddenly said. "I'll bet you know him too, Rachel. He used to come in the Roundhouse all the time. His name is Hamilton Baker."

"Yes," Rachel said. "Yes, I seem to remember somebody like that. But I have no idea where his bank is."

"It's in Cheyenne," David said, strolling over to the piano. He sat down on the stool. "It's called the Cheyenne Savings and Trust."

Without preamble David began playing the piano, and Rachel was astounded, not so much that he could play as by the kind of music. It was beautiful music, and it spilled out in a steady, unwavering beat with two or three poignant minor chords at the end of the phrases, while the melody moved in and out of the chords like a thread of gold woven into the finest cloth.

The piano was old and battered, and the tune dim and dreary, yet the music lured everyone out to listen to it. The other four girls, who had returned to their canvas cubicles shortly after being introduced to their new madam, came out now to listen. Even Bright Fawn, who had just put Will to bed, came over to listen.

Rachel had never heard music that moved her so, and for the few minutes that he played she felt transported to the finest theater in New York or London. Finally David stopped, took another swallow of his drink, then looked up at his audience as if surprised and somewhat embarrassed to find them there.

"I'm sorry," he said. "I didn't mean to cause a disturbance."

"A disturbance!" Rachel exclaimed. "You don't call that a disturbance, do you? I think it's the most beautiful thing I've ever heard!"

"Thank you," David said. "I haven't had an opportunity to play the piano much of late."

"Would you play for me? Here, I mean? I think it would be wonderful to have someone who plays that well in La Belle Femme Inn. I'd like to hire you as my piano player."

"La Belle Femme Inn?" David said quizzically.

Rachel smiled radiantly. "That's what I'm going to name this place after I get it fixed up. La Belle

Femme Inn! And I'm going to rebuild it as soon as I come back from Cheyenne with the necessary money!"

Rachel had the construction figures all worked out, and they were in her reticule as she stood nervously in the foyer of the Cheyenne Savings and Trust Bank, just before closing time, waiting to speak to Hamilton Baker. She had made her wishes known to a clerk, who now held a whispered conversation in the back of the room. Rachel was aware that all of the men in the bank were glaring at this upstart female who had dared to invade their domain, and she tried not to return their stares or to show embarrassment over being the center of their attention.

Finally the clerk returned. He said sternly, "You may see Mr. Baker now. But please be brief. The bank closes shortly."

"Thank you," Rachel said. "I intend to be as brief as possible."

Hamilton Baker was a portly man, with a thick, curving moustache hanging over drooping jowls. He stood as Rachel approached his desk, walked around it, and held a chair for her to be seated.

"Now, Mrs. Simmons, how may I be of service to you?" he asked, after resuming his seat.

"Mr. Baker, I recall seeing you in the Roundhouse a few times," she said winningly.

Hamilton Baker smiled and stroked his moustache. "Well, now. I wouldn't have thought that a pretty woman like you would have taken notice of someone like me. But yes, I was a guest there a few times."

"Then you are aware of the sort of establishment that it was. It was very nearly a private club, catering to wealthy and cultured people."

"Yes, I remember," Baker agreed.

"I have in mind, Mr. Baker, the construction of a building which will be remarkably similar to the Roundhouse. I will manage it."

Baker leaned back in his chair, and it creaked under his weight. "Where is this building to be?"

"In Benton."

"You surely can't be serious, Mrs. Simmons! You are no doubt aware that the Roundhouse is no longer in business, anywhere."

"I know that, sir. That's one reason I'm building my establishment."

"No, you don't seem to understand. The Roundhouse is no longer in business because it can no longer earn its way. The railroad is enough of a reality now that it has built its own momentum. It is no longer necessary to have an establishment like the Roundhouse to provide entertainment and comfortable lodgings for investors from the East."

Rachel coughed nervously, squirming a little in her seat. "Mr. Baker, it's you who don't understand. I won't be catering to investors from the East, although they would certainly be welcomed."

"Then I take it you hope to draw your customers from the people who are here with the railroad?"

"That's my hope, yes."

"What causes you to believe that a man would

spend his hard-earned money in a place like the Roundhouse?"

"That's not exactly what I think. That's why La Belle Femme Inn is going to be slightly different from the Roundhouse."

"How is it going to be different? The Roundhouse, La Belle Femme Inn, I fail to see . . ." He stopped in mid-sentence, sparse eyebrows rising. "La Belle Femme? Doesn't that mean the Pretty Woman?"

Rachel was smiling. "Yes."

Baker cleared his throat and looked away, suddenly uncomfortable. "Mrs. Simmons, are you by any chance talking of a sporting house?"

"I prefer to call it what it is, Mr. Baker, a brothel." She took a sheet of paper from her reticule and placed it on his desk. "On the left side, Mr. Baker, you see a list of the estimated costs. On the right-hand side, you see a projection of the profits I expect to earn. On comparing the two totals, you can see that it will be exceptionally profitable."

Baker scanned the figures with a practiced eye, then looked across the desk at Rachel in speculation. "Tell me, Mrs. Simmons . . . have you had experience at this sort of thing?"

"No."

"I thought as much. What makes you think you can run an establishment of this sort at a profit?"

"I ran the Roundhouse, and well," she said stoutly. "I imagine there will be little difference in the actual operation of the two. I believe in myself, sir, and I know that I can do it."

Baker began to smile, shaking his head. He looked at the figures again. "Forty-five hundred dollars? Is that what you require, Mrs. Simmons?"

"No. I've invested fifteen hundred of my own money, all I have. I need three thousand." Her heart was beating fast and she could scarcely believe her good fortune, afraid that the man was toying with her, leading her on only to refuse to grant the loan at the last minute.

But Hamilton Baker was taking a loan form from a pigeonhole in his desk and filling it out. He asked, "Are you going to serve food at La Belle Femme Inn?"

"Absolutely. In fact, I intend it to be the finest eating establishment around."

"Good. That means I can call it a restaurant on the loan application. No." He threw back his head and laughed. "I'll call it a supper club. That's becoming a popular thing back east, I understand, and should make a favorable impression on our board. They'll think it intelligent of me to be investing money in a supper club!"

"I wish to thank you, Mr. Baker," Rachel said fervently. "You won't be sorry, I promise you."

Baker shoved the paper across for her to sign, and smiled warmly at her. "You know, Mrs. Simmons, I don't think I will be sorry, either. I believe I may just be making a most sound business investment."

As she signed the loan form, Rachel recalled David Spencer's remark about banks, and smiled to herself. A few moments later she marched up to the clerk's window with the bank draft for three thousand dollars. When she left the bank, she could feel the added weight of the money in her reticule, and it was a good feeling—no, a grand and glorious feeling! She felt like twirling around and around on the board sidewalk, doing a little dance of delight.

"Well, Mrs. Simmons, how nice to see you again!"

She stopped to peer in the direction of the voice. It took her a moment to recognize Hawkeye Smith, since he was dressed in a dark suit and flowing tie; he looked quite different without the mangy buffalo robe.

He went on, "I take it you *are* Mrs. Simmons. At one time you had me believing that you were Mrs. Bonner."

"I remember," Rachel said diffidently. "I am sorry about that. I'm afraid I was playing a little game with you, Mr. Smith."

"Forget it," Hawkeye said with a shrug. He fell in beside her. "May I walk along with you?" She nodded assent, and they strolled leisurely along the plank walk. "What are you doing in Cheyenne, Mrs. Simmons? I recall hearing that you and Will Simmons were farming somewhere back in Nebraska."

"You haven't heard? Will was killed about two months ago."

"No, I hadn't heard," he said soberly. "How did it happen?"

"He was murdered. Two men rode up to our house in the middle of the night and shot him down."

"No idea as to who they were?"

"No. Nor their reason. They didn't steal anything. They gunned him down and rode off."

"I'm terribly sorry for your trouble, Rachel. I didn't know Will that well, but I knew that he was a good man. And I must admit that I was happy when I heard that you'd left Ewell Rankin to marry Will."

Rachel looked over at him. "I wasn't aware that I needed your approval as to the company I keep."

"No, no, I didn't mean that." His face took on a darker hue. "I was just—oh, hell, I don't know what I was doing!"

She smiled suddenly and reached out to touch his arm. "I am sorry. I shouldn't be so touchy. Tell me," she went on briskly, "are you still hunting buffalo for the railroad?"

"Oh, yes." He looked at her somewhat shyly. "I guess I look and smell a little better than I did the day I first met you."

She had to laugh. "Yes, indeed! You are much more pleasant company than you were then."

"Then am I good enough company for you to have supper with me? I'm due out on the evening train west, but it won't be until late."

It was Rachel's first inclination to refuse. Then she remembered that she was carrying a large sum of money on her person, and this was still rough country for a woman alone. If Hawkeye was journeying to Benton, why not befriend him long enough to travel with him?

"What a nice coincidence, Mr. Smith!" she said gaily. "I am taking the same train. I can't think of a better way to pass the time until then than having supper with you."

Hawkeye smiled with evident pleasure and offered her his arm. Down the block, he escorted her into the Golden Pan Restaurant. The Golden Pan was a pleasant place. It was not ornate, but there were two large windows in the front and they were kept sparkling clean. The result was that even though the afternoon sun was low in the sky to the west, enough light came in through the windows to make the place bright and cheerful.

Hawkeye ordered for them, and as the waitress left for the kitchen, Rachel sighed contentedly. "I still can't get used to such a variety of food to choose from. At Edenland we had to exist on spare rations."

"Edenland?"

"That was the name Will gave to the farm." Rachel laughed quietly, feeling suddenly strangely shy. "He said it was his Garden of Eden."

"How about you, Rachel? Was it *your* Garden of Eden?"

She sighed, and finally said, "No, I must be honest. I never had the same love for it that Will had. I tried, though. I really did try."

"Tell me again about Will's death."

Tersely, she told him about Will's murder. By the time she was finished, her eyes were wet with tears.

Hawkeye waited until she got herself under control, and asked, "You have no idea why two men would just ride up in the night and shotgun Will for no apparent reason?"

"No, I don't. The senselessness of his death made it even harder to bear." She smiled suddenly. "But there is something that has helped me bear up. I was pregnant when Will died, Hawkeye. I have his son now."

"A son, huh? How about that?" Hawkeye smiled widely. "Tell me about him."

"He was . . . he was born on the same night Will was killed." She went on to explain how an Indian girl had found her unconscious and about to give birth. "Bright Fawn is a wonderful person. I don't know what I would have done. I would surely be dead, both me and the baby."

Hawkeye frowned. "Bright Fawn? The daughter of Mean-to-His-Horses?"

"Yes?"

"If Bright Fawn has accepted you, then you're blessed with a true friend for life."

"You speak as if you know her."

"Yes, I know her. And I knew her father and mother, too. I never got a chance to know her brother. The soldiers killed him before he got a chance to grow up," Hawkeye said grimly. "I thought Bright Fawn had been killed, along with Mean-to-His-Horses. I'm glad to hear she's alive."

"I haven't told anyone but you that she's the daughter of Mean-to-His-Horses."

"You're wise not to."

"You say her brother was killed by the soldiers? She's never spoken of him. How old was he?"

"Around six months old."

"Six months! Dear God, why would the soldiers kill a mere baby?"

"Why would they kill his mother?" Hawkeye said bitterly. "They were both Indians, that's the only reason they needed."

"How terrible," Rachel said, stricken. "Bright Fawn loves little Will so. It must be dreadful for her to be around him and have to think about her own little brother being killed. She has every right to be bitter and vindictive, but she isn't like that, Hawkeye. She isn't like that at all. You would think she'd hate all white people. Don't Indians hate?"

Hawkeye laughed softly. "Oh, Indians are very good at hating their enemies. But hate to an Indian is like love. It isn't spread around indiscriminately. They are an honorable people. They love with honor, and they hate with honor. The pony soldiers responsible for killing her mother and brother are dead. Mean-to-His-Horses killed them. When they died, Bright Fawn's hate died with them."

"But what about the ones who killed her father?"

"That was different. Her father was a warrior, and he was killed in battle. His death was painful to Bright Fawn, but it was honorable. She can accept that."

"You seem to know a lot about Indians."

"I do. I lived with them."

"Well, I'm glad we had this talk. You've shed some light on Bright Fawn, and it helps me to understand her better, and to appreciate her more."

Their meal was brought then, and this provided a means to change the conversation. They went easily on to other lighter subjects. By the time their supper was finished and they walked down to the depot to wait for the train, Rachel was laughing at Hawkeye's dry wit.

Cheyenne still had not become jaded by the arrival of trains, and a goodly crowd was gathered at the station. Several people were clustered around a buckboard, listening to an itinerant preacher delivering a fiery sermon. The man was of average height and build, with a full head of thick, black hair. Standing up in the buckboard, he jabbed his finger repeatedly at the crowd as he spoke to them.

"And here's another reason why there shouldn't be no trains," he was saying. "It's been proved back east that them heavy trains shakes the ground so fierce that the hogs is kept too nervous to eat. They don't fatten up none, and lots of folks is having to go without pig meat, which ever' one knows is a heap healthier for a body than just about any other kind of meat there is.

"Also, the live steam from the engines wilts the grass and spoils the pasture, and the horses and cows don't eat, and there goes your beef! And as if it warn't bad enough for the train to kill pigs, cows, and horses, why, it'll even kill little children what gets onto the tracks! And yep, old folks who are going to church in their buggy!"

He wagged his finger. "And hear this now! Them steel rails lying out there on the ground draws lightning better'n a dog's tail, and ever' one knows to stay away from dogs during a lightning storm. Now, what do you think all that electricity around loose in the ground'll do to you? It'll make you sturl, that's what.

"You all knows what *sturl* means? It means the men folks will all be turned into geldings, and there won't be no more children being born. And that means the end of the human race. I tell you, good people, what you're seeing here ain't nothing more'n the Antichrist come to us in the form of a fire-breathing steel monster. Turn your efforts away from railroading now, and looked to more Godly pursuits."

Hawkeye and Rachel laughed at the fulminating preacher, as did most of the crowd, but it did not deter him in the least. He went on preaching against the railroad and passing a hat around.

The train arrived a few minutes later, pounding into the station in its haughty, snorting majesty, and Hawkeye and Rachel got on board.

It always seemed like another world to Rachel whenever she boarded a train. Although she was just a few feet from the people on the platform, she felt as if she were miles away. Compared to the noisy crowd around the station, it was very quiet on the train, and she and Hawkeye walked down the aisle looking for a seat.

There were about a dozen passengers in the car, and some were sleeping. A few awakened just enough to make certain that this was not their destination and then slipped back into sleep again.

"How about right here?" Hawkeye suggested. "Two seats facing each other. With a little ingenuity, we should both be able to catch a few winks."

"Good," Rachel said. "I must confess to being weary."

Hawkeye adjusted the seat for Rachel's comfort, then sat down opposite her, and by the time the train pulled out she had already closed her eyes.

Rachel dreamed. In her dream, she recalled the

pleasures evoked by Ewell Rankin's skilled caresses, his manipulation of her senses, and yet those pleasant sensations were accompanied by a sense of warmth and sharing such as she had never known with Ewell. It was if somehow the good qualities of Will Simmons were united with the love-making techniques of Ewell Rankin.

During the dream, Rachel was kissed as she had never been kissed before. Her dream lover's lips opened on hers and his tongue wedged into her mouth. It was shocking and thrilling at the same time, and involuntarily a moan of passion escaped her. Her blood ran hot, and her body was warmed by a heat such as she had never before experienced. The kiss went on and on, longer than she had ever imagined such a thing could last, and her head grew so light that she abandoned all thought save this pleasure.

Suddenly she realized that she was awake! This was no dream lover—this was Hawkeye Smith!

Rachel stared at him, her eyes wide open, her senses reeling. Finally sanity returned, and she realized what was happening. He had moved over to her seat while she was asleep, and he had kissed her. Somehow the reality had become mixed with her dream, and she had returned his kiss willingly—no, eagerly!

Her cheeks blazed with embarrassment, and she felt a rush of anger. "What do you think you're doing?"

He said artlessly, "Just kissing you goodbye, Rachel. I have to get off here."

"Get off here?" Bewildered, she sat up, her anger forgotten. "What on earth are you talking about? We are out in the middle of nowhere! The train doesn't stop here."

"I don't need it to stop. Besides, it has to slow along here. Some repair work on the track is being done. Can't you feel it slowing?" He reached up to the overhead rack for his rifle and handbag that he had brought on board.

"Hawkeye, you can't jump off the train in the middle of the night. You'll kill yourself!"

"You wouldn't be worrying about me now, would you?" he said amusedly.

Rachel thought of the bold way she had just been awakened, and her anger burned again. "No," she said coldly. "Not in the least. If you want to break your neck, then it is certainly no concern of mine."

"Aw, and here I was thinking you cared," he said with a poker face. "And after I went to the trouble of giving you a goodbye kiss."

"I didn't ask you to kiss me goodbye. I didn't even *want* you to kiss me goodbye!"

"Shh," he said, grinning. "You'll wake everyone in the car."

"Oh!" she said through gritted teeth. "You are impossible!"

He winked at her, turned away, and stepped through the front door of the car. She could see him standing on the platform for a moment, and then he was gone. She glanced quickly out the window and saw him rolling along the ground beside the track; and then, straining to see back along the right-of-way, she finally saw him get to his feet. He waved at her. She felt a sense of relief that he was safe.

It took her a long time to get back to sleep, and when she did, Hawkeye Smith returned to disturb her dreams.

CHAPTER TWENTY-TWO

Shortly after returning from Cheyenne, Rachel took her son down to the railroad car on the side-track to visit Aunt Mildred, hoping that Julius Deever would not be there. To her relief, her uncle was not at home.

But Mildred Deever looked terrible. She looked so bad that Rachel felt a rush of guilt for leaving her. Her aunt had lost a great deal of weight, and her eyes darted about her nervously, as if she had to be on a constant alert for some threat to her welfare. Rachel's visit did seem to cheer her up, and when she saw the baby, Mildred Deever smiled more happily than at any time Rachel could recall.

"Oh, Rachel!" her aunt said, taking the baby into her lap. Wouldn't your father have loved to see his grandson! He's so beautiful!"

Rachel said, "He's a good baby, too. Well-behaved, hardly ever cries, or . . ."

There was a sound of footsteps in the doorway, and Julius Deever barged in. Face red, he leveled an accusing finger at Rachel. "Slut! Whore!"

Mildred blanched. "Why, Julius! Such language! What has come over you?"

The finger still pointed at Rachel. "Mildred, do you know what your fine niece is doing? Do you know what kind of business she is in?"

"No, we haven't talked about that. She was just showing me her baby."

"She is a whore!" Deever trumpeted.

"That's a slight exaggeration, Uncle Julius," Rachel said, struggling to keep her temper.

"Is it?" He sneered. "Not if what I just heard is true. I've heard you're building that whorehouse on Ames Street. Did I hear right?"

"Yes, I'm the owner of La Belle Femme Inn, that much is true."

"What is La Belle Femme Inn?" her aunt asked, bewildered.

Deever's sneer was triumphant. "Tell her, if you dare. Tell your aunt what La Belle Femme Inn is."

"Yes, Rachel, what is it? What is Julius talking about?"

Rachel had not taken her gaze from Deever. "No matter what you've heard, I'm not what you say I am."

"It's a whorehouse, isn't it?" Deever demanded. "Either it's a whorehouse or it isn't."

Rachel sighed. In a low voice she said, "Yes, it's a brothel."

"That, my dear Mildred, is just a fancy name for a whorehouse! So what do you think of your fine niece now?"

Mildred Deever trembled with shock. "Rachel! No, I can't believe it!"

"I own the place, true, Aunt Mildred. But I have no intention of prostituting myself," Rachel said steadily. "I have a son now, and I intend to bring him up right—"

"Stop it!" Her aunt's eyes filled with tears. "To think that only a moment ago I was lamenting the fact that your father wasn't here to see his grandson. Praise the Lord he isn't here to see what has happened to his daughter! He would perish with shame!"

Rachel's thoughts went back to Rose Foster, and the warning the former madam had given her about what to expect from people. Knowing that it was futile, Rachel tried to argue her case anyway. "Aunt Mildred, I don't think you're being fair to me. The way I see it, there's little difference from what I'm doing now, and my duties at the Roundhouse. The only difference is, the money coming in will be mine, instead of going into Ewell Rankin's pocket!"

"I'll hear nothing against Mr. Rankin, if you please," Deever said pompously. "Ewell is a good friend, and I had a difficult time of it when you walked out on him for no reason. You embarrassed me, Rachel."

"Don't bother to defend Ewell Rankin to me, Uncle. I know what kind of a man he is!"

"Rachel, it would seem that you're only trying to keep us from thinking bad of you by attacking Mr. Rankin," her aunt said angrily. She stood up and gave the baby to Rachel. "Now take your child and leave this house!"

"Aunt Mildred, if you'll only listen—"

"No, I won't listen!" Mildred was crying openly.

"Just leave, and never come back until you have cleansed your soul of this—this life of sin you have fallen into."

"And to think," Deever said self-righteously, "that we took you to our bosom, raised you as our own daughter, and you shame us like this."

Rachel recalled watching Julius Deever consorting with the whore back in Connersville, and she said coldly, "I guess I will return to my whorehouse. At least I'm not being a hypocrite about it."

Deever's face flushed, and he assumed a wary look. In a faltering voice he said, "What do you mean?"

"You know very well what I mean, Uncle," she said, and turned to leave. Over her shoulder she said, "Neither of you has to be concerned. You won't see me again."

La Belle Femme Inn was opened three weeks later. It did not look anything like the Roundhouse from the outside. The Roundhouse had resembled a large, ornate hotel. La Belle Femme Inn looked like the residence of a wealthy railroad magnate, and that was just the impression Rachel had hoped to create. It was situated at the extreme end of Ames Street, quite a distance from the nearest saloon, and on the edge of the part of town that was laid out to become the residential district.

There was no sign, nothing to indicate what it was. Inside, everything had been directed toward good taste. And yet, despite all of Rachel's efforts to downplay the place, everyone in End of the Track knew the main business of La Belle Femme Inn.

Rachel had a more difficult time adjusting to everyone's reaction to her new profession than she had ever dreamed she would. People who had befriended her before now shunned her. At first she thought she was imagining things, but as time went on, it became more and more evident. Rose Foster had been correct!

Rachel spoke to David Spencer about it on the night La Belle Femme was due to open.

"I don't know, David," she said. "I'm afraid I may have made a big mistake."

She was leaning on the piano. She had not been able to afford a new piano, but the old one had been repaired, retuned, and polished until it looked new. But as pretty as the piano or the parlor of La Belle Femme Inn looked, nothing could rival Rachel's beauty. She was dressed in a gown of light green silk, pinched in at the waist and flaring out in many tiers below. The bodice was delicately worked in lace and embroidered roses, with one bright red bud strategically located to shield the cleavage that the dress displayed to an immodest degree.

David was well dressed in his own right. He was handsome in a ruffled shirt and a black velvet tie beneath his elegant black jacket. And tonight, as always, his pistol was prominently displayed. Somehow, the constant sight of that pistol seemed inconsistent on a man who could play the piano so beautifully. Rachel had never questioned David closely about his past, and his background was an enigma to her.

David glanced up at her and smiled. He was playing softly, moving gently to the rhythm of his music.

"You mean you believe yourself incapable of absorbing the ostracism that has developed? I hadn't thought that would bother you, Rachel."

"That doesn't bother me," she said. "I have little respect for them. Why should they respect me?"

David laughed. "That's my girl! Cynical to the end. But tell me then, why do you think you may have made a big mistake?"

"Because if everyone feels the way they seem to feel about me, they won't show up tonight. And David, if I don't get any customers, I'll lose everything!"

David shook his head, teeth gleaming in a smile. "Ah, now that's the Rachel I've come to know and love. She's driven by the one true god of man—avarice!"

"David, how you do carry on," Rachel said, laughing despite herself. "But don't you think I have a right to be worried?"

"A right perhaps," he responded. "But no need, no reason. You shall be trampled by customers tonight, mark my words."

"What makes you think so?"

"Because, my innocent Rachel, there are two other gods, lust and hypocrisy, only slightly less powerful than avarice. You will have customers aplenty, you may rely on that."

"I hope you're right." She shook her head in wonder. "I'm not even certain that I know what you're talking about half the time. But I do hope you're right."

David Spencer was right. La Belle Femme Inn was stormed with customers. Many of the men were the same ones who, on the streets, had looked the other way whenever she approached. Rachel wanted to laugh in their faces as they shuffled up to her table, desire overcoming their embarrassment, to purchase one of the brass checks that entitled them to the services of one of Rachel's girls. She had increased the original number of girls to ten.

Rachel had ordered the brass checks from Denver. They were about the size of a silver dollar, and they were quite attractive coins. One side was struck with a railroad worker laying track, while the reverse was struck with the head of a young girl and the words *La Belle Femme Inn.* This system prevented any of the customers from cheating the girls, as the girls would accept only the brass checks in payment for their services. In the morning, Rachel would redeem the checks from the girls.

On opening night, La Belle Femme Inn took in over four hundred dollars. By one A.M. when the last customer, other than the ten who were spending the night, had left, Rachel was tired but elated.

"Well, how did you do, Rachel?" David asked, strolling over from the piano.

"Oh, David, you were right!" she said happily. "I never dreamed I could make so much money!"

David smiled lazily. "If you Southern belles had thought of something like this for the Clairbourne County Cotillion, you would have raised a lot more money than you did, I imagine. I know that I certainly would have enjoyed it more."

Thunderstruck, Rachel stared at him in astonishment. "What did you say?"

"I merely commented on the fact that the Clairbourne County Cotillion would have earned a lot more money for the glorious cause of the Confederacy if the Southern belles had provided this service for those of us who were going off to war. I imagine many a poor lad in gray would have gone happier to his Maker with such pleasant memories to carry with him."

"*Who are you?*"

"David Spencer," he said. And then he added, with a shrug, "Hume."

Rachel gasped. "My God! You're Hell-Bent Hume!"

"That was what they called me," he said wryly. "I must confess that I never cared for that title. But I've been David Spencer since the war."

"I thought you were dead! Everyone thought so. They said you were killed in Missouri, somewhere."

"That's a belief I allowed to circulate without dispute." David got up, walked over to the bar and poured himself a drink, then brought it back to the table. "Most of my fellow patriots joined the Clairbourne Rifles, or the Mississippi Militia, or the Vicksburg Brigade. But I couldn't settle for that. I had the conceit that I could carry the war into the North by joining Quantrill's Raiders." He drained his glass with a shudder and went back to the bar for another.

"Quantrill's Murderers," he said with a bitter laugh, as he carried the fresh glass of whiskey back to Rachel's table.

"We heard about Quantrill," she said, remembering. "At first we cheered him on, then stories began to circulate. Nasty stories. Rumors, some said; fact, others insisted. Finally, when we learned that even the Confederate government had disowned Quantrill, he became as much of a villain to us as the Yankees. And because Hell-Bent Hume was from Clairbourne County, you were especially despised."

"I was more than despised," David said. "I was tried in absentia and convicted of treason. My sentence was to be hanged from the neck until dead. So, I never returned."

"But why, David? The war is over now, and there is no such thing as a Confederate government. Any judgment the Confederate courts may have handed down would be invalid now."

"I didn't need any judgment from a Confederate court," he said in a low voice. "I had tried myself, and found myself guilty as hell. Not of treason to the 'noble cause of the Confederacy.'" He raised his glass in a mock toast. "But treason to the human race." He drank. "Do you have any idea how many men I killed during the time I rode with Quantrill?"

"Of course not."

"Neither do I. And that bothers me. Worse, it haunts me every day of my life. I should be able to see each and every one of them, as clearly as if they were standing before me. Not only can't I remember names and faces, I can't even remember the number I killed!" His face was bleak.

Rachel resisted an impulse to reach across the table for his hand. "What happened after the war?"

"I couldn't go back home," he said tonelessly. "I just didn't fit in there anymore. Those who survived would return, positive that their cause, although lost, was at least noble. I could never agree with that viewpoint, and probably would have ended up killing a few, or being killed."

"So what did you do?"

"I rode with Dingus and Frank for a few months. But I soon tired of that. That wasn't the life for me, either."

"Dingus and Frank?"

"His real name is Jesse. Jesse and Frank James. They rode with Quantrill, too. They're cold as ice, especially Jesse. I still felt something . . . guilt, remorse, something. Maybe I couldn't remember the exact number of men I killed, but I still felt sorry that I did it. I wanted to at least hang onto that, and I knew if I continued to ride with the James brothers, I'd lose even that. So I lit out."

"And came out here?"

"Yes."

"But what about your father? I remember the Hume family, and Rosedale Plantation. Have you heard anything about the plantation since the war?"

"No," David said, his expression melancholy now. "If my father is still alive, he probably lost Rosedale to taxes. I'm sure that he converted every liquid asset he had into Confederate bonds."

"It's quite likely. I know my father did."

"I heard that your father was killed in Shiloh."

"Yes."

"I'm sorry. Better that it had been me."

"David!" she said, shocked. "You don't mean that!"

"Yes, I do mean it," he said emphatically. "The death your father suffered at least gave him rest and peace. I died too, you know. But I'm denied the rest and peace."

"Ah, David!" Now she did reach out and touched his hand fleetingly. "Are you a wanted man?"

He gave her a twisted smile. "Probably."

"Wanted for what?"

"Besides murder? Well, let's see, what sins are there? I've robbed and stolen, I've coveted, and I've lied. I had little respect for my father, and I've found it increasingly difficult to differentiate between false gods and the real one. What's left? Oh, yes. Adultery. I've done my share of that as well, Rachel Bonner Simmons."

"You have led an active life. But I am curious about one thing. When did you have time to learn to play the piano so beautifully?"

"Ah, yes, the piano." He held his slim hands out before him, and flexed his supple fingers. "You see these hands? They are the hands of a concert pianist. Had the war not intervened, I would probably be playing in concert halls in the capitals of the world, New York, Boston, London, Paris, Vienna, Rome. I studied with Franz Liszt in Rome. Perhaps I should have stayed there. He asked me to stay and continue studying with him. But no, I was anxious to return home." He gave a bark of laughter. "I got back just in time to go to war. These hands, these fingers, I soon discovered, could draw a gun and pull a trigger much faster than people who have not had the advantages of training with Franz Liszt."

"Oh, David, what a waste!" Rachel said in distress. "Now I can understand your bitterness."

"So now you know all about Hell-Bent Hume." He walked over to take his hat from the piano. Putting it on his head, he turned, his glance coming to rest on her. "Now I suppose you'll be wanting me to move on?"

Rachel was bewildered. "Why should I?"

"Well, you know who I am, what I am. Doesn't that frighten you?"

Rachel was silent for a little, thinking. Then she said slowly, "No, it doesn't frighten me, not in the least." Even as she spoke the words, she wondered just how true they were.

He came back to the table, looking down into her eyes. "There is something else you should know as well."

"What else should I know?"

"I seriously doubt that I can obey all your rules if I remain here."

"I'm not sure I understand, David."

"I've not proven myself capable of following rules of any kind. And if a rule is in the way of something I very much want, then I am likely to ignore it."

"What is it that you want?" Rachel went tense, anticipating his answer.

"I want you, my sweet, dear Rachel."

"I . . . I see." She laughed unconvincingly. "I think I made it clear that I'm not for sale."

He said simply, "I don't want to buy."

"I'm not sure that I like this conversation, David."

She got up and started off toward the stairs which led up to her room. She expected him to pursue it further, but he said nothing more, yet she could feel his eyes on her as she climbed the stairs.

She had never been approached so boldly before, and his proposition frightened her. It frightened her not only because she did not know if she could control him, but also because she was far from certain that she could control her own desires.

But why should she control herself? After all, she was no longer a young girl, fighting to protect her virginity. She was twenty-five years old, she had known two men intimately, and she was a mother. And something whispered to her that David Spencer was capable of arousing the same pleasure in her that Ewell Rankin had awakened.

Halfway up the stairs, she halted. She tried to close her mind and body to the thoughts that were raging through her. All those long months with Will and his inept love-making had left her frustrated and wanting. She had known what it *could* be like, and now she sensed that it could be hers again for the asking.

No, no, her reason said. *No, keep going up the stairs to your room, alone. If you compromise now, you will be compromising for the rest of your life!*

Yes, seize the opportunity! Accept this man. Yes, for all the days and weeks and months of back-breaking labor, and all the nights of raw nerves.

Rachel turned around. David was still standing where she had left him. His hat shadowed his features, but she fancied that she could feel his burning gaze on her, and a flush of heat rolled through her body.

"David?" she called softly.

"Yes, Rachel?"

"I'm going to my room now. If you like, you may come up in ten minutes."

Without waiting for an answer, she ran quickly up the stairs. She already regretted her rashness. Yet every nerve ending in her body tingled with anticipation.

Once inside her room, she turned down the bed and shucked her dress and undergarments. She started to put on a nightgown; then in a gesture of bravado she tossed it casually to one side, and walked to the window to gaze out at the moonlit landscape. A range of ragged mountains soared high in the distance, and their snow-capped peaks glistened in the silvery light of the moon. She studied their distant beauty until she heard the soft knock on the door. She drew a deep breath, as if about to plunge into an icy stream.

"Come in, David."

The door opened and closed, and she stood erect in the spill of moonlight through the window, bold in her nakedness. For the first time since she met him, David was without a coat. But he was still wearing his gun.

"You won't be needing your pistol, David."

He laughed softly. "You're right, of course. Wearing a gun has become so familiar to me that I sometimes forget I have it on my hip." He removed the gunbelt and placed it on the nightstand beside the bed.

Breathless, Rachel went to him, and helped him remove his shirt. Then she leaned into his bare chest, feeling the thick mat of hair on his chest cushion her breasts, as he pulled her close for a kiss. She returned the kiss with a hunger that blazed through her like a raging fever.

Soon they were on the bed together, their naked bodies pressed together. For the first time in over a year Rachel felt the delight of remembered pleasure. David was an artful lover. Those hands and fingers that could coax such beautiful music from the battered piano were also wonderfully capable of evoking exquisite feelings in her. As eager to give as she was to receive, she caressed his lean body boldly.

As their love-making increased in intensity, Rachel imagined that she could hear the music David had played all evening, and as the beautiful melody weaved its seductive way into her mind, so did the wandering of his hands over her body. All too soon she was ready, and she plucked at him with a trembling hand, urging him to her. As he moved over her and she felt his welcome weight against her, Rachel opened herself to him without reservation, and abandoned all thought of anything but the pleasure she was experiencing. She was lifted to dizzying heights of sensation, soaring from peak to peak with such rapidity that it was hard to tell when one was left and another attained. Finally, a shuddering moan of ecstasy was torn from her, and she knew that David had joined her in the maelstrom of sensation. She locked her arms around him and held him close to her as he shuddered in his own pleasure.

Later, with David's pleasant weight still on her, and only their harsh breathing and thumping hearts to tell of the delight they had just experienced, she heard David speak.

"What did you say?"

"I love you, my sweet Rachel. And I want you to know that I have never spoken those words to another woman."

"David, I . . ." she started to say in confusion.

He placed a finger on her lips. "No, don't say anything. I know you're going to tell me you don't love me, and I don't want to hear it."

"Oh, David! Dearest David, I wish that I could tell you that I did love you. With all my heart I wish that I did. But I can't lie to you, I can't tell you that."

"I know." He sighed, then kissed her once, lightly, and moved to stretch out beside her.

"David . . . can't we just accept what there is for now?"

"As long as I can be content with just that. But when the times comes that it isn't enough, and I strongly suspect that time will come, I will leave, without recriminations. Is that fair enough?"

"That's fair enough," she said softly.

Rachel lay quietly beside David, staring into the darkness, long after his measured breathing told her that he was asleep. Why couldn't she fall in love with him? He was a good lover, he was a cultured man, and for all of his lurid past, she was convinced that basically he was a good man. Despite all that, she was certain in her mind that she might become quite fond of him, but she would never love him.

Could she love any man? Perhaps she did not know what true love was.

CHAPTER TWENTY-THREE

Rachel was seething. Although she had been in the general store for several minutes, she had not been served. At first she thought the clerk had made an honest mistake. He had been busy when she came in, and might not have realized that the other customers had come in after her. So she did not get upset when he waited on them. They left, and he began making entries in his ledger, and that did not bother her too much, because it was possible that he might have to make entries while the transactions were still fresh in his mind. Besides, she was the only one in the store now, so he would not make the same mistake again.

But two more people came in, and he looked up from his ledger and smiled at them, then proceeded to wait on them. Once again Rachel had to wait, and this time she knew it was no oversight.

The latest customers left, and Rachel heard another one enter behind her.

"May I help you, sir?" the clerk said with a bright smile, looking past Rachel as if she did not exist.

"I believe the lady was here first," a familiar voice said.

"Oh, I assure you, sir, this is no lady," the clerk said with a sneer. "This is—"

But that was as far as the clerk got, because the man moved so quickly that he was little more than a blur in Rachel's peripheral vision. He was on the clerk in two quick steps, grabbing the startled man by the front of the collar and pulling him halfway across the counter.

"You were saying?" Hawkeye Smith asked, his voice cold and metallic.

"I—I believe you're right, sir," the clerk stammered. "The, uh, lady was here first."

Hawkeye released his grip on the clerk, and the man shrank back from him, looking at him with frightened eyes and adjusting his collar. Hawkeye grinned broadly. "I'm in no hurry, you see. I'll wait."

The clerk wore a sickly smile as he looked at Rachel. "What do you, uh, want?"

Rachel handed him a shopping list. "I need several things. And I want them delivered."

"No delivery," the clerk said curtly.

"Your sign out front says that you deliver," Hawkeye said.

"Really, sir! You can't expect me to go up to that place in broad daylight?" the clerk protested.

"Why not?" Hawkeye said. "I'm sure you go there at night. Seems to me I've seen you heading that direction."

The clerk coughed and turned scarlet. He drew

himself up indignantly. "But that's different! She had no right to expect—"

"She had every right to expect all the services you offer to anyone else," Hawkeye said. "See to it that delivery is prompt, too, would you? I'd hate to have to come back and remind you."

"No, no," the clerk said quickly. "You won't have to do that, sir. I'll deliver on time."

Hawkeye smiled. "Now, that's damned nice of you, friend."

Hawkeye held the door open, bowed Rachel out, and held his arm for her outside. Rachel tucked her arm in his. Hawkeye tipped his hat to all the ladies, and spoke to all the men. The ladies made a great show of cutting Rachel, either by turning their heads completely away from her or, in some instances, crossing to the other side of the street before they could meet face to face. The men were not quite so obvious, though they did look toward the ground in embarrassment. When Rachel tried to pull her arm away, Hawkeye tightened his grip.

Two blocks up the street, Rachel looked at him for the first time. Their glances met, and they both burst into laughter.

"That man's face!" she gasped out. "I've seen sunsets less red!"

She saw a man coming toward them, and got her laughter under control. When he had passed by, face carefully averted, she said, "You said you've seen the clerk come to my place at night?"

"Going that way, anyhow."

"How can you know that?" Rachel wanted to know. "You've never been there."

"No, I haven't."

"Why not?"

He grinned sheepishly. "Well, for one thing, I wasn't all that sure that you would want to see me. I sort of took advantage the last time we were together."

"Yes!" she said, suddenly recalling the incident in the railroad car. "Yes, Mr. Smith, you did!" She flushed again.

"Well, now, I wish to apologize for that," Hawkeye said. "But in truth, Rachel, I couldn't resist the opportunity. I don't think I've ever seen anybody or anything as beautiful as you were that night."

The combination of the sincerity of his apology and the outrageous flattery took the edge from her anger. Besides, he had been her knight in shining armor just now.

"I accept your apology," she said gravely.

"You do? Well, that's grand! That makes everything right with the world."

"Hawkeye, why did you jump off that train in the middle of the night, in the middle of nowhere? I have to confess that I've wondered about that."

"I had boarded my horse at a ranch near there," he said without looking at her. "It was closer to get off there than to travel to the nearest station, then double back. Beside, I had heard there was a stand of buffalo in the area."

"Why do you do that?"

"Why do I do what?"

"Hunt buffalo," she said.

"Simple. I have to earn a living some way."

"But that can't be a very easy way to make a living. Or even a productive way. Surely there are other jobs a man of your qualifications could find."

He laughed.

"Well, what is it? What did I say that you find so humorous?" she demanded.

"You said a man of my qualifications, as if I had that many qualifications to offer. The truth is, Rachel, I have little or no qualifications. I can hunt, trap, scout, speak three different Indian tongues, and that's about it." He wore a musing, slightly startled expression. "You know, listing my, uh, qualifications like that, it just occurs to me that the world may have passed me by. Any talents I have may be obsolete."

"I can't believe that, Hawkeye." She laughed self-consciously. "Listen to me, disapproving of *your* job! I am the madam of a whorehouse. When I venture outside, people turn away from me in disgust, and yet here I am scorning you for hunting buffalo! I'm sorry, I have no right to be critical."

"It's nothing you need apologize for. But since you've brought it up, Rachel, I'd like to ask you something. Why are you doing what you're doing? I'm not being critical, you understand, I'm just curious."

"I'm doing it for the money."

He nodded, looking down into her eyes. "Do you figure it's worth it?"

"Yes, it's worth it. To me, it is. You don't have any conception what it's like being penniless, and having to depend on someone else to support you."

Hawkeye laughed. "I don't know about that. I'm not exactly Jay Gould, you know."

"Oh, I know you have to work hard for what little money you earn. But it's different for men. You have your freedom, you can go anywhere and do almost anything you like, and nobody thinks anything of it. Women can't do that. And I especially can't do that with little Will. Will wanted his son to grow up with more advantages than his father had, and I intend to see that he gets them!"

Hawkeye raised his eyebrows at the vehemence in her voice. Smiling faintly, he said, "Even if he grows up with a mother no one will speak to?"

"Even that," she said grimly.

By now they had reached La Belle Femme Inn, and they stood for a moment looking at it. From the outside it could have been any residential dwelling, if a little better looking than most. It was white with blue trim, with bay windows and gingerbread trim. A white picket fence surrounded it.

On impulse Rachel said, "Would you like to come in for a minute?" She grinned. "It's not business hours now."

"Thank you, I believe I will. I've thought about dropping in any number of times. Now seems a good time."

It was mid-afternoon. Some of the girls were still sleeping, but there were a few in the parlor, reading and talking. This was about the only time they had for socializing. Rachel had insisted that they dress with decorum when they went out of the house, and even when they were inside during the off-business hours.

Bright Fawn was in the parlor with the baby, sitting beside him on the divan, watching closely as the girls played with him. Glancing up, she saw Hawkeye, and her face broke into a pleased smile. Speaking her own language, she said "Lance-in-the-Side, I am pleased to see you! I am Bright Fawn. Do you remember me?"

"How can I ever forget Bright Fawn?" Indeed he did remember her; the details of that night in her father's tipi were vivid in his memory. He said quickly, "Bright Fawn, my heart is filled with sorrow for you, when I think of your family."

"Your words ease my pain," Bright Fawn said formally.

"Well!" Rachel said. "I can see that I don't need to introduce you two."

"No, no need. I have known Bright Fawn since she was very small. I'm happy to see that she is your friend, Rachel."

"Hello, Hawkeye," a male voice said, and Hawkeye turned to see David Spencer coming in from the hall.

He nodded. "How are you, Spencer? Someone told me you were playing piano here."

"Well!" Rachel said in surprise. "You know each other, too?"

Judy got up from the divan, stretching like a cat, arching her back so that the thrust of her breasts was visible. "*I* don't know the gent. Why don't you introduce him?"

Rachel's lips tightened. She felt a twinge of . . . of something, she was not quite sure what. "Judy, this is Hawkeye Smith."

Hawkeye smiled. "Hello, Judy."

"Hello yourself," Judy said, with a heavy-lidded

look. "Listen, Hawkeye, if you happen to be in he mood . . ."

"Judy, it's not business hours yet," Rachel said sharply.

"Rose didn't keep such business hours," Judy said. "She always said that business was business, no matter what time of the day or night."

Rachel snapped, "I'm not Rose Foster! I set the rules here."

"It's all right, Rachel." Hawkeye laughed, touching her arm. "Thank you, Judy. You're a lovely woman . . . but not quite what I had in mind."

"Oh?" Judy said. She pouted prettily. "Well, if you happen to change your mind, big fellow, I'll be around."

"I'll remember."

"You'd better take Judy up on her offer. The one you're interested in isn't available, Smith."

Hawkeye looked at David measuringly, his eyes hardening. "And how do you know which one I'm interested in?"

"Let's say I'm a perceptive fellow."

"Let's say you're right. How do you know she isn't available?"

"Because I *say* she isn't available." David's right hand came to rest on the butt of his pistol.

Hawkeye noticed the move. He was unarmed, but a sudden gust of anger pushed him past caution. "What if I don't choose to see it that way?"

Rachel, belatedly realizing that she was the subject of their conversation, said angrily, "Gentlemen, I will not be discussed like a piece of property! And I am not available, Mr. Smith, because *I* say I am not available. And Mr. Spencer has no authority to speak for me."

"Is that right now?" Hawkeye relaxed, smiling lazily down at her. "You mean you aren't available for a drink and some pleasant conversation?"

Rachel had to smile. "For a drink and pleasant conversation, I'm always available."

"Well, then." Hawkeye spread his hands. "Then you'll be seeing me more often."

"Why?" David said harshly.

Hawkeye said easily, "For a drink and pleasant conversation, of course."

At that moment, almost two thousand miles away, Ewell Rankin was being served his second glass of champagne in the drawing room of Elmhurst, the New York mansion of William J. Cornelius.

Cornelius said, "Well, Ewell, have you enjoyed your visit to New York so far?"

"Oh, yes, definitely," Rankin replied.

He glanced around appreciatively at the opulence of the drawing room. The walls were of imported Algerian marble and the ceiling was trimmed in gold. Never in his wildest imaginings would he have conceived of such an edifice as Elmhurst. The Roundhouse had impressed everyone with its elegance, yet it could not even serve as an outhouse to the servants' quarters for Elmhurst.

The elegantly groomed Cornelius, plump cheeks pink from close barbering, came forward with a box of expensive cigars. Rankin took one and lit up.

When both men had their cigars going satisfactorily, Cornelius said, "I asked you here for a reason. A very special reason."

"Yes, sir, I assumed that. I must admit that I've been wondering what that reason was. You indicated in your telegram that you had something of urgency to discuss with me."

"Have you seen all of Elmhurst, Ewell? Have you taken a good look at it?"

"I certainly have, sir."

"And what do you think of it?"

"I think it's the most magnificent house and estate it has ever been my privilege to see. Surely, there is no other place like it in the whole world."

Cornelius laughed. "My dear fellow, there are at least fifteen homes that I know of which cost twice as much as Elmhurst, and Elmhurst cost nearly a million dollars."

"My God," Rankin said in awe. "That's unbelievable!"

"Believe it, Ewell, believe it. Tell me, what do you know of Dr. Durant and Silas Seymour?"

"I know that they are helping to build the railroad, and that they are associated with Credit Mobilier."

"That is correct. As are George Francis Train, Sidney Dillon, Oakes and Oliver Ames, and a number of others. Including, I might add, Schuyler Colfax, who will no doubt be the next vice-president of the United States, and also Speaker of the House James Blaine."

Ewell whistled through his teeth. "That's a damned powerful collection of men. I had no idea that Credit Mobilier was made up of so many powerful men."

"It is composed of powerful men because there is a lot of money involved. A tremendous amount of money, Ewell. Something in the neighborhood of seventy million dollars."

"That is a staggering sum." Rankin had to struggle to keep the greed out of his voice.

"Yes," Cornelius said. "It is indeed a staggering sum." He spoke the words quietly; then, suddenly and unexpectedly, he literally screamed, "*So why the hell are you trying to ruin everything?*" . .

The ferocity of the attack so surprised Rankin that he spilled half his champagne. "Mr. Cornelius, I assure you, I have no idea what you are talking about!"

"Oh, don't you? I must tell you, Mr. Rankin, that we know everything that you have been doing," Cornelius went on. "We know that you had Miller Conners killed when he discovered that you were using a different set of construction standards. We know also that you have been falsifying the losses of material due to weather, Indian raids, and whatever other ways you believe you can get away with, and we know that you shaved the safety factor on the trestles—"

"No, sir," Rankin said defensively. "Now, just a minute, that was Parker. He—"

"You murdered Parker," Cornelius said bluntly.

"You can't prove that!"

"I can't *prove* it?" Cornelius's smile was pitying. "Come now, Mr. Rankin, where do you think you are? In a court of law? I don't have to prove it. All I have to do is believe it. Mr. Rankin, lest you forget, you are dealing with the most powerful consortium of men God has ever allowed to walk this earth. We keep our counsel, and we make our own decisions. Now we know you did all of this, and that's all we need to know. We don't need your confession, or proof."

"All right!" Rankin conceded. "I did do it. I shaved a few corners here and there. I saw a few opportunities to make big money, so I took them."

"*Big* money? Everything you have done so far has brought you less than a hundred thousand dollars. Why you little pissant! One hundred thousand dollars wouldn't even furnish this room! You dare to jeopardize seventy million dollars for that kind of money?"

"I'm sorry. I guess I just didn't think of it that way."

"You didn't think, period," Cornelius snapped. "And that's the problem."

"What are you going to do?" Rankin asked apprehensively.

"Our first thought was to take care of you, the way you took care of Miller Conners," Cornelius said with an unpleasant smile. Terror gripped Rankin's vitals like an icy fist.

"But we finally decided not to do that. Something like that could backfire all the way to Washington, and we have too many high-ranking politicians allied with us. So, we came up with another idea."

"What?" Rankin asked fearfully.

"We're going to give you a chance to make amends. We're going to send you back. But this time we feel that, having now been informed of our displeasure over your past activities, you will endeavor to do a better job for us. In other words, Mr. Rankin, we think that now we can trust you."

Rankin realized that he was way out of his depth. He also realized how narrowly he had escaped death. He said fervently, "Oh, you can. I promise, you can trust me!"

"No more of your private deals on the side?"

"No, Mr. Cornelius, I can safely promise you that. No more private deals."

Cornelius smiled again, and suddenly it was almost as if the entire conversation had not taken place. "You must try the caviar, Ewell," he said suavely. "I think you will enjoy it."

"Oh! Uh . . . thanks," Rankin said, weak with relief. He took the proffered caviar, and although he did not care for it, he ate it with a great show of relish, lest he upset the man again.

"You shall be amply rewarded," Cornelius said chattily, as he spread caviar on a slice of toast. "But if you should fail us again, we will take harsh measures. To put a fine point to it, Ewell, you will be a dead man."

CHAPTER TWENTY-FOUR

Construction pushed on, and a succession of new towns assumed their roles as Hell on Wheels or End of the Track. After Benton came Rawlins, Desert, and Bitter Creek, each enjoying its brief time in the sun.

Rachel had made enough money from La Belle Femme Inn to repay her loan in full, and to move the establishment on to Desert when that became the new End of the Track. It would be too expensive, she decided, to set up in *every* new town; however, it struck her as a good idea to move to every other town, in a leap-frog fashion, thus managing to stay close enough to the construction crew to ensure a steady flow of customers for her girls.

Benton was rapidly becoming a ghost town by the time La Belle Femme Inn moved on. Even the depot had been torn down by the UP, and the only thing left to mark where Benton had been was a sidetrack that served a nearby army post.

Desert, aptly named because of the desolation of Wyoming's Red Desert, was very much like Benton during its boom times. But now, as the Great Race with the Central Pacific was nearing its conclusion, swarms of newspapermen arrived daily on trains from the East, submitting dispatches and bulletins as if they were reporting from the battlefields of a great war. They tallied each day's progress in miles and quarter miles of track.

One reporter, greatly taken by the parallel, wrote: "Sherman with his victorious legions sweeping from Atlanta to Savannah was a spectacle less glorious than this army of men marching on foot from Omaha to Sacramento, subduing unknown wilderness, scaling unknown mountains, surmounting untried obstacles, and binding across the broad breast of America the iron emblem of modern progress and civilization."

True to his promise, Hawkeye Smith was a frequent visitor to La Belle Femme Inn. And equally true to his promise, he made no direct overtures toward Rachel. One thing he did do, however, was play with the baby, and Will soon learned to recognize Hawkeye. He would gurgle happily and hold his arms out when Hawkeye visited.

On her part Rachel began to look forward with anticipation to Hawkeye's visits, and if he was absent for long she would become irritable and short-tempered.

"I would give anything if I could get you to feel that way about me," David Spencer said one night when Hawkeye had not been by for several days.

Rachel had just made an angry remark to a customer with a complaint. Normally she handled such complaints with good nature, and she was unhappy with herself for losing her temper. She turned her ire on David. "What are you talking about? What do you mean, you wish I felt that way about you? I just took that poor man's head off!"

"Oh, I'm not talking about that man, Rachel," he said with a wry smile. "In fact, he was out of line and needed dressing down. No, I'm talking about the man whose extended absence has upset you so."

"I don't know what you're talking about," she retorted.

"Don't you now?" His smile was melancholy. "Rachel, it is all quite clear to me. When Hawkeye Smith is around, you're as content as a bear in winter hibernation. But when he isn't around, you're as touchy as that same bear would be if rudely awakened. It is obvious, at least to me, that you're in love with him."

"Don't be ridiculous," she said crossly. "I've never even been to bed with him!"

"You haven't been going to bed with me, either," he said dryly. "It's been over a month since you've let me make love to you. You finally ran out of excuses, so I gave up asking. I know why you have refused me. But I reckon I didn't fully realize until tonight that *you* didn't know the reason."

"Well, you're wrong. I kept you out of my bed because I can't give you what you want, David. It has absolutely nothing to do with Hawkeye Smith!"

"It has everything to do with him." David sighed in exasperation. "I know it, I'm sure Bright Fawn knows it, the girls know it. Hell, I even think the baby knows it! Now can you honestly tell me that you don't know it?"

Rachel closed her eyes and pinched the bridge of her nose. She was tired, and her emotions were in a turmoil. Finally she said, "Perhaps I am in love with him. But it will never come to anything."

"Hawkeye is a good man. I hate to admit that, but he is a good man. He'll make you a fine husband."

"I won't marry him."

"Why not? You just admitted that you love him."

"That could be, but I notice that he hasn't asked me. Do you think he'd marry a whorehouse madam?"

"You could give that up."

"Why? So I can marry a buffalo hunter? He just barely makes enough to support himself. The railroad will be finished soon. Then what will he do? No, thank you. I tried being a dutiful wife to a poor man. I have my son to think about. I suppose that sounds cold and calculating, but I have to think of Will first."

David shrugged. "Then I'm sorry for you, almost as sorry as I am for myself. You have your devils to face, it would seem, and I have mine."

"I'd like a brass check, please," a new customer said. Happy for the interruption, Rachel sold the man his check. By the time the transaction was completed, David had returned to the piano, and once again his lilting music filled the air.

Rachel looked around the parlor of this new La Belle Femme Inn. She had learned a few things from the first one. This one was built in sections, so that it could more easily be knocked down and transported. It did lack some of the opulence of the original La Belle Femme Inn, but none of the customers seemed to mind. It was clean and refined, the girls were pretty, and there were drinks and nice music.

Rachel rarely drank. Occasionally she would take a glass or two of wine, but she never drank hard liquor. Tonight, however, she felt she needed it. She beckoned the bartender over to her table and ordered a glass of whiskey, ignoring the raised eyebrows from the girls and David's surprised stare.

She wanted the whiskey for the reason David had said. She had her own devils to face. She thought she had already defeated them, but if David could tell she was in love with Hawkeye, then perhaps David was right—everyone knew that she was in love with Hawkeye Smith. Perhaps even *he* knew.

The thought gave her pause. She drank the first drink quickly and beckoned for another. Unaccustomed to strong liquor, she suddenly found herself groggy. It was only eleven o'clock, but she was unable to continue with her duties.

Becky suddenly appeared before her. "You go on up to bed, Rachel. I have an all-night gent, and he can wait awhile. I'll manage the table."

"Thanks Becky," Rachel stood up and experienced a wave of dizziness. "I don't know what's come over me all of a sudden."

"Whiskey, my dear Rachel," said David's voice in her ear. "That's what has come over you."

"My God, do you mean to tell me I'm drunk?" she said, appalled.

"Not quite, but you're getting there. You'd better do as Becky says and go to bed. We'll manage things."

Rachel climbed the stairs to her room with an effort. Her legs felt leaded, and her thoughts moved sluggishly. Once in her room, she removed her clothes, not even remembering to lock the door. She did not even bother with donning a nightgown, but fell across the bed.

It was just short of midnight when Hawkeye strolled into La Belle Femme Inn, a cigar in his mouth. He was surprised to see Becky at the brass check table, instead of Rachel.

"Is Rachel ill?"

Becky smiled. "In a way. She had too many drinks and I shooed her upstairs to bed."

"Rachel drunk?" His eyebrows rose. "I can't believe it! Did she receive some bad news or something that set her off?"

"Not that I know of," Becky shrugged. "Rachel's had a lot on her mind lately."

"Well . . ." He felt lost without Rachel to talk to. "Since I'm here, I guess I'll at least have a drink."

At the bar he hooked one boot on the brass rail and sipped at a whiskey. He smelled the perfume before he heard her voice. "I saw you stop at the table, big fellow. You buy a brass check? If you did, I'm available."

He half-turned to look at Judy. "Sorry to disappoint a lady, but no brass check."

She was wearing a thin peignoir that left the tops

of her heavy breasts visible. As his glance moved over her, Judy shivered and stepped closer, close enough for a breast to brush his arm. She propped one foot beside his, and the peignoir gaped open. He could see the plump, white flesh of one thigh. Hawkeye felt an automatic response.

"That's all right, big fellow," she said in a throaty whisper. "*You* don't need a brass check. Not ever."

Why not? He had been celibate since the day he had started coming around La Belle Femme Inn. Did Rachel know, or even give a damn?

He sighed, and said, "Sorry, Judy. Maybe another night."

She stepped back as though he had slapped her, eyes flashing. "What is it with you? If you're waiting around for Rachel, she's never going to let you into her bed! She isn't even letting that gun-toting piano player into her bed nowadays!" With a sniff Judy flounced off.

Involuntarily Hawkeye's gaze jumped to the piano, and found David Spencer frowning at him. In a sardonic toast, Hawkeye held his glass up, drank, the turned back to the bar.

So Rachel had closed her door on David? Of course he had not known for sure that there was anything between them, but he had suspected it.

Hawkeye found his glance straying again and again to the stairway. The thought that Rachel was in bed up there plagued him.

He had known for a long time that he was in love with Rachel; he probably had been since the first time he had seen her on the train. But he had determined to keep his distance. The fact that she was a madam did not trouble him. He well knew how difficult it was out here for a woman alone. But he had to admit that the news that she was not selling herself had pleased him greatly. Still, he knew that it was best for him not to form an emotional attachment until his secret mission was completed. And to tell her about that might expose her to a needless risk.

Judy's disclosure that she had been having an affair with Spencer, and had ended it, put a different face on it. Could it be that she had ended it because of him, because of one Hawkeye Smith?

He realized that he was going to find out, now, tonight. Postponing it was intolerable. To hell with all good resolutions!

He finished the whiskey with a toss of his head and shot a quick look at the piano. While playing, Spencer had to half-turn on his stool to see the bar. Of course, when he *did* look this way, he would be able to pretty much guess where Hawkeye had gone.

With a glance around the room, Hawkeye saw that he was not being observed, so he headed for the stairs and went up quickly. He had the feeling that everyone was watching his progress, but he resolutely did not look around again.

At the door to Rachel's room, he raised his knuckles to knock, then hesitated. He tried the knob and found it unlocked. He drew a deep breath, opened the door quietly, and went in.

Was she asleep, or was she awake? She had long been plagued by erotic dreams. Was she having another one?

She opened her eyes. Enough moonlight came in through the window to show a figure looming over the bed. Was it David? How dare he . . .

A hand gently cupped her face, its thumb caressing her lips.

"What do you want?" She felt no fear, strangely enough, only a sense of wonder and awe.

"I think you know what I want, Rachel."

Lips touched her mouth, lingered a moment, then moved down her throat to her breasts. She felt her nipples stirring in response. Her arms lifted of their own volition and went around his shoulders. She could feel the strength in the broad shoulders, but she could not see the man clearly. Everything moved with such sweet slowness.

She knew, dimly, that she should resist what was happening to her. Yet how could you resist a dream? It had to come from the longings and desires of her own heart. What harm could result from giving in to the hunger of her body, if it was in her mind only?

Then the sweet, hot tenderness of her dream gave way to a rising sensation. Her blood stirred and a surge of heat blazed at the center of her being, sweeping outward, consuming every inch of her body.

She had experienced erotic dreams before, and she had been loved by three men, yet nothing in her experience had prepared her for what she was feeling now. Her body quivered with need under the caressing touch of her dream-lover. She was drowning in such exquisite feelings that time and place and reality were suspended; and she gasped and arched, raking her lover's bare back with her fingernails.

The lover of her dream responded to the raking as if it were a passionate embrace, and indeed it was. He placed his mouth over hers, smothering her with kisses.

Since this was a dream, Rachel was able to feel and imagine things which would not have otherwise been possible. She experienced everything that her lover felt. It was as if in their melding, which was as close as a man and woman could get, they exchanged souls. Rachel could feel the hot pounding of blood in his body just as he felt it, the tensing of his muscles just as he felt them, and she knew that he was experiencing her feelings as well. They were separate entities, to be sure, but they were one as well, and all pleasurable sensations Rachel felt were redoubled by the fact that they were shared experiences. Her body spasmed, and she felt the breath leave her body; then, like a rocket, she was lifted high to blaze across the heavens.

Afterward, she lay in slowly receding waves of pleasure. Sometime during their loving she had become aware that it was not a dream, that this was actually happening to her. By that time her ecstasy was so intense that it did not matter. Nothing mattered.

"I love you, Rachel," Hawkeye said.

She glanced over at him, and in the silver splash of moonlight she could see his face close to hers.

"You took an awful chance coming into my room like that," she said. "I might have shot you. I do keep a derringer under my pillow, you know."

"It was worth any risk." He laughed softly. "If you shot me now, I'd die a happy man."

Rachel's heart felt as if it had been sliced through with a dagger of ice. Will had uttered almost those same words on the night he was murdered!

"No!" she said. She threw her arms around Hawkeye and pulled him close. "No, please don't say that! Don't ever say that!"

Hawkeye felt her heart beating against him as rapidy as that of a bird's. He was confused by her strange reaction, and at the same time pleased with whatever it was that drove her into his arms.

"What's wrong, sweet?" he asked. "It's only an expression."

Rachel could not tell him that Will had used those same words. She was afraid that if she did, it would somehow result in the same terrible thing happening to Hawkeye, as illogical as that seemed. Instead, she pulled him closer to her, her bare breasts flattening against his chest. "Just don't say that ever again!"

He said soothingly, "All right, I won't. I promise. But there's something else I want to say."

Rachel stiffened. She knew what he was going to say, and she did not want to hear those words, either. She pulled away from him.

"No!" she said. "Don't ask me to marry you, Hawkeye. I can't marry you."

"How did you know I was going to ask that?" he said in astonishment. "But more important, why do you say— Do you love me?"

"Yes," she said. "Yes, yes, yes! I love you more than I ever thought I could love anyone."

"Then what the hell! Marry me."

"I can't," she said. She turned her face toward him, and in the light of the moon, two tears formed glistening tracks down her face. "Don't you see that I can't?"

"No," he said stonily. "No, I can't see that at all. Maybe I'm a dullard, but I don't see. Not if you love me."

"I said that I love you, and I do. Please don't ask more from me right now. Just accept that."

Hawkeye got out of bed and without a word began dressing. Rachel lay quite still, watching him. She was losing him. She knew that she was losing him because she would not marry him. Tears scalded her eyes, and every atom of her being screamed at her to stop him, to tell him, yes, yes, *yes*, she would marry him!

But her earlier resolve would not let her do it. She would be true to her promise to Will. She would provide for little Will, and she could not do that married to a buffalo hunter—no matter how much she loved him.

Finally, when Hawkeye was dressed, he returned to the bed and leaned down to kiss her. "All right! I love you, and I'll take what I can have—for the moment. I don't like it and I don't understand it. But I will accept it."

Rachel did not try to answer him. She lay without speaking as he strode through the door. It had come full cycle now, she realized. She had been hurt and unable to understand why Ewell Rankin would not marry her. Now Hawkeye was hurt and unable to understand why she would not marry him!

If he never came back, she would understand. She would never forgive herself, but she would understand.

CHAPTER TWENTY-FIVE

Winter came early to the Wasatch Mountains in 1868. But the Union Pacific did not go into winter quarters. The directors of the UP were anxious to grab control of as much of the lucrative route as they could, so they gave orders to press on.

Rachel moved La Belle Femme Inn with the railroad, but David Spencer did not accompany her. Hawkeye had become a regular visitor and David, unable to settle for second place in Rachel's life, made the decision to leave. He was not angry when he left, just resigned, and she felt conscience-stricken that she had only added to the burdens he already carried.

Yet David Spencer was not the only one carrying an emotional burden. In Hawkeye Smith, Rachel had finally found both a good man and an exciting lover, but this did not alter her decision to remain unwed.

Despite her refusal to marry Hawkeye, their relationship grew and deepened. They were man and wife in reality, except for the legal papers. He spent most of his free time with her, and she did not discourage him. She had discovered that she needed him—needed his love and his strength.

As their love grew, so did the railroad. Rachel and the prefabricated La Belle Femme Inn kept pace, setting up business briefly in Salt Wells, then Castle Rock, and by Christmas, in Wasatch, Utah.

It was ten degrees below zero on Christmas morning, but Rachel was warm as toast, sunk deep into a feather comforter, covered with quilts and blankets, snuggled in Hawkeye's arms. She kept La Belle Femme Inn closed all of Christmas day, and they left the bed only to eat, snuggled against each other for warmth, and making leisurely, beautiful love whenever the urge struck them. It was the best Christmas Rachel had ever known.

During the Christmas week, Credit Mobilier paid its stockholders a handsome dividend. But at the same time the Union Pacific Railroad was six million dollars in debt. Credit Mobilier was bleeding the railroad dry. By the end of the year, with the proposed link-up with the railroad coming east only sixty miles away, the entire operation was on the verge of collapse. Thomas Durant and Silas Seymour, although officers of the Union Pacific, were, as officers of Credit Mobilier, selling material to the railroad at excessive prices. Durant was receiving ten percent of all contracts, and had instructed the supervisors to report double the amount of material they were using. Silas Seymour was receiving kickbacks from tie-cutting contractors and timber haulers.

But somehow, despite the corruption and the mismanagement, the railroad kept moving west. It was extremely difficult work. The men had to drag timber out of snowbanks, chop away at the frozen earth with picks and shovels, and blast tunnels through mountains and canyons. The workers were all reaching the point of exhaustion, and many were talking of revolt, when the UP announced that all wages would be doubled. This was inducement enough to keep most of the men on the job, even though they were already several weeks behind in receiving their pay.

The railroad's troubles were Rachel's troubles as well, because if the workers were not paid, La Belle Femme Inn had no business. That was one reason Rachel knew she could keep La Belle Femme Inn closed for Christmas—there were no customers.

Enough money was scraped together after the first of the year to meet the railroad payroll, and for a short time Rachel's business flourished again; but by February the workers were not being paid, and Rachel's expenses for the next two months were greater than her income. She had to provide her girls with room and board, and although she was not bound to, she continued to pay them a stipend so they would remain with her. The stipend was important to girls like Becky, for instance, who sent a large part of her earnings back home to her mother and sister.

In April, with the promise of spring just around the corner, Rachel moved La Belle Femme Inn to Corinne. Corinne was only fifty miles from Promontory Point, and on April 7th, the directors of the UP and the CP agreed that Promontory Point would be the spot where the tracks would meet.

Business was good in Corinne. With the meeting point established, the railroad was able to get enough money to make the payroll more or less regularly, and there was a festive air about the new End of the Track. Within three weeks Rachel had nearly recouped the money she had lost during the previous three months, and she was beginning to think seriously of resigning as a brothel madam. She was growing increasingly weary of trying to fill a role she had never really felt comfortable in. Also, she now realized that her business, like every other, had risks. Another bad season like that just past, and she could lose everything. But if she did quit, what would she do? What *could* she do, that would bring in sufficient money to keep Will and herself?

And always, in the back of her mind, was the thought of Hawkeye, whom she now admitted that she needed and loved. He offered marriage and a kind of security that money could not bring. And was money so important? She had promised Will Senior that she would take care of little Will, that he should not be raised in want and poverty, yet she was now coming to believe that there were worse things than lack of money. She only had to look around her, at the directors of the railroad, at the so-called upright businessmen who dealt in trickery and death, discounting people's lives for the sake of money, to know that money could not buy happiness or even satisfaction. After all, she had lived the life of a dirt farmer's wife, with a man she had not really loved in the way a woman wants to love a man. Couldn't she live the life of a buffalo hunter's wife with a man she loved very much?

Then, with this thought, came sudden fear. Would Hawkeye still want her? When they first came together he had asked her to marry him at least once a week. Now, she realized, he had not mentioned the subject since before Christmas. Maybe he no longer cared about marrying her. Maybe he realized that he already had all of the conveniences of married life without any of the responsibilities.

She had been a fool! She had allowed herself to be dictated to by greed and her desire for financial independence, and it might have cost her the only true love she had ever known!

An agitated voice broke into her thoughts. "Rachel! Oh, thank God you're here!"

Startled, Rachel glanced up to see Aunt Mildred. She was shocked, not only because it was the first time she had seen her aunt since that dreadful scene last summer, but also by the woman's appearance. She had a black eye, a bad bruise on her cheek, and her lower lip was cut and swollen.

"Aunt Mildred! My God, what happened to you?"

"It's Julius." Mildred Deever said, beginning to sob. She sat down at the table and buried her face in her hands.

"What about Uncle Julius? What did he do to you?"

At a sound behind her, Rachel glanced around. Bright Fawn had come into the parlor. "Bright Fawn, fetch a pan of hot water and a washcloth."

With a nod Bright Fawn hastened to do her bidding. Rachel placed a gentle hand on her aunt's shoulder. "Aunt Mildred, what happened? Did he do this to you?"

"Yes." Mildred Deever bobbed her head. She managed to get her sobbing under control. She sat back, brushing stray strands of hair out of her eyes. "Yes, he did. He's gotten worse, Rachel."

"*Worse?* You mean he's beaten you before?" Rachel said, aghast.

"Rachel, he has always beaten me when he got into one of his rages. But always before he was careful to make sure he hit only where it wouldn't show. Now, as you can see, he doesn't care anymore."

Bright Fawn returned with a pan of water and a washcloth, and began ministering to Mildred's face.

"I didn't know," Rachel said. "You never once let on."

"It isn't something you want people to know," Mildred Deever said. "You have to bear the pain and humiliation in silence. It's a woman's lot in life."

"Not if the woman stands up for herself," Rachel said harshly. "Why? Why did he beat you this time?"

"This time? I didn't get around to ironing his shirt."

"You didn't get around to ironing his *shirt*?" Rachel was furious.

"If it hadn't been that, it would have been something else," Mildred said. "But it doesn't matter, because I just can't suffer it anymore. I won't take it anymore."

"Of course you won't take it, Aunt Mildred. You're going back to Cincinnati."

"Oh, dear, if only I could. But Julius keeps all the money. I don't have a cent of my own."

"I have enough money to send you home." Even as she made the offer, Rachel realized that the train fare back to Cincinnati would sorely deplete her savings. But she did not care. All she could see was her poor aunt, so badly abused by the man she had married.

"Rachel . . ." Mildred looked even more miserable. "I can't let you to that, not after all those terrible things I said to you."

"That's all right, I understand."

"No, you're just saying that." Mildred's tears started again. "Oh, Rachel, if you only knew how many times I've regretted those awful things I said! I longed to come to you and ask your forgiveness, and tell you that I love you, no matter what you do. But I was terrified of Julius. When I made the mistake of telling him how much I regretted speaking to you that way, he beat me so badly I could hardly walk for two whole days. Can you ever forgive me?"

"I'll forgive you, Aunt Mildred, if you'll only allow me to help you escape from that monster."

"I . . . I have to go back for my things." Her aunt shook her head doubtfully. "If he catches me, I don't know what I'll do."

"Don't worry about it, Aunt Mildred. I'll fetch your things for you. Bright Fawn, take my aunt up to my room, and stay with her. Don't let anyone near her, do you understand?"

"Yes, I understand." Bright Fawn helped Mildred to her feet. "Would you like to see Rachel's baby?"

Mildred brightened. "Oh, yes! More than anything, I want to see the child!"

"I'll bring him up to you," Bright Fawn said.

Rachel had the bartender hitch a horse to the buckboard. She drove to the sidetrack, and the railroad car that served as the Deever house. She tied the horse to the platform rail, went inside and began packing her aunt's belongings. She was just finished when she saw Julius Deever entering.

He was speaking before he saw her. "Mildred, who has their buckboard tied off outside?"

"It belongs to me, Julius Deever," Rachel said firmly.

His face reddened at the sight of her. "You! What are you doing here, you strumpet! You were told never to come here again!"

"I'm here for Aunt Mildred's belongings," Rachel said.

"Her belongings? What are you talking about, girl?" He tried to peer past her. "Where is she? Mildred, come out here!"

"Why do you want her? You intend to beat her again?"

His face got even redder. He said huffily, "You stay out of it. She is my wife, and what I do to my own wife is my affair."

"There is one thing you'll never do to her again. You'll never beat her."

"Goddammit, Mildred, I said get out of here!" he roared. He lunged past Rachel and looked through the open bedroom door. He whirled back to Rachel, his face registering astonishment. "She's not here!"

"No, she isn't."

"Where is she?"

"She's where you cannot hurt her."

He took a threatening step toward her. "Tell me where she is, you slut!"

"Aunt Mildred left End of the Track on the afternoon train, for Cincinnati," Rachel lied.

Deever looked baffled. "She couldn't have left, she doesn't have any money. I haven't given her any."

"I gave her the money for train fare."

"Whore's money?" He laughed derisively. "Do you think she'd use whore's money?"

"Better whore's money than murderer's money," she snapped, without thinking.

"What?" Deever lost color. "What are you prattling on about, girl?"

"I'm talking about the Eddison Trestle. I know that you and Ewell Rankin were in cahoots. The pair of you had the plans altered, so you could make some dirty money, and all those people were killed!"

"You—you must be crazy. You don't know what you're talking about!"

"Oh, but I do. You see, Will and I overheard Ewell and that construction engineer talking—" She stopped short, her eyes widening as the truth struck her. "Dear God, Rankin had Will killed! He must have. I never once thought . . ."

"You'd better watch what you're saying girl," Deever blustered. "He's been back east, but he's due back in Corinne later tonight. I don't think he'd be too pleased about you making wild accusations."

"And you're going to tell him, aren't you?"

Deever grinned suddenly. "I might. I just might."

"You do your worst, Julius Deever," she said defiantly. "It's too late for you to harm Aunt Mildred, and I'll take my chances." She picked up the bags. "Now get out of my way, I'm going to ship Aunt Mildred's things on to her."

Julius Deever drew his hand back menacingly, as if to strike her.

"Go ahead, you bully!" She jutted her face at him. "I'm sure Hawkeye Smith would be interested to know where I got the bruise. You do know Hawkeye, don't you?"

Deever stepped back, dropping his fist. In a shaking voice, he shouted, "Get out! Whore! Strumpet!"

Rachel quickly left the railroad car. Behind her she could hear Deever kicking furniture in his frustration. She was trembling as she drove the buckboard away, whipping the horse into a trot.

She was elated at herself for standing up to Julius Deever, yet fear nagged at her. If he found out that his wife had not yet left, he might come storming into La Belle Femme Inn after her.

Rachel wished that Hawkeye were here, but she had not seen him for several days, and had no idea where he was. With David gone as well, she had little protection.

But above all else loomed her fear of Ewell Rankin. She had been rash to blurt out what she knew to Deever; he would be sure to relate the conversation to Rankin. And if Rankin had ordered Will killed for what he knew, and she was convinced of that now, he would come after her too, now that he knew she shared Will's knowledge of his crooked dealings and the murders he was responsible for.

CHAPTER TWENTY-SIX

"What do you call this?" Mildred Deever asked.

"Lip rouge, Mrs. Deever," Becky said, hiding a smile. Using a small brush, Becky was applying the red salve liberally to the older woman's lips. In addition, she had applied rouge to Mildred's cheeks and makeup to her eyes. Her hair had been treated with a rinse that had turned it reddish orange, and the dress she wore revealed her neck all the way down to her shoulders.

"My goodness!" Mildred said, peering at herself in the mirror with a look of shock. "I look like a floozy, don't I?"

Becky laughed. "That's the way you're supposed to look, if you're going to be one of us."

"One of you?" Mildred flinched away from Becky's touch. "But I'm not going to . . ."

"Don't worry, Mrs. Deever," Becky said. "We've been called lots worse than floozies. Now, you just hold still so I can hide this bruise with powder."

"I . . . I must thank you for doing this for me. It's awfully nice of you."

"Think nothing of it," Becky said. "Rachel has been awfully nice to us. There's not a classier madam in all the West."

Mildred flinched and closed her eyes at the phrase. Judy strolled into the room just then, and Becky did not notice Mildred's reaction.

"I think this is a swell idea Rachel has to slip you out of town," Judy said. "I mean, dressing you up like one of us. Who'd ever figure that a nice lady like you could look like a whore?"

"I'm not sure it will work," Mildred said disconsolately.

Becky said, "Whyever not?"

"Well, all of you are so pretty, and I'm so . . ." Mildred put her hand to her cheek and examined herself again in the mirror. "And I'm so plain, and so . . . so old."

"You're not plain at all, ma'am," Becky said in a scolding voice. "When we get done, you'll be downright pretty."

"Do you really think so?" Mildred asked, brightening.

"Of course I do." Becky sighed. "But I just hate to see Rachel going out of the business."

"I could have told you that was bound to happen," Judy said.

"How could you tell?"

"Haven't you seen it coming? I knew the moment I realized she had fallen for Hawkeye Smith. I knew then that our days were numbered here."

"Do you think she'll marry him?"

"I don't know."

Becky finished the last application of makeup

and stood back to study her handiwork. "There now! You could sit right down next to that husband of yours, and he wouldn't know you."

Mildred shivered. "I hope it doesn't come to that."

"Don't worry, it won't," Becky reassured her. "We'll all be sitting together, and we're particular who sits with us." She and Judy laughed together.

"I don't understand," Mildred said. "What is so humorous?"

"When we venture out anywhere, Mrs. Deever," Judy explained. "No one comes even near us. We're like lepers, you see. So we make sport of ourselves, by saying that it isn't that people won't sit with us, it's that we are particular about who we *let* sit with us."

Rachel entered the room then. She stopped short, peering closely at her aunt. "Aunt Mildred! My God, is that really you?"

Mildred got up, smiling. Putting a finger under her chin, she did a small curtsy. "Do you think I could command any gentlemen callers?"

"Aunt Mildred!" Rachel had to laugh. "I can't believe I'm hearing this!"

"Well . . . any woman likes to think that she is . . . uh . . ."

"Desirable?" Rachel prompted

"Yes!"

"Believe me, Mrs. Deever," Becky said sincerely, "you'd be the queen of the parlor."

"Thank you, dear," Mildred said with dignity.

"Now, gather around," Rachel said briskly. "Oh,

Becky, would you please call the other girls up here?"

Becky stepped to the doorway and summoned the girls. When the others were in the room, Rachel said, "I've just come from the depot. I bought train tickets for all of you, to the destinations you wanted. For the first two hundred miles you'll all be together, and I'd like you to stay with my aunt, just in case."

"We will," Becky said with moist eyes.

"Rachel, I want to say something, for all of us," Judy said. "You've been grand with us. Most madams, even Rose—and the truth is, I liked Rose—but even she was just going to desert us. If you hadn't come along, I don't know what would have happened to us. It was really decent of you to buy us train tickets."

"That's not all," Rachel said, opening her reticule. "Here's a hundred dollars for each of you. I know that none of you have much money."

Judy was already shaking her head. "That must be just about all the money you have, Rachel."

"It doesn't matter. I'll manage. I should be able to sell La Belle Femme Inn for enough to see me through."

It took a little more convincing, but in the end the girls accepted the money. The whistle of the approaching train cut through the sudden silence in the room.

Becky said sorrowfully, "There's our train, girls."

One by one the girls embraced Rachel. Some were weeping as they left the room. Mildred Deever was the last one to put her arms around Rachel.

"Now, don't go crying, Aunt Mildred," Rachel scolded. "Your eye makeup will run."

"Then you won't be queen of the parlor anymore," Becky said.

Soon they were all gone, leaving only Rachel and Bright Fawn in the room. Rachel stood at the window where she could see the train depot in the distance. She could see the girls gathered on the platform, with Mildred Deever in the middle as they waited to board. From all indications her disguise was effective, since all the other passengers avoided the group carefully.

Suddenly Rachel gasped in horror.

"What is wrong?" Bright Fawn asked.

"My uncle. Julius Deever is on the platform."

Bright Fawn stepped up alongside Rachel, and for an anxious moment the two women watched Julius Deever to see if he would recognize his wife.

Mildred Deever saw him as well, and she turned her back. Then the girls clustered even closer around her. Deever gave them one scornful glance, then turned *his* back.

Now Rachel saw the real reason Deever was on the station platform, as Ewell Rankin stepped down from the arriving train. Rankin was as handsome and well groomed as ever. Rachel saw his suave good looks as a stamp of evil, and rage rose up, threatening to choke her, as she looked at the man she was sure was responsible for Will's death.

She knew that Deever would tell Rankin what she had said, and that filled her with apprehension. She represented a threat to him. She determined to stay out of his way, and to tell Hawkeye what she knew. He would see that no harm came to her.

The train whistled, and the passengers began boarding. Rankin and Deever were already walking away from the depot, deep in conversation, and paid no heed to the group of painted women getting on the train.

Rachel watched until the train began to chug away from the station, still headed west. A short distance out of town was the improvised roundhouse where the engine would be reversed for the trip east.

She breathed a sigh of relief and turned away from the window. "Thank God, they got away all right!"

"They will be in no danger now," Bright Fawn said.

"I hope you are right."

"It was good of you to buy them tickets on the Iron Horse, and give them money."

Rachel looked away. "It was something that I felt I had to do."

"I know. You love Lance-in-the-Side very much, and so you must give away all the money."

"What?" Rachel gave a start, staring at the Indian woman. "What on earth are you talking about?"

"I am talking about your man, your Hawkeye Smith, as he is known to the whites. You love him very much, and wish to marry with him. But you fear that he will not marry you, if you have much money from this place. So you gave it all away."

"I didn't think I was that transparent," Rachel said with a weak laugh.

"It is a good reason. When the heart is pure, it is as bright as fire in the night."

Rachel looked at her shrewdly. "Now, I'll ask you something. How long have *you* been in love with Hawkeye?"

A flicker of surprise crossed Bright Fawn's face. "I do not think you know this."

"When the heart is pure, it is as bright as fire in the night," Rachel said with a straight face.

"I loved Lance-in-the-Side when he lived with my people. But I was but a maiden then, and he could not return my love. Once, when I became a woman, I gave myself to him, and I thought that he would see me as a woman, and he would return my love. He was gentle and kind, and it was good when I gave myself to him, but I could tell even then that he did not love me as I loved him."

"I'm sorry," Rachel said, ignoring a twist of jealousy. "It must pain you to see me with Lance-in-the-Side."

Bright Fawn smiled, shaking her head. "No, you are my friend. Lance-in-the-Side is my friend. What can bring my heart more joy than for my friend to love my friend? This is the way the Great Spirit would have it."

"I'm glad I have you for a friend, Bright Fawn. Never has there been a better one."

Bright Fawn smiled.

"We can't afford any more mistakes, not now," Ewell Rankin said. "I told you about my trip to New York. We were fortunate to come out of it the way we did."

"Well, what do you think we should do about Rachel?" Julius Deever asked.

"I don't know," Rankin said thoughtfully. "The business about the trestles is one thing. It's doubtful anyone would believe her about that, particularly considering her, shall we say, social standing, so she represents no danger to us. And the Credit Mobilier people know about the trestles anyway. But if Rachel suspects that we had Will Simmons killed . . . Now that could cause a stink."

"Even if they investigated, wouldn't it still all have to come down to your word against hers?"

"That doesn't matter," Rankin said. "Any investigation, no matter how flimsy the grounds, would be all that it took to get the people back east nervous as hell. And Julius, do I have to tell you what will happen if they get *too* nervous? You weren't there to listen to Cornelius. He means business!

"Listen close now. This whole Credit Mobilier scheme is balanced like a pack of cards. The only thing keeping it from tumbling down around all of us is the number of influential men involved. But you let word get bandied about that there has been murder done, and Credit Mobilier will come crashing down. Do I have to tell you who would be at the bottom?"

"I see," Deever said apprehensively.

"We talked about this once before, and *you* were supposed to take care of it."

"Nobody realized that Rachel knew anything, not even you," Deever said in a whining voice. "You wanted Will Simmons dead, I saw to that—"

"Goddammit, Julius, they were man and wife! It

figures that he would tell her. I didn't know she'd been listening to me, along with Will Simmons! The clodhopper lied to me!"

"The two fellows I hired—they thought she was dead when they rode off."

"They *thought*!" Rankin said viciously. "That will be of great comfort to us when they write it on our tombstones."

Tonight La Belle Femme Inn seemed much larger than it actually was. Rachel knew that that was because everyone was gone. There were no girls, there was no bartender, and of course no customers. Only she, Bright Fawn, and little Will were in the huge house.

Bright Fawn had gone to bed early, after Will was asleep in his crib, but Rachel, who had grown used to staying up until late, could not go to sleep yet. She sat downstairs in the parlor, reading a book until a little after one. Finally, she closed the book, turned out the lamp, and started up the stairs.

She was about halfway up when she thought she heard a noise behind her. She turned and went back downstairs to see what it was. Then she noticed that the front door was standing open.

Rachel felt the hair along her spine rise. She knew she had shut the door. Someone had gotten into the house!

The baby! She whirled, shouting up the stairs, "Bright Fawn! Bright Fawn, the baby! See if Will is—"

Strong arms went around her from behind, and she felt a rag clamped across her nose and mouth.

The rag gave off a sickening-sweet smell, and she struggled mightily to escape it, but the arms were too strong and the smell too overpowering. In a moment, Rachel felt herself spinning away into darkness.

CHAPTER TWENTY-SEVEN

The sound of a pistol shot rolled down the mountainside, picked up resonance, then echoed back from the surrounding mountains. A hairy young man holding a smoking pistol turned and grinned at the two other men with him. They were squatting by a small campfire, one warming his hands, the other drinking quietly from a bottle. The fire made a bubble of light in the night.

"Trace, why are you so all-fired anxious to always be shooting off that piece of iron?" the one warming his hands asked.

"I like to stay in practice," Trace said. He spun the pistol expertly, then flipped it from hand to hand and twirled it again.

"Well, it makes me goldarned nervous."

"You know what your problem is, Jack?" Trace said with a taunting grin. "You got a yellow band down your back. People with a yellow band like that get nervous around guns. Now you take Pete and me, we don't get nervous like that. And you," he glared at the man with the bottle, "you suck on that bottle too much to suit me. Some operation this is going to be! A nervous Nellie and a bottle sucker!"

"Where is Pete?" Jack asked. He rubbed his hands together, stood up and peered into the darkness. "If he don't hurry, the train will get here before he does."

"Don't fret about Pete. He had a little job to take care of first."

"A little job to take care of? We're supposed to hold up a train in an hour. That's a big job. So what's this about a little job?"

"Where do you think we got the word about the payroll?" Trace asked.

"Jason got it."

"'Now you got it. So now he has a little job to take care of. He has to pay for the information. Now do you catch on?"

"Yeah, I reckon so." Pete looked into the darkness again. "But I just wish he'd hurry and show up. I'm getting nervous."

"Hell, you're always nervous." Trace laughed raucously, then peered at the quiet drinker. "Hey you, bottle sucker! You getting nervous?"

"No," the quiet drinker said.

Trace laughed again. "No, I guess not. You can't get nervous 'cause you killed all your nerves with the bottle some time back."

The drinker tipped the bottle up to finish it. A gunshot sounded, and the bottle exploded into a shower of glass.

"Now how about that?" Trace sneered. "You

beat me! Damned if you didn't swallow the last drop before I could bust the bottle."

Jack said, "Trace, you *are* crazy!"

"I'm crazy? Look at the bottle sucker there. I shot the bottle right out of his hand, and he didn't even flinch. Now *that's* crazy! Tell me, bottle man, what's it like?"

"What is what like?"

"What's it like being a piano player in a whorehouse?"

"Don't let Trace get under your hide," Jack said. "If I'd known he was this addled, I wouldn't have asked you in."

"I don't have to like a man to hold up a train with him," David Spencer said quietly. "All I want from this is my share of the loot, not friendship."

"Yeah, but to get your share, you'd better hold up your end. Jack here told me what a shooter you were, how many gents you're supposed to have accounted for. I ain't seen any proof of it yet."

"I don't waste my time shooting at bottles," David said, smiling slightly. "They can't shoot back."

Trace bristled, hand hovering near the butt of his gun. "I don't always shoot at empty bottles either, bottle sucker. Any time you want to find out, feel free."

"Trace, now cut this out," Jack said desperately. "Pete won't like it if'n he comes back and learns there's been a gun battle between you two!"

"To hell with Pete!" Trace said arrogantly. "He wises off to me, I may take him on too."

"Why don't we wait until after the robbery? In

fact, why don't we make a little wager now?" David smiled coldly. "The one who survives takes the other's share. How's that?"

Hawkeye Smith was in a good mood. His investigative work was finally beginning to pay dividends. Soon he would be able to tighten the noose around the necks of Ewell Rankin and his cohorts. So far they had managed to escape retribution, but now Hawkeye had a plan. The plan had been sent to President Grant via Steve King, and President Grant had approved it, promising his full support.

The president had set the plan in motion by ordering the Department of the Interior to request a slight modification on one section of the track near Ogden. The modification was routed through the UP Board of Directors to the Board of Directors of Credit Mobilier, and from Credit Mobilier down to its representatives in the field. At each step of the way the order had been monitored carefully by federal marshals who had been assigned to investigate the suspected corruption in the construction of the railroad. As a result, they had been able to record each instance of the padding added to the initial costs, and by the time the actual work was to be done, more than twenty thousand had been added on.

In light of the large sums already stolen, it was a small amount. Yet it was the first carefully documented instance of theft, from origin to implementation, that the government had put together, and it would be enough to enable the first arrests to be made.

By the time it got down to the last level, Hawkeye was the monitoring federal marshal. It was his task to wait until Ewell Rankin, as the Credit Mobilier agent, actually received the money from the Union Pacific disbursing officer; then, having witnessed the transaction, he could make an arrest. The chain of evidence, from the president's modification order down to Ewell Rankin, was strong, and would provide a good court case.

It was the first time Hawkeye had any clear evidence that Rankin was involved in the swindle, although he had long suspected the man. He had despised Rankin for his treatment of Rachel, and Hawkeye knew that the arrest was going to delight his soul.

However, a small hitch developed in the plan. Hawkeye did not receive the telegram informing him that the disbursement of funds was about to be made until after the afternoon train had left for Corinne, and Ewell Rankin was on that train, bound for Corinne to receive the funds. Rankin would arrive in Corinne late in the afternoon, and the next train would get Hawkeye in at one o'clock in the morning. His only hope was that Rankin would arrive so late that he could not collect his money until the next day. Hawkeye had to be an actual witness to the transaction for their case to be strong enough to hold up in court.

The disbursement office was closed when he got off the train, and most of Corinne was dark. But there was a light in the night telegrapher's office, which was located next door to the disbursement agent's quarters.

Hawkeye stepped inside the spill of yellow lantern light. The telegrapher was reading a book, which he put down, picking up a pad and pen. "Yes, sir? Would you like to send a telegram?"

"No," Hawkeye said. "I'm looking for the disbursing agent."

The smile left the man's face, and he said sourly, "This is the Western Union office. That's the disbursing office next door."

"It's closed."

"So it is, so it is."

"I'm a buffalo hunter for the UP—"

"Yeah, I know who you are. Hawkeye Smith."

"—and I was supposed to pick up some money. The UP owes me a pile of money for the buffalo meat."

The telegrapher shrugged irritably. "The UP's disbursing agent went to Wasatch on the noon train." He added hopefully, "Maybe you'd like to send him a telegram asking when he'll be back?"

Hawkeye probed in his pocket for a silver dollar and bounced it on the counter. "We could do that. Or, if you already know, we could just save all that, and pocket the money for yourself."

The telegrapher smiled broadly, and palmed the silver dollar. He looked about furtively and lowered his voice. "I'm not supposed to tell this, you understand. The railroad likes to keep it a secret when they're transferring money, but the morning train will be carrying the new payroll. The disbursing agent will be on that train, arriving around six, if it's on time. Which it ain't always."

"Thanks. Now that wasn't hard, was it?"

Hawkeye saluted the man sardonically and left the telegraph office, satisfied now that he could nail Rankin in the morning.

Outside, he lingered to light a cheroot. A noise along the track caused him to look up. He saw two men on a railroad handcar, pumping vigorously down the track. In a few minutes they were out of the glow of faint light from the train depot, swallowed up by the darkness. Hawkeye thought it a little strange that anyone would be taking a handcar out in the middle of the night. Of course, with the joining of the east and west sections of the railroad scheduled for tomorrow, it could be a couple of railroad inspectors making sure that everything was on schedule.

Hawkeye dismissed it from his mind, and strolled in the direction of La Belle Femme Inn. There was one good thing about having to spend the night in Corinne: He could be with Rachel. He had missed her sorely during his absence.

And another good thing—he was finally free to tell her that he was not just a buffalo hunter. He had long realized that Rachel was not too happy at the prospect of marrying a buffalo hunter, and he could not find it in his heart to blame her too much, not with her son to raise. She was entitled to a better sense of security for their future.

La Belle Femme Inn was dark when he approached, but then it was very late. But something bothered him as he started up the porch steps. Then he realized what it was—the front door stood wide.

"Rachel!" he called, stepping inside. "Rachel, where the hell are you?"

Quick footsteps sounded on the stairs. "Lance-in-the-Side, it is you!" Bright Fawn was fully dressed, and he noted that the baby was strapped to her back, papoose-style.

"Bright Fawn, what is it? Where is Rachel, and why do you have the baby on your back?"

"I was going to follow the men who took Rachel away," Bright Fawn said. "I wanted to help her."

"Somebody took Rachel? Why?" Hawkeye looked around, bewildered. "Where the hell is everyone? Why is this place so empty?"

"Tonight, Rachel send all girls away," Bright Fawn said. "She did this, and she gave away all her money, so she could marry you."

"Marry me?"

"She did not say so, but I know." Bright Fawn frowned. "But after girls leave, and I went to bed, Rachel sat in parlor to read. A short time ago she shouted for me, and when I ran down I saw two men dragging her away."

"Who were they?"

"I do not know," Bright Fawn said. "But they went to the station of the Iron Horse, and they put her on small car which men make go on the track like this." She pumped her hands up and down.

"Yes!" Hawkeye exclaimed. "My God, I must have seen them! Did you say it just happened?"

"Yes," Bright Fawn said.

"Bright Fawn, you stay here with the baby. I'll

find Rachel, never fear. I'll find her, and I'll bring her back."

Hawkeye hurried back to the depot, and finally found another handcar. He hoisted it up onto the track, jumped aboard, and began pumping. The other car had about a twenty-minute lead on him, and that meant they were at least three miles ahead. He had his work cut out for him, if he had any hopes of catching them.

When Rachel regained consciousness, she could feel the rush of night air in her hair and hear the sound of steel rolling on steel. She finally realized that she was lying on the work platform of a handcar, and two men were industriously pumping the drive handle. There was enough starlight to show her that one of the men was Julius Deever.

"Uncle Julius!" she said. "What are you doing? Where are you taking me?"

Deever motioned for the other man to stop pumping, and they rested, letting the car coast to a stop. Deever swiped at his forehead with a handkerchief.

"So," he said, "you're awake at last."

"Yes." Rachel felt a dull ache in her temples, and she wanted to raise her hand to her head, but she discovered that both hands were tied, secured to a ring fastened to the work deck.

"Why am I a prisoner?"

"You ask a hell of a lot of questions!" the second man snarled.

"And I'll keep asking until I get an answer! Who are *you*, and what are you doing here?"

The man chuckled. "My name is Pete, that's all

you need to know. And I'm going to correct an oversight I made the last time."

"What oversight? What are you talking about?"

"You'll find out," Pete said. She could feel his eyes on her, and she sensed that they were bright with lust. "You know, woman, the last time I saw you, you was pregnant, and you didn't look too fetching to me. But things are different now." He chuckled lewdly. "Yes sir, you look a heap better'n you did the night me and Trace rode up to that sod shanty!"

"You!" Rachel gasped. "You killed Will!"

"Now you got it."

"Uncle Julius, you *knew* about this?"

The man called Pete laughed. "Knew about it, woman? He paid for it."

"How can you do this to one of your own family?" Rachel said furiously.

"You're not my family," Deever said. "You never were. Nor that bitch I'm married to, either. You and all the rest of the Bonners! Southern planters! Hah!" He spat over the side of the handcar. "I only wish your daddy had survived the war so he could have been around to see his plantation sold for taxes and his only daughter a whore."

Pete said, "The way I hear it, she didn't lay on her back for money in that place of hers."

"As far as I'm concerned, she's a whore," Deever said piously.

"Well, now, I'm right glad to hear you say that. I reckon you wouldn't have any objections then if I have a bit of sport with her first, now would you?"

Deever asked, "What do you mean?"

"Well, Mr. Deever, her being your niece and all, you may never have noticed, but it's my guess she'd be worthwhile snuggling up to."

"I don't want anything to do with her!" Deever snapped.

"Maybe you don't. I can understand that, you being related and all. But you do want her dead?"

"There's no other way."

"Well, then? Why let all that go to waste?" Pete said, with a smacking sound of his lips. "What say you take a little walk, Mr. Deever? Leave me alone with her for a spell. Then I'll finish her off. You won't even have to dirty your hands."

"All right," Deever said tonelessly. "Do as you wish with her."

"Uncle Julius!" Rachel said. "You wouldn't really go off and leave me alone with this man, this killer?"

But Deever had already stepped down from the handcar and was walking out into the darkness.

"Well now, ain't that nice of him?" Pete said. "It would appear that I got your uncle's blessing now, wouldn't it?"

Rachel's throat was dry, and her heart was pounding, but there was nothing that she could do to defend herself. She was going to be attacked by this animal, and then she was going to be killed. She thought of little Will briefly, then took comfort in the knowledge that he was in Bright Fawn's care. Somehow, he would be looked after.

"Let's just have a little peek here," Pete said thickly.

Reaching down, he fastened his fingers in her

neckline and jerked it, popping all the buttons and pulling the bodice open. Rachel felt a sudden coolness on her flesh. Her breasts—the same breasts that had nursed her son and cushioned Hawkeye's head in love—were now fully exposed to the man who loomed over her.

He put his rough palm on her nipple. It had drawn up tightly against the impact of the cold night air. "Now ain't that something? It feels ripe enough to bust right open!" Pete squeezed, and Rachel cried out from the pain.

Then Pete froze at the sound of footsteps on the gravel. He said in alarm, "Mr. Deever? I thought I told you—"

"The name isn't Deever, friend. Now suppose you just stand up, nice and easy, and back off."

It was Hawkeye's voice. Rachel raised her head. "Hawkeye! Thank God!" She saw the faint light glint off his pistol as he took a step closer to the handcar.

"I told you to move it!"

"I'm moving, I'm moving," Pete said frantically. He clambered awkwardly off the car.

"That's fine. Now just stand away from the car. One wrong move, and I'll be happy to kill you. I just might anyway."

Hands in the air, Pete stepped cautiously back. Without turning his head, Hawkeye said, "I'll untie you in a moment, Rachel, as soon as I decide what to do with this bastard—"

Rachel shouted, "Hawkeye! Watch out!"

Rachel's warning was an instant too late, as Julius Deever brought his upraised pistol whistling down onto Hawkeye's head. Hawkeye grunted softly and collapsed to the ground.

"Goddamn, Mr. Deever, you came just in time!" Pete said jubilantly. "I thought I was a dead'un for sure!"

"Throw him onto the handcar," Deever said.

"On the car? What the hell for? Just shoot him and let me get on with what I was doing."

"No," Deever said firmly. "No time for that now. Heave him onto the car, and we'll take him to the others."

CHAPTER TWENTY-EIGHT

"Listen! What's that?" Jack, dozing by the campfire, suddenly sat up alert."

Trace gestured to him to be quiet and walked over to the tracks, listening. He was smiling openly when he came back to the fire. "That's Pete coming back. You see, Jack, you had no call to be nervous, did you? And you, bottle sucker, it won't be long now before we can have our little face-off. You nervous about that?"

David Spencer merely looked at him, his shadowed eyes cold and hard.

Jack shot to his feet as the handcar stopped just below the fire and the firelight illuminated it. "That's not just Pete, there's somebody with him!"

"That's Julius Deever," Trace said jeeringly. "I guess you didn't know that Deever, the UP construction boss himself, was in cahoots with us, now did you?"

"But there's a couple others on the handcar, Trace," Jack said excitedly.

"Couple of others?" Trace peered at the handcar. "What the hell! I don't know about them two."

"One's a woman!" Jack exclaimed.

"I see that it is. Damn! He was supposed to kill her, not bring her along!"

"Kill her?" Jack said fearfully. "Now look! I wasn't told nothing about any killing, much less a woman!"

"Shut your trap!" Trace said viciously. "You're a part of it, like it or not. But I'd sure like to know who that fellow lying on the car is."

David said, "It's Hawkeye Smith."

"Hawkeye Smith?" Trace squinted across the fire at him. "Who's he?"

"A buffalo hunter."

"A buffalo hunter? Hell, I wasn't told nothing about no buffalo hunter!"

Julius Deever and the man called Pete were coming toward the fire. David had thrown more wood on the fire, and as the flames leaped higher it was easy to see that both Hawkeye and Rachel were tied to the iron ring on the work deck.

"What's the woman doing here?" Trace demanded. "You were supposed to kill her."

"We got interrupted," Pete explained. "The big fellow here followed us and tried to rescue her. But for Mr. Deever, he would have."

Trace stared at Deever. "You aim to kill them both then, I'd reckon?"

"We have no choice," Deever said with averted glance.

Tracy grinned. "Well, there they are, like ducks in a row. Shoot 'em!"

"I . . . I can't," Deever said.

"Why not? You want 'em dead. You wasn't upset when we killed that clodhopper husband of hers. Now's your chance to see to the job yourself."

"No, not me. I'm no killer."

"You want it done then? Makes no never mind to me, one way or another."

"I want it done, yes."

"It'll cost you extra. I can't go wasting my bullets for free."

"You'll get paid."

"We've got a deal then." Trace was staring at the handcar, a killing shine in his eyes. His lips worked convulsively.

On the handcar, Rachel was staring at the young killer in horror. Hawkeye was still groggy, but he was growing aware of what was happening, and he struggled futilely with his bonds.

"I guess I'd better get it over with." Trace's hand dangled near the butt of his pistol. "We got more important things to do." He laughed suddenly, "You're going to bury them, Mr. Deever? That's not part of the bargain. I can't be getting my hands dirty with a shovel. 'Course, we could just leave 'em here for the wolves to get at—"

"No," David said suddenly, getting to his feet.

On the handcar, Rachel gasped as she recognized David. He was dirty and unshaven, a far cry from the immaculate man who had played piano at La Belle Femme Inn.

Trace half-turned, studying David with bright eyes. "No, what, bottle sucker?"

"You won't have to get your hands dirty, Trace,"

David said steadily. "You're going to untie them and let them go."

"Am I now? That's brave talk coming from a piano player." Trace faced David fully, his hand loose by his gun, an evil smile on his face. "Pete, you with me?"

"Yes." Pete moved across the fire from David.

"How about you, Jack?" Trace asked, without taking his gaze from David.

"I don't want no part of this. I'm getting the hell out of here!" Jack bleated. Turning, he sped off into the night.

"I guess it's up to me and you, Pete," Trace said with a mean laugh. "Let's get to it."

Trace's hand darted for his gun, but David's own pistol was out and booming before Trace's gun cleared the holster. David's bullet hit the other man over the heart, slamming him back against a boulder. He slid down to a sitting position, and looked up at David with an expression of utter disbelief. Then he doubled forward in death.

Knowing that Trace was the faster of the two, David had taken him out first. Now he swung around to Pete, whose own gun was coming up. Two shots sounded almost as one. Pete was hit, the impact of the bullet spinning him around, and he fell. David stood unhurt, his feet planted wide apart. Sure that both men were dead, he pivoted, the gun coming to bear on Julius Deever.

"You taking a hand in this, Deever?" David asked in a toneless voice.

"No, no, don't shoot me!" Deever fell to his knees. "Please don't kill me! This was all Ewell

Rankin's doing. He's the one behind it all. He ordered it done."

"How about Rachel's husband, Will Simmons? Was that done at his orders?"

"Yes, yes! He sent Trace and Pete to do it. Rankin, he killed Parker and Connors, too. Me, I've just been following orders. I had no choice!" He fell face down on the ground, groveling, his heavy body shaking with sobs.

"You're disgusting, Deever," David said contemptuously. "You're not worth the bullet it would take." He holstered his pistol and turned his back.

"Spencer," Hawkeye called, "if you'll untie me, I'll take care of Julius Deever for you. I'll place him under arrest."

David walked toward the handcar. "Arrest him? How can *you* do that?"

"I'm a United States marshal, assigned undercover to investigate the railroad corruption. I've been on this damned case for close to two years now."

David grinned. "Well, I'll be damned."

Rachel said sharply, "Hawkeye, why didn't you tell me?"

Hawkeye grinned sheepishly. "I thought it better not to get you involved."

David had stopped at the handcar. "Since you're a federal man. Maybe I shouldn't untie you."

"Why not?" Hawkeye asked.

"I was out here with this bunch to hold up the train due through here shortly."

"David, why?" Rachel asked despairingly.

David shrugged. "The way my life's been going,

what did it matter? But I want you to know, Rachel, that I knew nothing about them killing your husband."

"Do you still plan on robbing the train?" Hawkeye asked.

David looked back over his shoulder at the bodies on the ground. "No, I don't imagine I shall. Not alone."

"Then I don't imagine I'll have to arrest you. Now, will you please get on with getting us loose?"

"Sure thing."

As David bent down to untie the ropes, Rachel looked past him, and she saw Julius Deever on his knees, his gun held in both hands. She screamed, "David, look out!"

Deever's pistol boomed before her words were out. The bullet struck David Spencer in the back of the neck. So fast were his reflexes, however, that even as he was falling he drew his gun. He fell to his knees, grabbing at the handcar for support. The gun clattered to the work deck beside Hawkeye.

David looked at her, his smile sorrowful. "My sweet Rachel, now I can . . ." His eyes got a glazed look, and he coughed. "Now I can see their faces, all those I killed." He sighed, and fell to the ground.

"Oh, dear God! Please, no!" Rachel stretched her neck to look down. In the firelight his eyes were open and sightless.

"Hawkeye . . ." Her voice was a whisper. "It's almost as thought he hoped my uncle would kill him."

Hawkeye was staring at Julius Deever. He said

grimly, "It could well be, but I wish to hell he'd untied us first."

Rachel followed his gaze as she heard a demonic, mad laugh and saw Deever coming toward them. He laughed again. "Looks like he died on you, doesn't it?" The man's arrogance was back. He almost strutted over to them.

"Deever, why don't you give yourself up to me?" Hawkeye said cajolingly. "It'll go much easier on you."

"Give myself up? Really now, Mr. Hawkeye Smith. You don't think I'm foolish enough to do that, now do you? Not after everything has turned out so well here."

"Are you going to shoot us?" Rachel asked.

"Oh, no, my dear niece," Deever said. "No, I won't shoot you. Nothing so crude as that. I won't have to." He took his gold watch from his vest, and opened it. He was smiling craftily. "You see, the train that these fellows intended to rob will be along in ten minutes or so. Now, with the pair of you tied to that handcar . . ." He broke off with an expressive shrug. "I'm sure you get my meaning, Mr. Smith."

He turned and strode off into the darkness beyond the fire. He came back leading a horse. Getting up into the saddle with difficulty, he kneed the animal over to the handcar.

"I am sorry that I can't stay behind to watch the event happen, but I really must be going. You see, the ceremony for the joining of the rails is tomorrow, only a few hours from now, and I must attend. It will be an exciting event, and who will take note of two unfortunates dying out here on the prairie?"

Rachel could not stop herself from a final plea. "Uncle Julius, you can't leave us here like this!"

"Watch me," he said, and started the horse off alongside the track. His cruel, mocking laughter was heard long after he had vanished into the night.

Instead of wasting his breath remonstrating with Julius Deever, Hawkeye had been furtively struggling with the ropes, but to no avail. Part of the problem was the way he and Rachel were tied. The more pressure he put on the ropes to free himself, the more painful it was for Rachel. And if he exerted any more pressure, he could easily break her wrists.

"Go ahead, darling," Rachel said with clenched teeth. "Let me scream my head off, but do it!"

"I could break your arms," he warned.

"That's better than waiting for the train to hit us."

Hawkeye tried again, but Rachel could not restrain a cry of pain, and he stopped.

Then they heard it—the mournful, distant whistle of the approaching train. That sound that she had always loved now mocked her.

"Hawkeye, you must break the ropes! Break my arms if you have to , but get us loose!"

Hawkeye shifted to get a better position, and he spied David's pistol on the platform just out of his reach.

"Rachel, can you reach David's gun with your foot?"

"I can try. Are you going to shoot the rope in two?"

"No, I have a better idea. If it works. Try to poke the gun near my hands."

Rachel stretched her leg, and inadvertently struck the pistol. It spun toward the edge of the work deck and came within an inch of falling to the ground.

Hawkeye let his breath out in relief. "Be careful now. Nudge it up so that I can get my hands on it."

Rachel finally managed to get the pistol to his hands. All the time she was working the pistol toward him, the sound of the train whistle was getting closer. Hawkeye picked the gun up awkwardly in his hand, and started turning the cylinder slowly, ejecting the cartridges one at a time. The first two were empty casings, but the last four were live shells.

"What are you doing? Why are you taking the bullets out?"

"Hawkeye said, "I'll explain later."

When he had the four bullets out, he began pushing off one boot with the other, until finally the boot was off. He repeated the procedure until his sock was also off. Then he placed a bullet between his toes and carefully stretched his leg out and down, trying to stand the bullet upright on the rail. It fell over, and rolled down between the tracks.

"Goddammit! I'm glad Spencer was such a good shot. If he'd used more than two bullets, I wouldn't be able to make this work. I might not, anyway."

The puffing sound of the engine was so loud now that it seemed to fill the air. And now, frighteningly, the great, wavering, yellow headlamp had just come into view around the curve, no more than a half mile away.

"There!" Hawkeye exclaimed. "I've got one of them to stand up. Now, if I can just get the other two!"

He put another bullet between his toes and placed it on the rail. Then he managed to place the third one down, and it, too, stood upright on the track.

"If this works," he explained, "they'll go off just like warning torpedoes. That's what's used to signal the engineer for an emergency stop. Now, all we have to do is try to pump this car with our legs to gain a little distance, because as fast as he's going, it's going to take him a ways to brake down."

"Hawkeye, do you think it will work?"

"I don't know, but it's our only hope. Now, help me pump this thing!"

Hawkeye and Rachel twisted around so they could get their legs up to the two-man pump handle. From their position it was hard to get it started, but Hawkeye finally managed to get his side pulled down. The momentum was thus begun, and that helped Rachel push hers down as well. It got easier as they began pumping it faster and faster. Soon the handcar was rolling at a pretty good clip, but Hawkeye knew that if the train was not stopped, it would overtake them no matter how hard they pumped.

They heard three sharp explosions, and almost immediately after that the engineer applied his emergency brakes.

"It worked!" Hawkeye shouted. "Now, if we can just stay out in front until the engineer gets it stopped!"

The screech of steel on steel was ear-shattering, and both sides of the track turned orange in the shower of sparks from the wheels. Hawkeye and Rachel pumped frantically, but despite all their efforts, the great engine loomed closer, and closer still, until the screech of metal was like the wail of all the banshees of hell. The engine's cowcatcher was almost upon them; then, miraculously, it dropped back, a little at first, then a little more, until it was obvious they were gaining ground on it.

"We beat it, Rachel! We beat the damned thing!"

The train ground to a halt. Hawkeye and Rachel stopped pumping and let the handcar coast down until, like the puffing Iron Horse not many feet behind them, they sat motionless on the track.

CHAPTER TWENTY-NINE

A cold rain was falling, and those people who were gathered at Promontory Point for the joining of the rails cursed the bad fortune that had brought unpleasant weather to the grand ceremony. A few tents had been put up, and a half-dozen lavish private railroad cars for the dignitaries were parked on the track, but those shelters could accommodate only a small part of the huge crowd.

Suddenly, one of the telegraphers went over to speak to Leland Stanford, who carried a polished laurel tie, a golden spike, and a silver hammer, and whispered something in his ear. Stanford, who was president of the Central Pacific, nodded his head and returned to his private car.

"Ladies and gentlemen," the telegrapher shouted, waving his hands high to get their attention. "Ladies and gentlemen, I have an announcement to make. Dr. Durant and his party from the Union Pacific have been unavoidably detained in Piedmont, Wyoming. The celebration has been delayed for two more days. The joining of the rails will now take place on May 10th."

Some of those gathered jeered, others cheered, and a few laughed outright. A number commented on the fact that it was fitting that the railroad construction end on a sour note, since nothing else had gone smoothly. Most of those present headed for the work trains to ride to Toana or Ogden. Others lingered behind to avail themselves of the huge quantities of whiskey which was available in the tents, selling now at a reduced price, since the ceremony was delayed.

In fact, though none realized it at the time, Dr. Durant's delay in Piedmont was more than just an inconvenience. Dr. Durant had been taken captive by an armed mob of several hundred railroad workmen, his car switched to a sidetrack, and the wheels of the car chained to the rails. He was then informed that he would remain there until the workers received their overdue wages.

Dr. Durant attempted to telegraph the army for help, but all outgoing telegrams were intercepted, so he finally gave in and arranged to have two hundred and fifty thousand dollars transferred from the New York office by telegraph, in order to arrange for his release.

Back at Promontory Point, no one knew about this, and most people were in sour spirits over the unexpected delay. Two men who were not in sour spirits, however, were Ewell Rankin and Julius Deever. They were drinking champagne in celebration—not for the completion of the railroad, but for the demise of Rachel Bonner Simmons and Hawkeye Smith. An announcement had been made that the morning train from Ogden had collided with a handcar ten miles east of Corinne. The two operators of the handcar were as yet unidentified, although it was believed that they had been a man and a woman.

"Deever, I must confess that you handled that much better than I ever supposed you could," Rankin said, raising his glass in a toast.

They were the only people in the champagne tent. The other champagne drinkers were in the luxury of the private cars, and the working men preferred the hard liquor served in the other tents.

"Indeed, I am pleasantly surprised," Rankin added.

"Well, thank you." Deever preened, puffing up with self-importance. "Are you appreciative as well, Ewell?"

Rankin's eyes narrowed dangerously. "What the hell does that mean? You thinking of holding me up?"

"No, no," Deever said hastily. "That wasn't my meaning at all, not at all!"

"Because if you are, I must remind you of something." Rankin leaned forward, his eyes cold. "I must remind you that you had as much at stake as I did, had Rachel gone to the authorities."

"Oh, I know that. But you missed my meaning."

"Then exactly what did you mean?"

"It's just that . . . well, I had some plans that didn't work out. And now that the construction is finished, I'm out of a job."

The plan of Deever's that did not pan out was the

robbery of the train payroll car. He had been promised a hefty share of the loot in return for providing the needed information. But the deaths of the train robbers had put an end to that, of course, and Deever was left with a handful of nothing.

Rankin sneered openly. "You're a fool, Julius Deever, if you think I can do anything for you."

"But I put myself out on a limb for you," Deever said. "For that you should remember me!"

"I remember you, right enough." Rankin laughed harshly. "I remember only your incompetence. You saved your hide by seeing to your niece's death. That will have to be your reward. You'll get nothing from me—"

"Sorry to disappoint you, Rankin," Hawkeye Smith drawled from the tent entrance. "But your friend here wasn't successful this time, either."

Rankin reared back, his glance going to Hawkeye. Then he glared at Deever in a fury. "You told me this man and Rachel were dead!"

"I thought they were. I arranged it." Deever had gone as pale as death, and his glance shuttled about the tent in search of a means of escape. "The engineer, he turned in a report! He said he hit the handcar!"

"That was my doing," Hawkeye said, smiling slightly. "I figured that if you thought we had survived, you'd spook and run. Rankin, I wasn't here to witness the transfer of funds to you from the disbursing officer this morning. You can thank your friend for that at least. If I'd been here, I could have arrested you for conspiracy to defraud. Now it looks like I can't make that arrest."

Rankin smiled smugly. "Now, isn't that a damned shame? The best-laid plans, as they say."

"Oh, I'm still going to arrest you," Hawkeye said calmly. "On a far better charge. Murder."

"Murder?" Rankin laughed harshly. "You can't fit me to a murder charge."

"I think so. You see, I have a witness that you ordered Will Simmons's death, along with several others."

Rankin stared. "What witness?"

"Julius Deever."

Deever started. "What makes you think that?"

"You have already confessed before Rachel and me. And you'll repeat that statement in court, in exchange for immunity. Otherwise, you'll stand trial for those murders right along with Ewell Rankin."

"You can't do that! I didn't do any actual killing," Deever said desperately. "Why, I couldn't even kill you and Rachel, remember? I could have, but I let you live."

"Oh, you did that, all right. So kind of you," Hawkeye said sarcastically. "But how about David Spencer?"

"That was different, he was a criminal!"

"And so are you, Mr. Deever, so are you. And I intend to prove it in court."

"All right, I'll be your witness. I'll do anything you say." Deever glared at Ewell Rankin. "You were going to abandon me, leave me with nothing! Well, I can at least see to it that you—"

"You'll see to nothing, you fool! And neither will you, buffalo hunter!"

Rankin's hand was already moving for his gun.

Hawkeye had never taken his eyes off the man, and he went for his gun at the same time.

Rankin had a few seconds' advantage, and he had his gun out first. But in his haste his shot went high, passing through the crown of Hawkeye's hat and sending it flying through the tent entrance. Hawkeye dropped to one knee and took careful aim before he fired. His bullet slammed into Rankin's right shoulder and knocked him from the chair. On the ground Rankin writhed in pain, clutching at his shoulder. A red stain seeped through his fingers.

Hawkeye shot a glance at Deever, who was cowering back in his chair. He held up his empty hands. "Don't shoot, I'm not armed!"

Hawkeye relaxed, standing up, as Rachel came flying into the tent. She was carrying his bullet-punctured hat.

"Darling, are you all right?"

"I'm fine," he growled. "But didn't I tell you to wait outside until this was over?"

"How could I do that, not knowing what had happened to you?" she said angrily.

The two shots had drawn immediate attention, and others were crowding into the tent behind her. Hawkeye put an arm around her shoulders and drew her to him.

Ewell Rankin was sitting up now, pressing a handkerchief to his wound. His face was pale with pain, yet he managed to smile contemptuously at Hawkeye. "So our buffalo hunter is a U.S. marshal, huh? For your information, Mr. Marshal, I have a few friends in high places. And I'm not afraid to ask them for help."

"Oh, I'm sure you have, Rankin. And I hope you aren't afraid to contact them. Go ahead. Write letters to them. Send telegrams. That way, maybe we'll get to meet them. We would dearly love to find out who they are."

An army officer had been one of the first men inside the tent. Hawkeye fished his badge from his pocket and showed it to the officer. "Would you take this precious pair to the nearest federal stockade? Hold them there until they can be brought to trial."

"I'd be happy to, sir." The officer took out his own pistol and motioned to Rankin and Deever. "Come alone, gentlemen. I'll try to find a nice place out of the rain for you."

As the officer led the pair out at gunpoint, one of the spectators laughed. "Well, hell, we didn't get to see a ceremony, but I'd say we had a little excitement, after all."

"If I have anything to say about it," Hawkeye said, smiling down at Rachel in the crook of his arm, "there'll be a joining ceremony yet today."

Rachel's heart beat quickly. Gazing up into his eyes, she said breathlessly, "What did you have in mind, Mr. Smith?"

"There's a preacher here by the name of Reverend John Todd, and he represents a couple of religious magazines. He has been selected to say a prayer when the rails are joined. Now I think it would be right nice for us to be married by the very same preacher who will be dedicating the joining of the rails."

"Is this a proposal, sir?"

"Now what does it sound like?"

"I've heard nicer proposals, but . . ." She drew a deep breath. "But I accept!"

It rained the next day as well, but on May 10th the morning dawned bright and clear and the temperature rose to sixty-nine degrees. By seven A.M. on that historic morning a number of people were already beginning to assemble around the two-rail gap, which was all that was left for the completion of the transcontinental railroad.

At eight, a construction train pulled up to unload several gangs of track layers, and then backed away. At ten, two Union Pacific trains arrived and stopped a short distance from the gap. The first to arrive was Dr. Durant, finally released from detention in Wyoming. With Dr. Durant were Sidney Dillon, Brenville Dodge, Silas Seymour, and numerous other UP dignitaries. On board the second train were four companies of the Twenty-First Infantry and its headquarters band, and three cars that were divided into bedroom compartments for those who were fortunate enough to have tickets for the momentous occasion.

A gang of Chinese workmen leveled the gap in the roadbed, then laid the last few ties and the two rails. They bolted on the fishplates and drove all but the last few spikes.

At eleven-fifteen, the Jupiter, a flared funnel-stacked engine of the Central Pacific, and No. 119, a straight-stacked engine from the Union Pacific, were brought into facing positions across the meeting place of the rails. The soldiers formed a parade rest front, facing the track.

Then everybody waited. More than a thousand people were gathered for the ceremony.

Finally, almost half an hour late, the laurel tie was laid and the golden spike was placed in position over a pre-drilled hole. After another fifteen minutes, Leland Stanford was ready to strike the first blow. He stepped up to the silver-plated sledgehammer and brought it briskly down—missing the spike entirely.

The track layers, now unemployed and for the most part drunk, roared with irreverent laughter.

"Hey, Stanford! It's a good thing we didn't have you working on the crew! We wouldn't be out of California yet!"

Dr. Durant took the sledgehammer from Stanford and swung at the spike, but he too missed. There was some speculation later that Durant had missed on purpose, to spare Stanford embarrassment.

But finally the golden spike was driven home, and the telegrapher tapped out one word: "Done." The spectators shouted out their appreciation.

Afterward, the golden spike and laurel tie were carefully removed, and a photographer quickly took as many pictures as he could. While he took the pictures, the real celebration began. Wine, champagne, and whiskey flowed freely. A number of Chinese workmen set off a string of firecrackers, and they popped like rapid gunfire.

In the second Union Pacific train, in a small bedroom compartment, Rachel awoke slowly to hands stroking her body tenderly and knowingly. She opened her eyes as Hawkeye lowered his mouth to hers.

"Oh, darling! My darling Hawkeye! How I love you!"

"Hush, sweet," he murmured. "This is no time to talk. You're distracting me."

"Distracting you?" She laughed. "I haven't noticed you being much distracted since we were wed yesterday. Do you know we have scarcely left this compartment since?"

"I have to make up for lost time."

As she started a saucy retort, he closed her mouth with his. The incredibly sweet kiss lengthened, and Rachel came fully awake, fully aroused.

Hawkeye could make slow, languorous love to her until her need for release became sheet torture; or he could bring her to a quick, sharp culmination so intense as to be almost painful. This was one of the latter times, and Rachel cried out as she shuddered in her ecstasy; then she held him to her tightly, as Hawkeye groaned sharply.

A moment later, as Hawkeye lay beside her, a noise like rapid gunfire sounded outside, and Rachel jumped in sudden fear. She sat up, bumping her head on the low wall of the compartment, muttered an oath, and looked around to find Hawkeye laughing quietly.

"What do you find so humorous?" she demanded. "Somebody's shooting out there!"

"No, you silly goose!" He got his laughter under control. "The Chinese are just setting off a few firecrackers. It means that it's over. The golden spike is driven home."

She motioned worriedly to the next compartment. "It'll wake the baby."

"Let it. Bright Fawn can handle him." He beckoned to her with open arms. "Come back here, sweet, where you belong."

All of a sudden, she let out a wail of dismay. "You mean it's all over, and we missed it?" She reached over and pulled aside the curtain, and peered out. All she could see were people streaming past along the train, carrying glasses and cheering loudly. "It *is* over! You promised we'd watch it!" As a man skidded to a stop outside, staring at her with round eyes, she remembered she was naked and let the curtain fall back into place.

Hawkeye said, "We had better things to do. Didn't we, sweet?" He placed a warm hand on her flank.

"Hawkeye, you're . . ." She broke off. "You know something? I can't go on calling you Hawkeye. You must have another name. You even gave Hawkeye for the marriage license. Surely your folks didn't give you that name at birth?"

His look was wry. "Nope. My birth name is John Smith."

"*John* Smith?" She covered her mouth to hide a smile.

"You see why I was happy to change it. There must be a million John Smiths around."

"But there's only one Hawkeye. Come to think of it, I guess I will continue calling you Hawkeye."

Sighing happily, Rachel went into his arms again.

Outside, the celebration continued and, by the magic of the telegraph, the entire world was invited to the party. But inside the compartment, Hawkeye and Rachel knew nothing of that, nor did they care.